Mind

TRINITY TRILOGY
BOOK TWO

PRAISE FOR MIND

Mind

TRINITY TRILOGY
BOOK TWO

WATERHOUSE
PRESS

To Dyani Gingerich, Nikki Chiverrell, and Carolyn Beasley
My beautiful soul sisters.
You will always be a part of my past,
an amazing part of my present,
and forever in my future.

Thank you for being such an important part of this trilogy.

I'll always love you more.

BESOS

Bound - Eternally - Sisters - of - Souls

GILLIAN

CHAPTER ONE

Turns out that the moment the paparazzi find out you have taken one of United States' most eligible bachelors off the market, you also become famous. Unfortunately. It was not something I had ever considered would be a part of my reality when I agreed to marry Chase Davis. No, seeing my face splashed across countless magazines was not high on my list of life achievements. Worse is what comes with that fame. The backlash. I've been labeled everything from a gold digger to the first of *many* wives Chase is sure to have. One woman couldn't possibly keep a billionaire business tycoon like Chase Davis fulfilled. Surely, he'd need a truckload of harlots to do that job.

"Check this one out." My best friend and soon-to-be ex-roommate, Maria, laughs behind her hand while flipping through the most recent smut magazine. "*'Triple B, Big Business Billionaire Chase Davis to wed Triple D Toting Gillian Callahan'.*"

"What!" I screech. "Let me see that." Maria tosses the magazine at me over the mountain of moving boxes. Scanning the page, I see Chase with his arm around me, possessively gripping my hip. He's devastatingly beautiful even in a candid paparazzi shot like this. It was taken at a charity ball we'd recently attended. Only the image clearly shows me with a digitally enlarged bust at least twice the size of what God Himself gave me. Internally, I seethe. "They made my boobs huge!"

Maria laughs, and I toss the trash back at her, whacking her in the head with it. "¡*Puta!*" She calls me a bitch in Spanish.

"I'm just so tired of the garbage being written about me. I try not to read it. Chase ignores it completely. If only it was that easy." A long overdue sigh escapes my lungs as I place more books into a box already overloaded with books.

"*Cara bonita*, you cannot let strangers make you feel like shit. You're better than that." She punctuates her statement with a tug on my ponytail. "Oh, the *Kama Sutra*. That book is mine!" Her long fingers rip it from the stack I was going through. "Heaven forbid I accidentally steal your sex book." I roll my eyes and stick out my tongue.

She ignores me and shimmies over to the kitchen. "You know what this party needs? More bitches and vino! Ohhhh...and pizza!" Lightning fast, she's on the phone dialing. One of our girls must have answered right away, because she doesn't say hello and starts right in on what she wants. "Why are you not here helping your best friends move *puta perezosa*! ...Yes, I just called you a lazy bitch. Get off Carson's *polla,* and get your *culo* over here to help us." She hangs up without so much as a goodbye.

"Did you just tell Kat to get off Carson's dick?" I giggle.

"Yes, as a matter fact, I did. Next, Bree." She dials quickly and waits, drumming her fingers on the kitchen counter. While she waits, she stretches one long dancer's leg out behind her then crooks it up and grabs her ankle. With one arm, she pulls it up the back of her body. She looks like a contorted ballerina or a pretzel. It's awe-inspiring. She brings the leg down to the ground gracefully. "Do you have a class?" Maria asks sweetly into the receiver. Too nice for our Italian-Spanish fireball. Poor Bree. She doesn't even know what's about to hit her.

Maria continues. "No?" She waits a moment. Then her scathing, mean girl voice barks into the phone. "Get your flexible, tiny *culo* over here and help your *hermanas* pack their shit. And don't even try to pull an excuse that you're spending time with Phillip." Maria pauses and listens for a moment. "¡*Mierda!* We all know your va-jay-jay hasn't seen any action in months. Bring wine." She hangs up.

Laughter bubbles up my throat and spills out in a combination between snorting and trying to catch my breath. God, this woman is good for me. She knows exactly how to make life seem lighter, removing the heavy spotlight I've been under since my engagement to Chase was announced last week. Over that hurdle, we are still no closer to finding my stalker. When the announcement of our impending nuptials was released, we were inundated with congratulatory flowers. But one person sent a couple dozen dead roses with a card. Those words still give me chills.

Gillian,
Worst decision you ever made. Mark my words.
You're mine… Bitch.

Remembering those words sends chills skittering down my spine to settle sourly in my gut. Gooseflesh prickles along my skin, and I take a deep breath. A few rounds of yoga style breathing and I'm able to banish the negative and fill my head with positive thoughts. Chase. My fiancé.

The band of diamonds around my finger catches the light, twinkling, reminding me what I have to look forward to. A life with the man of my dreams.

The ping of my cellphone brings me back to the present. I grab it off the table and check the display. Instant happiness fills me as I see Chase's name.

From: Chase Davis

To: Gillian Callahan

Maria's condo is ready when she is. The sooner the better. I want you and your crazy sister safe.

"Ria, Chase says your condo's ready!" I holler while typing a thank you message back to my love.

She squeals with glee and dances a jig in the middle of our tiny kitchen. It's funnier because she's in the tiniest pair of booty shorts, and a sports bra that makes her overly large breasts bounce in a graphically vulgar display.

"Damn sister! Put those things away. You might poke an eye out," I laugh and she grins wickedly.

"It's really cool that Chase scored me a condo within walking distance to your penthouse. It's weird though; he won't discuss the *dinero*." I cringe and bite my lip. "What? It's gonna be rent-controlled, right?" She stomps her foot defiantly. "You promised it would be rent-controlled. I'm not living with another crazy *chica*. And by God, I will not move in with Tommy even though he won't let the idea go." She grumbles.

"No, it's not going to be costly at all." I try to sound vague but she gives me the side-eye, cocking a perfectly sculpted ebony eyebrow. I hate that she can do that. It's annoyingly cool.

"And how much will I be paying monthly, Mrs. Davis?" She uses my soon-to-be last name in a sickeningly saccharine-sweet voice. Not a good sign. When Maria starts using a sweet tone, it usually means the bear with giant claws is just around the corner and ready for a sneak attack.

"Um, less than your half here actually," I supply hoping she'll just wait and push Chase about the issue.

She leans a delicate hip against the island, cocks her head to the side, and purses her lips into a fake smile. "How much less, *bonita? ¿Cien? ¿Doscientos?*"

"Uh, probably less." I jump up pushing the fully loaded box of books in the corner with my foot. Pretending to ignore her, I work to close the box and label which house it's going to. This one's going to the penthouse.

"*¿Cuatro?* How much, Gigi?" she doesn't take her hand off her hip.

Scrunching up my face, I mumble, "Nothing," as quickly as possible and jet into the kitchen to find the wine. Suddenly, I'm parched. "So thirsty. Where'd we pack the wine again?" I try to change the subject. A cold hand grips my arm and twirls me around.

"*¿Nada?* As in, no dollars. *Gratis?* Free?" her tone is reaching a high, piercing pitch—the one that makes my teeth rattle.

I nod. "Don't be mad. Please? It's Chase. He won't take your money. Not when he has more money than God...and even Oprah!"

Maria shakes her head back and forth. "*Bonita*, this isn't going to work. I do not take handouts."

I grab her biceps, and she flinches. We both have that reaction when manhandled. It's just the leftover bonus from years of being physically abused. "I know, I know. I get it. I do. But, it's Chase, and he's so bossy. When I try to argue, he uses his sexy-as-sin body against me. Literally, *against* me!"

She turns her head to the side and puts a hand to her mouth making a lame attempt at holding back her snicker. "Really?"

Nodding, I explain that we had this very same conversation. I told Chase that Maria would never take a handout. A handful of orgasms later and he had seduced me into promising I'd get her to agree. By the end of my story, Maria is on the floor flailing around as if she's been zapped by a Taser. Which may actually happen if she doesn't stop making fun of me. That's another new addition to my everyday life. I now carry around a brush, lipstick, my GPS-tracked phone, wallet, and a handy dandy Taser, the phone and Taser courtesy of my control freak fiancé. Of course, those items are in the event that the six-foot-tall bodyguard I lovingly refer to as "Rambo" is taken out by some force of nature or is otherwise detained.

Maria is still on the floor howling.

"Cut it out, Ria. You have no idea what that man can do to me sexually. He could make a nun come without even touching her!"

"Really? Do tell?" I jump at least a foot in the air in surprise. Kat snickers behind me while Maria continues to suck in air and fails to control her laughter. We should have never given these women their own keys.

"Jesus, Kat. What the hell? You scared me. This stalker crap has me on edge already." I chastise her in a lame attempt to make her feel guilty.

"Sounds like a tall, dark, and handsome fella has you on

edge more often than the stalker. Am I right, sister?" Maria jumps up like a bird in flight and high-fives Kat. Stupid dancer agility. Most of the time, I feel tall and gangly. Only Chase makes me feel like a sexy vixen. My blonde besties are all really graceful, too. Maria though, she can jump around like a modern day ninja when center stage, but finds everyday walking a challenge. The girl trips over cracks in the sidewalk, even the ones that are blatantly obvious.

"*¡Perfecto!*" Maria agrees and grabs the two bottles of wine Kat is holding in one hand. "*¡Gracias!*"

"Tell me more about how Chase manipulates you into doing whatever he wants?" Kat's evil grin spreads across her pretty features. Caramel-colored eyes sparkle with mirth as she leans on the kitchen island. The bangles on her left arm tinkle like a wind chime blowing in a cool breeze as she stares me down.

"God, you two are incorrigible." Squinting at Kat, I give her my best glare. It doesn't work.

"Why are they incorrigible?" Bree saunters into the kitchen, pizza in one hand, wine in the other. Her golden hair falls in a perfectly flat sheet down her back. When she enters a room, it's like opening a window and being surrounded by a breath of fresh air.

Maria claps happily and relieves Bree of the pie.

"All veggie, super thin crust, and red sauce not that creamy garlic fattening crap!" she scolds.

Maria raises her hand in a one-finger salute as she takes the pie to get some plates, effectively telling her what she thinks about Bree's health-fanatic ways.

Kat and I stand shoulder-to-shoulder and give her an unimpressed look. "What? No need to go overboard on carbs and fat when you can drink your calories instead." She smiles and holds up the red Pinot Noir we all adore, aptly named Soul Sisters. We've all had better wines. Hell, the wine Chase serves me could make anyone weep with joy, but the four of us appreciate the symbolism. At a cool twelve bucks a bottle, the price tag doesn't hurt, either. It's also unique because it's made by Save Me San Francisco Wine Company where we live and it's owned by the band Train. Wine with a cool backstory like that, gives it an even higher appeal.

Bree pulls up her red chair and plops down pulling her knee up and hugging it close. She's wearing leggings, an oversized shirt, and Ugg boots. She calls it casual elegance. I call it pajamas. The four of us have *very* different opinions on clothing. They think I prefer to look stuck-up in tailored suits and skirts. Really, the goal is to look unapproachable and professional. Besides, I love a bargain basement label find. Regretfully, it hits me that even that will change once I marry Richie Rich.

Chase has recently made it clear he's replacing my entire wardrobe. At first, it bothered me that he has an opinion on what I wear, but seeing his excitement when he spoke with his assistant about what he wants purchased only made me feel loved, cared for...special. It's not the money or the clothing that sold me on the idea; it's that Chase wants to make me *feel* connected to him in all things. He specifically requested that his assistant, Dana—whom I'm trying very hard not to be jealous of—purchase items that would match or pair well with items he already has. I like the idea that we'd present a united front at different events, especially with my newfound and unwanted fame. The last thing I want is to embarrass Chase. He repeatedly tells me that I could wear a paper sack and he'd be proud to have me on his arm, but I know differently. The man likes luxury. A lot.

Chase is a certified clothing snob. Not only does he never wear anything off the rack, he has every suit tailored to fit his finely toned form. Like me, his desire to come off perfectly in order is part of what draws me to him. Only I get to see the real Chase, the one with all of the layers removed, metaphorically and physically.

Unfortunately, though, I haven't been able to convince him that I'm not going to run. As much as I believe in my desire to stay with him and be his wife, it still scares the living hell out of me. Committing to one man, giving him the power to make decisions about my life, is frightening. It's one of the reasons why I told Chase we needed to wait a year, but not the biggest. For the past week, he's been hinting that he'd like to shorten that timeframe considerably. Originally, when he proposed, he wanted to elope, as in, get married the very next day. The thought definitely had merit. However, something inside me still wants the fairytale. I've got the knight in shining Armani, and now I want the fairytale wedding. Nothing huge or audacious. Just his family, our friends, my girls, Phillip, and little Anabelle. I'd love to see her in a matching gown tossing petals into the air.

"Still thinking about all the convincing Chase does to get you to do things?" Maria laughs, and I firmly ignore her.

"Hey Bree, do you think Phil would walk me down the aisle?" I push back the tendril of red hair that fell out of my hair tie.

Bree's face lights up. Damn, the woman is beautiful.

She has an effervescent quality about her. Skin flawless and tanned naturally, big blue eyes, and a perfect Roman nose that's tipped just at the end. "I think he'd be honored. Really. And Anabelle would be the flower girl, right?"

I nod emphatically. "And of course all three of my sisters must be in the bridal party." They nod happily.

"I still can't believe he asked you so quickly. I mean, a few months seems like a short amount of time." Her lips twist into a thoughtful gesture. "Not that I'm saying he doesn't mean it or anything, it's just, why the rush?" She takes a sip of her wine.

Shrugging my shoulders, I take the wine glass Maria holds out for me. The blend of cherries, plums, and blackberries explodes over my taste buds. "Honestly, when you know, you just know. He's it for me. There's really no reason to wait."

Maria and Kat both nod. Bree bites her lips then tugs on her hair, twining a golden piece around her finger. She's holding something back. Fidgeting is one of her tells. Apparently, she's trying not to give her opinion.

I narrow my eyes at her. "Bree, something to add?"

"Uh, nuh-uh." She shakes her head and takes a bite of pizza. Stuffing her face isn't going to get her off the hook that easily. It's obvious she has something to say, and I want to know what it is.

"Out with it. And don't lie to me. You know I have radar on liars."

She rolls her eyes and takes a deep breath. "Fine. If you know he's it, then why the yearlong engagement?"

Her question digs uninvited through my subconscious. Instinctively, I know the answer, but I don't want to open that wound. It's not that I don't believe he isn't the one for me. My heart beats for Chase. His presence permeates the air around me at all times. When he's not with me, I feel him. Habitually, my thumb rubs the solid weight of his love encircling my finger, spinning it around and around.

"Sometimes you just want the time to allow yourselves to be sure. As Kat said, he asked me very quickly. I don't want him to regret that decision later." All three of the most important women in my life look at me as if I've grown horns, their eyes as wide as saucers. "We've been under a lot of stress," I add defensively. "Between almost losing my job, the return of The Bitch, and now my stalker..." I shake my head and let the words fall off knowing there is a lot of truth to them, but it's not the whole truth. If I'm honest with myself, I need to give Chase the time to make sure it's *me* he wants forever. Damaged, scarred, Gillian Callahan.

"Gigi, you can't be serious? You're waiting to marry Chase because you want to give *him* the chance to bail?" Kat asks in shock.

"¡*Estúpido!*" Maria chimes in and takes a large swallow of wine.

"I can't believe you!" Bree agrees sounding astonished.

"Me, either," says a deep, chocolaty voice from behind me. My blood goes cold even though the heat of my embarrassment is surely showing crimson across my face. I've heard that voice many times. In my dreams, whispered against my hairline, calling my name as he roars in pleasure.

My love.

My only.

My Chase.

I close my eyes as strong hands tug at my waist bringing

me back firmly against his solid, warm chest. The woodsy citrus scent wars with the veggie pizza wafting in the air. Tension is coiled thick in Chase's forearms as he tightens his grip. "Forgive me, ladies. I need to have a word with my fiancée." His voice conveys politeness and good manners, but when I turn around, his gaze is molten lava. The white heat of lightning burns behind those baby blues, and I fear the mounting storm.

"We didn't hear you come in." I say lamely trying to change the topic of what I know is going to be an emotionally devastating conversation.

"Obviously." He takes brisk steps towards the door. He grabs my coat and gestures with his finger to turn around.

"Wait. You want to leave? But the girls…"

His grip on my forearm is tight, unyielding. "The girls will understand," he says through clenched teeth; that tick in his jaw thumping powerfully.

"Where are we going?" I yank my arm back in irritation.

"Home. The penthouse," he confirms.

He tugs me out into the hallway and I pull to a stop. "You can't come in and pull me out of my apartment just because you said so. I was packing and enjoying myself."

Chase whips back his suit coat and sets a fist to each hip. "Fine. You want to go back in there and have the conversation about why the woman I love doesn't trust me?"

I cup his handsome face and pull him closer to eye level. "Chase, no." His eyes pierce mine with pure honesty and something else. Maybe fear? I take a deep breath and lean my forehead against his, wanting him to understand, pleading with him to understand. "You're the only man I trust with my heart. Will ever trust."

He pulls back and cups my chin. His thumb traces my bottom lip seductively. Prickles of heat rush through me all the way to the bottom of my feet. "And you are the only woman I will ever love. I want you in my life, as my wife. The sooner the better. Now that I know why you are stalling, I will not wait. One month. That's about all I can take."

"A month? Chase, you can't be serious." I search his gaze trying desperately to gain more time.

"Dead serious. Gillian, I'm not a patient man. I thought *you* needed more time to be sure. Now that I know it's you who thought I needed the time, I am no longer amenable to a delay. We will wed in a month. This is no longer open for negotiation."

He turns and pulls on my hand. I stop and yank back hard. "You can't do that!" It takes everything in me not to stomp my foot and throw a tantrum.

"I can, and I have." His voice is flat and unyielding.

"But the wedding…" tears mist over my vision even though I try to tamp them down.

Chase's fingers slide through my hair and burrow at the nape. One hand pulls the elastic band out letting the strands and curls fall wild and free down my back. He loves my hair loose for his greedy fingers. "You will have everything you ever dreamed of. I'll make certain of it. Dana will assist you."

"I don't want your perfect assistant's help," I snarl.

His lips twitch with mirth at my overtly obvious jealousy. "I know you don't want it, but with a shortened timeframe, you're going to need it. She is remarkably efficient. Just tell her what you want and she'll make it happen."

"Anything I want?" I counter trying to go for more

bravado than I'm usually capable of in his presence.

"Oh, baby, I like the way you think. From now on, I want you to have that attitude. You're going to be Mrs. Chase Davis, and billions will be at your disposal." He moves in for a kiss, but I rip away from him.

"What are you talking about? Aren't you going to have me sign a prenup?"

He shakes his head and I'm certain I heard him wrong. No man worth as much as he is would enter a marriage without protecting his investments. "No need. What's mine is yours, baby."

"No, no, no." I shake my head repeatedly and back up. Chase follows and presses me into the wall of the hallway. My breath catches with his nearness and the sheer power radiating around him. It's like a living, breathing thing, this thrumming magnetic energy surrounding me.

"Oh, yes." Chase says as one hand grips my hip keeping me connected to the firm, thick ridges and valleys of his body. His other hand burrows into the hair at the base of my neck once more, locking me in place. One of his favorite places to grip, to take control. "You are about to become more wealthy than you ever dreamed," he nips my lips playfully.

"You say that as if it's something I want. I don't want or need your money, Chase. Just you." I grip his shoulders fiercely trying to express what is so hard to say.

"Boggles the mind." He laughs before his lips swoop down and capture mine. His kiss is feral, possessive, forceful. I open to him on a gasp. He takes full advantage dipping his masterful tongue into my mouth. He tastes of cinnamon gum, which tingles and smarts against my taste buds as his devilish tongue flicks mine. That familiar fire that burns between us ignites instantly. The hand on my hip moves down to cup and fondle my rear end as his lips devour and pillage. It's so much and not enough all at once. Sparks fly and a heavy weight settles between my thighs. My sex moistens, readying to join with its counterpart. His nearness and touch makes me thick with lust, the ache a physical thing when he's so close yet not filling me.

"I want..." comes out as a whisper that he swallows.

"You'll have." He lifts me up, my legs twining around his waist as he presses his rock-solid erection between my thighs. We're in the middle of the hallway just outside my apartment. I can hear the cackling sounds of my best friends through the thin door.

"Jesus, Chase, we can't." I manage to speak between wet, drugging kisses.

His hands clutch my ass tighter, and he carries me a few paces down the hallway to the stairwell. "We can, and we will. I'll never be denied you again." His tone sounds angry, but I know he's not. He's just as taken by the undeniable thing that presses us together at the most inopportune times.

"Chase," I warn, but it's too late. He's already managed to undo his pants and pull out his thick, heavy cock. It stands up huge and dark pink, ready to pleasure. The sight of his dick, large and proud between my thighs, so close yet not close enough, has me salivating. I want to taste his unique, musky maleness on my tongue, on my lips, in my mouth.

"God, I need you," I confide watching him through a haze of desire.

"Oh, baby, it makes me wild when you beg." He pulls at my loose jersey skirt pushing it up to my waist. Without waiting, he pushes aside the lace covering my sex and drives into me in one powerful thrust. His lips crash over mine to muffle the scream. With Chase, I've never been able to rein it in; he brings out the uninhabited side in me. I pull away and take deep, gasping breaths as he withdraws and then rams his cock inside me once more.

"Baby," I whisper out into the open concrete space where it echoes off the walls as I stare unseeingly at the spiraling staircases above us.

Chase's fingers dig into the soft flesh of my hips, piercing but not hurting. "Baby, I can't wait to make you mine. I want the whole world to know I own you." His words are thick and crass. He knows that ownership is a lethal term to me, and, if I wasn't sure that I'd own him in return, I'd retreat and run for the hills. Nevertheless, knowing that I will own Chase Davis, body, mind, and soul, is everything. Sliding his thick manhood into me hard and fast, over and over, sends bolts of pleasure into every speck of my being.

He already owns me. And I tell him so. He goes crazy at my admission pounding into me ruthlessly. His pelvis crushes my clit on a particularly hard thrust, and I tumble head first into the wondrous black abyss. Light sparks across my closed eyes as his pelvic bone crushes my clit, prolonging my orgasm. Chase is right there with me, his moans muffled into the tender space at the crook of my neck. He bites down on the patch of skin there as his essence coats my insides.

"Gillian, you undo me." He mumbles through feather soft kisses along the exposed skin of my neck then up past my ear into my hairline. His lips cover every inch of my face until I open my eyes. Then he seals his lips over mine in a mind-numbing kiss.

"I love you." His eyes soften and I can see his happiness mirrored from within the blue depths. "But I need more than a month, Chase," I tell him.

He stiffens, and shakes his head.

"Kat is making my dress from scratch. She'll freak if I tell her I need it in a month."

"I'll call Vera Wang or Gabana personally. Hell, my cousin Chloe could make you a perfect gown. You'll have your dress in a month's time," he pulls out of me. My panties shift back into place keeping his fluids from spilling down my leg.

I choose my words carefully. "You said I could have anything I want. And a dress made by my best friend is what I want to wear on my wedding day." My tone is calm but firm.

He narrows his eyes. "We'll see." He rights my skirt, and we re-enter the hallway. Within moments, Chase has me back into my apartment standing in front of three shocked and tipsy women.

"¿Qué pasa?" Maria asks.

Chase ignores her and turns to Kat who looks a bit intimidated and leans back in her chair. "How long will it take you to make Gillian's wedding gown?"

Kat assesses me. I'm sure all three of them can see my kiss-swollen lips. I look down and my skirt is askew. She grins and then looks up at Chase. "Not sure. It will be done in a year; I can promise you that."

Chase huffs, which is unusual behavior and less than gentlemanly. "And if I want it in a month?"

Kat's eyes widen and her mouth gapes. "I uh, that's a

really short amount of time."

"How much time do you need exactly?" That jaw of his is clenched, working overtime.

"Depending on the work at the theatre…"

"I'll hire you an assistant to help at the theatre so you can focus most, if not all, of your attention on Gillian."

"You can't do that—" I start, but he squeezes my hand and talks over me. The Controlling Chase is in full swing.

"I'm on the Board of the San Francisco Theatre." What? When the hell was he going to share that tidbit of information? Maria looks just as surprised as I do, so it's news to her as well. Chase continues undeterred. "I can, and will, do whatever is necessary to make you my bride immediately." His tone is sharp and unrelenting. "Kathleen, timeframe?"

She looks shocked but resolved. "Probably six to eight weeks depending on whether or not I can get the fabric and the cost is within the budget."

"Money is no object. I will have fifty thousand wired into your account within the hour. Make it six weeks, and I'll throw in an extra twenty-five thousand for your trouble."

"Holy shit! You weren't kidding." Kat flits her chin in my direction. I smile weakly hating the fact that Chase is throwing his weight and money around with my best friends. He can't help it though. It's his way. At least his intentions are in the right place. And everyone knows the road to hell is paved with good intentions.

He waits patiently for Kat to ponder his request. "You got yourself a deal, buddy." They shake on it to make it official, which I find ridiculous and unnecessary.

Chase turns to me. "Now that that's settled…" He smiles

wide showing even, white teeth. His smile is so pretty it could turn any dark day bright. "You will be all mine, *the* Mrs. Davis in six weeks. I can hardly wait." He grins and pulls me into a hug.

His enthusiasm is contagious. Behind us, the girls whoop and holler as he swoops me in for a searing kiss. It almost becomes indecent when his hand covers my ass and he grinds his growing erection into my belly.

Maria blows past us and comes back with a glass. She fills it half-full and hands it to Chase. He takes it and nods his thanks.

"To the soon-to-be Mr. and Mrs. Chase Davis!" she says. "*¡Salud!*"

GILLIAN

CHAPTER TWO

Chase left me at the apartment after I insisted that it would be weeks before I officially moved into the penthouse, if he didn't let me finish packing. Although I wasn't sure staying behind was a better plan than escaping to our tower in the sky. The girls were merciless in their joking and digging for information. Kat was ecstatic over the new monetary windfall, but nervous about pleasing his highness with that amount of money and time limitation. Six weeks for a couture gown was a heavy burden, but I did my best to reassure her that I was less interested in a fashion masterpiece and more concerned with feeling beautiful and comfortable on the most important day of my life. She started sketching designs while the rest of us packed. On top of being a skilled seamstress, she was actually a very gifted designer.

"So you want fitted at the bodice and protruding out from the waist like a princess gown?" Kat asks while I store framed pictures of Maria and me on our drive through California several years ago. We were on a soul-finding mission. In the end, we mostly agreed that as long as we had the love of our friends and believed in our own self-worth, we'd survive anything life threw our way.

"I'm not really sure. Fitted on top, I think. Open in

the back. Chase loves a bare back." She nods as a mental image of white lace danced across my thoughts. "I want sexy elegance, nothing that's going to push up my boobs or be too revealing."

Kat brings her legs up into a cross-legged seated position on the couch and lays the sketch board over one knee. "I have an idea. What if we do lace arms into a perfect v shape in the back?" She draws the back showing a scalloped edge going into a deep triangle shape right above the butt cheeks. "We could have a tiny line of sparking gems holding up the top at the shoulder-line running across. I'll have to build a bra into the front." I nod starting to feel like this was really going to happen.

"I really like that idea."

"And if you wear your hair up, it will show off the back perfectly." She is ecstatic already sketching the front of the gown. I bite my lip and crinkle my nose.

Her caramel eyes twinkle when she stops sketching and catches the unease in my gaze. "What?" She cocks an eyebrow. Like Maria, annoyingly cool.

I shrug. "It's just that Chase likes my hair down. Always down." I know my face is turning bright pink, and for the millionth time, I curse my Irish heritage. "He always pulls it down when he kisses me." Kat's lips twitch into a sly grin.

"Okay, what if we compromise? Have some up on top and have it pulled over to the side so we can still showcase the back but your caveman will be able to paw your hair at his whim." She giggles and goes back to work.

"Perfect!" I squeal and clasp my hands together at my chest. Even with the wedding rush, it's still going to be the best day of my life. It's the day I agree to be Mrs. Chase

Davis, forever. He'll officially be my past, present, and future. Just like my soul sisters.

Kat continues undaunted, making sketches at the speed of light. The best I can do is a few good stick figures. Her fingers move over the sketch pad putting touches here and there. She makes a sweetheart shape at the front of the bodice, and then adds a sheer lace piece over just the swells of what look to be my breasts. That sheer piece had the same scalloped edge as the back. The more I look, the more I realize how incredibly talented Kat is. I wish she'd have more confidence in her ability.

In that moment, I promise myself that I'll make something good come of my new, unwanted fame. I make a mental note to talk about it with Chase, a plan already forming. Chase's cousin Chloe is a hot young designer that Kat adores. I wonder if I could get Chloe to come with me to Kat's house one day and see some of her designs. Maybe she'd give Kat the push she needs to break out. And with this new money coming her way, and a high profile client in Chase, the sky's the limit for my designing angel.

I grin as a scheme settles into place. "So you like it then," Kat beams up at me while I sit on the arm of the couch.

Looking down at her sketch, all the air leaves my lungs in a whoosh. My heart may have actually stopped because I can't move. I have never been witness to something so enchanting. It is a dream, a vision of lace and sparkles. Even in pencil, the design steals my breath. "It's everything I ever hoped for, Kat," I said, emotion garbling my words, tears spilling down my face.

"Oh honey, don't cry!" she hugs me to her. "This is a

happy occasion. No tears." Her smile is lovely and sincere.

I pick up the sketchbook and hug it to my chest not caring if some of the pencil marking rubs off on my white tank. "Oh my God, I'm getting married!" I sob happily. My three best friends crowd around me in a group hug. I show Bree and Maria the amazing design, and both promptly note little facets they like best. It is moments like these that I know beyond a shadow of a doubt that I'll spend the rest of my life loving these women. They would always be a constant source of supreme love and support. It's official…I am the luckiest girl in the world.

"I love you guys, so much!" I whisper as they squeeze the life out of me.

"We love you more." They each laugh, repeating the words I always say to them, filling my heart to bursting.

X

What a joke. I listen, straining to hear her voice. Only Gillian. She is crying, and my spine tingles, hoping that maybe the rich bastard broke it off with her. Nope. Finally, her voice rings above the others as my love and those three bitches fawn over something about her upcoming wedding. Little do they know there won't be a wedding. I'll make sure of it. Motherfucker moved the timetable up on the nuptials. Probably scared of what I'd do between now and then. Just means I have to work faster.

The women, though, are a problem I need to deal with. The four of them are inseparable, and I want Gillian to count on me, and only me, for all of her pleasure. If she needs something, I will be the one who gives it to her. No, each one of them will be dealt with soon enough. I was already working on my plan to pick them off, one by one, like the plucking of flower petals on a ripe daisy. Kathleen and Maria would be more difficult since they now had steady boyfriends, and Maria was dating that pig. A grin slips across my face as I catch my reflection in the mirror.

I turn down the mic on the recording device I installed a couple weeks ago in her apartment. That rich fucker only recently hired her a bodyguard. Good thing I was ten steps ahead of him. Her apartment had been easy enough to break into. The extra key she kept on top of the bookcase was a cinch to copy and put back before anyone was the wiser. I have spent more time in her apartment recently than I care to admit. Weakness is not my thing. The feeling makes my gut twist into knots, but I couldn't avoid it. I *needed* to be near her. Just being around her things, smelling her perfume, and lying in her bed, gave me a blessed moment of peace. The rage that swirls heavy in my veins only cools when I feel her presence envelop me like she used to. She always had that ability. She calms me, allowing me to push back the beast within. Obsessively working out helps with the excess energy, but not enough to quiet the mind. I need her with me. Knowing she is mine, for all time, is the only thing that will make me whole again.

I grab the wires I need and delicately connect them to the slick side of the cylinder. Slowly I twist them carefully to ensure the appropriate contact with the glass and metal. With pride, I examine the newest addition to my plan. Only decision to make now was who would be blown to bits first? I'd love to take out Chase Fucking Davis. Seeing his body parts fly into the air alongside one of his expensive toys, like his Porsche or Aston Martin, would be doubly satisfying. Taking out Jack Porter, the ex-military man, in the process would be the ultimate revenge for stealing my princess.

It is impossible to prevent the smile that slides over my lips, the same way I can't prevent the memory of sinking my cock into Gillian, over and over again. She never opened her eyes during sex, obviously overcome with emotion when we made love. Back then, my favorite guilty pleasure was watching her face contort as I'd blown my load. We always used condoms, but that would change when I got her back. The first thing I plan to do is lay her out and have my way with her. Fill her full of my cum. Even if it is by force, the bitch would be mine again. There is nothing her friends, her new, good mannered bodyguard, or that rich motherfucker can do to prevent me from claiming what's mine.

Then a name pops into my subconscious, like a song you finally remember that's been rattling around in your head ad nauseam. It's perfect really. The one bastard she always runs to. At first, I thought he might be gay. He hung out with the most beautiful woman in the fucking world and never touched her. Then I found out that he had. He was her first. I knew from the second I met him that he was in love with her. Once his little wifey died, he upgraded to a newer hotter model. Using that little shit daughter of his as a tool to gain my girl's heart and trust. Well, no more. Time for me to clean up that loose end. I'll even bet his demise will delay that sham of a wedding, giving me more time to clean house. Gillian will be mine and mine alone.

All of those bitches, bodyguards, and that rich fucker

have to go.

First, I'll start by making that little girl an orphan. It would be merciful of me to take out her disgusting father. A man who lusts after a woman, day in and day out, using her as bait. Sickening. I'll be doing that little girl a favor. Give her a new life.

Becoming an orphan was the best thing that ever happened to me. Once I'd beaten my drunk father to death and strangled my mother, it was nothing to set the house on fire. Leaving me a scarred, fourteen-year-old boy, who barely made it out of the house alive. At least that's what the authorities thought. Then I got myself a new name, complete with a set of real parents. Ones that didn't use me as their personal punching bag.

Yeah, I'll avenge that little girl and her dead mother. Barely in the grave, before the prick moves on to his next hot piece of ass. And Gillian has the perfect heart-shaped ass. White, creamy, flawless skin. My memories are no longer enough. I need more. But I have to be patient and exact my revenge at the right time. She doesn't have any other family except for a dad who abandoned her long ago. Getting rid of the rest of her so called "family" would feel so good. Chills of excitement race up and down my spine.

My dick hardens painfully. I slide my palm over the bulge in my jeans and squeeze. A rush of adrenaline mixed with desire slithers like a snake through me. I grit my teeth and pull my hand away, sickened at the lack of willpower. No, I won't pleasure myself. Not unless I'm with her, or in her home surrounded by her scent. That is the only time I allow myself a moment's respite and let go of the bitter hate and anger of not having her with me.

Now, it's time to focus on the matter at hand. I laugh openly into the silent room. The sound echoes off the concrete walls where all the beautiful images stare back at me. Gillian, walking down the street, doing yoga, working out at the gym, eating lunch with Davis. I've cut his face out of the picture and put my own in its place. It is going to be so nice to obliterate him. Instead of a bomb, though, I want to torture the pecker like he's torturing me. Keeping me away from my property, my possession, my woman, all of those violations deserve a great deal more pain rather than a quick ka-boom.

Her best friend. Her first fuck…there is something poetic about taking him out first. Like starting at the beginning. The cold metal cylinder chills my hand as I study its beauty. Smooth, sleek, and packed with a punch. It is almost too easy.

Bye bye, Phillip.

"Hey, you…" Phillip pulls me into a hug. "What are you doing here?" His chocolate-brown eyes seem to sparkle as he scans my face for signs of concern. His light hair curls a bit around his ears. He needs a haircut.

"I thought you could use a break. I know I could." I smile and grip his hand, squeezing it.

"Where to?" He pulls on his blazer, then shuffles the papers he'd been poring over, into a neat stack.

I roll my eyes and sigh. "I'd love to say Del Sol, but I'm under strict orders to stay indoors. Meaning, within the confines of Davis Industries."

Phillip's eyebrows knit together, and then he looks over my shoulder and waves at Austin, my bodyguard. As far as bodyguards go, I couldn't have asked for a better one, not that I want one in general. The fact that Chase believes I *need* one, and has been proven correct on multiple occasions, irks me. Austin stands off to the side scanning the area. He's a real gentleman—hulking in size and looks like a modern day Rambo. He has a Southern twang and mannerism that I find incredibly endearing. He does his best to stay out of my way, trailing me closely, only hovering when we are outside, getting into a car or going somewhere with Chase. If my guy is around though, Austin makes a point to give us privacy, while keeping his eye on his charge. If Chase didn't have Jack the linebacker on his tail, I would have put up more of a fight. However, now that the news of our impending nuptials is out and this stalker business has escalated, I feel safer having Austin with me. Of course, I'd never admit that to Chase. Smug, sexy bastard. I wouldn't want to inflate his ego any larger, not that it would be possible.

"Seriously? You can't leave the building?" He places a hand at my back and leads me to the elevators and directly in front of Austin. "Austin, I'm taking Gillian to Del Sol for lunch."

"Sorry, Mr. Parks. Ms. Callahan is to stay within the building unless escorted by Mr. Davis himself." At least Austin has the good manners to look chagrined. He doesn't like telling me what to do, and, worse, he doesn't appreciate chasing after me when I ignore the rules. Still, it is his job, and I want him to keep it for the time being.

Phillip's face contorts into a grimace. "That's insane.

You can't keep her in a fish bowl." Austin shrugs and settles as far back in the elevator as possible to give us space.

Phillip huffs as we get onto the elevator. "Your boyfriend has issues," Phillip says as I press the number on the elevator that will bring us to the cafeteria. They have good food, but I've been eating the same things for the past couple weeks, and it's really starting to grate on my nerves.

"With all due respect, sir, Mr. Davis only wants to keep his fiancée safe. We've had to ramp up security as of late, and it's just easier if we keep Ms. Callahan where we can have a firm eye on her."

This conversation is old and degrading. I'm not a child, and I'm not going to live my life like this. The elevator opens, and we all walk out. Just like he does every day, Austin immediately heads to the side wall to start his perimeter check. Before the elevator doors close I grab Phillip's arm, haul him back into the car and smash the "L" for the Lobby. The doors close just as Austin runs over to it yelling, "No!"

Phillip laughs as I take deep, calming breaths and giggle alongside him feeling like a teenager who just escaped her parents' house.

"You're a kook. You know you could have just told him you were going no matter what. He couldn't stop you."

Excitement tingles on the edges of my nerve endings. Sometimes, not following the rules is fun. "I don't know. I just reacted," I lift my gaze to his. At the same time, we both start laughing. It's ridiculous to think I can't go anywhere because of some deranged admirer. Besides, I have Phil with me. Nothing could happen in his presence. He loops his arm over my shoulders just as the door dings.

"Come on, I'll buy you lunch." He shakes his head, a

smirk planted on his sweet face.

We make it three feet before I see Chase and stop dead in my tracks. He looks insanely hot in his light grey suit, matching vest, white dress shirt and red tie. My eyes scan him from his glistening dress shoes, up those tight, muscular thighs that I love pressing me into flat surfaces. I continue the visual caress, journeying up his body to the promised land. Just a hint of his bulge can be seen against the expensive fabric. Following the path, I enjoy his trim waist, remembering how it feels to scratch my nails along the ridges of the perfect speed bumps of his abdomen, then across the wide, finely toned chest. Finally, my gaze settles onto those bottomless blue eyes. So blue they are like the ocean waters of Cancun. Right now though, those waters are frigid, glacial in their intensity.

"Well isn't this cozy?" Chase says as he makes his way toward us. Phillip grips my shoulder smiling confidently. "Escaping the castle are we, Princess?" Ugh. I hate Princess. I didn't like it when it was used in my past, and I don't want to hear him use it...ever again.

"You don't have to answer that," Phillip responds, annoyance coating his words.

"Oh, but she does, seeing as how the moment she leaves those doors," he points to the glass wall behind us with the rotating spinning door and exit to the building. "She's at risk."

Phillip rolls his eyes. "I can handle a little paparazzi..." Phillip starts, but Chase cuts him off by stepping close to Phil's face, leaving a scant few inches between them.

My best friend physically bristles at the nearness and intensity. Chase speaks quietly, but the tendons bulging in his neck reveal his frustration. "It's not the fucking paparazzo that's the problem. It's the sick fuck sending her threatening notes, disgusting sexual gifts slathered with his semen, and dead roses that I'm worried about." Chase's eyes narrow emphasizing his point. My gut churns like the sea in the middle of a storm.

Phillip pulls away, surprised as Chase eases me to his side protectively.

"Gigi, what's he talking about?" I sulk back against Chase, and he pulls me out of the protective cubby hole of his warm body.

His eyes dart to mine and are hard points when he responds. "So, you didn't think to tell him why I've hired a bodyguard?" He looks down at me, clearly frustrated.

I shake my head. "Not exactly. I told him about the flowers, and the texts but we haven't had a chance to really get into it..." My words fall off as I see Phillip's face morph into an all-encompassing frown.

"The last thing I ever want to hear is a frantic call from Austin. Do you have any idea what went through my mind?" Chase grates, his chastisement like an icicle through the heart.

Where is my Rambo anyway? He should have made it down by now. Scanning the perimeter my gaze settles on him standing off to the side along the back wall. His hands are clasped in tight fists, jaw clenched and eyes darker than I've ever seen them. He's always looked at me as if I was a sweet woman. Now, though, he's got a reason for the hard expression that draws his mouth into a thin line. I look down, ashamed, realizing that my juvenile actions actually hurt someone. I'll make sure that Chase doesn't fire him for losing me. Again.

"Gigi, what's going on? You have a man stalking you, and you didn't think it was important to mention how serious it was?" Phillip's eyes search my face. Concern and sadness evident in the way his eyes soften and turn a lighter brown.

I shrug. "Honestly, it didn't seem important. And, technically, I did tell you about the weird flowers I'd received. We don't know anything about him. He could be an old neighbor with a crush for all I know."

"You should've told me it was more than an admirer. I would never have suggested we go to lunch or let you blow off your guard if I'd known some asshole was after you. Chase, man, I'm really sorry." Phillip holds out his hand. Chase shakes it and nods. Some kind of man telepathy flashes between them as they come to a sort of truce.

Chase has never been Phillip's biggest fan. In the beginning, he may have even felt threatened by our closeness, but not anymore. Only recently since Phillip has been dating Bree have his feelings towards Phil eased into something bordering on friendship. At the very least, I'd consider them really good acquaintances. I have hope for more between them. They are the most important men in my life, and I wouldn't know what I'd do if I didn't have either of them. It is imperative that they get along.

"No matter. You know now. Until we can get more information on this guy, I want her kept close and with Austin at all times." Phillip nods. "Austin will accompany you to the restaurant and you will take one of my cars," Chase states, firm and unbending.

"We were going to walk—" Phillip stops when Chase

snaps a heated gaze in his direction.

"It would be safer if you took one of my cars. Jack will drive you and escort you back here."

"Don't I get a say in any of this?" I'm tired of watching the men volley back and forth about my life, without so much as a peep to find out how I was feeling, or what I might want.

"Phillip, can you wait for Gillian in the car? I need a moment with my fiancée." I look at Phil with widening eyes, silently begging him not to go. He smiles wickedly and shakes his head, clearly giving me a "you're on your own" look. I watch Phillip exit the building, and, just as I was about to speak, Chase's hands are cupping my cheeks and his lips slanting over mine.

Warmth. A wet, comfortable heaven, seeps into every pore as Chase kisses me. His fingers tangle into my hair as he pulls my head back, devouring me completely. His kiss is indecent and erotic. I could vaguely hear the sounds of heels clacking along the marble floors, and the elevator's repeated ding, announcing the cars arriving on the lobby level. I slide my hands under Chase's blazer and up his muscular back, scraping my nails down the taut surface while he plunges his tongue greedily into my mouth.

After long minutes, he pulls away. I chase his lips, plucking at the bottom one to get at that last bit of flesh before it is gone. Chase groans and cups my ass grinding his pelvis into my belly. I can clearly feel the hard ridge of his excitement through the thin fabric. Moisture fills the space between my thighs making my sex feel heavy and needy. I moan without regard to who may be watching, as he drags his lips along my neck.

"Never scare me like that again." I nod. "Promise me," he says with a firm clench of my ass.

I am wallowing in a pool of lust, barely able to keep my feet on the ground, though the honesty in his request ruffles me, bringing me back to the present. "I promise," I say, holding him tight, trying to make him believe that I'd never willingly frighten him.

He separates his body from mine, bringing me a full arm's length away but I'm still held at the biceps. "Now, enjoy lunch with your friend. And stop looking at me like that, or I'll fuck you against this column."

I gasp. "You wouldn't dare..."

"My building, my woman. Don't test me." And right then, I knew he wasn't joking. The man did what he wanted, when he wanted, and little would prevent him from getting his way. That power draws me in and holds me captive, and I never want to be free of the way he makes me feel.

"I really am sorry." His tie is askew so I reach up to adjust it and slip it back in place, tucking it perfectly under his vest. God, the man is sex personified. It takes mammoth effort not to crawl up his body and cling for dear life.

He tips my chin up to meet his gaze. "I know. Just please be careful. Text me when you're back."

I laugh. "I'm sure Austin, or Jack, or even the building security guard will tell you when I return."

He snaps his fingers at Austin and waves him over. I hate it when he does that. It seems like he's calling over a dog.

"Chase, don't snap at people. Your staff are not dogs or children."

His gaze darts to mine. He takes a deep breath through

his nose, nostrils flaring slightly. Then on his exhale, his eyes soften, turning impossibly kind. "You're right. I'll work on it." His lips crook into the sexy curve.

I lean up and kiss the edge of that lovely curve. "Thank you, baby. Love you."

"Love you. But still want to hear personally from my fiancée when you return." He loves calling me his fiancée. It seems as if he finds every reason possible to plop it into conversation. I wonder briefly if it makes it more real for him. Austin makes it to our side, and I look at him guiltily. Anyone can tell he's angry, but he has too much class to say anything. That or he fears what Chase will say.

"Austin. Gillian and Mr. Parks are going to lunch. Jack will drive. Stay close. And don't let my love slip through your fingers again." Chase is going easy on him. This experience is considered a warning. If I leave his side again, Chase will fire him. Every facet of my being is swimming with remorse. The tension pours off Austin as the two men share a stare off.

"Yes, sir." Austin answers simply.

After a quick kiss goodbye from Chase, Austin leads me to the car where Phillip has waited patiently. Before I get in, I stop and search Austin's face. He's having trouble looking me directly in the eyes.

"I'm sorry. I shouldn't have done that. It was childish and could have cost you your job." I look down, the shame controlling my mood. He touches my elbow. The gesture is friendly, meant to make a point.

Finally, I woman up and meet his hazel eyes. "If I may say so, screw the job, Ma'am. That little act could have cost you your life. Don't do it again," he warns, his eyes pleading.

"I won't." I mean it. If Austin has to stick to me like glue until this stalker business is over with, so be it. Either way, I have a feeling Austin will be around for a long time. Chase is unlikely to let me roam freely ever again. He doesn't like the idea of the paparazzi getting close, let alone some admirer with a small vocabulary and a pension for dead flowers.

Crawling into the car, I lean my head back with a sigh.

"Don't think you're off the hook with me, pretty girl. You're in big trouble. Big. Huge!" Phillip spreads his arms wide as I roll my eyes and cross my arms defensively.

"Yeah, yeah, get in line."

GILLIAN

CHAPTER THREE

Lunch with Phillip is excruciating. He spends the entire hour droning on and on about how I need to be more careful, and shouldn't have attempted to escape Austin's watch. The most surprising thing is how all of a sudden, my best friend is now enamored with my fiancé. Ultimately, we end lunch with a nod and a wave instead of our normal bear hug and snuggle. The entire experience has me in a sour mood now that I've had the day to think it through. What other woman has to deal with so many "great protectors" hovering over her every move? No one, that's who.

When Chase enters the master bedroom, I'm sprawled out on the bed, shoes kicked off, skirt in a heap on the floor wearing only a beige silk blouse and my undergarments. The ceiling is the most interesting thing in the room as I stare up, trying to put the pieces of my day back together. It's impossible. The day has been shit and I'm feeling very sorry for myself.

I try not to look at Chase although I can feel his presence as keenly as a breeze blowing against my hair. He's prowling, and I know his eyes are all over me. Technically, I should still be miffed by his behavior outside the elevators, but it only left me with a slow burning ache between my legs and a steady rosiness to my cheeks. A couple times today I was asked if I was too warm or coming down with something. When Austin asked in the elevator on the ride up, I'd about had it. I was ready to scream to the heavens or to anyone who would listen that I was turned on and to back the fuck off! The only thing that could put a salve to this wound was a six foot three Superman look-a-like who, right at this moment, was stripping off his tie and blazer, eyes scanning me from head to toe.

"Tired?" he asks cryptically.

"No. Hot." The words drip from my lips, sounding more like a growl than an answer.

"Agreed." His smirk is devastatingly sexy. He unbuttons his dress shirt one tiny white button at a time making a meal out of the process. Everything in me is hyper focused on each new piece of skin Chase uncovers. "You're in need?" One dark, sculpted eyebrow rises in perfect synchrony with the white fabric falling off his broad chest to pool at his feet.

His question is rhetorical, so I choose to nod, then arch my back off the bed, seductively sliding my hands from my hips, covered in black lace, to the buttons of my own blouse. Chase loosens his belt under my watchful gaze. The sound of the leather as it is pulled through his belt loops is almost as heated as his groan when I pluck open all but one button on my blouse. The creamy silk spreads to the sides exposing the fair skin of my abdomen. Chase sucks in a ragged breath through his teeth.

"Jesus, Gillian. Nothing compares to your beauty."

"Prove it," I say as I pop open the last button revealing a cream-colored lace push-up bra with black trimmed edge, the direct opposite of the matching panties. The bra does wonderful things to my breasts, pushing them up so high I could probably lick them myself. I cross one stocking-covered leg over the other, adding a pleasing press to my sex. I moan and scratch at the silk covering my thighs, clearly desperate. Chase knows what I'm doing.

"Oh I plan to. You were bad today. Should I issue a punishment?"

Punishment. That word has never entered my love's vocabulary, nor would I ever want it to. The word itself has negative connotations. Something given as a penalty for an offense, transgression, fault. To handle severely or roughly as in a fight. I knew exactly what the word meant, because Justin had me look it up and repeat it back to him like a robot right before he beat the hell out of me for something he thought I did wrong. His *punishment* he called it.

I spring from the bed, seemingly catapulted into a different time. A hateful memory bleeds into my psyche unwanted.

"You can't do anything right, can you?" Justin screams into my face while holding my throat in a viselike grip. His fingers dig into the tender column.

"Justin, I'm sorry! I didn't mean to. It was an accident." Tears pour down my face in rivulets, each crystal orb should calm him, see the sincerity in my apology. It doesn't. Crying does nothing but make him happy. Knowing he can affect me so deeply gets him off.

"I worked hard for the money that bought that chicken and rice, and your stupid ass burnt it all to a crisp!" His other hand comes out of nowhere and smacks me upside the head. I feel like one of those punching dolls. You keep it steady with one hand, punch it repeatedly with the other, and it bounces back for another go.

"I'm sorry, I swear. I was trying something new. Something I

thought you'd like and it didn't work! Really…" I'm cut off by a particularly harsh blow to my face that cuts my lip and makes my nose gush blood. The metallic smell and taste is vile, and I choke and spit at the floor.

"Now you're spitting on my floor you crazy cunt! Making another fucking mess. That's it. It's time for me to punish you!"

Justin pulls my ponytail and yanks my neck back, then drags me kicking to the kitchen table, where he proceeds to bend me over it forcefully. He slams my face into the Formica tabletop, blood spatters across the shined surface. The table settings clank as Justin grabs the spatula hot off the stove. He runs the hot metal down my spine sending spikes of pain warnings to my brain. Justin pulls up my dress and rips the simple cotton briefs off me, shoving them crudely out of his way.

"You fucking scream, whore, and I'll kill you," his scent is mixed with body odor and sawdust from the building he's working on. The smell swirls viciously in my gut, and I breathe shallowly through a busted nose and split lip, trying not to vomit. "You got that, slut?" he grits through his teeth.

I nod, crazily wishing, praying, hoping this will be over fast.

He palms my bare ass and for a moment I think maybe, maybe he'll just fuck me and not hit me. Wrong. Dead wrong. The first lash of the metal spatula sears my flesh. White hot pain, rips through my ass and up my back. I cry out, but quickly muffle the scream into my forearm biting the flesh trying to compensate for the whipping lashes against my fragile bare skin.

After twenty lashes he stops. His chest rises and falls, clearly winded. Between the heat scorching my ass and the pounding of my head from the repeated knocks from his fist, I almost pass out. But the blessed blackness doesn't come. What did set my teeth to rattle, is a punching shove against the table, hitting my teeth against the *top and bruising the gums.*

Then his dick pierced me. A guttural howl rips from my lungs...

Tears pour down the sides of my face as I come to. Chase is kissing the tears away. My entire body is shaking violently as I will the vile images to disappear, still stuck halfway between the nightmare and my happy place... Chase's embrace.

"Baby, baby, I'm sorry. I didn't know," Chase whispers as he hauls me into his lap. His voice is my anchor, and I cling to his chest, before wrapping my entire body around him, legs locked behind his back. Large, safe arms claim my back as I burrow into the warm, naked skin of his neck. Peace. Here is where I'm safe. No one can hurt me as long as I'm right here. He is my serenity.

"You're safe, baby. You're safe. I'm never going to hurt you. I'm sorry, God,"—his voice cracks with emotion— "I'm so sorry."

I nod and sniff into the warm haven of his neck. He smells of soap, and a delicate mix of citrus and sandalwood. It's heavenly. If they could bottle it up, I'd spray the scent all over my clothes and bedding. Chase rocks me from side to side then front to back. He kisses my temples and the tears that run down my cheeks, everywhere he can reach. His giant hands skim up and down my skin in long, calming, soothing strokes.

After a time, I finally pull my head from the shelter of his neck.

"Hey, there's my beautiful girl," he whispers, and I smile weakly.

He leans in and barely touches his lips to mine. The

touch is feather light but speaks of such promise. Chase is letting me come back to myself, to choose to accept his kiss. I do, greedily. And I don't stop, can't stop. I *need* him. With me, in me, to banish this memory, this nightmare. I pull at his neck and devour his mouth with my lips, tongue and teeth. My legs are hooked around his back, and I grind my sex against his hardness. He groans and pulls back, cupping my face and staring deep into my eyes.

"Slow down, Gillian. There's no rush. Do you want to talk about what just happened?"

I shake my head. "No, I want you to make love to me," I squeeze my legs around his body rubbing against his erection. It feels so good. He must know that I need him. Only he can take away the sick feeling, remove the claws of this monster and replace them with light and love.

Chase leans his forehead against mine. "I don't want to hurt you. I don't know what the right thing to do is." He sounds miserable. My big, strong man is out of his element, shattered. He thinks he hurt me, that the flashback was his fault. I have to convince him otherwise. Nothing could be farther from the truth.

"Look at me, Chase." His ocean-blue eyes pierce mine. I see sadness, hurt, and fear in their depths, and I won't have it. "Just love me. Your love takes it all away."

His eyes close and he sucks in a deep breath. I'm holding mine until he pulls me close and stands. Slowly, he sets me down on our bed, his body coming down with me. He removes his boxer briefs and my bra, panties, and stockings until we're both bare and as raw as the emotions filling the room.

He lays his naked body over mine and settles between

my thighs. Slowly his hands pull my legs farther apart as the knobbed head of his cock lies against the petals of my sex, awaiting entrance. He gazes into my eyes gauging my need. I try my best to show only my love, trust and desire for him. It must work, because he slides his length into me in one slow, heavenly thrust, until there is no him or me, just us.

Together. Joined.

I cup his cheeks sliding my thumbs along the five o'clock shadow marring his beautiful face. His eyes are still uncertain, worried. "You, surrounding me. Keeping me safe. This is what I need to pull me away from the depths of hell and bring me back to your love. Promise me you'll always bring me back," I whisper and kiss his lips.

"I promise," he says into my open mouth as the tension becomes too much. He pulls back and thrusts, fully embedding his thick cock deep inside. Lust coils between us as streams of pleasure shoot through me.

At a leisurely pace, Chase makes love to me. Most of the time we are so starved for one another he takes me wherever he finds me. Whether it's against a wall, in the closet, the library, our living room, each and every time its earth shattering. But this? This is an affirmation. His promise to me. It's how he's proving his undying love. I don't need a ring on my finger to know he's it for me. I can see it in his eyes, the way he looks at me, the struggle on his face as he pumps into me over and over, wanting, needing to ensure I go over the edge first. Always certain to make me scream with delight—never in pain.

I pull my legs up and over his back, and cross my ankles, holding him close. His hands cup my face, and he stares into my eyes, hips moving faster, pressing harder, deeper. He shifts his hips, swirls his pelvis and presses down, pushing his manhood against the perfect spot over and over until stars streak across my vision. I almost fear the fall, but he's there to catch me. Always.

"That's right, baby. Give it to me. Come for me."

His lips take mine in a wet kiss as I tumble into oblivion crying out his name. My limbs lock around his ass, clutching, reaching, and gripping for dear life as wave after wave of pleasure consumes me. His body answers the call, hardening and tightening as he swells so large within me I may burst. A silent cry slips past his lips, and then I'm encased in his heat. Jolt after jolt of his essence shoots deep inside, coating, marking, branding me as his.

When I come to, Chase is kissing my face, neck, clavicle, and chest in small loving caresses. His lips feel soft, like an angel's kiss along my cheek. Just when I register the feeling of them touching down, they wisp off to another expanse of bare, moist skin. The sensation is sweet, almost a tickle. I giggle.

"Did you just giggle?"

I smile and laugh. "Yes, I guess I did."

"It was cute."

"Cute?" I cringe and twist my lips unattractively. "Babies and puppies are cute. A naked woman you're still firmly imbedded in isn't cute."

He smirks and his lips tip at the edge. "Well, I say you're cute." I roll my eyes as he leans down and licks one rosy nipple. "And I think you're beautiful." He sucks on the sensitive skin then laves it with his tongue a few times increasing my arousal. I just had him and I already want him again. "And your tits are fucking incredible," he covers my

AUDREY CARLAN

other nipple then draws on it, sending zaps of excitement straight to my core. I can feel his cock stir within me once more. A wicked grin appears across his face.

"You didn't get enough the first time?" I ask jokingly then thrust my hips up to add pressure to where I want it most. He doesn't move. Just allows that huge cock of his to widen and grow within the slick walls of my pussy.

His gaze catches mine and he tugs one nipple up, making me cry out when it plops from his mouth still glistening with saliva. "I'll never get enough of you. Haven't you figured that out?" He tongues my other nipple again, this time blowing on the tip, sending shivers up my spine from the chill. "I don't want to hurt you, Gillian, but I do want your pussy to be so worn out it's hard to cross your legs when you're wearing those sexy-as-sin, fuck-me pumps, and tight-as-hell skirts."

I groan and lean my head back. He palms one breast while the other continues to receive the delightful, wet torture of Chase's lips and tongue. When he adds a gentle nip and tug from his teeth, I beg him to fuck me. He does... oh, yes, he does.

After round two, quickly followed by round three, my sex is throbbing, thighs shaking, and I know now that his lofty goal to have me sore tomorrow is not so far-fetched, as I may have thought initially. As it stands, I'm pretty sure it's impossible to get up to use the rest room.

"Here, baby, let me take care of you," Chase opens my legs. Instantly, the combined fluids of our orgasms start to slide out. As usual, my man watches his essence slide past my lips and along the crack of my bum. I squirm and he grins, immensely delighted. Finally, he wipes away the mess from our lovemaking. I shake my head and throw a hand over my face, and lie there as he cleans up then disposes of the washcloth, rejoining me in bed.

We lay there cuddled against one another's body. I'm about to fall asleep when he asks me a question.

"So, what happened tonight? I know it was a flashback. I want to know about it."

"Chase, no, I don't want to muddy your mind with those things. It was just a bad memory of when Justin beat me that's all." I snuggle in, and he holds me tight.

One of his hands slips into my hair and he runs his fingers through it. He continues this pattern then responds. "I need to know, Gillian. Everything was fine until I mentioned punishing you." I stiffen within his arms, and he continues running his fingers through my hair, then rubbing up and down my naked skin in long, even strokes. "It obviously triggered something. You know I would never hurt you, right? I was honestly suggesting some playful spanking. Nothing painful. God, and the way you reacted, it was worse than in the doctor's office."

He's referring to months ago when we first met. I had to get stitches removed from the mugging I'd endured in Chicago. When the doctor pulled on those stitches that jolt of pain sent me headfirst into a violent flashback. That revelation later turned into an evening of coming clean about our pasts. It was cathartic, and I don't think we'd be as close or moving forward so easily had we not gone through it.

"I'm sorry you were scared," I whisper weakly, not really knowing what to say.

"Scared? Baby, I was terrified. You looked at me as if I

was the devil himself, come to take you to the pits of hell." His arms tighten around me, his voice now shaky.

"I thought that's where I was. Back there, was hell," I admit.

"Tell me," he encourages.

Taking a deep breath, I explain what happened. It was years ago. I'd gotten a new recipe from a friend in college for an easy chicken bake. I'd always been really careful about how I spent Justin's money since he was supporting us by paying for the house and all our food. Back then, school and Justin were my life. He was five years older than me and was working a job in construction to provide for us. I was so excited to try the new dish. Dying to please him with my new cooking abilities. Unfortunately, I'd miscalculated the amount of water to rice ratio, and, after forty minutes, the dish was seared black on the bottom and the rice crunchy. Justin wasn't happy.

"So he beat you up because you burned dinner?"

I nod. "He hit me a couple times, splitting open my lip, almost breaking my nose…that time anyway. Then he drug me by my hair and shoved me face first, bent over on the kitchen table." There is so much tension coiled through Chase's muscles, I stop and kiss his bare chest, then massage each arm.

"Go on. I know there's more."

Taking a deep breath, I continue the story. "He ripped off my panties, took the hot spatula off the stove, and spanked me with it. Well, spanking is the wrong word. He hit me so hard he broke skin and bruised me black and blue. I had to sleep on my stomach for a week. In class, I'd use my sweater as a cushion on the hard chairs so no one would figure anything out." Chase's breathing was tight and labored.

"Is that it?" he asks through clenched teeth. I shake my head slowly peering deep into his eyes. I couldn't look at him when I said the last part.

"Then he raped me."

It took a couple years and a lot of therapy with Dr. Madison to finally admit that what Justin did to me was battery and rape. Admitting it to Chase has me crying into his chest for a good thirty minutes. Chase is a trooper though. He soothes me, speaks softly, and promises me that no one will ever hurt me again. Remarkably after sharing the story and falling asleep on Chase's chest, it was one of the best night's sleep in my life. I wake before Chase. It's Saturday, so we don't have to work. Although I never know with Chase. Lately, he seems to be making more of an effort to minimize the amount of work he does on the weekends. Instead of waking him, I choose to let him sleep. He never sleeps for long, and after the emotional downpour last night, he probably needs it. Then it dawns on me...today is Bree's birthday! I do a little naked jig, excited that we're all meeting up at one of Chase's swanky restaurants. I can't wait. Excitement skips through my veins as I make my way into the bathroom. Having everyone I love get together in one place is such a treat and so good for the soul.

The shower is scalding when I jump in and adjust the dials. I begin to hum a tune happily working the shampoo through my hair and methodically rinsing it. Conditioner follows, but I leave that in to soak into my red tresses while I lather up the body wash. Mmm...I love the smell of vanilla and cherry. So does Chase. He constantly comments on how good I smell. Usually that comment is paired with a sexy smile, and I'd go a long way to see more smiles on his face. When the suds reach my thighs I look down and am taken aback.

On the side of each thigh are four perfect fingerprint bruises. Seeing the purple marks normally would send me rolling into another bout of self-loathing, but these don't. Knowing these bruises are from Chase, a physical reminder of last night's lovemaking, changes them into something akin to a gift. It's just another bit of proof of the passion with which he took me, his haste to prove his love to me. They weren't given to harm but to please. I've come a long way. A secret smile slips past my lips as I lean my head back and close my eyes while rinsing my hair. When I open them, I'm grinning into the face of the most gorgeous man on the planet.

"Hey, beautiful, what are you smiling at?" Beautiful is an endearment I'm a-okay with.

"Oh nothing, just thinking about you and last night," I purposely glide my hands over my swollen breasts and down my ribs, abdomen, then legs. His eyes follow every movement as if he was caressing me himself.

His saucy grin abruptly turns cold, and I'm thrown back for a moment. The shower door flies open and a burst of cool air prickles against wet skin. I cover my breasts out of instinct and to prevent further chill.

"What. The. Fuck. Are. Those?" he points down at my thighs and the fingerprints.

I smile. "Those are a direct result of someone's passion," I waggle my eyebrows. He steps into the shower still wearing his pajama bottoms and hauls me against his bare chest. The water seeps into the grey cotton leaving dark, smudgy, soggy sections.

"Baby, I'm sorry. I promised I'd never hurt you. Christ! What is wrong with me?" He clutches my back sealing our bare chests against one another with no room to even let the water from the shower trickle through.

"No, Chase, no. I'm fine. We made love. Sometimes we both get overly excited. I'm not apologizing for the red streaks down your back am I?" He drags his head from the crook of my neck. A grimace mars his sculpted features.

"Really? You scratched me?" He turns around and sure enough, eight slightly raised lines pucker the skin of his muscular back. They won't be long lasting. Probably a day or two and they'll be gone, but for now, I love seeing them there. Anyone in the world could tell this man was taken and taken good!

I grin. "Not sorry, because I'll do it again. Maybe tonight." Biting my lip, I push at his wet pants and they sink to the floor in a squishy heap. "Never apologize for making love to me. I adore your passion, baby." I give him my most sexy look possible. He needs to understand that he could never truly hurt me.

"It's just, I don't want to mar your skin." He trails a hand over my breasts down my ribs until he drops to his knees. Before I realize what he's doing, his lips are on the bruises, kissing and licking each grape-sized mark as if his kisses and mouth alone could will them away. I let him, knowing it's important for him to make peace with this. It's going to happen again and again, and I wouldn't want it any other way.

I try to pull him up by tugging on his head, but he shakes me away. "Not done with you. Need to show you my love." His words are simple but dig deep.

He gently lifts one of my legs and sets it on the seat inside the shower, opening me, my center at eye level with his face. The anticipation is thrilling, yet brutal as he looks his fill of my sex, water running down and gathering at the opening. I close my eyes when his tongue runs through the weeping slit. Bursts of pleasure jolt through me as he uses his lips and tongue to suck and nip at my most intimate place. Using his thumbs, he opens me further then plunges his tongue deep into my core. Every time he pleasures me this way, he takes me to new heights of joy, startling me with mind-bending orgasms. I start to shake holding myself up by leaning on the tile wall as he fucks me with his tongue. When he brings his thumb into play twirling it in tight circles just where I need it most, I break. A bone-melting cry soars past my lips, echoing off the walls in our steamy haven. Chase is right there to catch me as my legs tremble and give out. Strong arms hold me up while I gasp for air, the steam in the shower so thick it adds to the disorientation.

"Thank you, for trusting me. For loving me. I love you, Gillian."

Right then, I know we'll be okay. Reinforcing his feelings by making love to me doesn't hurt anyone; it only heals.

GILLIAN

CHAPTER FOUR

When in Rome, live like the Romans. And that is exactly what I am going to do tonight. It is Bree's birthday, and we are going to one of Chase's swanky restaurants in the heart of downtown San Francisco. As with the classy establishment in Chicago, "Greens" as it's simply named, rises above the clouds in a modern skyscraper not far from our penthouse. As a matter of fact, Chase pointed it out from the rooftop garden this evening where we watched the sun set while snuggled in each other's arms.

After the bathroom incident this morning, my fiancée pours on the charm. He takes me shopping where we got Bree an incredible Buddha statue from an import/export store he owns on one of the many San Francisco piers. The unique statue will work well in her yoga studio. However, it's carved out of solid limestone and heavy as the dickens. Originally, it was imported from India. I didn't even want to think about how much it cost. A little sign near the bottom said $10,000, which almost gave me heart palpitations. I'm really trying hard not to complain about how much money Chase spends on things related to me. It's his money and up to him how he chooses to use it. Besides, I am really excited about the gift. It is one of the most remarkable statues I've ever seen, second only to an ornate life-sized angel hidden away in a dark corner of the lot that caught my eye.

The angel is white with a greyish hue to her stone. A flowing garment draped modestly over her features. Her shoulders are bare and perfectly smooth showing the dips in her clavicle bones. The most extravagant feature is the wide wings that jut out spreading a solid five to six feet. She has both arms away from her sides but not held up in praise. They are level with her chest, both hands held up, palms cupped toward the heavens. The angel's head is bowed down in a respectful pose. It's as if she is accepting God's purpose for her and becoming one with it. I fall in love with her instantly.

"You're taken with her?" Chase's lips graze the side of my neck under my ear sending spikes of excitement to skitter down my spine.

"She's unlike anything I've ever seen."

He nods against my shoulder and wraps both arms around my waist hugging me close, my back to his front.

"She's a guardian angel. I saved this piece from ruin in Greece. She was in the garden of a decrepit abandoned mansion that was being torn down. I bought the land for an environmental project that's been in the works for a few years. Still is. Didn't know what to do with her, so I shipped her here to find a home."

"Why was the mansion abandoned?"

"The family line that had lived there for centuries died out. The last remaining member didn't have any children or family to speak of, so when the last living member died, their fortune was donated to charity and the house sat untouched for years."

I reach out and touch a feather on one of her wings. It's cool to the touch. "That's unfortunate," I murmur enchanted with the angel.

I could feel him smiling against my cheek as we stare at the intricate wings spreading wide, and the angel's face poised in a secret smile.

"It is. The house once was beautiful."

Lightness fills me as I hug Chase's arms closer around me. "I didn't mean the house. I meant the family dying out. It's sad to imagine a future with no children running through your dreams. Don't you think?"

Chase stiffens; his forearms tighten against my body. He doesn't speak.

"You do want children?" I ask, just now realizing we'd never spent any time talking about the future beyond being together and getting married. Spinning around in his arms, I stare into his face. His eyes are thoughtful, not harsh. That is a good sign.

"I guess I haven't ever thought about it before, because I've been so focused on building my empire. With you, though, I find myself wanting and considering things I'd never wanted or considered before." His tone is a low grumble, the perfect pitch for seduction as his nimble fingers dig into the soft skin at my hips.

His answer has me smiling, my heart filling with hope for the future. "We have time. But start thinking about it. I want to carry your son or daughter one day." He gasps at my response and spreads a large hand over my stomach, looking down at his hand dreamily.

"When you say it like that, I want nothing more than to see you bloom with my child. The heir to everything we have." His smile is wistful when he leans down and takes my lips with his.

★ ★ ★ ★

The rest of the day was spent trying on the dresses Dana, Chase's assistant, had efficiently placed in my closest. Of course, all of them fit perfectly, which irks me. I want to hate his perky assistant, but, really, she hasn't done anything to me, and she's been nothing but professional with Chase. It did bother me that there was a woman his age in his life who knew him better than I did, or at least knew his business side better. He told me he never confided in anyone about his past. Only his cousins and I know what he'd been through before moving in with his Uncle Charles.

As it turns out, we'll be seeing his uncle and mother tomorrow for a family brunch. His mother insisted on it. Even though my guy typically bristles at someone else attempting to take charge, he most certainly jumps when that woman speaks. I cringe, realizing that if I'm honest with myself, I wouldn't have a problem spending time there if she liked me or even gave me a chance. Mr. Control Freak thinks I'm reading too much into his stoic Mother. Swears that she has nothing but pleasant things to say about me, but I'm not buying it. A woman knows when another woman doesn't like her. There's a look, a sensation that you get when you're around them. Almost like there's a tension surrounding the two of us. When Colleen and I are sharing a space, it permeates the air making it as thick as walking through molasses.

"A million dollars for your thoughts?" Chase asks.

"A million? Really? Do you always go overboard?"

He looks at me deadpan. "Yes, when it comes to you, I'd pay just about any price to know your thoughts."

I laugh and cuddle into his side. He swipes away a russet lock of hair pushing it behind my ear. These moments of quiet, sitting in the back of his limo, heading to our destination, are precious to me. During the day he's a giant, a business tycoon set on one goal and one goal alone, building and keeping his empire growing. At home, he's all man, a sexual god, and sometimes gentle lover. But when it's still, calm, that moment when you can hear your mate breathe, those are the times where I feel most content. Any couple can burn up the sheets, share careers, but how many can just *be* with one another. No pretenses, no pressing issues, the complexities of life all gone, leaving you stripped bare. What do you have left? Me, I have Chase, and he's all I need.

As if he can read my thoughts, he kisses my temple then caresses my cheek with the pad of his thumb. His eyes are dark, midnight in the shadow of the car.

"You're all I need," he whispers then brushes his lips over mine. Expressing my exact thoughts back to me has me fearing I said them aloud, but I know I didn't. We're connected in a way that defies reality.

His phone chirps, and the connection we have is not lost but definitely put on hold. Our moment of peace is gone, but it will be back. We have a lifetime to experience the quiet, and that thought makes me blissfully happy.

As Chase barks orders into the phone, all big businessman once more, we arrive at the restaurant, and Jack opens the door. Austin is flanking the door by the limo. If I was alone, he'd be helping me out of the car and escorting me in. When Chase is with me, he stands just off to the side, ensuring no suspicious characters get too close. Chase exits, looks around, then grabs my hand, swiftly pulling me into his side. His hand grips my hip protectively as a hoard of paparazzi come barreling towards us, cameras flashing.

"Looks like Dana's tip to the media that we'd be at Red SF didn't work. Showtime, my darling." Chase keeps me close and moves forward. "Austin, not even a finger," he growls as the paparazzi come from every direction.

"Chase, Gillian, look here!" one screams.

"No, Chase, Chase over here. Show us your bride!" another hollers.

"Yeah, let's see her rock!" A rotund man shouts, shooting his camera so close to my face I could hear the rapid-fire clicking. Austin shoves the man's hand from in front of me and holds him back.

The sound is deafening and the flashes blinding. I stumble in my too high heels, but Chase catches my waist, Austin steadying me at the elbow. I'm flanked on both sides by the men now. Jack is in front of Chase, pushing photographers out of the way so we can get through. I can't see as the flashes continue to flare, so instead I just tuck my head down and stare at the ground, letting Chase and Austin lead the way.

Finally, we make it past the lobby and into the sanctuary of the elevator.

"Jesus that was crazy. It's never been that bad before." I take a deep breath as Chase rubs his hand up and down my bare back. I've worn another dress open in the back. My man loves to touch my skin. And since I crave his touch, it's a win-win scenario any way you look at it. Besides, when

I put on this form fitting little black dress, I felt hot. It's a respectable length, goes down almost to the knee in a pencil skirt style and comes up into a boat-neck collar, running along the clavicle, and three-quarter sleeves. The surprise is when I turn around. The entire back drops away into a cowl shape that dips all the way down to the top of my ass. It's extremely revealing from behind, but shows absolutely nothing but tight curves in the front. I've paired it with the black, platform Louis Vuitton shoes Dana ordered and nothing else.

That's my other surprise. Eventually, Chase will slide his hand down to touch my ass. It's inevitable. He won't be able to contain himself for long. He puts on a good show of being completely in control, and in most things, he is. Except for me. Bare skin is kryptonite for my Superman. Mentally, I give myself a high five for going commando. Men can do it; why not women? Besides, it makes me feel wild. There's something unbelievably freeing about not wearing underwear.

"Speaking of the media frenzy, Dana has been hassling me about setting up the interview for *People* magazine about our engagement and upcoming wedding." I cringe when he mentions Dana, knowing my jealousy is childish and unfounded. He continues, "Baby, doing the interview is a good idea. It would be on our terms and help deflect the paparazzi. Right now, we're like a shiny new toy to them. Once we get our interview out there, it will take away from the mystery and excitement. Understand?"

I take a deep breath and shrug my shoulders. "If you say so. I'm not really interested in sharing our love with anyone, but if you think it will get them to back off, I'll do it."

"I do." He pulls me into a hug clasping his hands behind my back. I mimic his pose crossing my hands at the wrist just above his tight ass. "Thank you," he pecks my lips then rubs his forehead along mine. "You look incredibly beautiful tonight. Did I mention that?"

"Yes, but a lady never tires of hearing it." I grin and he nuzzles my temple before placing one last sweet kiss there. His hand trails down my arm, and our fingers automatically entwine.

The table is alive with excitement when we arrive. "Greens" is an upscale, gourmet restaurant, where everything they serve is one hundred percent organic. It's also like entering a secret night garden. The ceiling is dark with tiny, soft, twinkling lights that look like stars. I can see the constellation Orion built into the design. The big and little dippers sit above our massive table. Everywhere you look is lush foliage of varying degrees. Some flowers, some plants, overall a bold display of nature's beauty. It's magnificent and different, just like the man that owns it.

Bree is practically bouncing in her chair when she jumps out and hugs me, then twirls and plants a full mouthed kiss on Chase, squeezing his cheeks. Chase grasps her biceps and his eyes open so wide you'd think the poor man was being electrocuted. Bree pulls back, leaving a splotch of red lipstick smeared across his lips.

"I love this man!" She pats his chest affectionately.

"Uh," Chase is at a loss for words.

Phillip tips his head to the side, looks at me, then at Chase, and, with a snarky grin, grabs me by the neck to pull me in for a wet one. "Only fair Dude!" Phillip laughs as he tries to kiss me. Before Chase can respond, thick arms yank me back from behind. My friend practically falls over as I'm lifted in the air and placed to the side.

"You can kiss me, sweetie pie!" Austin says and makes a fish face. I had no idea he was still trailing us.

"Blech!" Phillip backs up with a laugh.

Chase pulls me against his side then wipes the lipstick away with his handkerchief. He looks over at Austin who saved me from the perils of getting a revenge kiss from my best friend. Chase points a finger at Austin, still clutching the white handkerchief in his hand, the one now stained red with Bree's lipstick. "You're getting a raise! Five hundred more a month for that move alone!"

"What about me! I was the one that kissed you!" Bree puffs out her lip. "Oh sweetheart, your present will be revealed soon," Chase grins.

Again Bree continues bouncing around, happily sipping a fruity looking cocktail. Her tight body highlighted in all the right places. I can see Phillip's appreciation. He can hardly keep his eyes off her. She's dressed to kill tonight and everyone knows it. Her dress doesn't leave anything to the imagination. The skin-tight, tank style, in a deep aubergine compliments her tanned skin and golden hair. The scooped neckline on the front is dangerously low, revealing perky breasts that are the perfect size to match her tiny frame.

Chase leans over and places a hand at my nape and his lips to my ear. "If Phillip keeps eye-fucking Bree so openly, I may have to take you in my manager's office." His fingers trail from my neck down to my waist where he tickles the dips at the base of my spine. Chills race up my back, instinctively I arch into his hard body. He smirks and then slides his hand discreetly into the open back laying a hand on the top swells of my bare ass. I watch in delight when he realizes I'm not wearing anything under the dress. "Gotcha, baby," I giggle into his neck.

Chase takes a deep breath and presses the evidence of his arousal against my hip on a quiet groan. "You realize that if I wanted you, right here, right now, nothing would stop me from having you. At this point, your friends could watch," he growls against the base of my neck as he sinks his teeth into the tender skin.

"I'll try to behave," I promise him while he drags his teeth along the column of my neck. My knees weaken while lust starts to make me dizzy.

"You do that," Chase warns with one last press of his hips against my side. From nothing to something in a tiny moment. He turns me on quicker than a match lighting.

Changing the subject before I combust and allow him to do exactly what he threatened, I turn my head and gesture to Phil and Bree. Chase's gaze follows mine. Quietly, I whisper against his ear, letting my voice float along the thin cartilage. "I think it's sweet how much Phillip wants her. And as for the other thing, it wouldn't do to leave our guests when you've invited them here for a party. Now, let's mingle so we can go home and you can sink that thick cock so far into me I forget my own name."

I kiss his cheek, and saunter across the room, sitting down in an empty chair at the long table prepared for our party. A steward offers me a glass of wine.

Chase grins evilly as he sits next to me and hooks an arm over the back of my chair. Just before his lips reach the glass he chastises, "Sunshine, you're going to pay for that one." Sunshine? Ugh. Where is he coming up with these?

I swear he must have a book of overused endearments he's testing out like the dictionary's "Word of the Day."

"No to Sunshine," I flip my hair over my shoulder curving away from him then looking coyly from the corner of my eye so he can get a nice long view of my open back. He takes the bait instantly. His eyes sweep from mine down my exposed back and up again. "I always do," I arch an eyebrow and bite my lip just for effect.

He clenches his teeth and drums his fingers along the table's surface. I slide a finger around the rim of my wine glass enjoying our little sexual cat and mouse game. Finally, Chase sighs loudly and then is interrupted with a handshake, man hug, type thing from Thomas, Maria's boyfriend. Thomas immediately updates Chase on the latest inner workings of crime fighting. Chase is friends with the San Francisco Chief of Police and they briefly chat about it.

Carson and Kat come over and greet us both. Kat looks stunning in one of her own designs. "Gigi, I can't wait to show you some of the fabrics I received today from Italy. Chase is a miracle worker!" she says happily.

"How so?" I'm genuinely interested, because last I heard, she was working on the dress designs and Chase was paying her. What more could he have to do with it.

"Well, when I called Chase to thank him for the money and the job of making your dress…"

"Technically, that was me," I interrupt, my feathers feeling a little ruffled. Just because Richie Rich is paying an exorbitant amount of money for a dress doesn't mean it wasn't me who chose her in the first place. I'd never let anyone beside my best friend make my dress.

Kat twists her lip and tilts her head. It's her "cool it

girlfriend" patented look. If Kat thinks you're being ridiculous, you get the lip twist and head tilt. You've said something that would normally offend one of your best friends, lip twist, head tilt. You're ranting on and on complaining about something lame, lip twist, head tilt.

"Sorry," I mumble.

She smacks her lips, "Anyway," she draws out the word. "As I was saying, I called to thank him, and he asked how it was going and what I was waiting on. We chatted, and I explained that I was waiting for the fabric to arrive from Italy. He asked for the vendor info, and today, only two days later, it arrives. Poof! Magic!"

Yeah, no poof, no magic. There were probably a whole lot of dollar bills being exchanged with extra doses of "Yes, sir!" if my guess was correct. I look over at Chase and he throws me a sexy wink. Damn, that man is powerful in more ways than just his overflowing bankroll.

"So, maybe tomorrow I can bring the samples by and show you the new crystals I got," she says happily.

"Can't. Have forced family fun at the Davis' tomorrow for brunch. Oh! You should totally go!" I clasp her hands just as Carson puts his arm around her shoulder.

"Where should you go, sweet cheeks?"

Sweet cheeks? I choke back a laugh and swing my head around to catch Ria's gaze. "Sweet cheeks?" she mouths and I nod. I remember when Chase tried to give me that one, but at least he did it in private.

"Gigi was just telling me that she has to go to brunch at your Dad's. How come we weren't invited?" she sounds concerned. I didn't mean to put doubt in her mind. Leave it to me and my stupid insecurities to mess something up.

"I don't know. Hadn't heard about it either. But, either way, if you want to go we'll crash it." He smiles and she ruffles his hair. His eyes never leave hers. Seeing two people so well suited for one another fall in love is a remarkable thing to witness.

"Yes, please, please. I'll so owe you. I don't want to be alone with her," I whisper, hoping Chase doesn't hear.

"Who? My Aunt Colleen?" Carson asks, his voice loud and booming. Kat elbows him, and I glance her way giving a silent thank you when I hear the resounding "oomph" from the stomach punch.

"What's this about my mother?" Chase's arms wrap about me from behind.

"Nothing, just telling Carson and Kat that we're having brunch there tomorrow and they should come."

Hopefully, that covers Carson's big mouth. I'm sure Kat's going to give him hell later. It's our job as women to teach our men the best way to gossip. You never give away your best friends. Ever. You blame yourself before getting one of your girls stuck in a compromising position. These are rules that a well-trained man in a long-term relationship will eventually catch onto. Obviously, Carson hasn't been in many long-term relationships, or he'd be better at discretion. That could be good or bad news for Kat.

"It will definitely make Gillian happy. She's still finding her footing with Mother," Chase answers but doesn't seem altogether happy about the option.

"Really, it's fine, you don't have to," I hedge trying to calm the waters before they turn choppy.

Carson shrugs. "Okay, cool. Then I'll be keeping my sweet cheeks all to myself," he nuzzles her nose in a sickening display of public affection.

And with that, Maria grabs Kat and me and pulls us over to the end of the table where Bree and Phillip are getting cozy. His hand is on her bare knee and slowly making its way farther up her thigh. A waiter appears with a couple bottles of champagne and another finishes setting down several large trays of noshes and nibbles.

"Let's get this party started, *chicas*!" Maria exclaims loudly. The steward fills four glasses and hands one to each lady. "*Gracias*," she tells him. He fills the other four glasses and hands them to each of the men whether they want it or not. "A toast!" she says.

"Ria, remember where we are…" I warn. Her toasts are a blast for us girls, but are usually peppered with colorful language or profanity. Sometimes both.

"Relax, this will be PG. I just want to congratulate our Bree on her twenty-sixth birthday." We all raise our glasses. "Very few have accomplished so much. Having your own studio and building a business is something to be proud of." Everyone nods, Kat and me tearing up a bit. "On top of that, your body is *muy caliente*. Am I right *Phillipe*?" She nudges Phil in the arm. He grins and wiggles his eyebrows. "*Besos* girl!" she finishes.

We all laugh, and Bree shushes Maria. I lift my glass, "To you, beautiful, *Besos*," I say.

"Yes, to you our sunshine girl, *Besos*!" Kat finishes.

We all take a sip. "Now let's eat!" Carson cuts in.

In front of us are several large platters filled with small finger-sized bites and little bowls of dips and sauces. I grab a triangle shaped item and take a bite. I'm treated to a rich spinach and cheese mixture of pure bliss. Chase tells me it's a Mediterranean dish called Spanakopita. It has flaky pastry layers that hold the melted cheese and veggie goodness. A steward comes and fills our wine with something jammy and red that is to die for. Bree takes a sip of her wine and closes her eyes, basically having a winegasm. I know the feeling. Chase is marvelous at picking wine.

I look over and catch Phil eyeing Bree again. Poor guy. He doesn't stand a chance. That dress she's wearing and those moans she's throwing have me feeling a bit like I'm intruding on a private moment. Chase leans in to whisper in my ear. His breath tickles the hair at my nape. I'd worn it half up, even though he prefers it down, because I wanted him to get the full effect of the dress. He did. Speaking of the dress, his hand keeps creeping its way down my spine, the pad of his fingers trailing along each bump in my spine.

"So what's their deal? Why does it look like Phillip has a serious case of blue balls?" Chase whispers in my ear.

An unladylike snort slips out and Chase snickers. "Probably because they haven't had sex yet," I confide.

"What?" He practically yells. Everyone at the table looks over at us. I know my face has turned bright red.

"Sorry, everyone, just asking a question. Chase couldn't hear me." Apparently, Chase needs training on gossip maneuvering as well. Though instead of being annoyed, I'm rather pleased he hasn't been in a long-term relationship where his girlfriend would have already taught him these subtleties. Now it will be his wife teaching them to him.

Once everyone starts mingling and eating, I lean over. "Try to contain yourself. They haven't had sex yet."

Chase stares at the two, probably trying to find some blatant rationale as to how something miraculous like this could be possible. "Why? Is there something physically wrong with him?" I shake my head. "With her?" His eyebrows shoot into his hairline.

"No, god. He's just gun-shy after Angela, okay. He wanted to take his time."

"I see. Looks like that self-inflicted celibacy is going to end tonight. His hands have been all over her tonight, and she hasn't been any better," he finishes with a smirk.

I smile and watch two of my greatest friends fall for one another. It's lovely and I couldn't be happier. They both deserve happiness, and I really believe they could be a great match.

"What's that look?" Chase asks.

"What do you mean?"

"You were staring at them with a smile as bright as the sun."

Taking a deep breath then a sip of my wine, I stare at Bree and Phillip. Their heads are close to one another, his hand on her shoulder keeping her close, her making repeated efforts to touch him in simple ways. "I want it to work. They deserve it."

"I think it will work. They look good together." Chase offers.

I turn, fully facing him. "Mr. Davis, that was very romantic of you." I goad, knowing that he usually doesn't give his opinion on matters of the heart, unless it involves my heart, of course.

"Lately, I will admit to feeling a bit more on the sweet side," he comes close and nips at my bottom lip. He loves sinking his teeth into me. Doesn't matter where. I'm not complaining.

Maria heard the word sweet and pounces on it lightning fast. "Speaking of things that are *dulce*, what about our *gato's* "sweet cheeks!"" she points at Kat. Her face turns crimson, and she tosses her napkin at Maria.

"Can it, sister!" Kat bellows over the table.

"What, wha'd I miss?" asks Bree.

"Oh just that Carson here calls our girl 'sweet cheeks'!" They're pretty rosy right now," I laugh.

Carson looks at her face then at the rest of us. "Those aren't the cheeks I was referring to when she earned the nickname." I didn't think it was possible for Kat's face to get any redder, but it did. The rest of the table howls in laughter. Even Chase guffaws a few times, letting go of his more conservative nature.

"You guys are terrible." Kat complains then takes a big gulp of wine.

The rest of the dinner carries on with a lot more wine and an exorbitant amount of food. Soon dessert is delivered, and we all sing a drunken version of Happy Birthday. Though Maria sings *feliz cumpleaños* repeating the entire song in Spanish for the hell of it.

After dessert, the waiter serves an after dinner drink, which is really unnecessary because we're all pretty lit, by the time it arrives. Chase has drivers and cars arranged for each of our friends knowing they were all taking taxi's here. My guy thinks of everything, sparing no detail. Bree opens all her presents. On top of the statue—I wasn't sure how we were giving it to her—I give her the book *Eat Pray Love* in hardback and a copy of the movie starring Julia Roberts. The four of us are all closet Julia fans. We have all watched *Pretty Woman* more times than we could count but we'd only admit to it under extreme duress, though, because cool girls didn't have a thing for chick-flick stars.

Bree gives us all a round of hugs and thanks Chase for the dinner. He stands and walks over to an area that had an Asian-style shoji screen. It is opposite the wall that had the door the waiters were using, but this one wasn't used all evening.

Chase steps behind it. "Go ahead and bring it in, boys," Chase says into the darkened space. From behind the screen, a couple of gentleman in navy coveralls enter. They are maneuvering the statue, which is draped in something while they push buttons on a mechanical dolly/mini-forklift, type of thing. Whatever it is, it was pushing the heavy statue into the room. Everyone's eyes are large, wanting to know what's hiding under the sheet.

"Bree, Happy Birthday from Gillian and me," he hugs me to his side.

She walks up to the large drape tentatively and pulls it off. It slides to the floor with a flourish revealing the ornate limestone Buddha statue.

"Holy shit," she whispers as she stares at it. Her hand shakes when she reaches out seemingly almost afraid to touch it.

"It won't bite you, and it's pretty strong. Being made of stone and all," I giggle and hold Chase while she inspects her gift.

Tears spill down her cheeks as she takes it all in. "What's the matter? Don't you like it?" Chase asks placing a hand at her shoulder. She burrows into his chest. He hugs her tight. They hug like that for a couple moments. Chase looks concerned. I'm about to cry myself at the beauty of seeing her connect with him. My bestie loves my guy. Something inside Bree clicked with this gift. That hug and those tears are from joy, only Chase isn't used to consoling a crying woman other than me. His shoulders are ramrod straight and his hand movements on her biceps jerky.

Bree pulls away and Chase looks relieved as he tugs me back to his side. I go willingly, not to save him, but because I love touching him.

"Thank you guys. It's the most beautiful gift I've ever been given. And, the message is loud and clear." She sniffles, wipes her eyes, Phillip by her side, there to hold her.

"What do you mean the message?" I ask.

"Do you see his hand gesture with his finger and hand up like that?" We both nod. "That position is called abhaya mudra. It's a gesture that means blessing, reassurance and protection. Literally, it translates to, 'Do not fear'."

X

Look at that piece of scum with his hand feeling my girl up in the middle of a restaurant. What a depraved human being. So sexed up that he can't treat her like the beautiful woman she is. And she is fucking gorgeous. That dress hugs her curves like a second skin, and the black contrasts perfectly with her fiery hair and creamy white skin. She's perfect. A princess. That's how she'll be treated again when I've got her firmly in my arms, under me, and in my bed. Then, I'll never let her leave.

"Another drink, sir?" The waitress steps in front of me, blocking my view of the private party. I asked to be seated right next to the room with a clear view through the one set of windows next to the entrance. I made certain that I was still far enough in the shadow to ensure Gillian didn't see my face, otherwise I'd be playing my hand a lot sooner than planned.

I never do anything on impulse. Even killing both my parents had taken months of preparation. The only plan that didn't come to fruition was Gillian. She is a chink in my armor, but no more. My inability to keep her is just water under the bridge. Once I get her back, she'll remember her place. Even if I have to spend months hurting her, breaking her down, eventually she'll succumb. Owning her mind is just as important as her body, and I'm a patient man.

When I lay my hands against the white of the tablecloth, the waitress gasps. "Sir, you're bleeding. You've cut yourself."

I look down, dazed, and realize that she's right. Bright red blood drips down from the center of my palm onto the fine white linen leaving a crimson circle stain. Just like my bleeding heart. How fitting. Apparently, while watching Chase rub his slimy hands all over my girl, I clutched a steak knife so tightly it cut clean through the skin on the palm of my hand. Great, I may even need stitches.

"It's nothing. Just bring my bill." The waitress looks at me wide eyed, mouth agape, clearly concerned, not knowing what to do or say. *Moron.* "The check. Now!" I grate through my teeth, keeping my voice as low as possible, yet still holding enough conviction to set the young woman scampering off.

Rich fucker can't even hire competent staff. The food was mediocre as well. I've had better, and for the price, the shit should have tasted like eating gold.

I can see that the party has ramped up. The staff just delivered some type of giant statue on a dolly. Leave it to the bastard to woo using his money. Well, he obviously doesn't know my girl as well as he thinks he does. She was with me first, and I didn't have a one hundredth of the money that asshole brings in. I wonder what the price of that smug face would cost a man. Doesn't matter. I have plans for Chase. If he thinks he can keep my Princess locked away in his tower, he's dead wrong.

In the meantime, though, I stare at her ex, Phillip. The man that's always hovering. He's like a dick in a glass case. Break in case of emergency. Yeah, he'd like to have her again. Who wouldn't? You can see it across his pretty boy face. Oh, he makes a good show of taking it up with the friend. Bree. She's going to be the easiest to pick off, owning her own business. All the late nights she spends alone, closing up her studio before heading out. It's like shooting fish in a barrel with that one. I'm going to save her for when the pickings are slim. Phillip, though, is about to get a new friend. Instead of following my girl, I'll be tailing his ass waiting for the perfect moment to strike.

I remember the smooth metal cylinder waiting at home. It's going to be so sweet to see him explode.

GILLIAN

CHAPTER FIVE

The morning sun streaks through the mostly closed drapes. A thin line of exposed sunlight lands directly over my eyes, waking me. A heavy arm holds me in place as I try to escape the sun's rays. Instead of turning over, I turn into the warm body surrounding me. My face lands against heated, bare, male flesh. Mmmm. His scent is intoxicating and seems to have a direct path to my pleasure button. Chase is my personal scratch and sniff. When my nails scrape along his toned pecs his arms tighten and hips thrust. Reminds me of one of those pop up toys you give to a baby. Slide the switch one way and a lion pops up. Turn a knob and a monkey exits its cubby. Scratch a Chase Davis and his dick rises to attention. Admittedly, it's a pretty fun game. Seeing my man's cock swell and harden from my touch...it's heady stuff, and endless entertainment.

Without jostling Chase too much, I wrap a firm hand around my favorite appendage. I'm rewarded with a low, raspy, groan. The kind from a man whose voice is thickened from sleep. With one finger, I trace a path from base to tip, appreciating the velvety softness. It's quite possibly the softest thing I've ever touched. Pulling back the covers, I spend a few moments admiring Chase's manhood.

He's still asleep, but I'm certain he'll be awake soon. It's taken a good few months for Chase to become accustomed to sharing a bed with a woman. Before me he didn't have sleepovers, and to my greatest relief, he'd never brought a woman to what is now *our* home. In the beginning, he'd often wake with nightmares or sleep very little. Now that I've moved into the penthouse and we've been sharing a bed, he says he sleeps more soundly than ever. As long as I'm in the bed where he can touch me he's fine. If I get up in the night to use the bathroom, upon returning, I usually find him awake, already pulling the comforter back to welcome me once again into his arms.

He tells me I'm noisy when I get up and that he's a light sleeper, but I know his secret. He senses when I'm gone, as I do him. On the rare days that he does make it up without disturbing me, he has taken to kissing my forehead before he leaves for work, knowing it bothers me to wake and not have him there. Usually I'll feel a whisper of minty breath fall across my face on those mornings with a "soon my love" against my hairline. Chase never says goodbye. We haven't really talked about it, but I suspect it has something to do with his upbringing. It must be significant to Chase. I make a mental note to ask him about it.

For now, though, this long, broad, toned god is mine for the taking. It's Sunday and we don't have to be at brunch at the Davis mansion until 11:00 a.m. A quick peek at the clock says its only 6:00 a.m. Plenty of time to gorge on my man without losing my appetite.

Quietly, I straddle Chase's thick thighs, appreciating how his cock seems to surge up toward its mate, instinctively knowing I'm close. I hover just over his groin, keeping deadly silent, not wanting to wake him before I've looked my fill. Chase's face is soft, angelic in sleep. All the tense lines of his jaw and eyes are gone as he slumbers. My businessman, my strong Superman is more a Clark Kent in the quiet of morning.

He has one arm down at his side and the other up over his head, hand curled into a loose fist. Even in sleep, the tendons and sinewy muscle of his forearms show his strength and capability. Those arms curve into squared off shoulders and the most perfect chest I've ever known. Not only is it wide and smooth, with only a smattering of dark hair, it's a haven. When I lay my head on his chest over his heart, I feel as though I'm home. Safe, wrapped in the blanket of his arms. That is how I fall asleep, every night, and will continue to do so for the rest of my life. Never fearing what will happen to me, because I know that Chase will protect me. I no longer have to worry about being harmed in my sleep by the man I thought I loved. With Chase, I'm cherished in his arms and am comforted, knowing I alone belong there.

My gaze drops down past his tight abs to his lovely cock. I push further down his legs so I can get closer to the object of my affection. In my experience, which hasn't been vast, a man's cock is anything but pretty. With Chase, every inch is mouth wateringly beautiful. His penis is more pink in color and free of wiry hair along its length. Only a light patch of curls surround the base. I don't know when he does it, but he's perfectly groomed.

Chase's manhood is devastatingly thick, as large as my wrist, and well above average in length. He doesn't have one of those God-awful porno-sized dicks, but it's the most impressive in size and aesthetics that I've had the pleasure of seeing. But the part of Chase that makes my body thrum, pulse quake, and pussy twinge, are the twin dips at each of his hip bones. God, how those dips where pelvis meet hips, torture me. They take me from zero to a thousand in one flash of bare skin. Even when I'm trying to be sneaky, I can't help but lean down and bite and lick the tender flesh. It's hard to hold back the violent growl and bite of the word *mine* that wants to rip through my throat and put fear into the hearts of any woman within a mile radius of my man.

Leaning back further, I grip the sides of Chase's hips and lick and suck each indention. The twinge of salt and man hits my taste buds seductively. It's not enough. I need more. Always more. Digging my teeth into the tender patch, I tongue and suck until pain lances my tongue, and Chase's hands tangle in my unruly hair. When I pull away, a bright red strawberry sized hickey is left.

"Marking your territory?" Chase's low voice tunnels through my lust. When I look up, all I see is the sky. The room has gotten considerably brighter and Chase's eyes are directly in the strip of light from the sun streaming through the drape's opening.

"Yes," I admit with absolutely no shame.

"Why?" There's no malice in his tone. No irritation, only curiosity.

"Because I want to. Because I can." Apparently, that was the perfect answer. His eyes darken as the pupils dilate, nostrils flare, and his fingers tighten in my hair.

"Come here," he growls.

I shake my head. "Not done."

He sucks in a deep breath. "Now," he says curtly, teeth

AUDREY CARLAN

clenched, fingers tightening along my scalp. Just the hint of discomfort at the roots excites me further. Chase knows exactly how and when to exert a little more control.

"No," I say with equal conviction right before my lips encase the wide knob of his cock and I suck...hard.

"Jesus!" he grates through his teeth.

Smiling around his cock, I pull as much of his length into my mouth as I can. Wanting to prologue the experience for him, I let his wet cock fall out of my mouth to slap against his abdomen. Before he can complain, I trail the flat of my tongue from the base, and up the column to tongue the slit at the top. He groans and thrusts his hips up a couple more inches. I know he wants me to pull him into my mouth, but I want him dizzy with lust, with the need for me to please him. He has me begging for his cock regularly, I want him begging for my mouth or pussy. He can have either one, but he must beg for it.

"You like this, baby? My mouth on your dick?" I ask coyly trailing my tongue along the side, swirling it around the tip.

"Fuck, yes. Keep going." I grin and enjoy the powerful feeling of knowing I'm tying him into knots of sexual need. He does an ab curl, his abdominal muscles flexing as he props himself on his elbows so he can watch. One hand sifts into the hair at my nape, trying to bring me closer to his cock, take control. Well, he's not getting it. Not until he begs for it.

I sink my fingers into his hips and place my mouth over the wide head of his cock, and inch by inch, take him down my throat. I make sure to avoid dragging my tongue along the surface to torture him a bit more. A fine sheen of sweat builds in the hollows between his abs. The sight sends fresh liquid to the needy space between my thighs. I can feel the wetness pool at the lips of my pussy as I suck on Chase's cock. I've never been turned on to this degree when going down on a man.

Chase sits up further, grips my thigh and trails his fingers to tickle just the edge of my ass, where thigh meets cheek, before he cups my sex with intent.

"Christ Baby. You're drenched. Turn around and let me suck on that sweet cunt." His words obliterate all plans to make him beg. At this point, he'd have *me* begging if he doesn't touch me. Without question and having lost all resolve, he lays down flat as I spin around on my knees. Before I can lift a knee to straddle him, Chase's large hands grip the fleshy handles of my hips and lift me into the air, settling me directly over his face. The pillows put him at the perfect angle and before I can even grip his cock, he's buried his mouth between my thighs, his tongue hitting its target with precision.

I cry out in pleasure at how fast Chase can bring me to the edge of orgasm with a couple of flicks of his tongue. His dexterous fingers pull apart the petals of my sex, leaving no space hidden from his greedy mouth. He's everywhere. It's as if he has swallowed me whole. I can feel my essence flooding my sex. He moans, sucking and drinking from me, as if he was dying from thirst. Like a sex-starved whore, I buck into his face crudely, desperate to reach the blissful end. Chase pulls away from my mound and I cry out.

"No!" My head falls down against his bobbing erection. Tingles skitter through every inch of my body, poised just on the edge of release.

"Suck on my fucking cock," Chase groans and thrusts towards my face angrily. When he turned the tables, I forgot he was on the edge of bliss himself.

"Oh," I whisper then get back to the business of making him fall apart.

His entire body tenses, his tongue piercing me so deeply I almost come on the spot. Violent spasms rack my body as we take each other as far into our mouths as possible, joining in a way that's almost more intimate than intercourse. Every surface of his front is pressing against mine. I can feel his heart thumping heavily in his chest, pounding against my belly. Chase holds my thighs wide apart as he ravishes me.

When I lap at his swollen crown, he finds the hood covering my clit. He uses his thumb to press and rub deep circles around the aching nub before he swirls and flicks his tongue against it. I feel my body splinter, as if it will crack and explode against the pleasure. Wanting to give as good as I'm getting, I plow ahead, shaking and twitching, my fingers digging into Chase's hips as I hold on, getting and giving the ride of a lifetime. With the little bit of resistance I have left I push back from Chase. His mouth releases me with a wet smack.

"Oh, no, you don't." He keeps a firm grip on my ass to keep me in position. "This weeping cunt is all mine!"

A tremble tears through every limb. If the dirty talk didn't seal it, the moment Chase's teeth graze the small heated knot, coupled with the slight press as he bites down, did. I scream so loud you'd think I was on fire, literally melting. The orgasm hits me like a wall of flames, searing me from the inside out. I buck against his face wildly, not capable of concern that my flailing could hurt him.

As I come back down, I'm greeted by Chase's erection. I lick my lips and then lave the head, kissing the top lovingly. Chase is breathing heavily behind me, the rhythm faltering with each stroke of my tongue. I take advantage and lick his stalk from root to tip, wetting the entire column with my saliva. Once I have him moaning my name and rubbing my thighs and ass cheeks, I take him into my mouth. As I pull him into the wet warmth, I tongue the sensitive underside. He jerks up, pushing a couple more inches of his length inside, bottoming out at the ridge of my throat. Now that I've had my release, I want him to beg.

Pulling back I ask, "What do you want, baby?" I flick my tongue against the patch of skin just under the head.

He groans. "Gillian, suck on me. Now," he calls out, his voice beyond strained.

I do as he asks alternating between slow sucks and long laps of my tongue. Pretty soon, it's not enough and he thrusts his hips towards my mouth. Just when I think I have the upper hand, Chase pushes two thick fingers deep inside my pussy. I stop and moan. He laughs, a bit of a sadistic sound from my vantage. Well, not this time. He's not getting the better of me. Hopefully.

Doubling my effort, I take him into my mouth and suck hard, hollowing out my cheeks, and flattening my tongue. I ride him fast and hard. The movement has his fingers steadily fucking me and I'm back to being driven by lust. With my right hand I lift and fondle his balls and stroke along the skin just behind.

"Fuck, Baby," He jerks his hips up going deep into my throat, almost gagging me. "I can't help it. Need to fuck your pretty mouth." He's losing control, and I love every minute of it. I reach past his balls and find the tight rosette of muscle, opening and closing with each suck and pull of my mouth along his cock. Quickly, I lick my finger and then place it firmly against his anus. On a strong thrust of his hips followed by a hard suck of my mouth, I press my finger deeply into his warm ass. He howls.

Sweat slickens our bodies as I suck his cock and finger-fuck his ass. A burst of precum spills into my mouth and I swallow it hungrily. Chase's hips hammer up into my mouth roughly, and I take it all. Relaxing my throat, I let the large knobbed head of his cock push past the muscle at the back of my throat so he can sink into the tight cavern. "Shit, fuck, baby. I'm gonna come," Chase grits through his teeth as I swallow and hum. He is grinding his teeth, the tendons in his neck straining with effort.

My second orgasm is right on the edge. Using my hand on his cock, I stroke him up and down in quick succession, then lick around his balls and anus wetting a second finger. When I bring his cock back into my mouth I take it straight down my throat and push another finger into his ass, right past the tight sphincter muscle.

"Fuck!" He roars around my thighs before he clamps his mouth over my clit and sucks hard. The orgasm rips through me as I'm graced with hot spurts of cum firing down my throat. I suck and swallow it down while shooting to the heavens on my own pleasure cloud.

Moments or an hour later, I couldn't be certain, we lie in a tangled heap, me on top of him, his cock half erect against my cheek. His breath comes out in heavy bursts along the moist flesh between my legs. Slowly, I adjust myself and turn around. He pulls me against his chest. I flip my hair back and out of my face, trying to catch my breath and come back to planet Earth.

Chase lifts my head and kisses me slow, sweet, and with purpose. "I fucking love you."

My heart soars into orbit at his words. I smile and kiss him back, tasting myself on his sweet lips. "I fucking love you more."

His all white smile is the snapshot I'll take of this moment in my mind. He turns my cheek inspecting the skin and wipes something away with the pad of his thumb.

"You have my cum on your face," he laughs, holding his thumb up to show me.

I swoop in, quick like a ninja, and lick the salty substance off his thumb, until it's clean.

He looks at me baffled and full of lust, his eyes turning that dangerous shade of dark blue. "That was ridiculously hot," he pulls me on top of his chest and kisses me, long, hard, and deep. Round two just started.

★ ★ ★ ★

Hours later, Chase and I are en route to brunch with his mother. I'm still reeling from the sex marathon we had this morning while enjoying how the scenery changes from concrete, brick, and glass, to lush trees and mansions as we leave the confines of the city. The street that leads to his Uncle Charles' mansion is lined with ornate black iron light posts and perfectly manicured lawns and houses surrounded by bush after bush of roses. I hate roses. Nothing that beautiful should be so painful. Now that my stalker has chosen them as his calling card, they are the last thing

I want to see, although it fits the mood of having to go see his mother.

The gates to the Davis mansion are located at the end of the street. The house sits atop a long hill like a castle, watching over the land. Pretentious. Chase's Uncle Charles is a good man. Taking him in when his mother was in the hospital all those years ago, and his Dad in prison for her attempted murder, truly shows the depth of love he has for his nephew. Having been the primary male figure in Chase's early life puts him high on my "people to cherish" pedestal.

Jack opens the car door and we exit. Chase clasps my hand and leads me up the stairs to the entrance. A small grin slants across his face. I love seeing him happy, a bit carefree even. I playfully nudge my shoulder against his, earning me a full, take-my-breath-away, smile. God, he's beautiful. Instead of knocking, Chase enters as if he owns the place. I guess since he grew up here it's like coming home.

As we walk through the parlor, I'm once again reminded of the vast Davis wealth. There is a double winding staircase at the entrance with huge, oil canvases, crawling up the walls. Probably all original pieces. Priceless antique furniture, paired with contemporary pieces, fills the large rooms. I try to imagine four young boys and a little girl running through these rooms and halls. It seems far too regal to allow for children.

"Did the house look like this when you were growing up?" I ask Chase as he leads me towards the back of the house, a section I hadn't been to previously.

"No. Once we were grown, my mother redecorated. My aunt had made the mansion very livable for her four children prior to her death. The moment we were teens and Mother had recovered completely, she made it her pet project. By then, my aunt had already passed away."

Made a lot of sense as to why everything seemed so stuffy. It fit the woman who designed it. I couldn't imagine growing up in a house where you were afraid to sit on the furniture. Mom was always a fan of creature comforts and fuzzy fabrics. That thought reminded me that I needed to put a little of me into the penthouse and unload some of my boxes from the move.

"When can I decorate the penthouse?"

Chase stops, spins around on one foot and kisses me. His hand tunnels into my hair as he deepens the kiss. Once we're both breathless, he pulls back leaning his forehead against mine.

"What was that for?" Not that I mind, but it was odd timing.

"Baby, I love hearing you speak about things that ensure you're a permanent part of my life. You can do whatever you want to the penthouse, but don't get too wild."

He tugs my hand, and I follow down a long hallway. I feel like a rat in a maze, or as if I'm playing a game of follow the leader.

"I would never spend too much money." The thought he'd worry makes me frown. "Besides, I have my own money. I do work."

"God, you are too cute." He laughs, and this time I stop and yank him to a halt.

My eyebrows knit together, and I sling a hand to my hip. "What does that mean?"

Chase takes a deep breath and smiles. "Baby, once we're married we're going to be house shopping or building a home. A place that's you and me. Yesterday when you mentioned having my children"—he clasps my hand—"all I've been able to think about is seeing your gorgeous body swollen with my child. My baby growing inside of you." He shakes his head and his gaze searches mine. "God, you'd be sexy."

That was not at all what I was expecting. Now he wants a home and babies? "Who are you and what did you do with my fiancé? The workaholic, master of his empire, sex God, that guy. Where'd he go?"

Lightning fast, Chase pulls me to him, hands clasped above my bum. "I'm all those things, but I also want a home. A place where we can always come back to after our travels, after a long work day. We'll raise our children there, once we choose to have them." His jaw tightens, and when he continues his voice is uncertain. "Is that not what you want?"

I'm quick to respond. "That's everything I ever wanted, Chase. And to have it with you…" my voice clogs with emotion.

"I know, baby. I know." And he does. He's right there with me, learning this new thing. Finding out that it's okay to want the American dream. The house, the 2.5 kids and a picket fence. Even masters of their universe want a home and a family.

"Come on, Mother will be waiting and she detests when people are tardy."

Reminds me of someone else I know. Trying not to roll my eyes I follow his stride, holding his hand tightly. Chase and I are moving towards our future. Nothing is going to ruin this moment.

GILLIAN

CHAPTER SIX

Boy was I wrong. The second we enter the "Sun Room" we're greeted by a sour-faced Colleen Davis.

"Mother!" Chase says jovially, making his way to his mom. She's sitting in a high back armchair. It's a pristine white, with shimmery golden lines running vertically, mimicking a circus tent print. I'd be afraid to sit in it, let alone enjoy a cup of coffee, for fear I'd stain it.

"My darling." She smiles and pats Chase's cheek as he kisses her on the forehead.

"Good afternoon, Ms. Davis," I say awkwardly, still in the same spot at the entrance of the room where Chase left me to greet his mother.

Her gaze catches mine and her lips pinch tight. She brings her attention back to Chase. "So, you're still seeing her?"

Chase smiles wide, walks over to me, and holds out his hand. "Oh yes. I'll be seeing a lot more of her, too. Pretty much every day for the rest of my life," he says proudly, putting an arm around my shoulder, bringing me tight against his side the way he prefers. His lips graze my hairline briefly. His mother's face pulls so tight into a grimace, I worry it will stick. "We're getting married," Chase says happily. Probably the most emotion I've seen him share in front of others, ever. Normally he keeps his feelings and emotions pretty close to the chest.

"You're kidding?" his mother says clearly taken aback.

"I'm not. Mother, Gillian has agreed to marry me." The confidence with which he delivers his words melts my heart and I can't help but swoon. He holds me tight and leads me to the couch across from where his mother is seated. I take a moment and scan the room. The entire right wall and a quarter of the ceiling is encased in thick glass allowing a perfect view of the land beyond. The Davis property is vast. A lot larger than I remembered from the night of his Uncle's birthday party where we had it out about Megan "The Bitch."

"When?" she asks tightly, bringing my attention from the lush landscape to her unhappy face. It's obvious this news does not come with congratulations. If we weren't here, she'd likely throw her teacup across the room. Briefly, I wonder what it would be like to see her lose control.

I move to answer, but Chase is faster. "Soon." He grips my arm keeping me close. The smile on his face is huge. In the light of the early afternoon, he looks effervescent and completely at peace. It lifts me up, knowing I'm the one who's put that smile on his face.

Colleen twists her mouth, trying but failing to hide a scowl. "But you've hardly dated. Don't you think it's a bit soon, to consider marriage," she adds "my darling," to soften the blow.

Chase finally keys into the fact that his mother is not altogether pleased with this news. "Mother, Gillian and I are in love. There's no reason to wait."

"And I'll just bet she wants to turn around a wedding pretty quickly, don't you my dear?" Her tone is scathing and meant to pierce.

"No, that's not at all true!" I answer desperately wanting to clarify that the six-week timeframe was his decision, not mine.

"Mother, stop. Gillian actually wants to wait a year. I want to get married immediately. We've set the date for six weeks from now."

Ms. Davis gasps, bringing a hand to her mouth. "You can't be serious, Chase. You barely know her."

"I know what I want. Gillian and I are getting married and I'd prefer you didn't share any more of your opinions…" his voice lowers in pitch "unless it's to congratulate your son and welcome his fiancée into our family." His words are delivered with a side order of "fuck you" without even trying. I couldn't be more proud of Chase for sticking up for me, especially in front of his mother. It's still a mystery to me why she doesn't like me. I've barely shared a few sentences with the woman since meeting her all those months ago at the charity event.

Just like a chameleon changes color, her entire being softens. "I apologize, my darling. My only concern is for you and your happiness. It always has been." Her voice falters and cracks as she holds out a hand. He moves to her then kneels at her feet. I hate how much control she holds over his emotions. Holding back a retort, I watch as she clasps his cheek. "My darling boy, if she is what you want, she is what you must have."

His smile brightens the room once more. His mother's lips tip up sweetly then her gaze turns to me. "Welcome to the Davis family, dear. Looks like we have a wedding to plan."

Chase stands and clasps his hands together. "Yes, absolutely! Mother is an amazing event planner. The two of you working together will be the perfect way to become friends." I'm certain my eyes are about to pop out of their sockets. That is quite possibly the last thing I want in the universe. Instead of bursting Chase's bubble, I smile and nod, not capable of anything else.

The door behind me opens and Chase's Uncle Charles bustles into the room. "Did I miss tea service? I had business that ran late."

Chase holds out a hand and greets his Uncle. "I was just sharing the news with mother that I have asked Gillian to be my wife and she has agreed."

"Well done my boy!" He clasps him on the back and pulls him into a man hug. "Forget the tea, what this news needs is champagne!"

His uncle's joy is contagious, and I finally release a bit of the pent up tension I've been holding since the moment I entered. "I couldn't agree more," I say as his Uncle pulls me up and off the couch into a full body hug.

"You'll be a stunning bride, and a most welcome addition to the Davis family my dear." He grins and kisses both of my cheeks. Charles Davis is nothing but glorious. His salt and pepper hair is slicked back into the quintessential businessman's style giving him that dapper appeal. The dark grey suit on his wiry frame probably cost more than my car, and he wears it well. Even though he looks pretentious and unapproachable, his welcoming eyes and easy smile dispel the aura.

"Thank you," I reach for Chase, and he pulls me against his side. Breathing in his woodsy citrus scent calms my nerves. Besides the moment I agreed to marry him, this is the happiest I've ever seen him, and I don't want to ruin this moment with how uncomfortable his mother makes me.

"Charles, Chase, why don't you go get some champagne and a couple cigars for yourselves, and let me chat with my future daughter-in-law, woman to woman." Her lips twist into a forced smile that is anything but pleasant.

"Good idea, Mother." Chase kisses me too briefly and starts to pull away. Before he can, I cup his neck and deepen the kiss. He pulls away and cocks his neck to the side to assess me.

"I'll be back soon, baby," he whispers and pecks me quickly.

"Hurry back," I say hoping I put enough fear into my tone, without letting on I don't really want to be alone with his mother.

"Enough. Chase darling, the champagne?" Her request is laced with irritation.

The two men saunter off. I watch Chase until I can no longer see him.

"So, you work fast," she says with a snarl.

I'm not standing for this any longer. "What is your problem with me?"

She huffs and then puts a red tipped nail to her lip. "I'm just trying to figure out your angle. I've looked into you."

"And what did you find that would make you dislike me, without even getting to know me?"

"It doesn't take a background check to see you're broken."

I cringe. Heat swirls in my chest making my skin feel tight and clammy. Chase has promised me he wouldn't say anything to anyone about my past. Thinking she could be playing into my insecurities, I take a deep breath. "I'm not sure I know what you mean."

"I know you have a jaded past. The restraining order you have on file against a man a few years ago says enough to tell me you've been hurt by a man." I clench my jaw as she grins. "You're poor, but educated. And you likely do your best work on your back, seeing as you work at my son's foundation."

"All true," she smiles wide for the first time at my admission. "Aside from sleeping my way to the top. I don't want Chase's money. Never have. I'll happily sign a prenup if he asks."

"I'll make sure he does," her lips twist into a snarl again. "You are not getting a red cent if you hurt my son, Missy." Hurt her son. Is that what she thinks I'm going to do? Is this her sick, jacked up idea of a maternal warning?

"Good luck with that. Chase has already decided no prenup, but again, if you can convince him otherwise I'll sign it. And I have no desire to hurt Chase. I love him Ms. Davis. Very much."

"Yeah, the last pretty little red-head who said that was unfaithful to him. He was crushed for years. Only recently have I seen my boy's light again." She attempts to continue, but I cut her off.

"Who do you think put that light there?" Her eyes are cold and assessing as she holds my gaze. "Me." I point to my chest. "Our love. It's been a hard road the last few months, but we've found something in one another that can't be denied." Tears pool in my eyes, and one slips down my cheek. "It's real, and I promise you on my mother's grave that I will do anything I can to make him happy." I swipe at the tears and try to calm down.

"We'll see. Just be warned missy, I'll be watching you very closely. There's no woman on this earth that's good enough for my son," she looks me up and down then scowls. "Especially not a broken little thing, from the wrong side of the tracks." Her tone is contemptuous and cuts deep. I realize I'm never going to win her over.

"It's a good thing I'm not marrying you then. This conversation is over. I'll see myself out, seeing as you're unable to." My eyes settle on the wheelchair next to her. Her gaze sharpens, assessing me once more. "It's too bad Chase's father damaged you. Maybe you wouldn't be such a horrible, miserable woman. At least I survived my beatings. You, on the other hand, came out alive but more twisted and broken than I'll ever be, because Chase is healing my hurts. Who's taking that knife out of your back and healing your wounds? Oh that's right, no one."

Her eyes are as round as serving platters and just as cold. "He told you…" she chokes unable to finish what she plans to say.

I nod and move to the door. "You know, we're more alike than you think. I spent years letting a man beat me into submission and almost take my life, before I got out." Her mouth opens in shock, losing every bit of her coiffed socialite good manners. "I'm still healing, but with Chase, each day is easier than the next. What's your excuse? You have everything life could ever offer. Money, the undying love of your son, a beautiful family…" I shake my head completely exasperated with this vile woman. "You know what? Never mind. I don't care."

Opening the door, I leave her there alone, with her miserable thoughts to keep her company. There's nothing I can do or say that is going to make her like me. And Chase is bat-shit crazy if he thinks I'll be planning the most important day of my life with that old crone.

Once I get outside, I see Austin standing with Jack next to the limo. Jack pulls his phone out and immediately starts speaking. "She's outside with us." I scowl and open the limo door with barely contained rage.

"You okay, ma'am?" Austin's southern drawl reaches me and tears pour down my face. His hand is warm against my shoulder, and right now, I need a friend, someone to care about me. I shake my head and he pulls me into a hug. He is so large, his arms seem to wrap around me twice.

"Mr. Davis won't like that." Jack's voice holds a warning. A choked sob escapes, and I hold Austin tighter, needing the closeness, wishing it was Chase instead.

"He won't like that his woman is hurting and we're not tending to her," Austin grits out.

"You're right, he won't." I hear Chase's clipped words from somewhere behind us.

Before I can react, I'm being turned and placed into the most welcoming arms in the entire world. My haven. Chase's arms encircle me and the entire world goes away. My breath hitches and I can't say anything. Shivers wrack my form as he holds me tight, protecting me, giving me peace.

"It's okay, baby, I'm here. Let's go home," he whispers into my hairline.

I nod and let him shuffle me into the limo. Before he closes the door, I hear him address Austin. "You're a good man, but let's not make a habit of putting your arms around my woman, unless it's to protect her."

"That's what I was doing, sir," Austin says, and I can feel Chase's body still momentarily, then he nods once.

Long moments pass before Chase grips me tighter and replies, "I believe you."

The door shuts and the engine roars. Time seems to pass in a blur of tears and hiccups.

I love this man. I love this man. I love this man. I chant internally.

Just when I think he's going to go all caveman, he surprises me with how very kind and understanding he can be.

"I'm sorry I was hugging Austin. He really was just being nice to me." The words spill out with little hitches in between.

Chase trails his fingers along the side of my face and cups my neck. "Baby, I know. He does seem to care for you, more than I want to admit."

I tilt my head back. "No, not even. He's very brotherly with me. He's never so much as glanced at me that way, I assure you." It's very important that this point hits home. I cannot handle Chase being jealous of my bodyguard, and I'm not going to accept a new one. I've just gotten comfortable with the one I have.

"I know that, baby. I've checked his record. He has five sisters back in Kentucky. When a man is interested in a woman, he doesn't hold her in the sisterly way he was holding you. He was comforting you, not making a move.

It's what I did for Chloe growing up. I know the difference."

"Thank you, I really like him." I glance at the privacy screen that is firmly closed. "More than Jack," I admit.

He laughs. "Jack is a tough pill to swallow. He doesn't trust easily. It's taken years for me to get on a friendly level with him. Once you're my wife and he sees that you're here to stay, he'll warm up to you." Chase hugs me close. "So, you going to tell me what happened with Mother that made you so upset."

A long sigh slips from my lips and I straighten my back. I knew we'd have to talk about it, but it's not pleasant. "She doesn't think I'm good enough for you, and made it very clear."

Chase's jaw clenches and he tilts his head back to rest against the seat. "Gillian. It's not you. Ever since Megan she…" he takes a deep breath.

"I know. She thinks I'm going to hurt you. But, you know what? She doesn't need to hurt me in return! She said she would make sure I signed a prenup, because I wasn't going to take you for your money. I want to now, sign it, just to prove her wrong." It's a good idea, and I want to move forward on it. "Have your lawyers draw one up. I'll sign the damn thing with her as a witness." My indignation is ramping up into full blown fury. "I'll prove that I don't want your money!"

"Gillian, shhhh. Settle down. There will be no prenup. We've already discussed this. Everything I have is yours. Everything you have is mine. That's a *real* marriage. Sharing money is just an extension of my commitment to you." He kisses the side of my neck.

"But, she'll never believe it's real. I can't have the only

other woman you love hating me. I can't Chase. It hurts too much." I know my lip is trembling as the pad of his thumb strokes it.

"You'll win her over." I shake my head. "You will. We just have to show her how much we mean to each other. Letting her help plan the wedding will go a long way towards earning her trust."

"Chase, I can't..."

"You can. Baby, I have faith in you. You've won me over; you'll win her over too. Promise me you'll try."

In frustration, I clasp my hands over my face and wipe them down to clear any residual tears, hoping my mascara didn't run and leave me looking like a raccoon. For Chase, I can do anything. He's the ultimate prize. Win over his mother; I can do this. I've won over worse. Justin's mother hated me in the beginning. Said I was too goody-goody for her son and a stuck-up bitch. Even though we ended up friendly, it turned out she was right. I was too good for her son, but it took him almost killing me to figure it out. Not this time.

"You know what, I will work with her on planning the wedding but Chase, I'm going to be me. And she's going to have to deal with my girls. They are a huge part of my life, and they will have as much say, if not more, than your mother."

"That ought to be interesting. I can see Maria now, telling Mother off. I wonder if I can get tickets to that show? I'll bring the popcorn," he laughs.

"This is not funny." I playfully slap his chest and he unbuckles my seat belt pulling me astride his lap into a warm hug.

As we embrace, his fingers trail up my thighs, pushing up my skirt as he goes. His hands cup my lace-clad bottom, and he thrusts his hips up against my core. A moan slips out into the open air of the limo. Damn, he just had me a couple hours ago and I already want him to take me again. With the rate his cock is rising, he feels it, too. Perhaps more.

"Unbuckle my pants." His eyes no longer hold the silly mirth of moments ago. Now his normally blue depths are clouding over and heavy-lidded with lust. It's unnerving. With just a look, he can have me at the pinnacle of desire.

My heart beats heavily against my chest as I undo his buckle, zipper then pull out his thick cock. As I admire it, Chase has been busy tickling the crease of my ass—his newest fascination. Just as I lean down to kiss my man, I hear the telltale sound of fabric shredding.

"Those were a beautiful pair of panties," I whisper and nip at his bottom lip, breathing in his air.

"I'll buy you more," he dips his tongue in to lick my mouth. "I rather liked ripping them off you. I told you Gillian, nothing will prevent me from having you. Wherever and whenever, I want." He tugs on my upper lip and soothes it with his tongue. "Especially not a scrap of lace." His hand moves between my legs and his fingers slip along the wet flesh. "So ready for me, baby…I like that," he rubs a thumb around my clit.

"Oh God," I tip my head back as Chase lines me up with his cock. His hands move to my hips and with a hip twirl and a well-aimed thrust, he's embedded fully inside. Jolts of pleasure rip through my body and I cry out, unable to contain it. I'm sure Austin and Jack are getting an earful, but I don't care. This man undoes me in ways that defy reason.

"Ride me, baby," he says as his teeth graze my neck.

I lift up using my knees on each side of his hips and place my hands on both shoulders for leverage. He helps by offsetting my weight with his hands holding me at the ribs.

As I come down, he powers up into me. His cock is thick and rock-hard as it jackhammers deep into my core. Chase tips his hips and lifts his knees bringing me down farther so that the only thing I see when I look down is our connection. The thick root of his cock is snug against me, the lips of my sex stretching wide to accommodate him. "Touch it. Feel us together, Baby."

He lifts me up a few inches and I place my fingers against the base of his cock. It's slick from our union. "So good," he whispers. I watch him dazedly as he brings me down, the petals of my sex opening and gripping his cock in a vulgar, graphic depiction of a hug. It's the most erotic thing I've ever seen, sending rivulets of fresh excitement to the space between us, making his path slicker.

As I watch my body engulf him, over and over, I feel my heart pounding in time with his thrusts. It's as if it beats for him. Only him. Within seconds his movements become more forceful, and I know he's getting close.

"Need to see you come. Want it all over me, soaking my dick with it." His dirty talk and a well-placed thumb swirling around my clit, does it. Heat fills every pore, pleasure streaks across my body, sending me into orbit. My orgasm hits so hard and strong I scream. Chase doesn't even try to muffle it, preferring to make it go on and on, using his strength to force me down onto his cock with long hard pulls, all the while, torturing my clit with little circles and tight pinches that are just barely more pleasure than pain. My pussy clenches tightly around his cock gripping roughly, trying to forcefully pull his essence from his body, until the sweet moment happens and he erupts in a deep groan, giving me everything.

In a few harsh thrusts, Chase's body goes rigid. One hand clamps my shoulder in a bruising hold, forcing me onto his thick cock over and over. I spiral into yet another smaller but equally satisfying orgasm.

His hot semen coats my insides warming me from the inside out as I collapse against his chest. We didn't even take our clothes off, too hurried to connect with one another.

Chase's arms soothe up and down my back, his length softening, but still deep inside. "Feel better?" He asks. "I know I do." He punctuates the question with a little thrust that sends aftershocks to tingle and flex at my core.

"Actually, I do." I snuggle into his neck. "You know sex isn't going to be the answer to everything right?"

"And why not?" He digs his hand into the hair at my nape, and I pull back to stare deep into his eyes, still filled with lust but softer now and more blue.

"Because, well,"—I think about it for a few seconds—"I can't really come up with anything." I smile.

"Oh, I can *come up* with something." He punctuates with a lift of his hips.

"You're a nut," I nuzzle his neck and lick the salty skin there.

"But you love me," he chuckles. It's such a beautiful sound.

"Yes, yes I do."

CHAPTER SEVEN

It's time. The locker room is empty, devoid of testosterone junkies, and people so fat they'll never lose that elusive twenty pounds they think will free them. I find the locker I want. I'd spied on him enough this past week to figure him out. He's so fucking predictable. His locker combination is his daughter's birthday. If it was Gillian's I'd have to figure out a more tortuous plan. I set the cylinder into the square space and connect the cord to the hinge of the locker. When it opens again…BOOM! No more Phillip.

Chills of excitement mingle with the unstoppable anticipation, and vision of seeing my girl at his funeral. Clad all in black, her beautiful face mourning the loss of a man that will one day be a lousy memory. I'll make sure of that. My dick hardens as I think about what her face will look like when she finds out her best friend for the last decade, her first fuck, is gone in the blink of an eye. Poof!

It's almost too fucking easy. Footsteps approach and I turn around and pretend to just be putting my sweatshirt on. I have a beanie slung low, covering my hair color. Another patron sits down and proceeds to change into his workout gear. Ignoring him, I keep a low profile by tying my shoes, never making eye contact. It wouldn't do for a witness to be able to remember me. Doesn't matter though. I frequent this gym all the time. Today, I came in through the back with a trainer buddy of mine, so there's no record I was here. Now it's time to solidify my alibi.

Once alone, I creep to the back of the gym and slip out the door. I pull off the sweatshirt leaving me in a bright red t-shirt. Very noticeable. I rip off the beanie and throw both items in my car then make my way around to the front. As I walk in, the girl at the counter flirts with me, and I make a point to talk her up for a few minutes while logging in.

"Have a nice workout," she says seductively.

"Oh, I think today is going to be a real blast," I chuckle at my own joke.

"Yeah, a blast. Totally!" she winks.

I turn and roll my eyes. Stupid bimbo. Like I'd bed a plastic woman when I can have someone as precious as my Gillian. A woman who doesn't need any surgical alterations. Her body was crafted by the angels. When I close my eyes, I can still remember her creamy skin, the rose-tipped nipples, the small strip of red, nestled at the apex of her thighs. Even her scent calls to me. She always smelled of vanilla. I can't enter Starbucks without salivating with thoughts of her.

Setting up on a machine far away from the locker rooms, I hop on an elliptical and wait. Twenty minutes into my workout he comes walking through the doors. His tall frame is wrapped from head to toe in Nike. Could the asshole be any more pathetic? A sadistic grin slips across my face as I watch my reflection in the mirror. All hell is about to break loose.

A few minutes later, the beautiful music of blood curdling screams, coupled with pandemonium, breaks out near the locker room. That grimy prick is yelling for people to get back and get out. That's when the roar of the blast knocks me on my ass. The earplugs I put into my ears barely dull the roar as the entire building shakes. The lights of the gym flicker out. Smoke fills the main level as people cry and struggle to their feet to help one another out. I run over to the locker room area to assess the damage. There is a huge hole where the locker room used to be. Bodies are everywhere. Some are gasping in pain, others are not moving. Including one brown-haired shmuck. He is under a large chunk of debris. I can't tell if he's alive or dead. My hope is the latter, but I'm pissed that the bomb had a delay in going off. He must have barely opened the locker at first, or maybe the wire didn't shift enough when he opened it. Either way, it eventually went off, destroying this corner of the building but not his face like it should have. Dammit all to hell.

"Buddy, a hand..." says a hoarse voice to my right. I look down and see the man that I'd sat next to earlier in the locker room.

Realizing that standing here was making a scene, I jump into action, helping others remove large pieces of plaster off of patrons. Blood pools on the ground near a few peoples' heads. They aren't breathing. Casualties of war. I'd seen a lot of it when I served time in Afghanistan. Sometimes you were just in the wrong place at the wrong time. I should feel bad, but I don't. Death doesn't sadden me. It's a part of life.

The first responders arrive in a flurry of activity. As I'm carrying a woman whose leg would probably need to be amputated, I see a paramedic put his fingers to Phillip's lifeless body. A beat later, the words that he says fill me with a rage so deep, I'm not sure I can contain it.

"Hey, stretcher over here. Got a pulse!" The paramedic yells for others to pull the rubble off Phillip's body as he works on keeping him alive.

"Mother fucker" I say under my breath as I make it outside into the fresh air. A fireman rushes over to me to carry the woman in my arms over to another ambulance.

The pretty bimbo I saw earlier runs over to me and flings herself into my arms. It is with extreme effort that I don't shove her off me and onto the ground. "Oh my God. I'm so glad you're okay!" she cries into my neck. I grit my teeth so hard I can hear the grinding sound deep within my skull.

"I'm fine. You should get checked out though."

She sniffs into my neck and nods. Disgusting. "Okay, yeah. I'll see you soon?" she worries her lip.

"Sure," I say barely managing a smile.

While I'm giving my statement to San Francisco's finest, a team of paramedics comes out of the gym with my target on their stretcher. One of them is on top of it straddling Phillip and pumping his chest. His heart must have stopped. Maybe my luck is turning around. The team pushes him into the ambulance, and with lights flashing and the siren blaring, they speed off into the night toward the hospital. I couldn't wait to hear the news of whether he lives or dies.

Chase tickles my feet as I try and fail to read a saucy romance novel. "Cut it out!" I poke at him with my toes. He has a pair of black, wire rimmed glasses perched on his nose as he pretends to read an article in *Forbes* while "massaging my feet". Chase glances over the rims of his spectacles. Drop dead sexy. There's something about a man looking positively smart that makes him utterly edible. It's proof he's Superman. He even has Clark Kent's glasses.

"I don't know what you are talking about." A slow grin slips along his lush lips. I was debating attacking my man when the cellphone on the table rings.

I look at the display. The number shows 'unknown'. Instantly, cold sweeps through me, stilling all movement. "What's the matter?" Chase asks, noticing the shift in our casual Sunday morning.

"Not sure." I hold the display out and he grabs the phone, answering it.

"Chase Davis here," he barks into the phone using his menacing all business voice. For a moment, he listens, not saying anything. I hold my breath as I wait. "Yes, she's my fiancée. You can tell me whatever it is." His tone is a warning, like when a rattlesnake shakes its tail. "I see. When did this happen?" He looks at his watch. "We'll be right there. Thank you for calling." Chase frowns, hangs up the phone and takes a deep breath.

Bone chilling fear slithers along my spine. I just know something horrible has happened. I can feel it deep within my soul. "What is it?"

"It's Phillip. He's been hurt. We have to get to the hospital. Right now." For Chase to say it like *that*, I realize it must be bad.

Jumping up, I rush to our room. Tossing the robe onto the floor, I throw on a pair of yoga pants and a long sleeve shirt. The entire process between getting dressed, stepping into a pair of tennis shoes and grabbing a hair tie takes less than five minutes. Chase ushers me to the garage level where he helps me into a gunmetal grey Aston Martin. He is clenching his teeth, his lips in a grim line. He's holding something back.

"What are you not telling me?" I whisper.

"It was an explosion at the gym. It's not looking good." He cringes as he puts the car in gear and speeds off towards the hospital.

Please be okay. Please be okay. I chant over and over in my head on the way to the hospital. *I can't lose you.*

I must have said that last part out loud because Chase responds, "You're not going to lose your friend. Have a little faith," Chase grips my hand in his. Palm to palm his energy seeps into my body and warms my soul. Solid, unyielding. This is the man I'm going to spend the rest of my life with.

We make it to the hospital in record time. Chase's connections get us more information than the average Joe. Turns out the explosion took place several hours ago.

"Why weren't we called sooner?" I ask panicking, realizing Anabelle has been with her sitter for a lot longer than Phillip's usual gym visit.

The nurse that was sent to talk to us, pulls us to the side. "Your friend was wearing gym attire. He didn't have any identification on him. It wasn't until the gym was able to pull up the list of patrons and go through a process of elimination, crosschecking who checked into the gym during that timeframe to who the cops had already spoken to as well as who we were able to identify here. There are twenty-five people here from the explosion. Your friend was *not* one of the luckier ones. He's still in surgery now."

White-hot prickles, tingle over my skin and my eyesight goes fuzzy. Blotches of darkness, then light, waver in and out throwing me off balance. "Shit, she's going to faint!" I hear Chase's voice.

"Not on my watch," the nurse says and shoves something under my noise. Synapsis fire on all cylinders and I come alive, completely alert. Turns out it's called an ammonia capsule that she shoved under my nose. Damn thing felt like it burned straight through the lining of my nasal cavity. Chase and the nurse lead me to a chair and I sit, putting my head between my legs.

"Breathe, Gillian, it's going to be okay." Chase rubs his hand up and down my spine in long soothing strokes.

I lift my head and focus once again on the blonde nurse with wide eyes. She reminds me of Bambi. All doe-eyed and small facial features. "I'm fine. Thank you. Please give us the rundown."

The nurse pulls out a clipboard. "What's your name? I need to verify you are next of kin or listed as his emergency contact." My mouth drops open and Chase bristles besides me.

"Look, I'm personal friends with the Dean of Medicine and a member of the Board of Directors for this hospital, not to mention a valued donor. You can talk candidly with us." Chase uses his, 'I own the universe and you are but a small pawn in my large game of chess' voice. Unfortunately, it doesn't work.

Her eyebrows rise over large doe-eyes giving us an "I don't give a rat's ass who you are and who you know" type look. Instead of getting into a verbal brawl, which will get us nowhere fast, I pull out my wallet and present her with my ID. She finds the space in his paperwork, and thank Heavens that Phil and I are one another's medical contacts.

"Gillian Callahan," she says out loud and double checks my driver's license. "Okay, I can tell you what I know, but you'll have to get full details from the doctor. Mr. Parks is in surgery now. He had internal bleeding and shrapnel injuries from the explosion. They have removed most of the shrapnel and his spleen. They repaired a tear in his liver, re-inflated the collapsed lung, and now, they're working on setting the breaks in his legs. "

My hand flies up to cover my mouth. "God, is he going to make it?" I ask not really wanting to hear the answer. There really is no other option but a huge and resounding "YES" that would be acceptable. The nurse doesn't look like she's got that magic answer.

"Ms. Callahan, we just don't know. It's touch and go right now. If he makes it through the next several hours of surgery, it will be a very long road to recovery."

"B-b-but it's possible? Anything's possible right?" I look at her with all the hope, fear, and desperation of a woman who's on the verge of losing her best friend, a member of her family for all intents and purposes.

She smiles but it doesn't reach her big eyes. "Miracles happen every day in this place. My suggestion to you right now is to pray." Those words slice through my heart and I cling to Chase.

"Thank you. Please send the doctor to us when he's available," Chase asks dismissing the nurse.

"Gillian, Phillip is strong and has so much to live for. He'll fight."

I suck in a breath and choke back a sob. "Anabelle needs to be picked up or the sitter will need to stay longer." I frantically grasp at anything I can be doing now. Phillip is laid up on a slab while people put him back together. *Please, let them put him back together.*

I pull out my phone and dial her grandparents' number. It rings and rings. "God dammit!" The answering machine picks up and I leave a message to call me. I try Bree's phone next. This time I leave a message. "Bree, Phillip's been in an accident. We're at San Francisco General Hospital in the Intensive Care Unit waiting room. Get down here now." I stand up and pace and punch in Phillip's home number. It rings once before the phone is picked up by a young girl.

"Eva, it's Gigi."

"Oh thank God! Gigi," the young girl starts to cry. "Mr. Parks isn't here. He left hours ago. Said he'd be home… but…he's not here. I've called and called," she sniffs.

"Calm down sweetheart. Phillip was in an accident at the gym. He's in the hospital. Can you stay with Anabelle until I have someone pick her up later tonight? I'll make sure you're compensated. I know you have school in the morning, but we really need you until I can get there." Quick math reminds me that Phillip's parents are two hours away but Angela's are only thirty minutes. I need to contact them. "Do me a favor and text me the numbers on the fridge for Anabelle's Nana and Papa."

"I tried to call them. Some housekeeper said they were in Hawaii for the next couple weeks," she starts to weep again.

"Okay sweetie, don't you worry. I'm going to pick Anabelle up tonight or have one of my friends do it. Can you watch her for another few hours? Until around ten or so?"

The young girl hiccups and then takes a slow breath. "Yeah, I can handle it. I'll call my mom and tell her what's happening. Can I call you if anything else happens or my mom wants to talk to you?"

"Of course, honey. You've got my number now. I'm surprised you didn't call it sooner."

The crying jag I thought ended came back with a vengeance. "I did!" she screeches. "I called and called and left message after message."

"Your phone number's been changed, Gillian," Chase taps my shoulder obviously able to hear her. I close my eyes and realize the error. At least Phil updated his medical information or none of us would know what was happening.

"Listen, honey, I forgot that I got a new phone. You're doing great taking care of our Anabelle, making sure she is safe. I'm very proud of you and appreciate you helping us right now."

"Of course. I love this family," she says then takes a slow breath. "Mr. Parks is so good to me. I hope he's going to be okay."

"He will be fine," I say with as much conviction as I can muster, not entirely sure if I am convincing myself or Eva.

Chase hugs me closer to his side, a protective, comforting squeeze that fills my heart with hope. "I'll be in touch with you soon, okay Eva?"

"Okay Gigi. See you later. I'll take very good care of Anabelle."

"Thank you, sweetheart. See you soon. Goodbye," I hang up and lean into Chase's warmth. The honest truth that Phillip's life is in God's hands is enough for me to break down. Chase holds me tight to his chest while I sob, never loosening his hold. So strong. Deep gut-wrenching heaves wrack my frame as the devastating reality that Phillip could be gone from this earth, wraps its evil, poison dipped claws into my psyche.

An hour later, a hurricane of footsteps rush into the intensive care waiting area. Maria and Bree are running down the bright white hallway. It's as if I see them in slow motion. Standing, I open my arms as Bree barrels into them.

"Tell me, tell me," her voice becomes far too loud in the quiet space.

"It's not good Bree. He's still in surgery..." tears fill my eyes and make everything seem blurry. I try to find the words to tell Phillip's girlfriend the news. Chase puts a hand on my shoulder and ushers me into the nearest chair. Bree stands crumbling inward, her long blonde hair falling in front of her like a veil. Chase holds onto her, bringing her to the seat next to me then crouches low. His hands clasp both of Bree's as Maria sits down next to us.

This is probably the kindest gesture I've ever seen my alpha male make when he's not behind closed doors, and doesn't involve me personally. My friend's head lifts up, her watery gaze on him, as if he is a life preserver during a shipwreck.

"Bree, Phillip was in the middle of an explosion at the gym. He's one of over twenty people injured in the blast." She gasps and sucks in a tortured breath. "He has internal injuries, a collapsed lung, and both legs are broken. We know he's in surgery to manage his injuries. He's been in for over eight hours. That's all we know." Tears slide down Bree's pinked cheeks. They fall in fat, wet drops, onto her fuchsia yoga pants.

"What if he doesn't make it?" She whispers the one thing that I fear more than anything.

Maria and I crowd around Bree and the three of us hug. "He has to make it. That's just how it's going to be," I say gaining more confidence with each moment. Every second they don't tell me my friend has left us means he's fighting to be here. For us, for Anabelle, for everyone who loves him.

Huddled together is how Kat, Carson, and Tom find us. Chase briefs them on Phil's prognosis while we wait.

And wait.

And wait.

Over the past three hours I'd gotten ahold of Phillip's parents and they drove down, making it here less than an hour ago. They agree to stay at Phil's and alternate taking care of Anabelle with the rest of us girls. Chase and I plan to take her for the weekends, and both Maria and Kat offer to take as many evenings as necessary. Bree is practically catatonic while we hash out the specifics of my best friend's life.

It's close to ten at night when a very tired looking doctor makes his way to our group. Chase extends a hand. "Dr. Roberts. We're Phillip's friends and family. How is he?"

The hallway is so silent, you could hear a pin drop. "He made it through surgery but not before coding on the table, twice." Bree and I both gasp. Tears slip down the faces of every woman standing here waiting to hear about the man we all love. "Phillip's a fighter that's for sure," the doctor smiles briefly. "Aside from the broken legs, and ribs, he sustained a collapsed lung and serious bleeding. The explosion did a number on him. He'll be in a medically induced coma for at least a week. Not only is there swelling in his brain, we have to let his body heal a bit. Otherwise the pain would be excruciating."

Bree slips to her knees, overrun with grief. Kat and Maria lift her up and hold her as she breaks down. I stand still, as if time has completely stopped. The doctor is speaking but I can't hear anything. It seems as though I check out somewhere around "medically induced coma" and "excruciating pain."

"Can we see our boy," Phillip's mother asks the doctor.

"Because of the risk of infection, I can allow you a few minutes at his bedside but only next of kin." Those words send Bree into hysterics. I wasn't far behind.

"Doctor, I'm sure we can work something out. This is Phillip's girlfriend and his best friend, my fiancée. I'm sure you can let them just take a peek after his parents have had a moment. Consider it a professional courtesy," Chase says while clapping the surgeon on his shoulder, the intent clear. You help me, I help you. I've seen it many times over the past few months and I've never been happier about how much influence my man carries in this town before now.

The doctor takes a breath and shakes his head. "Fine, just the two, and only under escort. But they'll need to control themselves. There are a lot of people in various stages of healing that cannot handle an outburst such as the one I just witnessed," Dr. Roberts looks at Bree. She wipes away her tears and pushes back her shoulders as she brings herself under control.

"I'll be just fine. I promise. I have to see him, if only for a moment." Her voice cracks on the last word, and I clasp her hand and tug her to my side.

The surgeon leads the Park's in to see their son first. After they come out, I hug his mother tight. Growing up, I always loved Phil's mom, the quintessential June Cleaver. Now she looks as though she's suffered a great loss. Her shoulders are slumped over, her hair is a wild mess from running her fingers through it, and all traces of make-up are long gone, revealing her true age of late fifties. Even still, she's beautiful and I kiss both her cheeks.

"Kiss my angel girl for me, and tell her I'll visit tomorrow."

Phillip's mom cups my cheek and pats it lovingly. "You always were a lovely girl. So good to my boy, especially after Angela. There's a special place in heaven for women like you, Gigi." Then she kisses my cheek and turns to her husband.

Bree starts to tug my hand towards the door to visit Phil. I glance over my shoulder at the pure love I see in Chase's eyes, and the gazes of our friends, basically telling us without words, that they are there for us, and for Phillip in spirit. Chase mouths "I love you," as the doors to the unit close behind us.

We're led to a wall of glass. Behind the panes is Phillip. Bree places her hands and forehead against the glass and closes her eyes. Her lips move and I imagine she's praying.

I take the quiet moment to catalogue every injury I can see from here. Aside from his wrapped chest, he has a row of stitches over his eye, another down the side of his face. His arms are speckled with bruises, cuts, and wounds from the blast. There's an oxygen mask over his mouth providing him life-saving oxygen. That means he's not breathing on his own. I close my eyes and send my own prayer, this time asking my Mother in Heaven to pull some strings with the big guy, and save my friend. He's got far too much to live for to lose his life now.

A warmth fills my chest and slowly expands throughout my body. The feeling of complete and utter serenity lifts the black cloud hanging over my head. The one that has been there from the moment we raced to the hospital. I look at Phillip and send him everything I have. Love, light, friendship, loyalty, peace and happiness. I just hope it's enough. Something in me believes it is. I just know he's going to make it.

GILLIAN

CHAPTER EIGHT

The next two weeks are touch and go. Phillip is out of the intensive care unit but hasn't woken from his coma. Originally, the doctors said it was "medically induced," but when they tried to bring him back a week after the accident, nothing. Yesterday, they were finally able to get him off the breathing machines since his lungs started working on their own. Bree is a wreck. We all are. She's been at the hospital every possible minute. When she's not there, one of us girls or Phil's parents are holding down the fort. Recently, she hired her yoga mentee. The little thing who subs for her is now taking on her full load. Bree doesn't care. She doesn't care about much of anything. I don't blame her. If Chase was hurt, almost killed, and still in a coma, I'd never leave his side.

I turn off the shower and grab one of the towels on the warmer. Heated towels. Only my man would make sure his towels are warmed before getting out of the shower. I make quick work of drying my hair and pulling it into a tight ponytail. Standing in front of the mirror, I notice how much thinner I've gotten. The stress of the last few weeks has taken its toll. My body has seen better days. I've always been a good size six, bordering on an eight, which normally looks good on my lengthy body. Right now, my size sixes are loose. Scanning my body from head to toe in the mirror, I can see the indents for each of my ribs and the hip bones are actually coming to a bit of a point. There's definitely less for Chase to grab onto. Even my full, size C breasts seem smaller. When was the last time I ate? I'm trying to remember as my phone on the vanity rings.

Quickly, I grab a pair of skinny jeans, a form fitting tank, and a tunic style sweater that comes down to mid-thigh. Hitting the speaker button, I throw on a pair of heather grey panties and matching bra.

"Hello," I say while slipping up the jeans and buttoning them. I turn to look at my bum in the mirror. It's still a good heart shape but not nearly as rounded as it usually is.

"Gigi, when you leave the hospital today can you come by the theatre for a quick fitting? I have a nice template, but it would be better if I could pin some of the fabrics to the sample where I want them while you're in the dress," Kat says in a rush.

I groan and slip the tank over my head. "Kat, I really need some time at home. I have a million things to do for work and for the wedding."

"Um, hello? Dressmaker here. What the hell do you think I'm working on night and day? If your man didn't have to marry you in the next four weeks…" she starts on the same rant I hear every few days.

"Okay!" I cut her off before she goes into the extra-long diatribe. "I'll be there around two. Does that work?"

A loud huff comes through the speaker. "Yeah, I guess. Plan to stay at least two hours though."

Two fucking hours? What the hell is she making, a dress

for the Queen Mother? Christ on a cross this is going to end me. "Fine!" I yell and then hit the end button. I can't talk to her anymore. I have things to do. It's my rotation to be with Phil, and I need to get down to the hospital to relieve Bree. Once I throw on the tunic, I pull a pair of ballet flats at random out of the closet and tip toe through our dark bedroom.

Through a miracle, Chase is still sleeping. He's been working incredibly long hours trying to get past a major merger as well as locate anything on my stalker. There's been little activity, which makes me hopeful that he's gone for good. Maybe he was caught for something else. I'm still suspicious about Justin, and the fact that nobody knows where he is. It's as if he's fallen off the face of the earth. Chase is convinced he's the culprit. His rationale is, why would anyone else have such an obsession? My question to him was, "I don't know; why are you obsessed with me?" He snickered and played it off, but, really, it's a solid question.

Making my way into the kitchen, all I can think about is the sweet cup of heaven I'm about to drink. Bentley, our chef, sets up the machine so it will make coffee for me each morning. He adds some special spices in the coffee and leaves me creamer that he made fresh in the fridge. It's the closest thing to a Starbucks vanilla latte as I can get without having to go to a physical location.

When I enter the kitchen, I'm bombarded by my fiancé's assistant. "There you are, Gigi. I've been waiting for you!" Dana says happily while sitting on one of the barstools. In front of her is a huge, three-ringed binder with multiple colored tabs sticking out the edges. I glance at the clock on the microwave.

"It's seven thirty, Dana." Why the hell does she have a key to our private quarters? That reminds me that I need to have a chat with my hubby-to-be about his over-achieving assistant and her instant access to our home at all hours.

"And there's not a moment to spare!" She nods happily, her pretty blonde hair bobbing right along with her. She's dressed in a fierce black suit with a jewel toned satin blouse. The gold of her hair lies in perfect curls around her shoulders. I cringe and look down at my bare feet. The edges of my toenails have chipped paint and have seen better days. I need a pedicure, but can't bring myself to worry about trivial things when my best friend is laid up in the hospital. "Now, I've got tons of things to run by you," she starts by pulling open the first section and opening it to one of the tabs. I pad around the kitchen and pull out a coffee cup.

"Do you want coffee?" I ask.

"No, I've already had some." She has? It's seven thirty in the morning. How the hell can she be so damned chipper? "Now Gigi, look at these tablecloths and tell me which one you like best."

Tablecloths. Is she fucking insane? Who cares about tablecloths? "You pick one." I say and pull out my favorite mug. It's one of the only things I've unpacked. It's a fairy with giant expanded wings that Bree bought me for Christmas a few years ago. It's been my staple mug ever since.

Her eyebrows rise and then she pinches her lips together. "Okay. What type of font do you want on the invitations? We should have sent them out two weeks ago but under the circumstances…" she means, because my best friend exploded, but has the good sense to not bring it up further.

"Don't care about that either, Dana," I warn. Tingles of

irritation start to curl and slither along my spine. I can feel my inner temperature heating up.

She flips to the next section completely unfettered. "How about the ceremony? Let's talk flowers. I know you like daisies, because Chase had me ensure the florist put them in the vases in the foyer and around his office, but what other flowers…" she starts speaking, but I tune her out. There have been perfect bundles of daisies in our foyer each week. It's the first thing I see when I open the elevator and it's so welcoming. Something I've come to look forward to. I also noticed that my office on the fiftieth floor has had a new batch of them each week and several more placed around our home. I can't believe I've taken for granted something Chase did to make me happy and comfortable in this new environment.

The man owns my soul.

"…so do you want all daisies at the wedding or would something more traditional like roses be better?" she asks. A shiver runs through me.

"No roses. I hate roses!" My voice comes out scathing and downright mean.

Dana's eyes widen, but she continues anyway. Wow. She could get work done in the middle of an earthquake and look perfect doing it. "Let's talk food. Chase's favorite is seafood, and I'm sure Cancun will have the freshest fish possible."

"No seafood."

"Sorry?" Her eyes narrow. "I really think you need to take advantage of the location, and the seafood will be so…"

I roll my eyes. "Look Dana, I know you're trying to be nice, and you are…nice that is. I don't care for seafood, and I don't want to smell stinky fish on the best day of my life. We're going to Mexico, why not have Mexican food?" I hold out my hands and realize I've been swinging them around like a deranged crazy person. Gripping the cool slab of marble at the counter top centers me, momentarily.

"Uh, I had no idea about the food. Chase didn't mention that..." she scribbles something in the binder, circles it and then puts a giant slash through it.

Something she said spikes my interest. I grab my cup and calm my tone. "Have you been talking to Chase about the wedding?"

Dana shrugs and flips to another section of the book. "He likes to be informed of the decisions we've made. He's not happy with how little we've gotten done. We're really behind."

I laugh and shake my head. Who can think about a wedding when so much in my life is up in the air? The iPhone I put in the back pocket of my jeans rings loudly. I hold up a pointed finger at Dana. "Just a moment."

"Hello," I turn around and lean my back against the counter on a sigh. What now?

"Gigi, he left a fucking note...here! I cannot believe this shit!" Bree is screaming and crying at the same time.

Gripping the phone tightly to my ear, "Whoa whoa, what are you talking about, Bree? Calm down."

"I'm not going to fucking calm down! Your goddamned stalker did this to Phillip!" she roars, her tone so high-pitched I hold the phone back several inches so I don't lose an eardrum.

"Bree, I don't understand. What do you mean?" Fear locks its evil grip around my heart and squeezes as Bree explains.

I can hear shuffling and a door closing then the noises from the hospital. "I swear to God, Gillian, if he dies…" she lets her words fall off as she sucks in a breath. Her tone was something I've never heard from her. It's gut-wrenching, filled with fire and ice and dipped in poison. Hatred. It's what hatred sounds like. "I came into the room. I was late today and just got in. Right on the foot of the bed was a note. For you," she seethes.

"What does it say?" I ask, tears clouding my vision. It's my worst nightmare come to life.

Her voice cracks as she clears her throat. "It says…
Gillian,
Phillip was a blast. Too bad he made it.
Perhaps next time he won't. Who's next?
You're mine…Bitch!

X

"I'll be right there, I'm sorry Bree, I'm so sorry. You can't know how much," I try to finish but she cuts me off.

"Save it for Phillip. He's the one lying in a coma," she says and then abruptly hangs up. My heart sinks as my knees weaken. I slump to the floor in a heap of tears. I grip my knees tight and sob into them.

"Gigi, what's the matter?" Dana comes around and puts a cool hand on mine. "Are you okay?"

I shake my head over and over. "I'll never be okay again," I barely say through my tears. Guilt, fear, and sadness rip through me, tearing my insides apart.

"I'm going to get Chase!" The last thing I hear is her

heels clicking on the tile floor.

My work here is done. I'm standing in the room next to that stupid comatose fucker listening to his hysterical woman as she calls the love of my life on the phone. She's giving an Oscar-worthy performance. Knowing my Princess the way I do, she's rife with guilt. And now she knows just how far I'm capable of going to get to her. There will be no roadblocks.

It was easy enough to slip into Phillip's hospital room. That stupid bastard Chase Davis didn't even post a guard. Idiot. Thanks to his carelessness, I'm even closer than ever to finishing my plan to get my girl back. Eventually, I'm going to remove each and every last one of those bitches. Soul sisters she calls them. More like brainless twits, if you ask me. No one has cottoned on to me being the stalker. Not even her so called "best friends in the whole world" what's that term? Oh yeah BFFs. Ridiculously stupid. They make it so easy. Rubbing my hand through my hair, I put the surgical cap on concealing my hair fully.

I slip out of the room looking left and right, making sure I don't recognize anyone. The scrubs were a nice touch, pilfered out of the open supply closet. I got in and out of Phillip's room without so much as a look my way. Medical personnel are always too busy to really pay attention to anything around them besides the patient in front of them. Walking zombies for the most part. Completely worked in my favor today. It was so easy to walk in there. Phillip was still as a statue when I placed the note on the bed for my girl. I was actually shocked there wasn't a horde of his admirers hanging around like usual. Looks like I timed it perfectly.

I barely make it out of his room and into the room next to his when his "girlfriend" shows up in her trendy yoga gear. At least she's something to look at. I don't prefer the petite types, I'm more of a long, lean, with curves and red hair type man, but I can see why men go to yoga. It's not for the exercise that's for sure. It's for the hot, flexible little bitch they somehow think they have a chance with. I'll bet she gets hit on by more of her male students than not. Regardless, I'm done looking at her, and, most of all, I'm done hearing her whiney voice. The bug I planted under Phillip's bed last week in the middle of the night has given me a keen perspective on their relationship.

The chick is head over heels for the dumb ass. I might actually take a knife to my throat if I have to listen to one more of her cry sessions where she begs him to wake up, for her, for his punk kid and on and on. She never, fucking, stops. It's a broken record or a TV commercial jingle that you can't shake. Something has to cut through the monotony. Well, just as soon as the time is right, I'll be cutting through something. Her pretty little throat. If I don't get my girl, I'm picking off the weakest link for the hell of it.

Time's up Yoga Barbie.

"Breathe, baby. In two, three, four, five and out, two three four five. In again," Chase inhales audibly. "And out," he exhales. I watch his face in a daze, mimicking him breathing in and out. I'm not sure where I am or what I'm doing. All I know is Chase is here, and I am safe. "Again," he instructs me to inhale then out for another five beats.

Chase's hands are warm as they cup my neck. His forehead leans against mine. He continues to breathe deep, and I synchronize with him, not knowing what else to do. I'm bobbing in a sea of calm, open water, no land in sight. Only Chase, my life raft.

"Come back to me, Gillian," his voice feels like it's being shoved through a panel of wool, thick, scratchy and muffled. "Come on, Gorgeous. Give me those green eyes. Focus on me. Only me. It's just you and me, here in our home."

Home.

Chase.

Focus.

The tingle throughout my body starts to ebb, my heart rate losing its erratic rhythm against my chest. Moments ago it was a sledgehammer pounding me into the ground, so deep down I couldn't breathe, lost my vision. Now all I see is blue…endless blue. Chase's eyes blink and a slight curve tips his lips.

"There's my girl, just focus on me. Look into my eyes. I've got you. I've always got you." Chase's voice is quiet and steady. Slowly, I start to feel the space around me. The air is no longer pressing me into the hole. Chase's hands slide up and down my back in long, unhurried sweeps. I grip my fingers into the flesh of his back and start to pull him tighter against me, fear still burning the edges of consciousness. Burying my face into his neck, sandalwood and citrus fill the air forcing me into the present. I come to slowly, bit by bit, realizing where I am.

On the floor, in the kitchen, wrapped around Chase. He's sitting cross-legged with me in his lap, my legs wrapped around his waist. I'm clinging to him so hard I've lost all feeling in my hands. After a few more breaths, I pull my head out of the comfort of his neck and blink a few times.

"What happened?" I ask, my voice sounds scratchy and crackles on each syllable.

Chase pets my hair and pushes the loose strands behind my ear. "You had a panic attack. Worse than any I've ever seen. Much scarier than your flashbacks. What the hell triggered it?"

It all comes flooding back like a tsunami wave breaking against shore. Tears well and spill over my cheeks. "The stalker left another note," comes out in a garbled whisper.

"A note?" I nod. "Where?"

The fissure in my heart breaks open allowing the pain to enter once more. "Phillip!" I cry into Chase's neck unable to stop the bone-crushing guilt.

Chase pulls me back and cups my cheeks. "You're not making sense. Phillip? A note?" I nod. "You mean the stalker left a note with Phillip at the hospital?"

My lip trembles, and I can feel the muscles around my face contorting and crumbling inward as the sadness crushes me. "Bree found it this morning."

"Okay. We'll deal with this." He hugs me tighter and lifts me up, then stands. I cling to him, not ever wanting to let go. "Dana!" Chase yells over my shoulder. The heel clacking starts again.

"Chase?"

"Get Jack down to the hospital now. There's been another message. Tell him to call me the minute he gets it."

"Yes, sir." I hear her voice answer as if far away.

We're moving. Chase is walking me through the penthouse back into our room. Once there, he sets me on the bed. He pulls off my tunic and then gently pushes against my chest suggesting I lay back. He undoes my jeans and pulls them off leaving me in my tank and panties. Then he removes his t-shirt and pajama bottoms, clad only in his underwear. I'm so brokenhearted I can't even appreciate his beauty.

Tears slip down my cheeks and wet the pillow under my head. Chase maneuvers me into the middle of the bed under our down comforter. He pulls me into his chest facing one another. He holds me while I cry. With other men, like Danny, and even Justin, they always wanted me to tell them how they could fix my problems. Would hound me until finally I just pretended nothing was wrong. So much so, I built up giant walls around my heart that no one could penetrate. Over the past few years and through therapy, I learned that it's okay to cry. It's okay to hurt, and let myself feel that hurt.

Chase slides his hands all over me. Up my bare thigh, over my arm and down to my hand, back up, then down my back and into my hair, where he pulls the ponytail holder out, letting the hair tumble down my back. When I've quieted, he finally says, "Talk to me."

I close my eyes and bring his hands up to my lips. I kiss each and every knuckle and the center of each palm. Over the past six months, I was certain I could never love this man more, but that isn't true. Right now, he is taking care of me the way I need to be taken care of...not judging. Simply, being with me. Letting me have my moment, even though I know what happened in that kitchen is killing him. Not knowing what that note said is probably digging a giant crater into his psyche, yet he tends to me. I come first.

"No man will ever love me the way you do." I whisper the epiphany.

Chase's blue gaze meets mine. It's probably the most open and honest I've seen them. "I was put on this earth to love and protect you."

"To infinity?"

He blinks slowly and gifts me with his small, secretive smile. "Yes. Forever, baby." He nudges my nose with his and kisses me briefly. It's not a romantic kiss but it's just as grounding, solidifying our love. "Tell me, Gillian."

The words spill out like a too full bowl of cereal. "The stalker left a note, insinuating that he was responsible for the explosion, that he wishes Phillip was dead, and that he might get him next time. Then he said something about who was going to be next." I suck in a harsh breath trying not to let the emotions overwhelm me again.

Chase brings a hand to my cheek. "Honey, we're going to find him. I *will* find him if it's the last thing I do. I promise," he assures me.

I pull Chase closer and kiss him hard. He returns the

kiss, holding me close. Our faces are so close to one another I can feel his breath against my lips. "Gillian, you need to see someone. A therapist. These flashbacks and panic attacks scare me beyond reason."

Slowly I inhale a breath and then nuzzle into his skin. "Okay, I will."

Chase's arms tighten. "Right away. Not next week, not a month from now, not after the wedding. This week. If you don't make an appointment, I will." The tone he uses is his, "Non-negotiable" one that I usually like to rally against. Not this time.

The wedding. I can't even be happy about the most exciting day of my life. It feels as if everything is falling apart around me.

"Chase...the wedding...it's too much," I finally admit what's been plaguing me the last couple weeks.

He takes a heavy breath, turns onto his back and pulls me over the top of him. I lean both arms on top of his warm chest and set my chin on them. His eyes scan the ceiling looking everywhere but at me. Finally, he looks down, one hand burrows into the hair at my nape, the other holds me close at the waist. His eyes are sad, more so than ever before. "I know. I hate waiting, but with everything that's going on...I can no longer watch what the stress is doing to you."

I kiss his chest right over his heart. "You know I want nothing more than to be your wife," I swallow the giant lump of sadness clogging my words. "But, Chase, the stalker, Phil still in a coma, Anabelle fatherless." I shake my head trying not to dig too deep into those thoughts. "Bree is a mess and hates me right now. I have to fix my life, or I'm not going to be any good for you..." My voice trembles, and I bite my lip to hold back from falling into a fit of tears again.

"You're the only thing that's ever been good for me," Chase cups my chin, his thumb petting along the cheekbone. "I don't deserve you, but I'm too selfish to let you go."

I look deep into his eyes, trying to express with one look the seriousness of what I'm about to say. "Don't ever let me go. I no longer know who I am without you. We're one now. It's you and me. Full circle. Just us."

His smile is huge and as beautiful as a sunrise. "What you said before, about no man every loving you like I do?" I nod. "I'll ruin any man that tries to come between us." He's as serious as a heart attack. He continues, "We'll get married, Gorgeous, but as much as I hate to say it, we'll postpone it a few months. Let's start with three and go from there. I don't want to wait a second longer than I have to. I can't wait to make you Mrs. Davis."

"God, Chase, you're my everything," I admit.

"Come here, beautiful girl," he says pulling me into a deep, wet kiss. For a long time we just kiss and caress one another, reconnecting on a physical level, now that we're solid emotionally. His hands run lines all over my body. It's as if he's painting a canvas. Small brushes here, long strokes there, all while making it his life's mission to kiss me fully. A kiss from Chase is an event. He's soft when he needs to be, harder other times. Simple tugs of his teeth against my top then bottom lip, all work to rile me up. I sigh into his mouth. His hands trace circles over my lower back and start to push up my tank. When his hands cup my breasts I sit up, straddling him, then the phone rings. Chase's hands fall to the mattress in a heap of muscle and bone.

"Mother hell…" he clenches his teeth down and that jaw tick I'm so fond of starts winking.

"It's okay. You told him to call you. It's probably Jack," I remind him.

That gets his attention. He lifts up, puts one arm around my body and leans over the bed to the side table to grab his phone, never letting me go with the other arm. He lays back and presses a button bringing it to his ear. I lean down and take this moment to place kisses along his wide chest.

"Read it to me," he says gruffly.

I already know what it says, but can sense the exact moment Chase understands how serious this has become. His chest tightens and his hand on my thigh clenches down. I hug him the best I can, draped over his body.

"Put a guard at the door to the room. No one gets in that's not family or one of our friends. Get the note over to Thomas Redding and his team. They need to be on this ASAP." He clicks off the phone and tosses it on the bed.

"Austin never leaves your side when you're not with me." His voice is menacing, and I can tell that Protective Unreasonable Chase is about to make a show-stopping appearance. "He will not get to you. I will spend every fucking dollar I have to keep you safe," he grits his teeth so hard I can hear him grinding them. I put a hand to his jaw and lean down to kiss away his anger.

"Whatever you say, baby. I'll do it. Now, I need you," I grind my hips against his ever present erection. It had softened a bit during his call, but is growing again as I roll and press into it. With a quick move, I rip the tank off, twist an arm around my back and unclasp the lacy bra. With effort, I grip his hands, the ones that are clenched into fists by his side, pull them up, and place them directly onto my bare breasts. They squeeze reflexively and Chase thrusts his hips between my thighs. So good.

"That's it. Now, take what's yours, Chase." His eyes blaze fire at the words of ownership I chose. My guy is beyond possessive. He doesn't consider me his property, per se, but he does consider me his, because I'm his other half. Without him, there is no me and vice versa. We're the best parts of each other.

Chase leans up and places a firm hand around my neck, lifting my chin with his thumb. "I'm going to fuck you so hard you never forget who takes care of you, baby." He kisses me rough, wet, and deep. I give it back to him with everything I have. He knows what I need and gives it to me over and over. Reconnecting physically, when I'm struggling emotionally, is exactly what will get me through today. Tomorrow, on the other hand is a new day, and one I'm not looking forward to.

GILLIAN

CHAPTER NINE

"Gillian, my dear, it's so good to see you," Dr. Madison says as his arms encircle me. It's like hugging your brother or someone you love dearly. That sense of familiarity and peace sink deep into the tortured parts of my soul. Unfortunately, it also makes me miss Phillip and his big bear hugs. I squeeze Dr. Madison harder trying to convey all the hurt and turmoil that's plaguing me, without having to get into the nitty gritty of it.

"I think that's quite enough," I hear Chase grumble from behind me. I pull away, having forgotten that Chase was close.

Dr. Madison holds me at arm's length then looks over my shoulder. "A friend of yours, I presume." His voice carries a twinge of sarcasm yet still a hint of humor that always makes me feel comfortable revealing my deep, dark, secrets. Before I can answer, Chase grips me around the waist and pulls me back against his chest. Dr. Madison's eyebrows rise and his lips curl into a familiar frown as he clasps his hands together confidently in front of him.

"This is Chase Davis, Dr. Madison. My fiancé," I finish.

"Fiancé?" his tone is surprised. Probably because the last time I was here I made it clear that I was swearing off serious relationships for the rest of my natural life. I nod and he gestures for me to take a seat in the big comfy chair, the one I usually crawl into like a kitten. "You can wait outside Mr. uh…"

"Davis, Chase Davis," he says with an air of authority. He's used to that name carrying some serious clout. Unfortunately, Chase is going to be sorely mistaken when he realizes that Dr. Madison doesn't care about trivial things such as status. He's in the business of mental health not wealth.

Chase looks at me and then at the doctor. Instead of leaving, he walks around and takes the chair next to mine, props his ankle on the opposite knee and brings his hands into a steeple under his chin. "No, I think I'd like to stay. Can't be too careful with my woman," he says and I roll my eyes. Oh, the doctor is going to have a field day with this one.

Dr. Madison sits down and crosses his legs pulling a yellow notepad onto his lap. "Your woman?" He quirks a brow again. "Interesting. How do you feel about being *his* woman?" The doctor turns toward me.

"Uh…" I pinch my lips together not knowing how to answer that.

"She feels perfectly fine about it, right Gillian?" Chase answers for me in the only way he could…with finality. I don't think he could accept anything else. His pride would probably crack and break right here like a porcelain doll hitting concrete.

The doctor turns towards Chase. "I didn't realize this session was couple's therapy. When Gillian called, she said she had some personal things she needed to work through."

He attempts to continue, but Chase cuts him off.

"I don't think I like your tone, Doctor," Chase's eyes narrow and he leans both elbows onto his knees.

"Excuse me if I've offended you. I think we got off on the wrong foot," he says in a perfectly reasonable tone.

Chase looks Dr. Madison up and down. My therapist is hot. There's no denying it. He just is. Maria and I often joke, calling him Dr. McHottie. His dark blond hair is styled to perfection. The Dockers and dress shirt he's wearing are in pristine condition, even though I know I'm the last patient of the day. The doctor's hazel eyes assess both Chase and me until he crosses his arms and brings one hand up to his face, curling a knuckle against his lips.

Chase visibly bristles. He's unbelievably cute when he's jealous. "Why do you have to have a male doctor anyway? Aren't there women you could talk to?"

I laugh out loud, slip off my heels from work, and curl into the chair. Both Chase and Dr. Madison look at me like I've lost my marbles. Probably because I have. "Chase, sometimes, baby, you are too much. Do you see what I'm dealing with?" I ask the Doctor. Chase's brows rise and his eyes widen.

With a small smirk the doctor responds, "I do. Looks like you're spiraling right into familiar patterns," he says, and I nod knowing he's referring to my fetish for controlling men.

"Chase doesn't realize he's trying to control the universe, Dr. Madison. When it comes to me, he just, well, he loses his shit," I say deadpan as Chase whips his head to me, his gaze expressing his frustration.

Chase stands up abruptly. "Excuse me?" Chase walks

over to my chair, and pulls me up to a standing position. "I think we're done here," he growls. His hold, the way he's claimed me in front of the doctor is not lost on my therapist.

"Sit down, Mr. Davis." The doctor's tone is forceful yet respectful. "It seems we have only just begun. If you want Gillian to be herself, feel safe, calm and whole in your world, you're going to need to work with us, not against us. Emotional health is necessary for any loving relationship to flourish and succeed. Do you want Gillian to be whole?" he asks in a way that Chase can't deny.

"Of course I do. Nothing means more to me than her." I hug him tight and untangle myself from his arms and go back to my chair. He does the same, only a scowl mars his handsome features.

Dr. Madison adjusts his long body in his own, high-back, worn, leather chair. "Now, Gillian, why are you here?"

I take a deep breath and start to go through everything. During the middle of my story, when I get to the part about the stalker blowing up Phillip, Chase reaches out and clasps my hand. He traces the infinity symbol on my hand as I grip his hand tight. My rock.

"And now we've had to cancel the wedding, because I can't relax. I don't know what to do about Phillip, my best friend, Bree, is hurt, and...and..." I tremble as the weight of everything pulls me under the tide.

Chase jumps in, "We're not cancelling our wedding. Just postponing it a little while. Hopefully, we'll have this stalker situation dealt with really soon. I've got any army of men working on this."

"I'm being *stalked*, Dr. Madison. A real life, scary guy, is *stalking* me. This freak wants to hurt me. He wants to hurt my friends. Christ, he *has* hurt my friends. What am I going to do?" I screech. "Who else has this type of crap to deal with? It's unbelievable," I say everything as if I'm releasing all the pent up frustration of the past five years. Maybe I am.

The doctor takes a breath and hands me a box of tissue. I blow my nose loudly into the tissue. "Gillian, this situation is unfortunate. I'm sorry you have to go through it. Have you narrowed down who this individual is? Maybe someone from your past?" he says the words slowly, and I envision Justin, the sickening grin that would slip across his lips when he was about to lose his mind. Instantly I'm back there...

Woods all around me. The sun is setting as I run through the trees. Speckles of light flutter along the ground as my feet hit the dirt and leaves. Blood pours out my nose, into my mouth, and down the front of my shirt. I have to get away. If he finds me, he just may kill me this time.

"Where are you, Gil?" I can hear is voice not far behind.

I run faster, even though the coppery taste of my own blood makes me gag and spit. I can only breathe through my mouth. He's broken my nose again, and every heaving breath I take as I run, I swallow down more of my own life source.

My hands are painted red as I slam into a tree and whirl around it, trying and failing to catch my breath.

"There's nowhere you can run that I won't find you." He laughs loudly. It seems to echo off the trees as if he's closer, standing right in front of me. From this spot, I don't know where he is, only that he's close. I crouch down low. Tears blind me as I lean heavily against the rough bark of the tree.

For long moments, all I can hear is the sound of my own breathing. Maybe he went back to the campsite? I know there's a road not too far from here. If I can just get to the road, I can flag down someone for help.

Standing up, I try to see through the now fully darkened forest. My entire body is shaking and the cold shock from the pain is setting in. Just as I take two steps forward, I feel a hand around my neck and one at my hip slamming me into the tree. My head hits the bark so hard I see tiny bursts of light.

"You think you can escape me?" Justin snarls before bringing back his arm and punching me hard in the stomach. All the air leaves my lungs in a giant whoosh. Pain lances through my abdomen. He pins me to the tree with the weight of his body and pulls my hands up over my head. Justin cocks his head and looks at every facet of my face, his dry, cracked lips curling into a sneer. Leaning close he drags an unshaven cheek against mine. I can feel his lips against my ear. "Remember when you said you were mine forever? That was a promise. One I'll never let you break. I'll kill you before I ever let you leave."

"Baby, Gillian, I'm here," Chase's voice enters my thoughts. I can feel his hand running up and down my back. The lights of the room start to penetrate my senses. I can see the French doors that lead off to the balcony, the mahogany desk in the corner, a wall of bookcases with medical texts and trinkets from around the world. I know this place. I love this place. This place makes me feel safe. Currently, I'm huddled into the corner in a fetal position.

"Come here, Gillian. I've got you, I've always got you. Remember, I promised to always bring you back," Chase's words reach my subconscious, and I fling myself into his arms. He holds me close, lifts me up and brings me to the chair I was sitting in previously. I hug him tight as he cradles me like an infant. Once my breathing comes back to a neutral pattern I uncurl my legs and look around. Dr.

Madison is sitting in his chair, yellow pad held tight by his clenched hand, the paper scrunched up and creased, kind of like my heart after that flashback.

"I'm sorry, Dr. Madison," I whisper and his head springs up.

"Gillian, you have nothing to be sorry about. I hadn't realized that you were having the flashbacks again. This stalker business is bringing up some very old wounds, ones you obviously haven't dealt with. How often are they coming to you?" He asks.

Shame hits me like a physical blow. "Um, I've been having them off and on for the past few months. When I moved in with Chase they were all but gone. Then this thing with Phil happened, now they're back full force."

"And the nightmares…tell him about everything," Chase warns forcing me to be honest with the doctor and myself.

I close my eyes and let Chase's scent fill my nostrils and calm me, his warmth replacing the chill deep in my bones, and his love washing away the shame.

"I've had one a night since the note appeared a few days ago at the hospital. I feel like I'm losing my mind, that I'm living in the past. The only thing that can bring me out of it is…" I suck in a breath as the tears spill down my cheeks.

"Is what?" Dr. Madison asks.

"Me," Chase answers for me and I nod silently, not able to form words. "And I'll do it every time. Gladly, baby. You're mine. Not some sick fuck from your past that put his hands on you with hate. I swear to God if I ever see him…"

I turn in his lap and cup his cheeks. "No. He's ruined

enough of me. I can't let him hurt you. Not you." I lean my forehead against his.

"Is that what you think, Gillian? That Justin ruined you?" Dr. Madison asks softly.

I nod and look out the window. "I don't even know why Chase would want someone so messed up. It doesn't make sense," I admit. Chase's arms grip me tight. I scramble out of his lap and into the other chair needing the space to wallow in my own self-pity.

"Gillian, you are the best thing that ever happened to me. Not only are you the most beautiful woman I've ever known, your heart is bigger than those of a hundred people. You're smart, silly, devastatingly intelligent, and your soul is pure. I *want* that in my life. I *need* that in my life, every day, forever." Chase comes over to me and kneels at my feet. "No woman has every loved *me*, the man I am with *you*." Chase swallows and kisses my hands. "You are not ruined. Baby, you're perfect. Perfect for me."

Nodding, I clasp his hands and kiss each of his fingers. "I love you, Chase. Thank you for being with me. Pushing your way in today. I needed you with me."

"There's nothing that will keep me from you," Chase finishes kissing me softly as if he's sealing his promise with a kiss.

Dr. Madison takes a deep breath and lets it out with a sigh. "Welcome back, Gillian. We have some work to do, with and without, your over-protective fiancé," he grins at Chase. My man does not care. He just shrugs and pulls me up. He grabs my shoes and helps me step into each one. His hands skim up my legs in the process. A little caress letting me know our time together isn't finished. And no, no it's not. I'll never be finished with Chase.

★ ★ ★ ★

"What are you doing here? It's not your turn to babysit," Bree says, disdain clearly evident in her tone.

Entering the room, I take in its cheery appearance. Flowers cover every surface, tickling my nose with their sweet scent. It's a direct contrast to the unmoving man lying in the hospital bed and the irate woman at his side, clutching his hand. Bree is flushed with anger. Her skin has reddened, her mouth is in a heavy scowl and her eyes are shooting daggers. One of her petite hands is clenched so tight into the thick blanket covering Phillip that it almost glows white.

"Bree, seriously?" I shake my head and place my hand on Phillip's thigh, wanting him to feel my presence. She smacks my hand off him so quickly I stumble back.

"Don't fucking touch him! Everything you touch turns to shit!"

Whoa! I knew she was upset, positively broken-hearted after receiving that note, but I had no idea when I came today I would be dealing with a stranger. This is *not* my soul sister, my Bree. She's not herself. "That is not fair, Bree, and you know it." I try speaking softly, hoping to express the deep sadness that fills me.

"Fair? You want to talk about fair?" She stands and swipes a hand through her messy blonde hair. Usually, it's a perfect golden blanket down her back. Right now it's scraggily, possibly even unwashed, definitely having seen a thousand better days. "You're standing here, and Phillip's lying there. Is that fair, Gigi?"

"You don't mean that." Fear, guilt, and shame, my three ugly friends, creep into my subconscious.

Bree's normally warm blue eyes, ice over and narrow. "Don't I? Phillip is lying here in a coma because of you. Because some fucking man wants to hurt you!" I gasp, but she continues with her verbal assault, striking while the iron is nice and hot. "Did it work? Are you hurting?"

Tears slip down my cheeks. I let them fall. "Yes," I choke out.

"It's not enough is it? He won't stop. Who's next, Gigi? Anabelle?" She stabs that verbal knife so far into my heart I clutch my chest and slam into the wall behind me. The tears race to the surface and spill over my cheeks as I crouch down low and hug my knees. Not Anabelle. Not my sweet angel baby. Images flash across my mind. Her adorably round face, eyes as blue as an unclouded sky on a sunny day, and her blonde curls bobbing along as she sings one of her many songs. My goddaughter.

Bree is now crouched in front of me. We've never been this close and not touched one another in some fashion, a small pat, a friendly gesture, something. Right now Bree's hate is all I feel. It's like a physical blanket, coating my tortured mind with more guilt.

"I'll give myself up. I'll let him take me," I say through my tears. "I will. He can have me. I would never wish this on any of you. Not Phil, not my sweet baby girl, no one!" I say with as much conviction as possible. The idea has taken root as I watch Bree's face crumble. She looks at me as if she's never seen me before.

"Over my dead body," I hear come from the door. Kat is holding a colorful array of fresh flowers. Her eyes assess both Bree and me. She sets the flowers on the one open spot on the side table. She comes around, her long maxi skirt flowing with her movements. The ocean. Everything she's wearing is blue, indigo, aquamarine, and green. The fabric sways in soft swooshes as she stands in front of us, her hands on her hips. Peace. I close my eyes; they're too full of tears to keep them open. Instead, I let the calm waves of her presence cool the overheated emotions within, like a wet towel over an open flame.

Bree stands abruptly. "Be careful, Kat. That just could happen." Sorrow rips through me again as Bree makes her way to Phil and slides a hand down his face from temple to chin.

"Come here," Kat holds out her arms to me and I stand weakly then crumble into her. She pets my hair, soothes a hand down my back, hugging me tightly until I calm down. She pulls away, a hand still in my hair, one holding my bicep. "This. Is. Not. Your. Fault." She says it then puts her head against my forehead. Our eyes lock. Carmel to green. "You hear me?" I nod. "Good. Now, there will be no sacrificing ourselves to wackos. We're in this together," Kat shakes her head up and down until she's got me mimicking her "yes" gesture.

"What are we in together?" Maria says as she walks in, tripping over her own feet. She leans heavily against the wall, catching herself before she falls. I take a deep breath and pull back from Kat's arms, wiping the errant tears away. Bree is standing with her arms crossed and a hip cocked. "Wha'd I miss?"

"I'm surprised you made it here alive," Bree says in a haughty tone. I'm not even sure I know this woman. Bree has never spoken to anyone with such malice before.

"*Discúlpeme?* What's she talking about?" Maria asks while entering the room and setting her rehearsal bag down on floor. She's wearing her standard dancing gear, black workout leggings and a loose jersey shirt over her sports bra. Probably stopping in before she's due at the theatre.

I can't respond, the sadness swallowing my ability to form words. Bree doesn't hesitate. "Well, the odds of any of us surviving, until Gigi's stalker can be found, are slim to none. Tell them about the note," she grates. Her head tips to the side as she looks at me, fear controlling her tongue. I stand mute not capable of speech. She continues undaunted. "The stalker left a note a few days ago, right here on Phillip's bed." She points to the foot of the hospital bed. "Admitted to being the one to plant the bomb in the gym and then insinuated that someone was next!" Her pretty eyes narrow.

Kat gasps placing a hand over her mouth. Maria's form tightens, her spine becomes straight as an arrow, hands clenching at her sides. "I cannot wait to get my *manos* on this psycho." She inhales audibly. "*¡Está muerto!*" He's dead, she pronounces.

"No, the last thing we need is for you to go crazy, Ria. Bree's right; this is my fault. Whoever it is, wants me. Even though Chase and Tommy are working to find him, it feels useless. Everything is turning to shit. Just like Bree said! I should just let him take me!" I wave my hands in the air like a deranged person. I'm actually starting to feel deranged. Looks like I'll be needing double the amount of visits to Dr. Madison in the very near future.

"You will do no such thing! That's crazy talk, Gigi. You can't put yourself in harm's way to protect us. He could kill you! Then what would we have. A dead best friend," Kat's voice is layered with emotion but she's valiantly holding it together. I wish I were as strong as she is right now.

Maria comes over to me and hugs me tight. I can see Bree cringe and look away. How could this happen? This freak is breaking me apart, shredding the lives of everyone that I love around me. Something has to be done. The idea of planting myself somewhere the stalker can get to me is growing, ready to bloom as a plan starts to form. I could do it. Save my friends, Chase, little Anabelle. Then no one would be hurt again.

"I can hear you thinking, *Cara Bonita*. You are *not* doing this. No matter what. *¿Me escuchas?* You hear me? Don't you dare, throw yourself in front of this *loco* fucker!" Maria cups my cheeks and waits for me to nod. Her ice blue eyes are hard, unyielding. It reminds me of Chase when he's in a "non-negotiable" mood. Chase. I need Chase.

Bree huffs, "It's not a bad idea, using her as bait. The freak will surely come for his *precious* prize," her words lash out, as painful as a whip, splitting me open, cutting right into my heart.

Kat bristles at Bree's words hugging her body. Ria turns around and faces our soul sister. "What the fuck is your problem? Are you seriously suggesting Gigi, our *hermana*, risk death as punishment for *Phillipe* or just to save yourself!"

Bree's eyes fill with tears. It's the first time since I arrived that I've seen a shred of the real Bree. The woman I would throw myself in front of a speeding train to save. Her shoulders slump down, her upper body caving in. She looks down, completely defeated.

Unfortunately, Maria does not pick up on Bree's

distress. "Did you get a hit to the *cabeza*? Are you *loco*?" she continues undaunted.

Bree's shoulders quake, her entire body rattles as she holds herself up against the back of the hospital chair. "I'm sorry, Gigi, I don't know..." she starts, tears spilling down her cheeks as her eyes meet mine. The apology is clear in her gaze. She is devastated. "I didn't mean it, Oh my god, what have I done!" her voice cracks. I run over to her and pull her into my arms, holding her so tight I may actually bruise her. She doesn't seem to care, sobbing into the crook of my neck, letting three weeks of pain out, in a tidal wave of loss. Anguish pours from her, a palpable thing, as I hold her.

"I'm not c-crazy," Bree chokes out against my hair, wiping her tears and her snotty nose along my shoulder. I welcome it. Anything that will give her a moment's respite from the fear and uncertainty plaguing us all. Especially Bree, who probably doesn't even realize she's completely fallen in love with Phillip. Right now, she needs to find her center.

I stroke her hair and hold her to me. "You're not crazy or insane honey," I tell her soothingly.

She hiccups as another wave of tears pour down her face. "No, I'm not...I'm pregnant," she announces. The entire room goes dead silent. I pull her back and look into her teary, tortured face. Three pairs of eyes focus solely on her. She nods, then crumbles into a heap of tissue and bones as I hold her up.

All three of us gather around, putting all of our love into our circle of protection. Our trinity. Together, holding one another, we let it all go.

X

So, Yoga Barbie is pregnant. Yee-frickin' haw. This is too good. I couldn't have planned this better myself. She just moved right up to the top of the fucking list. Taking her and her bastard child out in one swoop? If that doesn't send a big, giant, flashing message to my girl, nothing will. I'm almost giddy at hearing the news through the bug I planted under the hospital bed. Chase's people keep underestimating me. You'd think after blowing up the gym, and leaving my calling card, by way of a note on the bed, they'd take me more seriously. Their stupidity, my good fortune.

I pull out the pictures of Bree Simmons and her studio, *I Am Yoga*. Stupid fucking name. She is yoga? How about, "I Am Dead," because that's what she's going to be much sooner than I planned. My princess and her other two bitches will lose it, make mistakes, once I take out the tiny blonde. Kill her and her kid off and they'll all be too busy mourning the loss to really focus on keeping me away. That's when I'll strike. The funeral will be perfect. I know where that blonde bitch's family goes to church—St. Patrick's down on Mission. They're sure to plan services there. It's big, and pretentious, just like her family. It makes you wonder how the blonde turned to yoga and a Buddhist way, when her family are die hard Catholics. No matter.

All I have to do now is make sure I have access in advance along with an exit route. That Catholic Church sits on an old, unused, sewer system. Perfect for dragging an unconscious, five foot seven or so redhead. Then, I'll finally have my girl right where I want her. Somewhere no one will ever find her.

Sitting back, I plop my shiny wingtips right on top of Bree Simmons's attractive face in the black and white image. She'll be prettier when I give her a new smile…from ear to ear. I can hardly wait to watch her bleed out.

GILLIAN

CHAPTER TEN

It's been a week since Bree's breakdown and our fight in the hospital room. An entire seven days of avoiding Maria, Bree, and Kat completely. I've seen Dr. Madison twice this week. He's warned me several times not to put distance between myself and the ones I love, but I haven't listened. Knowing that Phillip was targeted and hurt because of me, that he's in a coma and may never wake up? It's weighing too heavily, swallowing me whole.

The doctors say his body is healing well, and that when he wakes up he'll have already made it past the most painful part of recovery aside from physical therapy. Chase has made certain that Phillip receives round-the-clock care, by way of making a hefty million dollar donation to the hospital. He didn't tell me he made the donation. I overheard him talking to Dana a couple weeks ago. Instead of bringing it up to him, I let it be. I want Phil to have the best possible care, and if my fiancé can make it happen, then I'll choke down my pride and let it be. Especially now.

"Baby, get dressed." Chase enters the closet behind me and pulls out one of my favorite gauzy maxi dresses and a soft cardigan. Dana absolutely hates the dresses I refuse to get rid of. She says they are too boxy for my thin frame. I think they feel like Heaven, but it's Friday morning, and I need to put on my work attire.

"Chase, its Friday." I pull out a heather grey pencil skirt and a pastel pink shell. Chase grabs the hangers from my hands and puts the maxi dress and cardigan in its place.

"We're taking a personal day. I've already arranged it. Hawthorne knows how hard you've been working and agreed to the time. Said to consider it a comp day." He waggles his dark brows, pulls me into a clinch and kisses me.

I breathe in his citrus and sandalwood scent that has become the most calming smell in the entire world and rub my nose into his chest.

"I'm taking you out on a date," Chase announces.

I'm certain that my face must show my surprise, because he cups my cheeks and nuzzles my nose. "I haven't done right by not wooing you. Today is about us, and enjoying the city. You need a break away from everything, and I need time alone with you," he kisses the corner of my mouth and drags his morning scruff down the column of my neck, sending chills racing down to my toes. After a quick lick, a bite, and a tender kiss to that spot he adores, the juncture where neck meets shoulder, he pulls away. "Wear the comfy dress. I know you love it, and I love you. Today is about just being us."

Just being us.

Six months ago, I would never have thought I'd be standing here in my sleep tank and panties while the most gorgeous man alive, my fiancé, claims he's taking me on a date to just be us. What does "us" even look like? The past several months have been beautiful and devastating, rife with happiness, pleasure, pain, guilt, trauma and everything in between. I feel as though we've lived more life in half a year, than most couples do in an entire lifetime of being married.

A small smile lifts the corners of my mouth as I cling to the dress. "Where are you taking me?" I ask while he takes a short-sleeved polo in bright yellow down from a hanger. I watch as he pulls out a pair of khaki chinos from the neat stack. Once I remove my tank and throw on a new bra and panties, I lift the maxi dress over my body, and it falls in a sweep of comfy cotton. It's a swirling mix of purples and blues with a one-inch strap at the shoulders. I grab the sweater and enter the bathroom.

"Leave your hair down. I like seeing it blow in the wind," Chase murmurs from behind me.

"Okay," I give him a coy smile and he digs a hand into the back of my hair landing on the nape of my neck. He rubs circles into the skin under my ear. He gives just a hint of pressure then proceeds to his side of the bathroom where he completes his morning routine.

Once we're both done and have a light breakfast, consisting of a half bagel, crème cheese and fruit, we're on our way. When we get down to the garage, I expect Chase to usher me into one of his fancy cars. I don't know much about cars, but the little wings on one car and the shield with a lion on another tell me they probably cost more than everything my three girlfriends and I own all put together. Instead of cars, I'm greeted by six men all in black suits. New security.

"Okay guys, if the stalker is watching, he will assume that Mr. Davis and Miss Callahan are with me or Mr. Campbell. We will be driving the decoy cars. You two," Jack points to a couple giant NFL sized men I've never met before, "will be taking them wherever Mr. Davis directs. I expect detailed reports sent to me every twenty minutes. If I don't receive them, I will assume something is wrong. Regardless, I'll be tracking both of our charges with the GPS on their phones and the vehicle."

To my left, I see three perfectly matched black SUVs with blackened out windows. "Is this really necessary?" I nudge Chase in the shoulder while whispering in his ear.

He looks down at me and his eyes are hard, unshakable. It's the same way he looks at an adversary in the boardroom. Serious, and in complete control. "I do what it takes to protect what's mine. Your safety is non-negotiable." There's that word again. I should make a game out of how many times he says the word "non-negotiable." I roll my eyes, and he puts an arm around my shoulder bringing me close before placing a soft kiss at my temple. "Just play along, my love," he says and those words remind me that he's still my Chase. The man that loves me, the one who can be jovial, sweet, and heart-meltingly honest behind closed doors. My fiancé. The man who will grow old with me and always put me first.

"You're mine, too, you know," I snuggle into his neck and nip the tender skin there. He wraps his arms around me in a tight hug. His hugs could heal the world, but he doesn't give them to just anyone. I've only ever seen him hug his family and not an all over body embrace, like the ones he gives me. No, those are just for me.

Chase holds me tighter as Jack finishes up his orders. "To forever, Baby," he says then pulls away and clasps my hand. "Enough. Time's wasting," he barks and ushers me to enter one of the black SUVs. We get settled in the back and our new security fills the front.

★ ★ ★ ★

First stop is 16th street. Chase takes a calming breath and exits the car. He offers his hand and helps me exit the large vehicle. Our bodyguards stay close but out of the way.

"Where are we?" I ask looking around at the busy street. San Francisco is wonderfully diverse. People from all walks of life, all ethnicities converge into this urban melting pot. There are people in fierce suits blindly focused on wherever they are headed. Hipsters fill local cafes and bookstores alongside busy families, shuffling their kids to and fro.

Chase clasps my hand and turns down the street. "You'll see," he grins and I almost stop walking to just stare at the open happiness he's gifting me and the world around us. We walk a few blocks until we're between Moraga and Noriega. Chase stops and points to the very bottom of a staircase. "Look." I follow his finger to a spot over my shoulder. I slowly walk over and I'm greeted by the most stunning sight. It's a rainbow staircase but, it's not exactly a rainbow.

Small mosaic tiles coalesce together to create a myriad of images. My gaze jumps from point to point, unable to still on one facet. It's breathtaking, unique and quite possibly one of the most beautiful things I've ever seen. "How?" I whisper trying to take the wonder in.

"It was built in 2005. Over three hundred community volunteers, local businesses and individual donors came together to bring artists Aileen Barr and Colette Crutcher's design to fruition." I take a couple steps up and view the sweeping colors made completely of tiny tiles. "There's a hundred and sixty three steps in all. I love the moon in the center. On a clear night, it seems to reflect the real moon's rays making it unearthly." I scan the stairs all the way up until I see the giant moon in the center with dark swirling tiles around it.

Finally, I'm able to take a breath and really appreciate the view. The bottom of the staircase starts with a flurry of oceanic themes from little fish to swirling waves all in small colored pieces. The ocean waves seem to go half way up the flight of stairs until it reaches tiles that are rich browns and oranges speckled with flowers and woodland creatures. Up further reflects a sky with birds, and an array of flying insects all in aqua and pale blue hued tiles. Continuing on is the moon Chase loves. A giant white swooping circle made of glistening whites and grey pieces surrounded by a dark indigo and midnight blue. At the very tip top of the stairs seems to be a bright sunburst depicting a giant sun. I'm pretty certain I've never seen anything more heart-stopping aside from the man holding me up while I feast on this local art.

"Shall we walk it?" Chase clasps my hand as I nod, still unable to speak. We take each step and every so often, I lean down and run my finger along a tile. Chase doesn't let go of my hand, just crouches low to see what has caught my attention. We continue on, and finally, when we're in between the moon and sun, Chase sits me down. He goes down about ten or fifteen steps and pulls out his phone. "Give me one your smiles, beautiful." I don't even have to try. Sitting here at a place I've never been with the man who clearly wanted to share such beauty with me, I couldn't hold back a giant grin. He snaps a couple of photos. I pull out my own phone and gesture to him to sit next to me. A lone kid with a mowhawk tinged in bright pink and a leather jacket walks to the side of us trying to pass.

"Excuse me, sir?" I ask as Chase growls under his breath and tightens his hold. "Can you take our picture please?" Mohawk Guy nods and grins before adjusting the satchel he has across his body. He smiles as I hand him the phone. His mouth is teaming with jewelry, little rings on the top and bottom. He brings new meaning to the term 'metal mouth'.

"You look like my sister," Mohawk Guy says on a grin. His eyes are an astonishing shade of green that match my own. If he didn't have so much metal marring his features, he'd be quite cute.

"I hope that's a compliment," I respond in my most polite tone.

"It is. People tell me she's hot all the time. But I'm like, gross, that's my sister," he shudders and takes several steps down pointing the camera at us. Both Chase and I laugh at this perfect stranger sharing a bit of his life with us. Somehow, it just adds to the moment in a lovely way. Mohawk Guy must have taken a couple shots while we weren't watching or posing because I can hear the telltale clicking. Then he comes closer and says, "Now, pretend you love each other."

Chase turns his head to me, and clasps my cheeks. His eyes are a stunning shade of ocean blue and like so many times before, I lose myself in them. "I don't have to pretend," Chase whispers.

"Me either," I say back, right before his lips meet mine. His mouth opens and I delve in, giving Chase what I consider to be the first real kiss of the day, and it's right here, on the most beautiful stairway in all the world. He tastes of mint and man. *My* man.

Chase and I make out on those stairs as if we were teenagers who just found one another and are kissing for the first time. We both put so much promise and love into it that I forget where we are, until I hear giggling from behind me and a little *"thwack thwack thwack"* sound. I pull away and look back. A little brown haired girl and what must be her brother are jumping down each stair one at a time, holding hands. I turn back and look to see that Mohawk Guy is gone but he left my phone on the step right next to my sandaled foot. Never judge a book by its cover. That kid could have run off with that fancy phone Chase got me, but he didn't.

I pick up the phone and pull up the images. There are at least seven or so. There's the one where we were laughing at one another candidly, then the posed picture and then the up close one. Chase is holding my cheeks and telling me he loves me. That picture is going to be printed and put up in our home. "Look," I show him the pictures. He points to the one that I like best.

"Send them all to me but this one is...special." I nod, so happy to see that he and I are absolutely in tune with one another. I can't wait to surprise him with a blown up copy of it in our bedroom or living room. "Come on, snookems" he says. Oh no, not another endearment. Snookems is one I will *not* tolerate. I cringe and he laughs. "No to snookems? Alright, I'll stick to baby," he grins and nudges my cheek with his nose. He clasps my hand and we make our way up the rest of the stairs.

"Onto our next site," he loops an arm around my shoulder. "You okay to walk?" we both look down to my sparkly flip-flops then his practical walking loafers.

Smiling, I look up into his eyes and cling to his waist. "I'll walk with you anywhere."

★ ★ ★ ★

We walk for about a mile when Chase stops at the entrance to the Japanese Tea Garden. It's a huge gate that looks like a pagoda. The sign on the entrance doors says, "Closed for Maintenance," but Chase enters anyway.

"We can't go in. It's closed," I warn in a hushed tone hoping we don't bring any attention to our trespassing. Chase looks behind him and gestures to a bench near the door for our guards to sit at.

A man of Asian descent dressed all in white seems to show up out of nowhere. "Mr. Davis," the man holds out a hand, walking toward us. Chase shakes it. "I believe everything is set up to your liking. You have free reign of the gardens for the next three hours, as requested. And thank you again for the very generous donation. It will be put to good use maintaining the grounds."

"Shall we?" Chase smiles and holds a hand out to a few different paths. I shake my head grinning. That man would try to buy his way into the gates of heaven if he could.

The first place we stop is in front of a red five-story pagoda. It reminds me of the friendship pagoda firecracker I've always enjoyed during Independence Day. The one that comes in an octagon shape, and, then when lit, pops up into a mini Asian looking mansion. The real deal is even cooler.

"This was actually built in 1915 for the Panama-Pacific Exposition. It was moved here after the event to protect the history. Pagodas typically relate to a place where religious activities can be held, usually for Buddhists, who tend to use the tiered location for worship. They are also known to hold artifacts and keep religious relics safe."

Chase stares at the red square tiered building while I stare at him. "You're really into architecture and history," I lean against his shoulder and wait for his reply.

He takes a breath and looks around. "It's a passion of mine, definitely," he answers simply. I like that about him. Something interesting and different about Chase. Somehow it makes him seem more real, more human.

We continue down a path and come to a sprawling Zen garden. He leads me to a bench and we sit, looking out over the landscape and the river rocks, which have been raked into perfect calming patterns. "Do you know about the Zen garden too?" I ask. His eyes twinkle and he nods. "Tell me about their significance."

Chase cups my shoulder and looks out over the garden. "The Zen garden was added with religious as well as mythological meaning in mind. They are meant to help others in their search for enlightenment."

I hum, unsure of the mythological and religious aspects. The gardens are beautiful and would definitely make a person want to think through a problem. "Does it enlighten you?" I ask Chase sarcastically.

"Yes," he says deadpan and my shoulders slump at my lost joke. Then I feel it. His shoulders start shaking and he tips his head back and a full belly laugh rumbles through his chest and out his mouth. I smack his chest and snuff against it. "You totally fell for it. Do I look like the type of guy who is enlightened by bunch of rocks and shrubs?" he croaks out while still snickering.

I roll my eyes. "Whatever!" I huff and stand up preparing to get some distance between us.

"Oh, no you don't," he says as I make a run for it down the winding path. As I'm running, I feel free as a bird. The scenery is lush, green, and full of floral scents that waft along the path. The air is moist, thick with humidity that's misting my skin as I barrel through another area. I come to a giant red brown half-moon shaped bridge over a span of water that seems to have popped up out of nowhere. The sun glints off the bridge and glistens off the water, creating a full circle in the reflection.

Chase's arms come around me from behind, his form flattening against my back. We're both panting and breathing heavy as I take in the bridge. "Amazing isn't it?" he whispers, his breath tickling along the edges of my ear and neck.

"It is," I hold his arms around my waist keeping him close.

"Let's walk over it," he says gripping me around the waist then clasping my hand. I follow him around the side of the water and to the railing. The bridge is wood with deep small steps that are about a foot apart leading to the peak of the circle. Chase holds my ribs as I find my footing and make my way up. Once at the top, I look out over the gardens. It's quiet, so quiet you can hear the birds chirping, bees buzzing nearby, even a few creatures that can't be seen are skittering around making their presence known.

Chase turns me from the railing and cages me in, his eyes skate over my face. He seems to take in everything, understand all that I'm thinking in this moment, without needing to say a word. He brings his lips to mine and kisses me. It's not the kiss of a man who's starved for his woman. No, it's a kiss to remember. One to pair with this day, and remember twenty, thirty, forty years from now, when we're old and gray, and come back to this place. We'll have this. A moment where we expressed our love for one another on a bridge shaped in a never-ending circle. Just like our relationship. Unending.

He leads me down the steep stairs, clasping me at the waist and pulling me against his big body to the ground. "Come on; you hungry?" he asks. I shake my head out of habit. Who could have an appetite when so much is shattering? At least that's the way it's been for the past month. "No? Well, you're going to eat. Baby, you're too thin." I don't respond. He's right and we both know it. When we make our way away from the bridge, he leads me to an open clearing surrounded by weeping willow trees. Their branches are weighted toward the ground. Underneath them is a large white blanket and several throw pillows. Next to the pillows is a bucket with champagne and a couple of picnic baskets.

After we sit down, I kick off my flip-flops, grab Chase's ankles, and slip off his shoes admiring his bare feet. They're so masculine with short wide toes with perfectly rounded nails. His feet are ridiculously soft and only a tiny smattering of hair trails down from his ankles to sprinkle the tops of his feet. It's annoying. Men are supposed to have ugly, mammoth clod hoppers but not my Chase.

Chase opens the champagne and pours me a glass. It's crisp with just the right spark of bubbles to tickle the taste buds. Then he sets out a cutting board and proceeds to unwrap and lay out a cornucopia of meats and cheeses. He removes a little glass jar with a purplish paste and adds a few heavy dollops in between the meat and cheese. "Bentley tells me it's a raspberry chambord infused mustard to go with the coppa, sopressata, and prosciutto," he points to the different cured meats. "As well as the brie, manchego, and Irish cheddar," he traces a line on the board between the white cheeses.

"It looks fantastic." His smile is wide and sincere. He lays out a few more items to add to our feast. Gherkin pickles, pears, and strawberries.

Over the course of an hour, we eat, feeding each other little nibbles. Once we're full, we lay next to one another on the blanket, leaning our heads on the soft pillows. Chase traces a finger from my wrist, up my forearm, over my bicep and to my shoulder then back down. Everywhere he touches tingles with pleasure and ramps up the lust that's always just brewing under the surface between us.

"I can't even imagine not getting to look at your beauty every day," his words come out as if in prayer.

"Good thing you don't have to," I answer as honestly as possible.

I never plan to be without him. I'm not sure I could. Now that I've experienced the real Chase, the man, not just the overbearing business tycoon who runs an empire, or the sad little boy who watched his mother be hurt for years. I get the benefit of seeing the man who loves architecture, and history, and cookies for breakfast. Who enjoys a simple meal as much as a five-star one. The man who likes to wear pajama bottoms that match the ensembles I wear to bed, or a suit he's paired with a dress I'm wearing so we're united in all things. The most honest human being I've ever had the privilege of loving.

Chase sits up and slides a hand from my ankle up under my long dress. He pushes the fabric up to my chest and then motions for me to lift. He removes the entire garment leaving me in nothing but a lavender bra and matching bikini briefs. "You are more stunning than anything in all five acres of these gardens," he says softly tracing a finger from sternum to knee. With ease, he moves to his knees and pulls the polo up and over his body giving me the sweetest view of his upper half. The golden chest of the Gods. Chase is nothing if not meticulous in his commitment to keeping fit and healthy. It pays off in spades for his chest is muscled to perfection with smooth lines and nice dips along a toned abdomen. He loosens his pants and pulls off the chinos. With reverence, he cups both my knees and then slides them open shifting so his body fits between them.

Before I realize it, he's got my bra off and his mouth covering a ripe nipple. He worries the tender peak until it's as red as the strawberries we just ate. He looks at my chest with such wonder and awe then sucks the other nipple into his mouth. While he's got the entire thing in his mouth his hands are busy, pulling and pushing down my panties. I wiggle and help remove them until I'm bare under his warm body. I pull Chase's chin, my breast leaving his mouth in an audible plop.

"Love your tits, baby. I could suck on them for hours," he nuzzles them again gripping each globe and points them up to his mouth where he flicks each tip with his tongue. I moan and push my hips up.

"In me. Need you in me," I gesture with a tip of my

pelvis against his steely erection. He groans and slides down my body.

"Not yet. I want your cum on my tongue," he says spreading my legs out wide. Lust rips through me wetting me further at the rawness of his words. We're out in the open, the sun sprinkling through the trees and here Chase has me, sprawled out naked, his eyes focused on the heat between my legs.

"I love that I don't have to even touch your sweet cunt and it positively cries for my touch, my tongue, my cock." He leans down and inhales. "That smell, your excitement, that's for me. Do you know what that does to me, Gillian?" Chase stands to remove his boxer briefs. I move to close my legs. "Stay open for me. I want to watch your pussy cry, begging to be filled."

For long moments, he stares, completely rapt, focusing on my center, the core of my being. Chase slides a big hand around his hard cock giving it a few tugs, priming it, readying it to plunder and take what's undeniably his.

After a few moments, I can't take it anymore. My hips are rolling up and down, side to side, legs still splayed open to his gaze. He's tugging on his dick so hard I have to grip the blanket to stay put and let him have his moment. I close my eyes, the desire to wrap my hand around his soft length is strong. Finally, Chase grips my hips and stills the restless movements before I feel the wet heat of his tongue plunge directly into my core.

"Uh, oh my…" I say then lose my words when he grips the fleshy part of my bum and forces his tongue into me as far as it will go, reaching a place inside me so deep I'm positive no man has ever tasted me in quite that way.

Chase holds me down as I thrash. His lips seal over my opening and he sucks, hard. So hard that a heavy ache builds in my pelvis and spreads out like a warm blanket. Chase pulls back, laying his lips over the pulsing knot of pure need, the one begging for his attention. He twists his lips around the tight pearl, nips it with his teeth, and gives little teasing flicks against it with his tongue. Finally, when I'm so far gone I'm pulling his hair so hard I think I might remove chunks from his head, he puts me out of my misery. Chase lays his lips over my clit in a hard, lock-down move, then rubs the flat of his tongue against it in combination with sucking it back from my body.

A silent scream leaves my mouth as tremor after tremor rocks my body from the tips of my toes up to the fiery ends of my hair. Chase stays with me, lapping the tight bundle of nerves, stuffing his tongue deep into my pussy all while growling and groaning his appreciation like a wild animal.

When I finally come down, he centers himself between my thighs and waist, waiting for me to look him in the eye. His lips, chin, and nose are covered in my essence. He lifts up onto his knees and pulls my legs wide then impales my body on his cock. I actually scream out, howling in ecstasy.

"That's it baby, you take my cock," he presses deep. "Take. It. All. The. Way." He grunts until he's seated to the very hilt, his heavy balls slapping against the crack of my ass. "You feel me, Gillian. You feel me inside you. I'm always going to be there. Taking you, taking what's mine, giving you what's yours." He breathes heavily as he stirs his cock inside me. "You want that? All of me. Every" *thrust* "fucking," *thrust,* "inch" *thrust,* "Of me," *thrust,"* is yours," he lets out in a feverish rush.

He tugs at my hips spearing me on his thick cock, the lips of my sex protesting with each massive thrust. It's divine. Him taking me this way. Proving that nothing will keep him from me.

"What do you feel?" He brings a wicked thumb into the mix, swirling the digit around my clit in dizzying circles that sends lightning to my sex.

"I feel…" I try to catch my breath as my orgasm builds, swirls like a boiling pot, my spine tightening, limbs protesting as the first waves of release shimmer through me. "I feel us." He smiles, comes down onto me and powers into me.

"What else?" He grates. His skin is shining with sweat at the effort to hold back, not just pound and pour into me. No, he wants it to be good for me and it always is.

"Baby, it's everything," I whisper into his ear as I cling to him in a full body clench before tipping my head back and roaring through my release. I grip him to me so tightly I can feel the exact moment his spine stiffens, one vertebra at a time, in extreme pleasure, before pouring his release into me. The orgasm goes on and on as we both ride the wave for long minutes.

When I come back from Nirvana, I'm still clinging to him, only now I'm sprawled naked on his chest, both of us panting like we just ran a full marathon. Chase extends his arm and shuffles through his pants. He pulls out his phone holds it out and takes a picture.

"Now look at the camera for me this time. I want to keep this moment with me forever," he says. I can only oblige him. Certain that my breasts are plastered against his chest I peek up through my hair and my hiding place on his chest. One of my hands is lying against his rapidly beating heart.

AUDREY CARLAN

We both look at the camera, and I give my secret smile, the one I only give to him. He takes the picture and turns it around so I can see. It's breathtakingly beautiful. I see the Drum Bridge clearly in the distance but most importantly, I see Chase, his eyes sated and untarnished by his past or our current situation. My own gaze is soft, resplendent. Mostly, it's just another candid moment of us in love.

"Send it to me…that one is special," I use the same words he used about the other image. He nods once and then tosses the phone back down near his pants. We lay together for a long time.

"Do you think it will always be this good between us?" I finally ask. His arms tighten along my bare back and waist.

I lean up and rest my chin on his chest like I usually do after we make love.

"I don't know why it wouldn't. I'm positive there is no other woman for me. No one else would put up with me the way you do." He waggles his eyebrows, but I know there is some truth in his statement.

Kissing him softly, I pull back. "You're right. No woman in their right mind would put up with you," he cringes, but I continue. "Special dates and private garden showings, rooftop brunches, endless love making where the woman's pleasure is paramount…you're right. You're ridiculous!" I giggle, and he nuzzles my nose.

"You're cute."

"Didn't we already have this conversation? Cute is for puppies and newborns not naked women in their twenties who allow you to ravish them in public gardens."

Chase laughs, and I enjoy feeling his cock wiggle within me. He likes to stay connected to me for as long as possible, but I know our private time is running out.

"Don't we need to go?"

He kisses me then sits up. I shimmy off him and stand. The mixture of our combined releases coats my thighs and starts running down my leg. Chase watches closely, a predatory gleam in his eyes and a crooked, sexy smile on his face. I roll my eyes and grab the soft napkin that came with our picnic, wiping the mess up before putting on my panties, bra, and dress.

Chase dresses and I start to put everything away. "Leave it. I've paid someone to take care of it for us." Of course he did. I shake my head and he puts my cardigan over my shoulders, the chill of the late afternoon in San Francisco starting to encroach.

"Next up...dessert," Chase says as he leads me out the gate of the garden. I close my eyes and try to imprint today's experience so that I can go back to it often. Whenever I have a rough day, I'm going to go back to those rainbow steps that tell a story so beautiful one must experience it with their own eyes, and the magical garden where Chase made wild and crazy love to me under the cool shade of a willow tree.

"I thought that's what we just had," I say, the innuendo clear in my tone.

"You saucy little vixen, come on. I know a place that serves up the best caramel cupcakes baked fresh every day."

"You had me at 'saucy little vixen'," I grin.

GILLIAN

CHAPTER ELEVEN

Hollow is a little café not far from the Japanese Tea Garden. Twilight comes upon us at the tail end of our walk. Chase holds open the door of the quaint little eatery for me to enter. Cinnamon and rich coffee swirls heavily in the air, delighting the senses. I inhale deeply, taking it all in while closing my eyes. Chase squeezes my fingers and proceeds to the counter. He orders as I peruse the wares. A long antique looking sideboard displays an array of coffee and baking-related items for use in the kitchen. A small, metal robot-shaped infuser that holds tea catches my attention. It's so wildly random that I pick up the little object and know instantly that I'm buying two of them for Chase and me. It will be a pleasant memory of this day. Stealthily, I grab two of the robots and hold them behind my back, right as Chase turns around.

"Shall we sit inside?"

I nod and let him proceed to the wrought iron table in front of me. With a quickness I wasn't sure I had, I turned, went up to the cashier, and in two movements, had the robots on the counter and a couple of twenties pushing into the young boy's hand. "Take it quick!" I say, clearly rushed. Casting a glance at Chase, he's sitting with his arms crossed, a leg up over one knee shaking his head. I shrug and take the return change and the little bag before making my way over to a smirking Chase.

He taps a finger on the table and grins. "So, what's in the bag, Sweetie?" he asks. It's official. The use of every endearment known to man is a running game with him. I should start giving them back to him.

"Mementos of our day," I pull out the two robot shaped tea infusers. A huge smile breaks across his face as he picks up one of them. It looks positively miniscule in his giant hand.

His brows crinkle as he turns the item over and around. "What is it?"

That's when I start to laugh. "They're tea infusers. See, you open it here," I flick open the latch at the robot's head and it opens perfectly in half. "Then you put the fresh tea in here, close it up and then drop it into a glass and pour your hot water in."

He pulls up the little long, bendy arms with what look like washers that have been cut in half to mimic hands. "And these?"

I giggle then curve the arms up, rubbing my thumb along the indentation. "This part hooks onto the cup so it stays in and you can use the arms to pull it out when your tea is ready."

"Huh, genius," he says as if this is the first time he's ever seen an infuser.

"I thought it would be nice to have something in our kitchen that's from us. Me and you, and our time together." I can feel my cheeks heat as embarrassment coats the moment.

Chase covers my hand with his. "It's perfect." He says

then brings my hand up and kisses my palm. The café attendant brings over two steaming mugs and sets them in front of us. They look like lattes only the foam has designs in them. Mine has a heart and Chase's has a leaf pattern.

"Now that is cool!" I say and lean down for a sniff. "Is this…?" I inhale the perfect vanilla and coffee scent.

"Your beloved vanilla latte? Of course," he grins lifting up his cup with a smug smirk. I lift mine and clink our glasses together.

"To our future. May it always be as lovely as today."

He smiles. "I'll definitely drink to that."

The latte is one of the best I've ever had grace my tongue. Seriously, the blend of espresso, vanilla and crème is unbelievable. I moan around my mug, clasping the precious with two hands while I let the heady concoction woo me into a state of bliss. When I look up Chase is blatantly staring at me. His eyes are dark and swimming with the smooth edges of lust.

"You make me wildly happy, Gillian." His words filter through me as if they were said into a can, connected to a string, that my heart is listening through.

I smile as the attendant brings two huge cupcakes. They have four perfectly designed flowerets in a tan colored frosting. "Are these the best cupcakes in San Francisco?" I ask Chase as he lifts his up and takes a monster-sized bite. Usually, he's pretty conservative and proper in public but not now with this sweet confection sitting in front of him. He nods his head up and down swiftly.

Pulling down the wrapper I take a small bite of the sugary treat. Oh. My. God. I may have just had a food-gasm. Holy shit! He was not kidding. The caramel is buttery and smooth, not overbearing, while the cake is a fluffy, white, and moist. "Incredible," I say over a mouth full of sweet awesomeness.

"Told you. The best!"

"We should have these at the wedding!" I smile around another huge bite.

Chase sets down his treat and puts a fist under his chin holding his head up while leaning on the table. His gaze holds mine as the most splendid serenity slips across my man's features.

"What?" I ask unable to suppress a smile when he's looking at me like I'm the only thing he loves in the universe.

"You." I cock my head to the side. "That's the first time you've mentioned the wedding with a smile on your face," he says.

All of a sudden, the cupcake seems thick, dry and coated in cement as I try to swallow. "Really?" I take a sip of my 'cup of love' forcing down the uncomfortable feeling his words give me. I know they shouldn't. It wasn't a barb, but it was brutal in its honesty.

"It's just that I want you to be excited about becoming Mrs. Davis. Just now was the first time you had excitement in your eyes over getting married. It was nice to see." He leans back in his chair and I can't help but think it's to put distance between us.

Not wanting any distance, I lean forward and cover his hand with mine. "I want to be excited. You know that right now, it's hard." His lips form a tight line. "I wish the wedding was the only thing we had to manage right now. Then it would be fun and I'd feel like the happiest girl in the world to be marrying the man I love. It will be that way. Once Phil gets better and our problem goes away." I refer to my stalker as a problem. Somehow, it gives it less credence.

"Baby, I know. I'm not mad. Well, that's not true. I'm furious over what you've had to deal with, but I also know that this is going to be a small time in our life. A blip on the whole that will be our future together," he finishes confidently.

He's right. He's so unbelievably right. When we look back twenty years from now, it will be with a wave of the hand and a 'Remember that freak that stalked us? What a loser. What was his name again?' At least that's what I'm going to believe.

We finish the rest of our date whispering beautiful things to one another about how our lives are going to be five, ten, twenty years from now. When we're done and back at our home, we make love under the stars in our own rooftop garden.

★ ★ ★ ★

Saturday morning brings a bundle of joy. Literally. Anabelle arrives like a tornado. She's running around the penthouse like a wild gazelle.

"Aunt Gigi, is this your house!" she squeals skipping from room to room. "You live in this big, huge place all by yourself! She looks at the art on the walls in awe. Even the vase she's standing next to is taller than her four-year-old frame.

"No, Auntie lives with Uncle Chase remember," Chase enters from the elevator clad in a golf shirt, pants and holding his clubs.

Anabelle's face brightens when she sees Chase. "That's right. You kiss him and you're going to marry him and give me a baby sister to play with!" she claps.

Chase stops in his tracks with his mouth open. "Uh, did I miss something?" He looks at Anabelle then to me and down to my stomach. "Are you…?" His words falter off.

I shake my head furiously. "No! No she's mixed up something." I hold out my hands and see Chase visibly relax. Crouching low, I come down to eye level with Phillip's daughter. "Belle, Aunt Gigi is marrying Chase. That makes him your Uncle, but our kids will be your cousins. And Auntie is not having a baby right now."

Her little lip forms into a pout. "But I thought when you get married you get to have babies," she stops and crosses her arms over her chest.

I take a deep breath. "Well, that's true. You can have a baby when you're married, and when Uncle Chase and Aunt Gigi decide to do that, you'll be one of the first to know, okay?" I tap her nose lightly. She giggles and wipes it with her sleeve.

"Okay," she spins on a toe and runs over to Chase. He catches her and lifts her up into his arms effortlessly. Since Phillip's hospitalization three weeks ago, we've only had Anabelle a couple nights and we watched her at Phil's house, but during those times, she's become Chase's little sidekick. This time, we'll have her through Monday when we drop her off at her preschool.

"Alright Miss Anabelle, if you could do anything today, anything in the whole wide world, what would it be? Uncle Chase will make it happen," he says with a great deal of bravado.

Anabelle puffs out her bottom lip. Oh man, she's bringing out the big guns. No man or woman has been able to deny the full pout with lip tremble. "I wanna see my Daddy," she announces then hides her face into the crook of Chase's neck.

I rush over and rub her back. "Oh Angel, you know he misses you. He's just healing from the accident and will be home really, really soon." My voice is scratchy and low, but I do my best to convey a positive outlook.

Anabelle raises her head and looks at me with giant, bright blue, teary eyes. "But how come I can't see him? Lots of people go to doctors and people come and bring flowers, and balloons, and crayons, and even dollies. I want to bring Daddy my dolly and then maybe he'll get better really, really fast!" she exclaims, and it breaks my heart in two.

We all wish we could just make Phil wake up from his coma. The doctors don't know why he hasn't woken up yet. The swelling in his brain has completely healed, his lungs are doing well, he's breathing on his own and his body is accepting the medication well. Vitals are all great but he still hasn't opened his eyes.

"Baby girl, as soon as Daddy says it's okay for you to visit we'll bring you. I promise." My shoulders slump, weighed down by the heavy load of telling Phil's daughter what his grandparents and I agreed on. Phil wouldn't want her to see him like that or worry.

Chase's eyes are sad at first but I see the moment they change. His stance gets a little stronger and he lifts his body to his full height. He's taking one for the team. "How about an ice cream sundae with all the toppings? I believe Bentley has prepared a magical ice cream feast for you!" Her eyes widen and she kicks her legs to be let down.

"Really? I'm going to try and find him! Don't show me where he is!" she exclaims playing her own game of seek and find as opposed to hide and seek.

Chase places an arm over my shoulders then pulls me into a hug. "It's going to be okay."

"I know it just…it hurts. Phil needs to wake up. Anabelle needs her father, and I need my best friend. Bree needs her guy, more now than ever before," I say into my favorite place. That warm spot where shoulder meets neck. Chase smells divine with his woodsy citrus scent, much sharper with the addition of sweat from golfing a quick nine holes this morning.

"Why more now, than ever before," he pulls back a foot and looks into my eyes.

I close my eyes and take a breath. "I didn't realize I never told you. Bree's pregnant." His mouth turns into an 'O' shape. "It's really early. Couldn't be more than a month along."

Chase hugs me hard. "That motherfucking stalker is going to hell and I plan to be the one to send him there." His body is stiff, and I can feel the heat start to surge in a halo of fiery tension around his entire body.

With slow movements, I run my hands up and down his back, over his arms and clasp his hands. "Not today you're not. You have your soon-to-be niece to impress with giant mounds of ice cream."

A small grin slips across his lips then he pecks me once, twice, three times before leading me down the hall to the kitchen. Little peals of laughter can be heard as we get closer. It's the most wonderful sound. I'm convinced that a child's laughter could heal all wounds.

Anabelle and Bentley are making not one but two different sundaes each. Bentley surprised her with multicolored whipped cream. She's currently adding blobs of the blue cream to one sundae while biting her lip in concentration.

"That looks pretty good. Is one for me?" I ask knowing it wasn't. Anabelle looks at her two treats speculatively.

"Can I have more if I finish mine?" She asks Chase, *not* me. She knows my answer would be a resounding *no*.

"Of course," Chase offers casually. I roll my eyes wondering if this is how it's going to be when we have kids. They ask and he gives them everything on a silver platter.

Anabelle pushes the sundae that looks like a rainbow exploded on it toward me. "You could have this one. Bente," she says instead of Bentley. "Can I have another bowl for Uncle Chase?"

"Oh honey, I don't need ice cream," he says patting his chiseled abs. I know he works really hard for those abs, and I appreciate them more than anyone. However, Chase has already had four homemade cookies with his coffee this morning. Anabelle studies Chase, looking at him in that "adults just don't understand the important things in life" type of expression.

"Everyone needs ice cream. It's like, the most bestest thing ever." She shakes her head and starts filling the empty bowl. Every so often she licks her fingers removing little bits of the candy and cream, double dipping happily into each bowl before adding the topping to her creation.

I laugh and happily eat mine. The extra calories can do nothing but set me on the path to getting back to normal.

"Here Uncle Chase, its perfect. See, I used all the blue candies and cream because you're a boy. Boys like blue," she finishes with a stiff nod.

"Well, I can't pass up a treat from a beautiful girl now can I? Thank you, Miss Anabelle."

Chase and Anabelle talk animatedly as I sit back and enjoy them. They're quite a pair. I have to admit, I'm surprised by how calm and at ease Chase is with her. He's a natural. Even when she's jabbering non-stop he's patient and pays attention to everything she says. During the times that Anabelle is with us, Chase seems carefree, laughs more, smiles a lot and seems beyond happy. Is this what our life will be like when we have a child? I can't help but dream of our own little mini-Davis's. Hopefully, our first will be a boy with dark espresso-colored hair just like his Dad with those endlessly blue ocean eyes.

"Earth to Gillian?" Chase cups my neck running a hand through my hair. "A million for your thoughts," he says with a grin.

Smacking his chest, I leave those thoughts and enter the present. "You always go overboard. I told you. My thoughts are free for you my love," I kiss his lips.

"Ewww, you know that's super icky Aunt Gigi. You will get boy cooties, and get sick and die!" she says her expression grave and unyielding. It takes everything Chase and I have to look at her without busting into laughter. "Daddy told me to never kiss boys, except for him, because daddies have a special medicine that makes them not have cooties."

Without missing a beat, Chase turns around and faces our little angel. "I take the medicine, too. Your daddy gave me some, but it only works for Aunt Gillian. She's the only girl I can kiss ever again. That's why we have to get married," he says clearly. Even I almost believe his bullshit. Anabelle, on the other hand, is convinced. No argument necessary.

Anabelle sucks in a huge breath and puts a chubby hand to her forehead. "Whew. I thought you guys were goners."

That's all it took to hit the breaking point. Chase and I howled in laughter, him picking her up and swinging her onto his shoulders. "You wanna go see the top of the world?" he asks.

Anabelle's eyes widen and she nods her head. "Yes, that would be so super cool awesome!"

"Chase, I'm going to call Bree, let her know we have Anabelle this weekend and check on Phil." Chase nods as he hits the spiral staircase. He brings her off his shoulders and leads her carefully up the stairs. "Meet you in a bit!" I holler up.

"I've got this, babe!" He yells back down. And you know what? He does. He's been incredible with her, my friends, hell, with my entire life. He's taken everything in stride and without complaint. He could have an issue with watching my guy friend's child on our weekend, but instead, he makes it an adventure, fully commits to the cause, and seems to like it. Just proves that underneath all his gruff, over-bearing, controlling nature is a kind, sweet, and caring man. My man, and soon, he will be my husband.

My husband.

Those words have come to mean so much. I know Chase is disheartened by not getting married yet. We'd be getting married next weekend if things weren't so screwed up and this psycho had been caught. It's hard to believe that whoever it is has been able to avoid the police and

Chase's men up to this point. Besides Justin, I can't think of anyone who would want to hurt me or the people around me by extension. It just doesn't add up. It has to be simple, something or *someone* I'm completely disregarding.

Rubbing my temples, I soothe out the tension headache that always starts when I spiral down the rabbit hole of trying to figure out who the stalker is. What's worse is it's probably right in front of my eyes and I'm just not seeing it.

Sighing I grab my phone and punch in Bree's work number. "I Am Yoga, Charity speaking," a voice I don't recognize answers.

"Um yeah, is Bree there?"

"She's about to teach a class. May I ask who's calling?" she chirps happily.

"Tell her it's Gigi. She'll speak to me," I say.

I hear the phone get put down before there's a rustling and then the voice that I know can heal a broken heart answers. "Hey you," Bree says sounding a little strained. It's my fault. I've avoided talking to the girls all week. It was necessary for me to have that time to put things into perspective, see my shrink, and connect with Chase.

"Sorry I've been incognito," I offer.

"No, it's okay. After what I said…Christ Gigi, I don't think I'll ever forgive myself," she sniffs and I can hear the tears clogging her voice.

"None of that. Words were exchanged during a really stressful time. We're moving on from this and not letting that bastard get in the way of our friendship. Okay? I won't have it." I say with as much conviction as I can through the phone.

Another sniff and what sounds like the clearing of her

throat. "Yeah, okay. As long as you know that I wasn't in my right mind. I had just found out about the baby," she whispers the last part. "And I just miss him so much, Gigi. I didn't mean to take it out on you." And the tears are back.

When is this situation going to get any better? "Honey, its fine. We're fine. Phil's going to be fine. This baby is going to be perfect."

"Yeah, perfect," is her sarcastic reply followed closely by a hiccup which I know for a fact is holding back a full-blown crying session. Not good.

"Bree, are you…" I can hardly form the words. "Are you considering termination?"

Silence on the other end.

"Bree…"

"I'm here. Um, look I really need to get to class. Why did you call?"

God no. Phillip would never forgive her if she terminated the baby. He's the biggest pro-lifer known to his sex. It's not a religious thing or a political preference. He's just a big believer in keeping a child against all odds. We've had several conversations about it over the years.

"Bree…" I try again, this time putting as much fear into my own response as possible.

"Not now," she says stiffly ending all hope of digging further into her psyche on this issue. "Why did you call?"

"We have Anabelle this weekend. Just wanted to give you a heads up in case, you know, Phil—" I start to finish but she cuts me off.

"Yeah, okay. We'll talk later. Love you. *Besos*," she says and then hangs up before I can return the gesture.

"Well that went straight to hell," I say into the open

room then flop backward onto the bed.

Time for a meeting of the minds. "Operation soul sister invasion to commence in three, two, one—" I press down on speed dial.

"*Hola?*" Maria answers.

"Hey Ria. We've got a problem. We're going to need to get Kat and get all up in Bree's business. Yoga Monday morning?"

"What's up with my *hermana?*" she cuts right to the quick.

Sighing, I check the paint on my nails. I need a mani and pedi. Maybe I'll take Anabelle tomorrow. "She's not taking this baby news as a positive thing. I'm worried about her, what she might do if Phil doesn't come out of it soon."

"You think she's going to hurt herself or the *niño?*"

I shake my head even though Ria can't see it. "I don't know what she's going to do. It's just, the way she sounded over the phone a little bit ago. She needs us. Maybe we could help her work through some of her negative feelings over being pregnant. It's obviously not planned. I mean, have you ever heard her even talk about having children?"

Ria clucks on the other end. "No but she's great with Belle," she offers.

"That's true. I'm sure it just has to do with everything that's going on. So you'll talk to Kat and we'll all go Monday to yoga class first thing?"

"*Si, Cara Bonita.* Say *hola* to Chase for me. *Besos mi amiga!*

Feeling better already, I toss the phone onto the bed and make my way up to the top of the world where my man and an angel await.

CHAPTER TWELVE

Look at the pretty blonde, setting up her gear. The room is still dark, but I can see her clearly from my hiding spot behind the shoji screen. She has no idea what's in store for her on this fine Monday morning in San Francisco. That golden blonde hair of hers is pulled back tight into a low pony tail. With a flick of her wrist she spreads out a teal yoga mat on the wooden, lifted stage. It looks like an altar, track lighting shining perfectly down on it creating a halo effect. As her back is turned I walk barefoot, to stand behind the monstrosity the rich fucker and my Princess bought as her birthday present. Buddha. I can't believe people believe that Oriental bullshit. What was it someone once said to me? Ah yes, Buddhism is introspection on one's life. So basically, if you think about your life for any length of time you're a Buddhist? Whatever.

Yoga Barbie turns on some music. It sounds like Enya. Christ I hate that squawky bitch. Slinking around the statue, I see her lighting candles, and turning on some burner with smelly liquid in it. When she completes her set up, she starts her meditation practice. This is exactly the moment I've been waiting for.

Waiting several minutes until she's nice and deep into

her relaxation, and I can tell her breathing has become shallow and regular, I pad along the side of the wall. Even if she opens her eyes she won't instantly see me. The element of surprise is key. I slowly walk along the area of carpeting as quiet as a mouse. The closer I get, the harder I get. Knowing I'm going to be taking out one of the people who have kept me from my woman, is too fucking sweet. My mouth waters enticingly just thinking about the blood I'm going to spill. My dick turns hard as stone as I creep closer to her. The blonde bombshell, the tiny little thing with a perfect body and a sassy mouth. Well, that mouth will lose all its sass soon enough.

I can taste the revenge on my tongue. After I'm done here, I'm going to treat myself to a session of private time with Gillian's things. The items I borrowed from her apartment before that bastard emptied the place completely will do just fine until I have the real thing. Yeah, I'm going to pull out my hard cock and go to town, thinking about all the things I'm going to do to Gillian when I get her back. Once she finds out what's happened to her soul sister Bree and her unborn baby, they'll all take me more seriously. Maybe, just maybe my Princess will come to her senses and dump the rich piece of shit for a real man. Someone who can take care of her, protect her. Chase Davis can't even keep her friends safe. It's only a matter of time before I get my hands on my girl again.

The music changes to something more tribal, thumping. My heart starts to beat in time with the heavy bass, it's the perfect sound. Eyes on the prize, I step up onto the platform. She's humming some type of chant low in her throat and letting it wind down her frame where her stomach pushes out. As she inhales it comes back in, concaving more deeply than anything I've ever seen. Weird fucking chick. The world will be a better place without another tree-hugging wacko pushing their organic, love the Earth and all God's creatures propaganda.

Slinking up right behind her, I'm so close I can smell the scent of her hair. Coconut. Reminds me of the beach, just like her blonde hair and tanned skin. She probably hits the tanning beds, soaking up all those poisonous UV rays. Well not on my perfect milky white girl. Her creamy skin glows like a pearl. There's nothing more beautiful than that.

I put my hand behind my back and pull out my blade. It's the same knife I use to gut fish. It's a solid six inch blade with a sturdy wooden handle. Interesting enough, the fucker that sired me made it over forty years ago. It was one of the only things I took before I killed my parents and burned the house down. The knife's been more useful than those two abusers ever were. The silver glints from the lighting above, almost as if it's a beacon, telling me to continue ridding the world of stupid people.

Before she can scream, I crouch down low, grip her around the chest, caging in her arms. With quick feet I've circled them around her bottom half. One long, firm, slice, and it's over. Her blood pours like a red waterfall down her tank, painting the pink fabric crimson. Her body jerks several times along with the disgusting sound of air, attempting to be sucked into her throat where blood is pooling. I hold her there until her body stills. I set the knife down grab one of her hands and feel for a pulse through my gloved fingers.

Nothing.

Uncurling my legs from around her body I let her fall

back naturally. Her brown eyes are open but there is no light left. At least I took her when she was meditating. Since she believes that shit, I'm sure it was a lovely way to go. As I watch the rest of the blood pool on the shiny wood floor, growing inch by inch like a giant rose blooming open in front of my eyes, something tickles the hairs on the back of my neck. For a couple moments I just look at the body, not knowing why something doesn't seem quite right. Instead of worrying about it, I strip my clothes completely, then pad completely naked, over to my original hiding spot. Quickly, I throw on the pair of dark grey sweats and a baseball cap slung low over my forehead. Grabbing the garbage bag I tucked into my tennis shoe I throw the soiled clothes in it. Wouldn't do to leave this evidence, littered with my skin and hair fragments.

Hoisting the bag over my shoulder like Santa Claus with a bag full of goodies, I look down at my handiwork. Perfect. The cut is clean with no jagged edges, just like a surgeon. Thanks dear old Dad for teaching me the art of gutting fish. It came in handy. Apparently, it's the only thing that has come in handy from that sick fuck. Scanning the room one more time the sense of worry tingles at the edges of my consciousness. Something is off.

Oh yeah, I pull out one of the gloves and put it back on. With one finger I dip into the congealing pool of blood. Several more dips, a few swirling letters and I've left my mark. Grinning ear to ear, I imprint this moment into my brain.

Taking one last look around, I make sure there isn't any potential evidence for that pig, Tomas Redding to use against me. Nothing. Then the sound of voices coming up the stairs startles me out of my reverie. Quick as bullet, I slip through the back door and sneak into the fire stairwell, no one the wiser.

Gillian's best friends are losing this battle. One can only dream of her forfeiting the game and giving herself up. Right now, I'm up two to zero.

"Um hello, BFF here waiting," I holler out the window of the limo. Kat is sucking face and rubbing her long body all over Carson right in front of her building. He's no better. His hands are firmly cupping her ass while he kisses the daylights out of her. "Seriously guys! We want to bombard her before class not be late to it!" I screech.

Opening the door to get out, a firm hand locks around my bicep and pulls me back in. "I am happy to retrieve Ms. Bennett on your behalf, ma'am." Austin says in warning. I scowl, roll my eyes and harrumph loud enough for him to hear it. He smiles and exits the limo and taps on Kat's shoulder. She pulls away from Carson, her eyes glassy, as if she doesn't know where she is. "Ms. Callahan requests your presence." Austin says.

"Hello!" I point out the limo and giggle. Kat has the good grace to look embarrassed.

"Sorry, sorry. I get carried away. That man…mmm," she licks her lips and waves while Austin gets back into the limo. When Chase isn't around, he rides in the back with me. They believe it's safer. I believe it's suffocating.

I grin at Kat. "Looks like you two are getting along

famously!" Kat shrugs and turns her head. That is not a gesture a woman hopelessly in love gives to her best friend. "What's up?"

Another Kat deflection. I wait with arms crossed and a head tilt. I've been working on perfecting her move for a while. It only seems to work on her though. The rest of the girls think it's hysterical so it works only if my goal is to make them laugh. Kat sighs loudly then leans back in her seat. "I don't know. Everything's great, he's great, the sex is…"

"Great?" I offer.

"No, it's phenomenal but he hasn't said *it*. You know…" she waves her hand back and forth.

I shake my head not having a clue what she's talking about.

"Uh, Gigi, it's like you never pick up on my prompts," she whines.

"It's not my fault you suck at charades, now just tell me…in English please. What's wrong?"

She huffs a breath over her swooping bangs. "He hasn't said he loves me and I've said it to him like…a million times!" her plump lips turn into a pout.

"Oh honey, it's nothing. Have you asked him about it?"

Her eyes turn really bright. "Yeah, that's the thing. I have. He says when he's ready he'll say it. So, even though it's been months, he still hasn't said it. Don't you think that's odd?"

I know Kat is the type of woman to overthink and analyze a situation to death. It's very possible that she's misconstrued what Carson meant, yet something like this is pretty cut and dry. Either he loves her or he doesn't. I wonder what's holding him up.

"Yeah, I'll agree with you that it's odd but maybe he's waiting for some special day or something." I finish just as we pull up to the building where Bree's studio is. Maria is standing outside waiting, a coy smirk across her lips when she spies the limo.

Austin gets out of the limo first and ushers Kat out, then hovers over me as we walk into the building. He leads us up the stairs to her third floor location.

"Austin, we've got it from here, thanks," I say and go to open the door.

"Sorry ma'am, you know I have to check the place out. Then I'll sit in the back and wait for the class to finish. Mr. Davis was very specific with his instructions. Security has been heightened since Ms. Simmons received the last note at the hospital."

I groan and he looks nonplussed. Maria pulls on the door handle and we hear the *"thunk"* from the bolt lock. I peer through the frosted glass trying to see something. Once I get close to the glass, I can hear the music. She's there somewhere. Perhaps she forgot to unlock the door and she went to the bathroom.

Maria bangs on the door and hollers. "Bree, open up!"

While we wait, I turn to Kat and speak low. "It's really going to be okay. I'm sure there's a reason for him not saying those three little words. It could be anything. Maybe he's gun-shy, maybe someone's cheated on him, maybe he's never said it before, maybe he doesn't know what love even is yet?"

"I guess so, it just, it sucks. I feel like I'm the only one fully committed you know?"

"Yeah, I get that. But he wouldn't still be with you if something wasn't there, okay?"

Kat nods and looks at Maria whose making a bit of a scene behind us. She bangs on the door again.

"Perra, you better open this door or the *hombre grande* is going to do it for us!" she threatens.

Turning toward Maria I fish into my purse and pull out my keys. I hold up the key that has an "Om" symbol written in black sharpie pen on it. "We could just use our key." I laugh.

"Oh yeah, totally forgot she gave us keys," she smacks her forehead and I turn around, unlock and open the door.

"Bree, honey where are you." I call out. The room is darker than it normally is when she's preparing for a class. Maybe she's still meditating. She usually does that right before, but the banging on the door should have broken her out of her practice. As I turn the corner into the main room I come to a stop. The lights above the platform are shining down onto a body, prone in and a sea of red. Slowly I take tiny steps closer, "B-bree…" I whisper as gooseflesh rises on my skin. She doesn't move, in fact she's perfectly still, lifeless.

I can hear the moment that Maria and Kat enter because their happy chatter slips away as they must be seeing what I'm seeing.

One step, two, three and I can see blond hair. The face is turned away from me but the blond hair looks exactly like Bree's, only it's coated in a ruby substance.

No…no…no…. I'm not sure if I've spoken because all of the air has left the room. In its place is a dull roar. The sound of a faraway train with a whistle that sounds like some sort of scream. The train gets closer, the blaring scream louder as I take in the giant gaping hole at the base of the swanlike neck in front of me. The clawing screech of metal and heavy machinery rips through me as if the train is running an inch from my head. I can almost feel the violent windshear as it passes at the speed of light.

It's not a train. It's the blood-curdling scream that is drawn straight from my soul.

I can feel that I'm being lifted in the air and carried, Bree's form getting further away as if in a tunnel. At this angle, my nightmare comes to life in front of me, and I am now able to see the message that could only have been left for me.

The words are smudged and swirled, written in my best friend's blood.

Two down. Two to go.

★ ★ ★ ★t

"Where is she!" someone bellows. I'm barely able to hear anything. That sound, that train still echoing through my head.

"My fiancé. Where the fuck is she! Gillian Callahan. Tall, beautiful, redhead. You can't miss her!" Ah, my love. That's the sound of a man who loves his woman. Only this woman doesn't deserve to be loved She's a killer. No, I may not have held the knife, but I may as well have signed her death certificate. And the baby, oh my god.

The baby. Phillip's baby.

I'm huddled in between two warm bodies just outside the building being looked after by the paramedics. Both women next to me are breathing so fast and hard it's as if we just ran a marathon. In the little cave of our three heads touching water seeps, pouring down onto our clasped hands in the center, making the air in our space thick with humidity. Two arms encircle me from behind, but I don't let go. I can't let go. If I do, he'll take them too.

"Don't fucking touch them!" I scream. "Take me…just take me!" comes out in a banshee wail of terror and grief.

"Baby, it's me; it's Chase," his voice is like cold water over a burn. I turn and claw my way into his arms. They encase me and it's instant relief. Cool lotion over a sunburn. As long as this man is holding me, nothing else exists. It can't. His presence is too powerful, too large to infiltrate. Like Fort Knox. The only place I feel safe.

Behind me I see that Carson is pulling Kat into his arms. I don't know how he got here or why, but it's right. The only thing missing is…

"Maria!" I hear over my shoulder. Tommy's large frame and booming voice is barreling along with him until Maria jumps up and dashes into his arms. "Thank God you're okay," he whispers kissing her.

Chase places a thumb under my chin and shifts my face until his blue eyes come into focus. "Talk to me," he whispers then kisses my lips lightly.

Tears rush down my face. "She's gone. B-bree. He killed her." The words leave my lips but they sound wrong, twisted, and laced with acid.

Chase's eyes turn hard, glacial. His nostrils flare and he clenches down. "Thomas. A word," he says. Maria's boyfriend pulls back after another quick peck and a hand squeeze. "Where's the body?" he asks.

I shake my head back and forth. "No, no, no, you can't

see. You don't want that in your head," I cry and crumble to my knees. Maria and Kat both sit on the ground and hover around me once more, also deep in their own grief.

"Baby, I have to see what happened. I'm sorry. I'll be right back. Thomas, get me access," he grates through is teeth. "Carson, Austin, keep an eye on the girls. Jack, you're with me," Chase says to his bodyguard. I hadn't even realized those men were here.

Thomas nods. "I actually haven't been in there. Got the call from Austin just after you."

An eternity goes by but I don't care. Even though I've lost feeling in my legs from being in the same position for so long and my eyelids feel like they are stuck together from crying so much I've lost the ability to generate tears. Literally every tear I have went to Bree. My soul sister. The sour taste in my mouth swirls and rumbles like a volcano ready to erupt. Instantly I jump up and run over to a nearby trash can spewing the contents of my stomach. My body heaves until there's nothing left but the putrid taste of bile on my tongue.

Carson hands me a bottle of water along with a shoulder pat. He doesn't say anything. I don't expect him to. What do you say to someone when they've just found their best friend murdered. I swish the liquid and then spit that into the garbage can, too. Once the nausea calms, I walk back to the wall where Kat and Maria are leaning. They both look as wrecked as I feel.

There's nothing I can think of to say to either of them, so I just lean against the wall and wait. Chase and Tommy both walk briskly to us, their faces set in grim lines. Only Tommy is holding out his phone. "Maria, look at this," he holds out the phone. The three of us girls look at the picture. It's an image of the top of two bare feet. Only I'm unable to focus on the feet only the blood pooling around them. It's sticking to the sides of one foot, turning brown in color as the blood dries. A shudder, ping pongs through me ramping up that nausea once more.

"What's missing on her feet?" Thomas says as Maria holds a hand over her mouth but leans closer to the image.

"Dios mio! It's not her," chills skitter up to the surface of my skin at those words.

Kat pulls the phone into her hands and looks closely. "No tattoo...our trinity. It's not there." Kat chokes as her voice clogs with emotion, tears slipping silently down her face.

Chase pulls me into his arms. "Gillian, it's not Bree. I don't know who that poor woman is, but it's not her," he whispers as my knees buckle and I cling to his strong shoulders. Bone-deep relief surrounds me. Slowly I get a wild idea. I pull back and dig into Chase's pocket and pull out his phone. It's locked but with a thumb, I move the cursor over and bring up the keypad.

I type in the word that means so much to my guy.

I-N-F-I-N-I-T-Y

The screen comes to life and an image of me stops me momentarily. I'm in bed, my red hair fanned across the white pillows. My back is completely bare, the comforter pulled down to the swell of my ass. I'm sleeping. Nothing private is showing but I glance up and Chase just gives me one of his crooked grins. Later. I'll deal with him later. For now, I need confirmation.

I dial the number and wait. It rings twice before I hear

the most beautiful sound in all the world.

Bree. Alive. "Hello? Chase is that you?" Bree asks happily. " I need to talk to Gigi right now!" she says excitedly.

"Oh my God, it's you. You're alive!" The tears I thought dried up have come back in a torrential downpour. It's hurricane Gillian over here, and nothing is going to calm the storm soon. Maria grabs the phone from my hand.

"Bree, girl," tears fill Maria's eyes as she talks to Bree. Our very alive soul sister, who somehow escaped death and doesn't even know it. "What? Phillip's awake?" she says awe filling her voice.

Those two words start at my head and work their way down, settling deep into my heart. The muscle swells and warms as I whisper those words. "Phillip's awake."

"*Gracias, Jesús,* Phillip's awake everyone!" she laughs and I cling to Chase tighter. "Okay okay, *hermana* stop. We have to talk to you. Who did your class this morning?" Maria's face crumbles. "Tommy, girl's name is Charity Kerns," she says. He nods and heads off to give the information to the police.

Once Kat's had a turn on the phone the three of us agree that we need to go to the hospital to see her face-to-face. We have to tell her what happened to Charity, her yoga mentee, but we also need to see Phil.

Life and death. Yin and yang.

Please Lord help us get through this.

GILLIAN

CHAPTER THIRTEEN

When faced with death and the very *real* prospect of losing someone you love, it changes you. For me it's a sense of self, maybe even a oneness with God and the universe as a whole. Watching Phillip battle to come back from the murky depths of his coma, seeing Bree alive when I thought I lost her forever…it's more than an experience. It defines you and the rest of your life in a way that's impossible to explain. I'm just different. I know beyond a shadow of a doubt that I will always carry this experience, hold onto that fear, that overwhelming feeling of loss within me.

Entering Phillip's room I see Bree, healthy, and most importantly, *alive*. A gasp slips from my lips as her head turns bearing an unbelievably beautiful smile. It's one of those moments that hit you so hard with gratitude that it almost brings you to your knees. As it is, I have to hold onto the end of the hospital bed and take heaping steadying breaths. Then, I look up into Phil's smooth brown eyes and I lose it. He's giving me the frowny worried face, the one that always seems to break me, when I'm the one that should be worried over him. It's he who's been in a coma for the past month, he that almost lost his life because of some sicko with a fetish for an unavailable redhead that's so pale white she glows in the dark.

"Phil, Bree," I croak.

Bree takes a few steps then pulls me into her warm embrace. It's perfect. Everything about this moment is perfect. I run my hand down her back slipping my fingers through her long silky blonde hair. Hair that's free of congealed sticky red blood.

"Honey, you're trembling," she squeezes me and I fall even harder into her small frame.

"You're alive," I pull away and look at her face. Tears fill her eyes in sympathy though she doesn't know why I'm beside myself with relief. Slowly I place a hand over her stomach and a hiccupping sob rips through my throat. Baby's fine, nestled in the safety of Bree's womb. Without realizing what I'm doing or touching, Bree grasps my hand looks over my shoulder and then kisses my fingers.

"I'm fine," she promises then gives me a hard look, moving her eyes from me to Phillip trying to communicate something I'm completely missing.

"Yeah you are!" Maria rushes in and tackles Bree. I let go and move over to the bed. Phil's eyes are confused but watchful.

"Hey you," I say though it sounds like the words have been put through a cheese grater.

"Hey, get over here," He says in his usual bossy way. Something about it, perhaps the familiarity of it makes more tears fall. I get close and he clasps my hand, so warm. I lean down and kiss his dry lips softly, almost as if he isn't real, then nuzzle his forehead. "You look like shit," he says to me, eyes full of chastisement and worry. "You haven't been taking care of yourself. You're skin and bones," his eyes hop around my face and neck as if he's cataloguing and indexing every inch.

"Yeah, well you don't look so dandy yourself there, handsome," I joke falling into our very familiar sibling style sparring.

He closes his eyes and lets his head fall back against the pillow on an exhale. "Did you get married without me?"

I shake my head and smile. "Can't. Who'd walk me down the aisle?"

Phillip swallows slowly and shakes his head.

"I missed you…so much," I say before kissing his forehead. With light fingers I sweep away an unruly lock of hair, something I've done countless times before but this time feels like more. Everything feels like more when you know your friends are going to stay in your life.

Phil's brows pull together as he looks over at Maria and Kat hugging Bree as if they're never ever going to let her go. It's quite possible they won't. We've been through a devastating morning. I don't think any of us plan to leave the others for awhile. When I look past the girls, I can see Chase and Carson leaning against the wall. Chase's eyes are guarded. They skip all around my face, hands, and body as I touch my best friend. He sucks in a heavy breath I can hear from ten feet away. His chin is tight, teeth clenched. More than anything, he's trying to tamp down his jealousy. Even if he and Phil have come to an understanding over the last several months, he does not like any man touching me. Especially a man who is pulling me down to his chest. My ear lands softly against the cotton fabric of Phil's gown, directly over his heart. I close my eyes and just listen to it beat. Beautiful.

"We're going to be okay. I know I've been out a long time but I'm back." I nod into his chest and let the tears wet his hospital gown. Before long, I feel a hand at my shoulder. I expected it to be Chase but it's not, it's Maria.

"*Cara Bonita*, my turn," she says her own emotions thick in her tone. I pull away and let them have their moment.

Chase holds out his arms. I'm drawn into them like iron filings to a magnet. "Everything's going to be okay," I say while snuggling into his chest. The citrus and sandalwood smell fills me with an instant sense of peace.

"Yes it will, I'm going to make sure of it," he says with a jarring lack of emotion. Leaning back, I take in his face. It's hard, his eyes cold. He's working his jaw as if he's grinding rocks between his teeth. Even though his outward appearance is off-putting, he's still holding me with a tenderness that I know is solely for me and what we have between us. After one more hug, Chase moves me to his side. "Phillip, Bree, we need to update you on what happened this morning."

Bree's eyes narrow and look at each one of us speculatively. "Something really bad happened. That's why you're all hovering over me and acting like this is the first time you've seen me in years." Maria and Kat look at one another. I hold my head low, guilt rearing its despicable presence once more. "What is it? Tell me now," she says with a tightness in her tone. Phil reaches out a hand and cups her shoulder.

I glance at everyone around the room. Kat in Carson's arms, Maria holding up a wall near the hospital bed, both bodyguards as well as Chase and me. All of us look at Bree with nothing but...sadness. Chase moves to speak but Maria holds out a hand to him. He just nods allowing her to approach this delicate situation in the best way possible under the circumstances. I couldn't speak right now if I tried. My throat is dry and coated in remorse.

Maria walks over to Bree and takes her hand. "Bree, there was an attack on Charity at your Studio." Bree's eyes widen and she backs up a step. "*Cariño*, Charity didn't make it."

Bree's head shakes back and forth. "No, no, what on earth do you mean she didn't make it? You mean she was killed?" her voice goes to a high pitch. She sucks in a breath then whispers, "What happened?" Phil pulls Bree onto the bed and she sits in the curve of space next to his hip. He loops an arm around her waist. His hand is lying directly over her stomach protecting his unborn child already. Paternal instinct already in motion even though he doesn't know it.

"The...uh...stalker slit her throat honey." One of her tiny hands flies up to her mouth, her eyes going impossibly wide. "*Hermana*, that cut was meant for you. He left a-another message," she stumbles on the words, the emotion clogging her voice before she clears her throat.

Chase takes this moment to jump in. "The stalker has taken steps to kill both Phillip and now Bree," he looks over at Bree with sympathy. "This has escalated beyond any investigation my team can handle. The investigation is now being handled by the San Francisco PD. Thomas is still the detective in charge and will keep us apprised of information as it becomes available. Until then, I have a plan to keep all of you safe."

Maria's head turns so fast toward Chase it's as if she was sucker punched. "Oh really? You have a plan? I'm certain I'm not going to like this." She places her hands on her hips, cocks her head to the side and stares him down, the Italian side of her heritage coming to the surface with a roar.

Chase's lips are set into a grim line. "No, none of you are. Every single one of you are going to be relocated." Collective gasps and grumbles start instantly. I stay silent letting Chase handle it. Nothing we've done so far has kept my friends safe. I'll do anything to change that. "I'm going to request that each of you move into the Davis estate outside of town. It has large, high stone walls and the gate and property will be monitored and patrolled by armed guards day and night. Additional armed security teams will be positioned at all the doors going in and out."

"You can't be serious," Phillip adds.

"Deadly serious, just like your girlfriend and unborn child," Chase looks down at the hand that Phil has over Bree's stomach, it tightens reflexively, "would be dead right now if the situation had played out differently."

Oh, for Heaven's sake. I could kill him myself for letting that cat out of the bag. All of the whispered chatter stops instantly. Phillip's eyes narrow as he turns Bree toward him. "Unborn child? What is he talking about?"

Tears spring to Bree's eyes and fall delicately down her cheeks. "I was going to tell you..."

"You're pregnant?" he whispers. I feel like a heel with all of us around watching this play out. It should be a private moment between them. "How? When," he asks clearly baffled as much as the rest of us were when Bree admitted it to us last week.

"The first time," she croaks and he pulls her to his chest nuzzling her hair.

"My God, and you've been dealing with this alone. I'm

so sorry, honey, so sorry," He holds her against his chest as she cries. Tears form in his eyes but he tips his head back and blinks several times.

I turn on Chase and punch his bicep hard. "That was private! She wanted to tell him herself!" I chastise him in a hushed whisper.

Chase cups my cheeks. "I'm sorry, Baby, it just slipped out, but all of your friends need to take this seriously." He kisses my lips and then hugs me close. "Every one of you will be assigned a bodyguard and driver. One to take you to and from wherever you need to go and back to the estate. It's the only defense we have against this sociopath until he's caught. The mansion has plenty of bedrooms, each with private bathrooms. There is a full-time staff that will see to all your needs, meals, laundry, etc."

Carson holds Kat. "We'll move in right away, sweetcheeks," he says then kisses her neck.

"Yeah, whatever it takes." Kat says reassuringly. Chase visibly relaxes with their agreement.

"And you two," he gestures to Bree and Phillip.

Phillip's hand is cupping Bree's cheek. He sets his forehead against hers then his hand trails from her cheek, down her shoulder and over to her stomach. "Honey, we have to keep you and our baby safe," he cradles her in his arms. She pulls up her knees to her chest, and he holds her while she cries.

"We'll do as you ask. I don't know when I'll be released but Bree and my child's safety are paramount. Fuck!" he practically roars and we all turn. "Where's Anabelle?" His body stiffens and I can tell he's moved too much.

"Relax, relax," Chase says. "A security team has been

watching your house, Anabelle's school, and following your parents closely. Your daughter has been staying on and off with all of us during your recovery. I'll have your parents and child moved to the mansion immediately."

Phillip nods and relaxes. "Thank you, man. I mean, what you're doing…" his voice is rough and full of emotion.

"We protect our family," Chase says matter of fact. Their gazes meet and exchange some type of silent communication that women, me in particular find annoying.

Maria is the last one to be stared down by all of us. She's standing stick straight with a visible chip on her shoulder. "Ria, I can't let this monster hurt you," I say with very little breath left. The crippling fear and panic is crawling through my body, squeezing all the air from my lungs. "Please…for me."

She rolls her eyes and then her shoulders slump. "*Cara Bonita*, you know I'd do anything for you." She pulls me into a tight hug.

"Thank you, thank you, thank you, " I say into her thick black hair.

X

"I can't believe you're more beautiful in person than you are in your picture," I stand holding out both arms. Women love to be hugged with no hint of sexual pressure. It gives them a fake sense of security. The big bad wolf won't actually pretend to take them to grandma's house and not eat them alive. Unfortunately for her, I am the wolf.

A huge smile beams across her face. She's actually really pretty if I went for blondes. I don't. Redheads are more my speed but I need this particular blonde. "Thank you, you're too kind."

"Have a seat, hope Italian's okay?" Internally, I roll my eyes as she moves her long, lean body into the wooden chair across from me. I chose this place because a woman would find it charming. Gillian did. Just being here makes me miss my girl but this is a necessary step and a relationship I need to cultivate to meet the next phase of my plan.

She sits back in the chair, picks up the glass of water and takes a slow sip. It's impressive how put together she seems yet she's beyond nervous. One of her hands is clenched into a fist around her napkin in her lap, the other is holding the glass. "It's fine, I love pasta. I think it's probably the most universal food."

I chuckle for her benefit even though what she said isn't funny but laughing along with someone makes them feel more comfortable and less tense. When a little blush of color spreads across her cheeks, I know I've got her.

"So, tell me about yourself." The goal of this date was to get as much information as possible and build a rapport that will get me closer to the ultimate prize.

"What do you want to know?" she asks coyly then licks her lips. Ah, so it's going to be like that. Hmmm, maybe I'll fuck the information out of her. The way she's appraising my body over her glass as she sips, is very telling. I've fucked a few women since Gillian but only to fill a biological need. If she's going to be letting that rich fucker put his puny dick in her, I may as well be getting a piece of ass of my own. Fair is fair.

"Everything of course. Family?"

"I have a sister who lives in New York. When I'm traveling to our New York office, I get time to visit her. My parents live in Florida. The typical snow birds. Flying down south for the winter." She grins, and I try my best not to yawn and nod instead.

The waiter comes over to us, and she scrambles to pick up her menu. I can tell she's scanning the items as quickly as possible.

"Would you like me to come back?" She looks up nervously from the menu.

"How about we get a bottle of red?" She nods and I turn back to the waiter. "Bring us something in this range that is ordered most often." I point to the menu that shows wine between thirty and forty dollars. When I look over at her, she's dreamily watching me. "I like to be surprised," I shrug.

"That's really interesting. You could end up with a horrible bottle." Her tone is warning but still sultry.

"Or, I could find myself sitting in front of the most beautiful, mesmerizing,"—I move my hand to one of hers laying on the table and draw a finger down her forearm, along her hand and across her middle finger—"enchanting things I'm ever going to experience," I finish and she sighs. I've got this woman on my hook, and I'm reeling her in with no effort at all. Piece of cake.

"Tell me about your family," she asks.

"Well, I'm adopted. My family raised me and then moved onto the next batch of kids they chose to save." Which is not all together far from the truth. The family I ended up with was great considering the hellhole I came from, but they were saints, and saints aren't happy saving one. No, they have to keep saving or die trying.

The woman's clear blue eyes soften and turn a bit sad. Oh Christ, I don't want to deal with a sappy bitch. I need to liquor her up and fast, so she starts talking or shuts the fuck up by way of a dick shoved down her throat.

The waiter takes that moment to bring our wine. He allows me to sip it. I tell him its fine and he pours small amounts in each bulbous glass. We both try it and it's pretty good. Most of the time if you tell someone to bring you a wine that's popular, they'll bring you something that's easily palatable.

"Mmm" she says then licks her lips again.

"Good?" I ask.

With a flick of her wrist, she pushes back her long blonde hair. "It is. Thank you."

We both order a pasta and a chicken dish. After the food arrives, she's well into her second glass of wine and starting to feel it.

"Now that we've got the family stuff out of the way, how about telling me what you like to do for fun?" I grin and lean closer to her, covering one delicate, small hand with my much larger, calloused one.

Her eyes glance down at my hand as I tickle and tease the skin over the back of her hand. "N-not much I'm afraid. I work a lot, too much, most of the time."

Could this be any easier? Right off the bat she's going to talk about the exact information I want to know. "Is that right? What type of work are you in?"

"The company I work for does a bit of everything. Corporate, purchasing, investments, acquisitions, restaurants, nightclubs, hotels, you name it we have a hand in it." Now that she's feeling the liquor, she giggles and places her hand over mine. It's warm and I imagine it has a lot to do with the desire for sex, topped with the wine pouring through her veins.

"So tell me, what it is you do in this bit of everything corporate purchasing?" I roll my hand over and over mimicking the "on and on" gesture, even though I know exactly what she does. I've been watching her steadily for several months now hoping Chase was taking a bit of pussy on the side, but so far, the bastard's been loyal. Maybe I won't feed him his balls after I cut them off and watch him bleed out. Nah...I totally will.

Her eyes light up. "I'm an executive personal assistant," she says proudly.

"Sounds powerful and sexy at the same time," I add with a sensual grit to my voice.

"How so?"

"Well, the executive part means you're in charge or working with the man in charge." I waggle my eyebrows and she laughs. "So you obviously have some power." Her lips twist as she reflects on what I'm saying. "The personal part is obvious. The word "personal" makes me think of "private" which can lead to sexy things when viewed in the right way." I wink and she blushes again. This time it's all the way down her neck toward her ample bosom. I'm kind of surprised Chase isn't tapping this. She's a pretty easy woman to nail down. I know I'll be between those thighs tonight and we're on a blind date. Couldn't be hard for a prick with lots of cash.

It must have been a while since this woman was last

fucked because her body is strung too tight. Her lips are bright red, the residue from the wine adding to the color. Every so often, she takes a deep breath and slowly exhales as if she's trying to relax. The squirming in her seat is another indicator of her excitement. It's going to be so easy to break this one.

"So tell me, who do you *personally* assist?" I ask, my tone laced with innuendo.

She sighs and props an elbow on the table and rests her chin in her hand. Slowly, I move over to the seat right next to her and place my own arm on the tabletop and get really close to her face. Her eyes drift over my features, desire making them a much darker blue than they were originally. A floral scent surrounds her smelling like springtime and roses. I like roses. A lot.

"Why do you care?" she asks trying to add a layer of mystery. Lame. She thinks she can play cat and mouse with me? I'm not your typical house cat enjoying a saucer of cream. I'm a fucking jaguar that rips apart raw flesh and bites heartily into bone.

Leaning even further forward, I place a hand over her knee. The skin is bare, free of nylons. She gasps when my thumb makes contact with the skin just above her kneecap.

With tiny movements, I push up the fabric of her dress sliding my thumb along the inner thigh. Her legs clench but don't close as I make it a scant few inches from the blistering source of heat under her dress. "You going to keep your work a secret," I groan leaning toward her to nuzzle her neck to make her think I'm drenched in need.

"Um, no…"

"Then why are you hesitating? I'm not hesitating." I

slide my hand all the way up to cup her.

"Oh, my God," she whispers as I rub my hand against the damp fabric. I know the moment I've hit the right spot because she tightens her legs caging my hand.

I press harder into her soft flesh. The wisp of lace between her thighs is nothing for me to push over and press a finger into her wet heat.

"Uh uh, fair's fair. You've been driving me crazy with lust all night," I lie. "Looking sexy as sin in that dress, and those fuck me shoes. You want to be fucked tonight don't you?" I press harder as she hums in delight. Before long, she's making slight movements, thrusting her hips, forcing my finger deep within her.

"I can't believe you're doing t-this right h-here."

"Oh sweetheart, you have no idea what I'm prepared to do to get what I want." I thrust another finger high and deep into her. "I want to know you. Everything about you. Starting with who you work for." I nip her ear and she thrusts her hips. "It can't be that big of a secret...can it?" I curve my fingers against the wall of her pussy and tickle that ridge inside. Little moans slip from her lips getting progressively louder. Almost loud enough that if there were more people here, we'd get caught.

This time of night is usually after the rush and I'm cashing in on that. "Tell me what I want to know. Who do you work for?" I tickle the inside wall and yank both fingers down hard. Her entire body tightens as she spirals into orgasm silently. Her head hangs down, breath coming in rapid bursts against her chest. I remove my hand sticky with her fluids and wipe it off on my napkin. "So..." I wait a beat before she responds with the one name I was ready to hear, confirmation that I've just gotten myself one major leap forward toward getting my girl back.

"Billionaire Chase Davis," she lifts her head smiling. What she doesn't know is this is my game and I've just won another round.

Bingo.

GILLIAN

CHAPTER FOURTEEN

"Gillian, get out of bed," Chase's voice booms in the quiet room, digging a tiny knife into my subconscious. I pull the covers up and cower under the blanket. The bed dips near my hips. He pulls the blanket back. I'm so lethargic that even using my full strength to hold the blanket in place it's no match for him. Throwing my forearm over my eyes I exhale loudly, making a point to show him how frustrated I am. "Come, get out of bed. Take a shower, put some comfortable clothes on and join the group for dinner."

I shake my head keeping my arm over my eyes. "I'm tired, Chase," I say my teeth grinding down.

"You've slept all day. Hell, you've slept all week. The girls are worried." His fingertip trails down the side of my hairline. "I'm worried. You've hidden in bed all week. Enough is enough. Come on," He tugs on my arm and pulls me up to a seated position.

The lights are too bright, the pressure in my head is overwhelming and the guilt in my heart is stifling. "Why can't you just let me sleep?" I shove at his hands but he doesn't relent, pulling me into a standing position and walking, more like pushing, me into the bathroom.

"I spoke with Dr. Madison. Explained how depressed

you've been," his blue eyes are soft as he assess me. He sets a prescription bottle of something on the counter. "It's an anti-anxiety, anti-depressant. He said to take one a day and he'll discuss how you feel next week."

Tingles of anger prick at my skin making me feel more like a porcupine, ready to bite back at being attacked. He's been talking to my therapist behind my back? With a flick of my hand, the bottle goes flying along the bathroom counter and lands in the sink. Chase's eyes narrow and fill with heat. "You. Need. Those," he says slowly. Too slowly.

"I'm not sick, Chase, I'm fucking *sad* okay! Big difference!" My voice is harsh filled with contempt. Same tone I took with Dr. Madison when he gave me the first script. I tore it up in front of his face into tiny little pieces and let it fall to the ground like confetti. He was just as pleased at my display as Chase is now.

Chase steps closer, arms out. I take two steps back and cross my arms over my chest. "This is for your own good. You've checked the fuck out, Gillian. Life is happening without you in it. That is not okay. Do you not see what you're doing by distancing yourself?"

I shake my head back and forth. Panic and anger firing on all synapsis until my skin is so hot I'm burning alive. "What life!" I roar. "You think I like having to have a body guard trail me everywhere I go. To look over my shoulder every minute of every day. To always feel like I'm being watched!" I lean over with my hands on the counter top.

"It's to keep you safe…" Chase starts.

"No! Don't even fucking say it. No one's safe. My friends have been targeted and almost killed. Several people in the gym died because of me!" I point to my chest so

AUDREY CARLAN

hard it hurts. "And Bree, she'd be *dead* right now but no, a twenty-year-old girl with her entire life in front of her was murdered in her place…because of me!" I scream, tears pouring down my face. "So don't tell me I'm missing out on life. I don't fucking deserve to live!" The lethargy takes control and I slide down the wall across from the vanity into a heap on the tile floor. Hugging my knees tight I hang my head over them and let it all wash over me. The worry, the fear, the constant state of anxiousness. Seeing my friends looking at me with pity in their eyes. It's too much. I can't take it anymore.

Before long Chase crouches in front of me. "Gillian, none of this is your fault. You have to know that."

"Do I, Chase? Do I know that? No. I know that wherever I go that might be where and when it happens. That the sick fuck gets to me. But then again, at least if he gets what he wants, he won't hurt anyone else I love. That's on me!" The tremble starts in my lips but moves down my chest and into each limb.

Chase's face contorts into a deep scowl. "You listen to me. Whoever is doing this is to blame. Not you. Baby, look at me," he moves his hand to cup my cheek. Using his thumb, he lifts my head, forcing me to look at him. "We will get this guy. It's only a matter of time." His words mean so much but fall short of curing the cold ache inside.

"But at what cost? Just like he said, who's next? You?" I choke out the word on a sob. He's definitely on the stalker's hit list. If the stalker's infatuated with me then he must despise the man I'm going to marry. The man I publically gave my heart to. Just the split second thought of something happening to Chase sends my stomach churning, and I'm ready to vomit. The crippling grip of fear seizes my mind once more. "I couldn't bear it."

Chase pulls me into his lap to straddle his waist. I cling to him like a second skin. "You won't have to. But this isn't healthy. You hiding out in our room…"

"It's not our room." I choke out even more miserable. It's an overly directed, completely pretentious, uncomfortable guest suite that mimics old French antique style. Everything is a gaudy rose combined with gold tones and mixed with floral and striped patterns. There's an overwhelming pink hue to the space that reminds me of an attempt to see life through rose-colored glasses. Apparently, Chase's Mom has similar themes in her guest rooms as Chase does with his restaurants. If this room was a restaurant, it would be called "Pink." Maria and Tommy are in the blue room, Bree in the white room, even though I don't think she's actually slept a night in it, and Kat and Carson are in the grey room.

My guy exhales loudly against my neck. "No, it's not our room. I know you were just starting to connect with our penthouse." His hands sweep up and down my back soothing my anxiety. As he holds me, I start the yoga style breathing that Bree taught me. It does wonders when I'm having a meltdown. "Baby, we're going to have all the time in the world to make our home ours. Besides, I told you after the wedding we'll be looking into a home, probably somewhere close to here. It's a great location and the houses are top notch."

I groan. The last thing I want to do is move closer to Colleen Davis. His Uncle Charles is great. So far I've been here a week, and I've avoided all communication with my soon-to-be monster-in-law.

Chase pulls my head back and rests his forehead against mine. "You don't like the idea of moving closer to Mother do you?" I can hear the smile in his tone without having to look at his handsome face. I shake my head. Less than a year, and he already knows me so well. "No matter. When the time is right, we'll carve out a place for us and our future children. If we can't find it, I'll build it. I told you Gillian, I'm going to give you the world."

He nuzzles my cheek then kisses me softly. "I just want you."

Chase grins and the ice around my heart cracks and falls, melting under the man's spell once more. "Boggles the mind," he shakes his head then holds very still as he inhales deeply. "I hate to say it honey, but you reek." He cringes and I laugh. The first laugh I've had in over a week, possibly two. Quickly, he stands me up, divests me of my clothes and turns the water on. "Go, shower," he pushes me into the large space surrounded by pink tile. Note to self: Never decorate anything in pink...ever.

I get under the spray and it's pure heaven. The heat pounds against my sore neck and battered conscience. When I open my eyes, Chase is staring, his eyes seeming to trace every curve, lingering on my chest, legs, and most especially, the apex of my thighs. "Why don't you join me big guy," I offer.

He shakes his head. "Would love to, but then we'd never make it down to dinner, and there are three women who will literally cut off my balls and my dick if I don't get you down for dinner. They're starting to believe I'm holding you hostage," he snickers. "Not that I wouldn't," he waggles his brows. I roll my eyes and turn around. His breath catches.

"Damn, you have a fine ass. Makes me want to…" I turn and he's holding his hands in tight fists as he looks his fill. The form fitting slacks are tenting, showing a mighty large bulge.

"What do you want to do?" I run my hands over my breasts seductively making sure to soap them fully, stimulating them into tight points. I open my mouth and tip my head back, catching some water in my mouth as well as letting the hot stream pelt my aching nipples.

Chase growls. "Lower," he grates between his teeth.

I comply, not only to make him insane with lust but he's making me feel wanton, desirable. All week I've only felt like an empty shell of a woman I used to know and respect. Time to come out of my shell. "Like this?" I move my hand between my thighs and stroke along the slick seam and moan.

"Yeah, just like that," he says, his tone so thick with lust I open my eyes and am treated to the most beautiful sight. My man, his three-piece suit still on, eyes laser focused on me, only he's opened his pants and let out his giant cock. His erection is enormous, thick and glistening at the tip as he strokes it with one hand. My mouth waters as I watch him pull on his dick, using fierce strokes, much harder than I ever would do myself. "Now put a finger in that pretty pussy, pretend it's my finger," he groans.

"Can't baby," I close my eyes trying to do as he asks. "Too small, you always feel huge inside me," I whine.

"Press two fingers in, yeah, spread your legs wider. Open those lips and tip your pelvis so I can see you fingering yourself. Christ, you're so fucking sexy," he says, his voice strained, coming in sharp staccato beats as he tugs and moans through his own pleasure.

Chase thinks I'm sexy as I work to get myself off, but his beauty is undefinable. It's as if he's art in motion. His body is arched, bowed towards me in a way that suggests he physically *needs* to be closer. The layers of his dark hair are wild as he thrusts forward, neck tipped back, the ropey tendons contracting with every movement. As those even teeth bite into his plump bottom lip, I whimper, wanting nothing more than to be biting that lip myself. His eyes open in a flash, sending ripples of excitement to swirl heavily in my body, like a balloon filled with too much air and is about to burst.

"Tug on that sweet clit, Baby. I want to watch you come. Come for me, only me," he says—as if I need to be reminded. All of my pleasure is for him, because of him, and willingly handed over to him for eternity.

A soft cry forms deep in the base of my throat and works into a keening sound as I furiously work my clit with one hand, the other two fingers thrusting in and out.

"That's it, now give it me, come with me," he says with a deep rumble, one I'd recognize anywhere.

Just that tone, the wicked edge of his release tips me over and that overfilled balloon that's bursts. Stars shoot in every direction as pleasure soars from between my legs, up my spine and through each limb. Beautiful, sweet release. Chase is right there with me, eyes half hooded, mouth tucked into a grimace as if he's in pain, that feeling you get when the pleasure is so good it's almost painful. I watch as the tremors ripple through my body while jet after jet of his release flows into the shower, mixes with the water and goes down the drain.

Chase white knuckles the towel rod as I balance myself against both sides of the shower walls breathing heavily.

"Feel better?" Chase says as he pulls off his clothes that were spattered from the showers spray and enters the cube. I'm standing struck completely stupid as my own personal Superman leaves his super suit behind and holds me bare ass naked. And what a fine ass it is, I think, mimicking Chase's earlier sentiment.

"Much, but why didn't you just join me earlier?" *I could have used a nice hard cock.*

He slicks his hair back as the water licks over his skin, making him glisten like a water God. Chase grins and pulls me into a deep, wet, kiss, one I could have used earlier when I had my fingers between my legs. "I told you, I didn't want us to be late for dinner with everyone downstairs. You know me, Gillian. Once I've got you naked, spread open for me, I need hours to gorge on your beautiful body. The second I have my cock in you, time stops and a different type of play begins."

I shake my head and finish my shower, and hop out before I get any ideas to take advantage of my wet, naked, man.

★ ★ ★ ★

"She lives!" Kat squeals and runs over to hug me. I left my hair wet and just pulled it up into a big clip. At least my attire matches everyone else's. I'm wearing one of Chase's dress shirts and a pair of yoga pants. When he exited the shower and saw what I had on his eyes turned soft and mushy. If there was ever a way for my stoic, controlling, overconfident man to look mushy, it would be the moment when he saw that I was more comfortable surrounded in something that smelled like him than anything else.

"Welcome to the land of the living, *Puta!* Done avoiding your *hermana's?*" Maria says with attitude, but she still gets up from her chair and pulls me into a hug. She sets her forehead against mine. Mesmerizing ice blue eyes focus on mine. I feel like they're staring right through me. "You okay?"

"I will be," I hug her back trying to fill my guilty soul with the love and kinship of my friends.

Bree stands and I pull away from Maria and go right into her arms. "I'm so sorry," I shake as she holds me.

"Oh Gigi, you have nothing to be sorry for." She hugs me tight. "This freak, they're going to get him. Yes, we've lost a lot but we still have each other." Her own voice cracks and she clears her throat.

I lean back and lay my hand over her belly. It's still as flat as always but I imagine I can feel the baby inside, warm and safe. "And we have this baby to look forward to, right?" I look into her watery blue eyes. She nods eagerly, finally smiling.

"I can't believe I'm going to be someone's mother! Oh my god!" All the girls jump up, Maria fist pumps and whoops in the air then starts to rock her own victory jig.

"Best Auntie Ever title coming my way." She does a little dance we all know too well. Kat turns, cocks a hip and gives the head tilt.

"I don't think so. Not possible. Everyone knows I'm the best. Besides, I'm going to make her princess outfits and let her play dress up in my closet..."

I roll my eyes but Bree just smiles and watches the two in mock battle. "Hey guys, I think you're forgetting one important factor." They both stop their bickering and turn around to look at us. "It could be a boy," I offer. Both of them look at me as if I've suddenly grown additional limbs.

Maria walks over to us and puts her hand over Bree's belly. "Nope, *chica*. Never been wrong." She shrugs, turns to Kat. "I'm going to teach her how to dance like a ballerina. All *niñas* love ballerinas." Her face twists into a smug expression, eyebrow cocked.

I need to get in on this. No way are these two going to show me up! "Sorry ladies, but I'm going to share with her my love of shoes. You've seen how much Anabelle loves me? You know her shoe collection is stellar. Who do you think got her those? Hmmmm?"

Bree giggles and shakes her head. A pair of arms pulls me into a warm body from behind. Obviously, Chase is done with his shower. "Having fun?" he asks as Maria hands me a glass of wine.

I smile at her, tink our glasses and say "*Salud,*" then grip hold of Chase's hands. "Very much," I take a sip and snuggle back into his embrace even more. "Thanks for getting me out of the room and out of my funk. This is exactly what I need."

"I'll always bring you back. You know that." He kisses the side of my neck and pulls away to chat up Carson. He's handed a glass of wine and they head over to the pool table as the four of us girls reconnect.

"So what did Phil say when you both were alone? About the baby?" Kat asks the question I've been dying to know.

Bree takes a bite of a strawberry from a plate of nibbles the cook set out. "Surprisingly, he's taken it really well. He made me take another pregnancy test with him waiting the three minutes so he could see the stick turn into a plus symbol. Then when it did he gave me another one with a huge smile and said, Again." She uses a rough voice mimicking a male.

We all laugh and giggle. "That sounds like Phil. Never wants to be left out." I shake my head thinking fondly of my best friend. He deserves this happiness and seeing how lit up Bree is now, I know it's going to work out between them.

"Yeah, he wants me to move in right away. Get Anabelle used to the idea of me before we tell her she's going to be a big sister. What do you guys think? I haven't told him one way or the other. He gets out of the hospital next week and then he and Anabelle will be here with all of us until this situation is settled. But then what?" Her nose scrunches up and she pulls a knee to her chest resting her chin on it. "We haven't really been dating that long. What if we're not compatible in that way?"

"What makes you think that? You love him right?" Maria asks.

Bree huffs pulling her long blonde hair up, twists it into a spiral and stuffs it over making a snail swirl at the crown of her head. It's like a magic trick, all that golden hair staying up all on its own. I've asked her to teach me how to do it but it never works on my hair. "I do love him, so much, but this is all so fast. I don't want him to regret it down the road. We shouldn't move in together just because we accidentally got pregnant. You know?"

Kat nods and twists her lips in thought. "But honey,

what if it's the best thing you've ever done. Look at Gigi. She and Chase were only together a few months and moved in, and now they're getting married. Love happens when it happens. The timeline doesn't matter." All of us nod and wait while Kat continues to be the voice of reason. "Don't miss out on something that could be everything you ever wanted because you're scared."

Bree contemplates this quietly and bites her lip. "Yeah, I'll think about it."

"And remember," I add. "You have some time to practice living together here before you have to make the big change. All of you will be here as a family, sharing a space for a while. That could be a practice run," I finish. Bree's eyes light up.

"You're right. It will give us time to see if we're compatible day in and day out. You're a genius, Gigi!" she hums happily, bouncing side to side in her chair like all the world's problems have been solved. Boy, I wish it was that easy.

Maria winks at me and tips her glass in the air. I smile. "Toast!" Maria says. All three of us groan but hold our glasses up into the air. "Hey, come on. I'll make it PG now that Bree is all preggers." Bree scowls and gives her a dirty look.

I clear my throat. "I'd like to give the toast," Maria nods. "To change. It's happening all around us. Let it guide us into the next phase of our lives and feel blessed in the knowledge that we are all still together to share it." All eyes go to Bree. Three women so thankful that their soul sister is still alive, that she's carrying the next addition to our family within her and by God, we're all determined to be around for years to come. The image of that poor young girl, the one who looks so much like Bree, comes fluttering back into my mind. I send up a silent prayer for the young girl and her family.

In that moment, I make a pact with myself. No more woe-is-me, no more pity party for one. These women, Phil, Thomas, Carson and most importantly Chase, deserve me whole. Instead of crying or hiding in my room, I'm going to face this head on. Whatever it takes. This bastard cannot take away my will to live or the fierce love I have of those around me.

"Let's take a load off!" Maria whoops and fills all of our glasses to the brim with a jammy cabernet from Napa. Bree looks at the glasses with longing then rubs her belly. Right at that moment, the chef enters the entertainment room.

"Dinner is served Mr. Davis," the chef bows to Chase.

Several "I'm starved," and "So hungry" from the men can be heard as we all make our way to the dining room. The chef has set out a steak dish with potatoes and veggies. Down home cooking with a gourmet approach. I snicker and Chase leads me to the front of the table and to his right. His mother is sitting to his left.

"Mother," Chase says softly, leans down and kisses her cheek. Colleen takes in the group who, except for Bree, are a little tipsy to say the least.

"Looks like all of you dressed for dinner," she says haughtily glancing at each of us with a pinched scowl. All four women are in different styles of yoga pants, tanks, and sweater-shirt type combinations. Maria's eyes flash to Colleen. She balances herself against the chair back sending daggers.

"Excuse me? You have a problem with my attire?"

she says before slowly lifting her right leg out. She grasps it at the calf and pulls it all the way up along her side, toe pointing straight into the air in a standing splits. Maria closes her eyes and breathes out slowly. "Sorry, leg cramp," she offers sweetly, knowing the movement horrified the woman watching her. Dance acrobatics at a formal dinner table set for royalty with a snobby witch trying to stare her down...I never loved her more.

"Damn, Tommy is a lucky man," Carson grumbles and Kat whacks him in the shoulder. "Sorry Sweet cheeks but that's impressive. Imagine what I could do to you if you were able to do that..." He grins, his eyes focused on her pretty face. She blushes then nudges him.

Chase controls the grin that slips across his face. "Yes well, Mother, normal people dress comfortably when staying in for the night. You should try it," he offers while taking in her buttoned up silk blouse and skirt ensemble. I'm always surprised at how easily Chase pushes off what his mother says but still sounds respectful doing it. "Eat up everyone. Don't let the food get cold."

I watch Chase eat. He glances around the room smiling. I've never seen him happier. Our friends have truly become a welcome part of his life, and seeing them all here, enjoying a meal in the house he grew up in, has to be making him nostalgic. Eventually, his gaze settles on me. He cocks his head to the side, pops in a baby potato and gives me a heart-stopping, gorgeous grin that makes me flush with excitement. He winks and I practically drool.

"Eat, baby. You're going to need it for what I have in store for you tonight," he whispers.

I cut a piece of meat, plop it into my mouth and give

him a sexy, knowing look of my own. He thinks he's going to lead this evening, he's got another thing coming. I'm feeling better than I have in a long time. My friends are healthy, happy, and Phil's on the mend and awake. We're all going to have another life to celebrate, and pretty soon, I'm marrying the man of my dreams. Yeah, he's so going to get a piece of me tonight. A whole lot more than he bargained for. I plan to ride my man until I'm walking bowlegged to work tomorrow.

Chase sees the change in me, always aware of subtle changes or maybe it's just the pheromones calling to him. "What?" He says sweetly.

"You're mine," I say quietly and grab his knee under the table.

"Staking your claim?" he whispers leaning over toward me while the table is alive with boisterous conversations, each person trying to out-talk the other.

"You got a problem with that?" I offer with a little attitude.

"Not even a little bit." He reaches down and adjusts his pants. I grin, knowing he's already getting hard, picturing what we're going to do to one another later.

Licking my lips, I take a sip of wine and exhale. Just thinking of being with him intimately has my heart pounding, my panties wet, and desire running through my veins.

Chase's eyes have turned dark, swirling with intensity. "You are so going to get it," he growls into his wine glass taking a large sip of the rich fruity liquid.

"You gonna give it to me?" I throw back.

"Many times over. Plan to ache with how many times

I'm going to stuff you full of my cock," he grits through his teeth.

I look him dead in the eye. We stare each other down. His eyes are still filled with lust, probably mirroring my own. I can no longer hear the conversations around us. There's nothing but his eyes, mouth, and beautiful face and the desire pumping through the two of us.

I want him more than anything in this lifetime.

I need him more than air.

"Bring it!" I challenge plopping another bite into my mouth.

Without preamble, Chase stands, grabs both of my hands, pulls me up, leans down pushing his shoulder into my stomach and lifts me up into the air.

"Chase! What in the world?" his mother cries out.

"Put me down!" I bang on his ass then fondle it a couple times enjoying the feel of his tight glutes flexing. It's a great ass.

One of his hands holds my legs the other firmly gripping my ass. "Sorry everyone. It's been a long day and my fiancée and I are going to retire for the evening. Please enjoy the food, wine, and dessert I know the chef has prepared."

"Chase, sit down. You're embarrassing yourself," his mother scolds. I snicker behind him trying to hold myself aloft balancing on his waist and see the group.

"*Buenas noches,*" Maria waves and throws a thumbs up my way.

"Have fun," Kat laughs and twirls a lock of her hair. I don't think she's too far from taking her own man the way that Carson's eyes are devouring her.

"See you tomorrow," Bree waves.

I wiggle my fingers at them as Chase carries me out of the dining room. Colleen's red face is the last thing I see.

Once in our room, Chase tosses me on the bed. I can't help but giggle and shriek with joy. He jumps on the bed and cages me between his thick thighs. I scratch my nails along them enticingly.

"What am I going to do with you?" he looks at me, licks his lips and then starts to unbutton my, well his, shirt.

"Everything!" I whisper as he kisses my neck moving down between my breasts.

"As you wish."

X

CHAPTER FIFTEEN

I cannot believe that fucking prick survived a bomb and a building collapsing on top of him. His will to live must far surpass my desire to have him dead. At least he's going to suffer for the next few months through healing and physical therapy. Who knows, maybe I'll cut the fucker in his sleep one night soon. Make that child an orphan once and for all. Already took care of his other spawn by cutting off the life source of the acrobatic blonde. One girl down, two to go. Remembering the moment that knife pierced her pretty jugular makes my dick stir with excitement. No time for that though. Now that the prick isn't in the hospital, I need a new source for my information.

Stepping off the elevator, I scan the space. A huge sign made of chrome boldly says "Davis Industries, Inc." on the wall directly opposite the car. Slowing my gait, I hold a briefcase and pretend to be on my cell phone talking quietly. Anyone I pass ignores me. Nothing to see here. Just a random guy cruising the halls to his next meeting. Only I'm not here for a meeting exactly, I'm here for intel, to scope out the place. I can feel my girl's essence here, although I know she's not here now. Watched her walk out with the bastard and their two bodyguards. Now I just need to find her office. I'm sure it's next to that rich fucker's. Having a woman like that makes a man want to keep her close. One of my biggest mistakes was letting her get away. Not again. I'm taking my time. Being smart about how I get her back.

It's early, but since she's gone, I have the perfect ruse. As I approach, a huge wide smile adorns her pretty face. The same face I've been fucking every other night since we met. I must say, I was surprised to find out Dana Shephard is a wildcat in the bedroom. She'll take my dick any way I give it to her. It's unusual to meet a girl and fuck her in the ass within a week. Just proves how much of a whore she is under all those elegant business suits.

"Hey you," she says as I approach. Before I reach her, I can see the double doors that are most certainly Chase's. Then to the left I see a dark office. Right there beside the door is the nameplate I was looking for—Gillian Callahan—proudly displayed in gold letting. It warms my heart seeing my girl's name looking important. Only it won't be for long. She needs to be important to me and me alone. Once I reach Dana's desk I lean over and give her a wet kiss. She accepts it willingly moaning into my mouth. Another hint that she's an easy lay, sucking face with her brand new boyfriend on the job. Dumb bitch.

Holding up a white bag I set it on her desk then bring around a latte. I've purposely loosened the lid so that when I shove it toward her, the brown liquid splashes all over her white blouse.

"Oh shit, no!" I say giving an Oscar worthy performance. I grab the napkins inside the bag. They aren't going to do much with coffee on a silk blouse.

"Sugar," she says as she holds out the soaked shirt.

"Honey, I'm so sorry. I was just trying to bring you lunch and give you an afternoon pick-me-up," I grip her around the wrist and drag her to my side. "You know, after I kept you up working that fantastic body last night" I whisper in her ear and she giggles like a schoolgirl. "You should go rinse that in cold water."

"It's okay, I have back up shirts," she says as she turns to the wall of cabinets behind her and opens one. Several women's blouses and skirts hang neatly in a line. "When you work the hours I work, you always have to have plenty of backups," she grabs a new, almost identical white blouse.

Looking down at my watch I cringe. "I'm really sorry honey, but I have to go back to work. Like I said, I just wanted to stop in and give you the treats."

Dana comes over to me, clasps my cheeks and then kisses me long and hard. My dick turns semi-erect at the thought of flipping her around and taking her over her desk like the whore she is. "See you tonight?" she says hopefully.

Shaking my head I turn towards the hall I came from letting her think I'm in a hurry. "Afraid not. Have to work late into the evening, then work out, but tomorrow I'm all over you," I grin.

A blush creeps over her face. "Okay, then I'll see you tomorrow. Looking forward to it," she waves and starts down the hall to what I assume is the ladies restroom. Once she's out of sight, I walk over to the dark office and step inside. I'm instantly surrounded in her vanilla goodness. It's everywhere. I remember she used to use vanilla scented body wash. The scent catapults me back to a time when we were happy, enjoying every moment together and life seemed better.

Letting the past go, I get down on my knees and pull out the chip from my pocket. Removing the sticky side I slide it directly under the file cabinet on her solid wood desk. This should give me direct access to listen to my heart's content to what my girl is planning, doing, and hopefully learn more about where she is. So far, I know she's still with the fucker, but she hasn't been staying at the penthouse. Today was the first day she showed up to work. Her credit cards haven't been used and she's not staying with any of her friends. As a matter of fact, all of her friends have up and disappeared. Guess I scared the rest of those bastards off when I killed the blonde bitch.

I'm sure her funeral will be soon. It's been over a week since I slit her throat. That will be a nice event to watch from a distance. Seeing all those people crying over a stupid cunt like Bree Simmons. Might even be comical. The more I think about it, the more I know I did the world a favor killing her off. Had she stayed out of the way, not been so close to my girl, maybe she'd still be here. Every human is born with free will, and I warned all of them that nothing would keep me from getting to Gillian. Maybe now they'll listen. The other two should have been told about my note. They're next if they don't fix their shit and disappear. So far so good. I haven't so much as heard a peep from any of her gang in over a week.

Then I saw her exiting the building right before I was going in. I'm glad she didn't see me. It's been nice flying under the radar, her not having a clue where I'm at. It's strange though. I'm the one that loved her like no other, took care of her, helped her handle all her problems. Doesn't make sense why she wouldn't automatically assume it's me.

Probably the gold dick is making her stupid in the head. I'll fix her though. When she's mine and I have her hidden away in my special place, she'll have no choice but to remember the love we shared. How beautiful and unique it was then and could be now.

Still undetected I make it out of the office and set the envelope with Gillian's name under a couple sheets of paper in Dana's inbox. She'll find it within the next day or so and give it to my girl, and I'll be able to hear her open it. While I'm daydreaming about Gillian finding the present I left for her, I'm propelled back to the here and now by the glass door being held open for me. Looking up, I stare right into the face of the enemy. Chase Fucking Davis.

"Here you go, sir," Chase holds open the door, his bodyguard standing directly behind him. Jack Porter's eyes take in my appearance, a brief moment of recognition passes through his features but disappears as I tilt my head down and away. Boring suit, briefcase, nothing to see here

"Oh, sorry, 'cuse me," I grumble distorting my voice just in case.

"No problem," Chase says as I walk through. He steps in and hustles down the concrete stairs. Just as I turn around to make sure everything's fine, I see that Jack Porter is in the same position at the doors, staring me down. His cold, dark eyes calculating everything about me.

God damn it! Not good. The last thing I need is a suspicious ex-military man on my tail. I'll have to keep my ear to the ground and give it another week or so before I strike. Let them think everything's fine again. Of course, that'll be shot to hell when they find the envelope.

It's fine. I'll lay low and enjoy listening in on my girl and fucking Chase Davis's secretary for the hell of it. Maybe I'll take pictures and send them to Gillian. Eventually, yeah, I'll show her the pictures. Then she'll be beside herself. Seeing me taking something that was Chase's. Letting another woman put her hands on me. I'm sure it will make her insane with jealousy.

"How are you settling in?" I ask Phil over the phone.

I can hear his long exhale. "As well as can be expected. Gigi, this isn't my home but it's nice having Bree and Anabelle by my side. Anabelle is so excited to be here. She thinks we're having a vacation."

Laughing into the phone, I press the receiver into the crook of my neck and flip through some emails. "Chase's offer for a tutor still stands. If you want Anabelle getting the extra schooling she would be receiving in preschool we'll make sure to have a teacher come out," I remind him of the offer Chase made.

"No, it's okay. It's not going to be for that long and 'sides. Bree is taking the next month or so off. She can't bear to go back to the studio after what happened. I'm thinking she's going to close down her business and look into doing something else."

A deep pang starts up in my heart. "She can't," I whisper. "Opening I Am Yoga was her dream. It's all she ever really wanted to do."

"But sweetie, a girl was murdered there and in her place. Would you want to go back and teach on that pedestal knowing that someone was killed there, that you should have been killed there?"

I exhale and suck in a shaky breath. "No, I wouldn't. I'll come up with something. Either way, did you get her to agree to see a therapist? Dr. Madison is on speed dial for me, and I'm certain he'd see her. On our dime of course," I explain.

"I'll talk to her about it. Thanks, Gigi. And thank Chase too for his hospitality. I've already thanked Charles and Colleen." I can hear a scuffling noise through the receiver. "Hey, the nurse is here for therapy down in the mansion's gym. Apparently, Chase had a bunch of equipment sent over so I wouldn't have to leave. Sneaky fella that one."

I laugh. "He is that. I'm glad you're on the mend and so thankful that you and your family are safe now. Thank you for agreeing to stay as we get this situation dealt with. I hope for all of our sakes it isn't for too long."

"It'll be fine. Since Chase owns my architectural firm, he's made it so that I'm not missing any pay, still receiving full salary. Bree and Anabelle and the baby are all healthy and safe. Can't ask for much more."

"I'm glad, Phil," I say just as the door opens and Chase enters. His long body looks fierce and imposing in the midnight black suit. He has a light blue dress shirt on and a yellow tie. That blue shirt makes his eyes pop, melting me on the spot. His dark cappuccino-colored hair has fallen in sexy layers that I'm dying to run my fingers through. He closes the door, locks it, then shifts the blinds to closed before leaning his back on the door.

"Okay, gotta go. Love you, Gigi," Phil says as I lick my lips, enjoying every speck of seeing my man standing against the door, his arms casually crossed, and a come fuck me look in his eyes.

"Yeah, love you too," I respond breathily. Chase's eyebrows quirk at the sentiment. He really doesn't like me telling any man but him that I love them.

"Uh, you okay, Gigi? You sound off." Phil asks right before I'm about to put down the phone.

My eyes never leave Chase's as he pushes off the door and walks over to the desk. His warm hand clasps my wrist and he tugs me up into a standing position plastering our bodies against one another. He's deliciously hard. Liquid fire burns through my body sending moisture to the thin lace between my legs.

"I'm perfectly fine. About to be so much better. Talk soon. 'Bye Phil," I rasp into the phone and then blindly try to put the receiver into the cradle. Chase grabs the phone and hangs it up for me right before pulling me into a searing kiss. His hands tunnel into my hair as his tongue delves deep.

Rapture. With swift hands, Chase untucks my shirt and unbuttons it, leaving it open. The red pushup bra leaves very little to the imagination. "Those panties match this bra," his tone is heavy with lust and the dirty office sex we're about to have.

"You know it does," I bite down on his bottom lip.

"I fucking love you," he slides the shirt off.

"Mmm, I fucking love you more," I moan as he takes my nipple through the red lace, rubbing his tongue in hard strokes so that the texture of the lace scrapes delectably against the aching flesh. "What's going on, Chase?" I ask after unbuttoning his shirt, getting right to his golden chest. He leans back long enough for me to swirl my tongue around his nipple and bite down.

A growl escapes his mouth. "Need to be in you. Right now. Gonna take you hard against this desk, baby." He bites down on the tender skin of my neck then traces the column with his teeth. With one hand, he undoes the zipper of my skirt, and it falls to the floor in a puddle. In less than a second, my back is on the desk and my man is between my legs, rubbing his length against my sopping panties.

I groan. "What changed? Why now? Not that I'm complaining..." I thrust my hips just as I hear the scratchy snap of lace shredding and the pinch of fabric breaking at my hip. "Another pair of panties? Seriously Chase!" The man is going to have to purchase a women's lingerie store if he keeps this up.

"I seriously need to be in this pussy right now, so yeah, panties are gone. It would be easier if you'd just stop wearing them," he grumbles as he holds my legs wide open assessing me. He is fascinated with having me spread open for him, completely vulnerable. It gets him hard as concrete. "Fucking perfect, and all mine," he leans down and licks my wet center from bottom to top, swirling around the bundle of nerves that's aching for attention. "You taste so good. I could eat you for hours."

Breathing hard, I continue playing with him. Trying to get to the bottom of his immediate need to fuck me here at work where anyone could interrupt. "If I wasn't wearing panties..." I stop, inhaling as he spears his tongue deep into me over and over. Pleasure roars through my body in waves. I grip his hair and shove him harder into me. He growls, sucks hard at my pussy then bites my clit in retaliation. I hold him there panting, tremors skipping along every nerve ending. "If I wasn't wearing panties, anyone could figure it out. Know I was ready to be fucked any time…"

He pulls back looking almost angry. Apparently, I poked the bear. "The fuck you are, you're ready for my cock. You see this Gillian," He unzips his pants and pulls out a huge erection. His dick is so hard and swollen I physically ache to touch it, have it near, deep inside, and all around me. "You see how I'm bursting to be with you. To fuck you. Mate with you. My fiancée." He lines up his cock at my entrance and spears into me. His hand goes over my mouth just as I scream into it muffling the sound. "My cock knows where it feels good and that's in you. Only you, baby." Chase rears back and plows into me again. I bite down on his hand at the onslaught of the pleasure and pain coalescing into one. He winces when my pussy clamps down in the first tightening of orgasm. He doesn't stop, just grins.

"I'm gonna come, Chase." My body arcs, nipples pointing to the sky, back curving up, hair dangling over the edge. He grips my hips, holds my legs high and open then crushing my clit. He grins sexily as the orgasm rips through me. He doesn't stop, and he's not done.

"Nowhere near done fucking you. Want your pussy so sore you have trouble sitting tomorrow," he pounds harder, again hand over mouth has I shriek into the second orgasm. His thumb comes down over my clit and he starts moving it around in rough circles.

"No baby, I can't, not again," I plead as the pleasure mounts, my body tired from two magnificent orgasms. He leans forward fucking me at a new angle that propels his cock deeper into my tightening channel to rub along that spot inside of me. Instantly I soar into bliss, his giant dick plunging into me over and over again. It's like he can't stop, *won't* stop fucking me.

"Who owns you?" Chase asks as I'm right on the edge of my fourth life altering orgasm. His face is pinched, breath coming in harsh gasps, sweat beading at the hairline as he slams into me.

I spiral into the abyss as he continues to pound into me. It's reckless, uncoordinated, and somewhere through it, I lose my guy to it. He's a machine and I don't know where the off switch is.

"Chase, no more, stop!" I cry out and shove against him. He holds me fast, not leaving my body but the glazed unfeeling look in his eyes slips away at my harsh tone and physical response. Suddenly his ocean eyes are back and tracing my features. His dick is still, throbbing, swollen and splitting me in half. With all that, four orgasms for me, and my guy hasn't found his own release. "Talk to me." I beg. He lets me lean up and clasp his neck wrapping my legs around his back. He sits down in the chair behind him, not letting me or our connection go. My limbs go over the sides of the chair and I settle heavily against him, gasping air, my sex throbbing and tingling. Aftershocks tingling through me as we sit quietly.

Finally he speaks. "We got another note." I close my eyes and lean against him. Now I know what the need to have me was about. The fierce way he wanted to prove his ownership, that I was his woman, and that he could please me over and over again makes a lot more sense now. When Chase is threatened, he reacts like a caveman would.

"It's okay, baby, I'm here, I'm safe. You're making sure I am." He clasps my back pulling me hard against his chest.

"I can't lose you, Gillian. I wouldn't survive it. You're my world. Life doesn't exist if I don't have you to share it with," he whispers into the soft skin at my neck. Shivers skitter down my spine and I tighten my grip. I love this man.

"You're not going to lose me," I let my feet dangle along the floor. Just my toes touch but it's enough. Slowly I lift up and come back down, allowing him a bit of relief. He moans and kisses my neck. I place my hands on his shoulders and stand up fully. Just the tip of his erection is still embedded. His eyes open and he takes a pink nipple into his mouth tugging softly, sending strings of renewed excitement to pool between my thighs.

Chase tips his head back letting my nipple go with a plop. I take his wet lips into a long kiss while I slide along his length, letting gravity pull me down. I land against his lap. He groans and closes his eyes. I squeeze him as hard as I can with the muscles inside, slide back up and slam down again. "You feel me, Chase, I'm right here. Where I want to be." Another up and then a hard slide down clenching the entire time. "Making love to you," I say grinding into his lap.

After several more up and downs, slowly making love to my man I can feel when the moment changes for him. His body goes tight and his grip around me hardens. I can almost sense when his cock swells.

"Baby I'm there," he licks his lips and I slide up, put my mouth to his, squeeze as hard as I can and fall back down, and he crashes into bliss. Chase's hands grip my hips and holds me to him, his back bowing up as he thrusts, pouring hotly inside of me while he rubs out the last of his pleasure.

We lay there for a long time just being together. Chase is still almost completely dressed while I'm in my red push up bra with the cups down around my boobs sitting in his lap. He got as far as taking out his dick. I got as far as opening up his shirt. His tie is askew but tightly knotted just under his neck. The scenario is too funny for me to contain. I start to laugh. Big, loud, guffaws have me hiccupping and wiping away joyful tears.

"What is so funny?"

"Look at us. We look a wreck." I point to my lack of clothing and his state of undress. He looks down at himself and then at me.

"I'd say we look damn fine. Office sex suits you," he nuzzles my neck and sucks on the tendon.

"Nu-uh, no way! I can't physically handle another orgasm. Didn't anyone ever tell you to keep the multiple orgasms to the bedroom? I still have to work the rest of the day!" I scold him and lift off his lap. Before I can move he stops me. As I expected, his release slowly starts to trickle down my thigh. He watches with a dirty grin. I smack his chest. "You're sick, you know that?" I grab some tissue and wipe up.

"Can't help that it turns me on to see my mark on you. See," He stands up and his dick is hard all over again.

"No!" I point a finger and run around my desk half naked.

"Where you gonna go?" He bites his bottom lip, leans down and picks up my clothes. "Looking for these, sexy?" He says.

"Chase, I swear to God, I cannot handle that," I point at his package. "Another time, tomorrow. You broke my vagina okay?"

He laughs and lunges. "Then I guess I'll have to kiss

it better," he leads me over to the couch at the back of my office and sets me down. Before he can get on his knees and do what he promises, I challenge him.

"Or, I could suck you off?" I offer.

Chase groans, tilts his head back and looks at the sky. "Thank you for giving me the perfect woman," he says to noone but I presume he's talking to God.

Less than a minute later, speaking is not an option.

X

That mother fucking, cock sucking, piece of shit is going down! I'm going to find him, and cut off every appendage starting with his precious fucking dick!

I listen as Chase moans while my girl puts her perfect fucking mouth on his tiny dick! "Arrrggggghh, he's fucking DEAD!" I scream and throw the earphones. Then I pull out my dick and hit the speaker button. Anger surging like white-hot fire pokers through my veins.

"I love sucking on you," Gillian says, her voice raspy and horse. I imagine it's me she's got those pink lips wrapped around. "Gonna make you feel good," she says and I tug hard on the tight flesh between my thighs.

Male groaning sounds spill through the speakers, then he starts to open his stupid mouth. "Take it down your throat, yeah, all the way, like that. God, Gillian, so deep, you've got all of me, Baby. You're so beautiful," he says and I pull my hand up and lick from palm to fingertip wetting the surface then wrapping it back around my cock jerking over and over along with the sound of the couple's moans.

"Come on me, between my tits, on my face, wherever you want," she says sounding like a two-bit whore. It's not her fault. I know it's *his* influence because that's what he likes to hear.

More moaning, "Never on your pretty face. Love you too much, swallow me. It's all for you," he says then a long string of wet sucking followed by a male's obvious orgasm, with me following right along with her, spurting hotly into my hand. All for my girl, my Gillian.

"That's it, Gillian. You're mine," the bastard says and then I hear kissing sounds. Blech. I'm about to vomit so sickened by hearing her blow him, but more turned on than I ever have been in my entire life. It was easy to remember those perfect lips and imagine them wrapped around my cock once again. I need to get her back.

"She's yours, Chase. Yeah right, over your dead body!" I promise to the room. Looking at all the images of my girl staring back at me. Her image calms me and I've got thousands of them now, plastering the walls like wallpaper. My own Gillian room.

"Can't wait to bring you here, my love. Soon. Soon we'll be together again. I swear it."

GILLIAN

CHAPTER SIXTEEN

"He's driving me crazy already!" Bree groans dramatically, slumping into the booth. We're at our favorite Irish Pub sitting at our table. I caress the shape of the trinity symbol in the table with my finger, appreciating the familiarity of the trinity in our lives and the circle protecting it.

Maria pushes the plate of melted aged cheddar towards Bree. "Eat. You're bitchy already and you're only like what, all of three months pregnant?"

Bree huffs loudly. "It's just that he wants it all the time now, and I don't want to hurt him," her bottom lip puffs out.

"What did the doctor say?" I ask genuinely interested in the details about sex while pregnant.

She pinches a crusty piece of bread, plops it in her mouth then swings the piece around. "He said I'm totally fine. Baby is healthy, heartbeat looks good. It was so sweet when Phil heard the heart beat and got to see the image on the sonogram." Her eyes light up and she hugs herself. "He was mesmerized by the image of our baby. He's really going to be great. Hopefully, he'll teach me a thing or two."

"So what's the problem? His *pene roto*?" Maria asks.

Nudging her arm I respond, "Stop it! You always think men's penises are broken." I laugh. Maria shrugs and sips her Poorman stout, our standard drink when in our favorite pub.

Bree exhales loudly. "It's just he's finally starting to feel better and he's crazy horny which makes me insanely turned on. I don't know, this baby just makes me want dick. You know," she looks at both of us. As if on cue both Maria and I shake our head no at the same time then burst out laughing.

"What'd I miss!" Kat runs up sliding into the booth next to Bree giving her a hug. Then she leans down and gives the belly a pat. "How's our girl doing," she says.

"Which one?" Maria and I say simultaneously. Again, the laughter takes over. We're on a roll!

Maria controls herself first. "Bree's telling us how horned up she is, but too afraid to break her man's *pene*," she says by ending with a crunch to a piece of baguette smothered in cheese.

Bree's mouth forms an O. "That is not true! It's just I'm worried about Phil. He's still healing but we're both jonesing to be alone."

Once I've controlled the giggles I jump in. "As long as you both take it slow, I'm sure it'll be fine. Just talk to him about your concerns. Chase and I will take Anabelle to the movie room and put on one of those Disney movies she likes. We'll pretend we're at the movies. She'll love it. Sound like a plan?"

Her hand comes out over mine. "Sounds like Heaven. Thanks, girl."

"No problem. Besides, it's the least we can do. I know it can't be easy with all of us living under the same roof."

Kat chimes in after waving over the waiter. "It's really

not a big deal. I mean, the house is huge, and all the rooms are spread out. The only time I see you guys is if we're down for dinner. The rest of the time, I'm working or spending time alone with Carson. Which, by the way, still is a problem!" she pouts.

"What problem?" Maria asks. "He not being good to you? Need me to *hablar con él,* speak to him? He better be treating my *hermana* right!" Oh, I can see Maria's spine straightening and her feathers ruffling just like a peacock readying for battle.

"Relax, Ria. If Kat wants us to butt in, we'll butt in. I'm pretty sure she doesn't. Right?"

"Right!" she gets the waiter's attention with a hand wave, points to the drink in front of Maria, and holds one finger up. The waiter nods back. "Exactly, Gigi. It's just, remember guys, I told you that Carson hasn't said he loves me? Well, he still hasn't. It's starting to piss me off. So I've stopped telling him that I love him, and you know what's weird?"

Bree straightens up and gets close to Kat. "What?"

"He keeps trying to force me to say it. For example, we'll be playing around or have just had sex and he'll say, "You love me, huh sweet cheeks?" She mimics a male voice lowering her own for effect. "And instead of saying, "Yes, I do. I just nod. It's driving him nutty." She snickers. The waiter drops off her drink. "Thanks," she smiles and takes a sip. A bit of froth gets stuck to her lip.

"You got a little something right here," I point to my upper lip. "Got Poorman!" I joke.

Kat licks it off and smiles. "No, I got rich man who won't say he loves me! So what do you guys think?"

I shake my head not sure where Carson's at with their relationship. I know him, but not well enough to really have a solid opinion on the inner workings of his mind. Bree tilts her head and seems to think about it, twirling a long blonde lock of hair. "What if he's just afraid to say it? Like he's a serious commitmentphobe?" she offers.

Kat puts her elbows on the table and sighs. "I don't know what to do. I mean, if he doesn't love me after this long, he's never going to. But I'm so deep in love with him, I can't imagine not wanting to be with him—ever."

Maria reaches out. "You're going to have to talk to him. I know you don't like confrontation but I think it's time to be direct. Straight up ask him why he doesn't love you."

When the words leave Maria's mouth, Kat cringes. It's heartbreaking watching her hurting like this. I've seen the two of them together and they're perfect for one another. It's obvious theirs is a deep connection, and what I see is definitely true love. I'm just not sure what Carson's problem is. But it's really not up to any of us girls to get involved. This is something that Kat has to do on her own and in her own time. I just hope for Carson's sake that when she does bring it up, it isn't too late. I'd hate for this to come up during a fight or something petty. It could easily tear them apart.

"I'm sure you'll work it out. Just think on it, and if you want to hash out your plan of attack with one of us, you know where we live." Bree giggles and Maria puts up an "L" shape using her thumb and forefinger.

"Lame joke. You need to work on those," she chastises.

"Speaking of work!" a voice I hadn't heard since earlier today bounds over attached to the body of Chase's assistant, Dana.

Maria looks at the tall blond business goddess with disdain. "Does she ever take a load off?" she whispers and I bonk her elbow. "Owee," she rubs her elbow.

"Hi Dana, what can I do for you?" I ask with as much politeness as I can manage after a busy week at work and hiding out from my missing in action stalker. Haven't heard a peep since he sent those images of the young girl he murdered thinking it was Bree over a month ago. All he wrote on each picture was one word.

Remember.

Chase didn't share the images with me and I'm thankful for that. I don't need the reminder of what the psycho did to that girl; it plays over and over in my nightmares including every time I think back to what could have happened to our Bree.

"Chase told me you'd be here with the bridesmaids so I figured it was a perfect opportunity to finalize the details for the wedding. There's still several things that need to be ironed out and there's only a month left!" She sets down the bane of my existence. The evil wedding binder. It's now three times the size it once was with tons of tabs that have perfectly typed titles.

"Can't you see that we're trying to relax here?" Maria buts in, she just can't help herself.

"Look, Ms. De La Torre," Ria's eyes get big at the formal approach. "Chase has put me in charge of making this the best day of their lives, and I intend to do just that. You're either with me, or against me. I'd rather not have to tell Chase that you're in the way of him marrying Gigi. You and I both know that won't go well for any of us. Will it?"

Maria looks at her, looks at me, then at each of our

friends and back to Dana. "You just put me in my place, threatened me, promised a bad time for my girl, and gave me a layer of guilt all in one breath." Dana nods. "Are you sure we're not related?" Maria laughs and then smacks the book. "All right all right, you can ask your questions, but if you're going to be making us all work, then we're going to do it getting tipsy!" she proclaims.

Dana bites her lip. "Fair enough." She shrugs and turns to the first tab with a sticky note poking out. Maria waves over the waiter and orders all of us another round and Bree a fat piece of Irish Potato Cake with a decaf coffee with Irish Cream creamer. It's one hundred percent alcohol free but tricks the senses into thinking you're having Bailey's. For a pregnant woman, that's key to not feeling left out.

"Love you, girl," Bree smiles and shimmies in her chair finishing off the cheese and bread appetizer.

"First on the list, the location. I have reserved half of a resort down in Cancun. It's one that Chase owns."

"Half? Why so much? This was supposed to be really small. Just family and a few friends." Instantly the nerves start to prickle against my hairline.

Dana takes a sip of her Poorman Stout. "Wow, this is really good!" she licks her lips then responds to my question. "It is going to be small. About forty people at most. Chase just wanted to make sure things were extremely private so we've cordoned off any rooms that might face the ceremony location.

"Oh, okay." I nod, less worried now.

"I know the flower issue from before was problematic but can we talk about it now? I need to have them ordered for the arbor we're having built, the walk, the reception tables and such." Dana scribbles notes down and I sigh.

Not sure what would work best, I blow out a slow breath. "I just don't want you flying in flowers or whatever."

"Gigi, you love white flowers. All kinds. Yes, you love daises but they're not in season, so why not have just a mixture of local white flowers that don't have a lot of scent?"

Dana looks at me for confirmation. "That would be really nice. I love white flowers."

"Excellent. I'll pick an array and make it lovely. Good, now the wedding dress you have. I'll have it shipped and ready."

We spend the next hour going over the final wedding details. By the end of it, I'm three Poorman Stouts in and finishing up half a cheddar burger.

"Okay ladies, and last but not least, the bachelorette party. Due to the circumstances," she looks at me with sadness. "Chase is not okay with you ladies going off and being alone even with bodyguards. He wants a combined bachelorette and bachelor party."

Bree, Kat, and Maria immediately start grumbling and griping. A lot of "Uncool" and "Not fair" are peppered with a few slurs of "Controlling" and "Party pooper." Get three women who love a good party, then tell them they can't have what they want, and you'll have three pissed off chicks.

Finally, I can't handle the bitching any longer. "Ladies, cut it out!" They all stop mid-gripe. "We've experienced the danger. I'm not going to risk any of you or put myself in a bad spot right before my wedding. I'm sure we can come up with something fun that's a little more low key." I start to ask if they have any ideas when Dana cuts me off.

"Oh, I wasn't planning on low key, just private," she

grins. "I have a plan, and Chase has loads of money to make it possible," she grins.

The girls all lean forward as if Dana is about to tell us a secret. "Lay it on us, girlfriend," Ria exclaims.

She looks around adding to the secret vibe. "Private yacht. A couple days before the wedding. Will have all of you and your guys. Ohh, and maybe I can invite my new boyfriend to come along!" she says excitedly then her eyes widen and she covers her mouth with her hand obviously trying to take back that bit of information.

"Dana! You have a boyfriend?" I ask, happier than I should be. Even though I know Chase is mine, knowing his very attractive, longtime friend and colleague has her own guy, makes me deliriously happy.

"Girl, spill it!" Maria slams her empty glass down.

Dana blushes crimson. "We've been dating for the past several weeks actually. He's," she inhales looking off into the distance. "He's wonderful. Good looking, built," she holds her hands out showing how wide her beau is. "And he's really good in the bedroom," her words tumble out like an avalanche barreling down a mountain.

"Woo hoo!" Bree high-fives her. "Thank goodness someone is getting some. Damn, I need to get some," she pouts again and we all laugh.

"You ladies are crazy," I nudge Maria. "Gotta pee, let me up." Austin makes his way to me from his booth across from us.

"Ma'am, you look like you're having too much fun. Think Mr. Davis will approve?" He asks with a sly grin knowing as well as I do that he would in fact, not approve.

I shrug and smile. "Does it look like I care?" I respond

defiantly. He laughs. Once we get to the restroom, he turns and waits for me to enter.

"You cannot wait by the door, Austin. It's creepy. Go stand over there," I point to the hostess desk. "Go hit on the pretty hostess; get yourself a date." He looks at me as if I'm speaking Greek. "Seriously, you need to lighten up. When was the last time you dated?"

"Well, I'd suspect it was sometime before I started working for Mr. Davis." He answers.

My mouth opens but the words are stuck. "N-noo way! You haven't gotten laid in like half a year!" I'm crushed for my big Southern charmer.

Austin grins wickedly. "Well now, ma'am I never said I didn't have relations since then. Just not an official sit down, have a meal, go to the movies type thing in a long while." He waggles his eyebrows.

I smack his thick bicep. "You sly dog, you!" I laugh and then grip his bicep. Solid cantaloupe sized guns is what he's packing. "Go show that pretty brunette these guns then slip her your digits!" I suggest.

"Ma'am, you're tipsy on your way to drunk. How about you go to the ladies room, and I'll worry about my dating record, okay?"

I roll my eyes. "Fine, but my advice…solid gold. Women can't turn down the hotness of hunky arms. It's like girl kryptonite. Swear," I cross my finger over my heart. He grabs my biceps turns me around and presses in between my shoulder blades giving me a little push.

"Go!" He reminds me. By now, I really do have to go.

Quickly I use the bathroom, wash my hands and check my makeup and hair in the mirror. Once everything is situated and in place, I open the bathroom door. The men's room is directly opposite and opens at the same time revealing the last man in the world I ever wanted to see again.

"Oh, my God. Justin."

"Princess, what good luck, I have. I was hoping I'd run into you," he says.

I glance over to the hostess desk, as expected, Austin is there, but he's not looking this way. Justin follows my gaze. Lightning fast, he grips my wrist and yanks me into the men's bathroom. Before I can scream, he has a hand over my mouth and the lock on the door in place.

"I've been looking for you, woman. Ever since a friend of ours sent me the posting in the newspaper on the society pages of your pending nuptials to that rich guy. I knew I had to find you. Throw my hat back in the ring." Justin leans close to me and inhales. "Christ, you smell fucking good. Just like you used to. Like coming fucking home," he lets his nose caress my neck. I whimper. "Now don't you say a fucking word or we're going to have a problem. You get me?" He says and I nod.

Slowly he lets go of my face. I shove him as hard as I can, whirl around and try to get the lock undone. I start to scream when his hand comes around my face again. I bite down on the flesh until his other arm comes up and his fist clocks the side of my head so hard I see stars. Before I can get my bearings, he has a hold of my hair. "So it's back to this, eh. Back to fighting. Oh, you remember how much I liked it when you fought back. There was always such passion between us wasn't there Gil?" He pushes me over to the tile wall, grabs a wad of paper towels, and shoves them into my mouth. The scratchy paper goes deep, gagging me. Nausea starts to rise and I tamp it down.

"Look, Gil, I just wanted to talk, and look at what you made me do. Now, I want you back." He presses his body into mine. "Christ you've always had a body that wouldn't quit but now, even more grown up, fucking amazing." He puts his hands on my hips and rubs his erection into my belly. I turn my head and try to scream through the paper but nothing comes out.

Someone knocks on the door and tries the handle. Just as I try to scream, Justin pulls my head back and slams it into the tile. "Be right out," he yells out to whoever is on the other side. When I look back there's two of him standing there. The force of the blow makes me see double. Then I feel Justin's hands at my waist going under my shirt. He pushes it up. "Oh yeah, I think I need to be reacquainted with these fuck-me tits." Justin cups them roughly as tears leak from each eye. "You have grown," he pushes down the cups, my breasts spilling out, nipples tightening instantly against the cold.

Justin pinches each nipple hard, and I start to gag again having trouble holding back the vomit. I breathe through the desire to throw up. The last thing I want to do is choke on my own vomit. "Oh, don't fight it. You know you like it, baby." He uses the one nick name that Chase always calls me and it makes my heart pound. I know I'm going to be sick. "Remember all the fun we had, how hard I fucked you. I'm going to take your right now, for old times sake. Then we can go back to my pad and take it slower. This time, I'll fuck every inch of you and I won't be so nice. You should have never run away," he scolds while kissing my neck.

A heavy banging starts against the door and I look at it longingly. "Don't you dare, it will be much worse if you make any noise." He cups my sex over pants, pressing his finger hard into the seam. "Oh yeah, you like that huh." The banging gets louder and I hope its Austin. If it is, he'll help me. "Cool your jets I'm busy with my girl in here!" he yells then starts sucking on my neck. I can feel the skin puckering and tightening under the power of his mouth. He always loved marking me, and as often as possible. Any way he could he would. Whether it was with his fists, his dick, or his mouth, he'd always left visible remnants of his power over me. "I'd kiss your mouth, but I can't have you screaming."

"Open the fucking door," I hear Austin's voice. A brief moment of gratitude covers my heart.

"Wait your turn!" Justin roars, then turns around. I lift my knee with all my night and as hard as I can slam it into his balls. He howls, pulls back his fist and socks me in the face, blood pours from my nose and things turn black and hazy. "Oh no you don't, you're going to make if feel all better, bitch!" he holds up my body. I'm not able to move. Between the alcohol and the blows to the head, I'm losing consciousness. Just as I feel a warm, wet sensation surrounding my right breast, a loud noise that sounds roughly like splitting wood and metal coming off hinges explodes in my ears right before a fierce pain around my entire breast hits me. It's like a hundred needles pinching me all at once. As soon as it came it left, the hands holding my arms above my head are gone. My body falls in a lifeless heap to the floor. I can't move.

Fading in and out, I hear the sounds of male grunts

and pain. Lots and lots of moaning and screaming then I'm weightless. Something is thrown over my chest and I'm being carried. The last thing I hear are my girlfriends crying, men crowding around then the sense of being lifted into a car.

"It's okay, Gigi. I'm taking you to the hospital."

I shake my head. Finally, I realize the gag is no longer in place. "Take me home. To Chase," I beg.

"You need a doctor." Austin pets my hair and holds me close.

Jack's voice comes from somewhere close. "Austin, there's a doctor meeting us at the Davis Mansion. Chase is waiting and be warned. He's furious."

All I can think about is that I'm in pain and I need my safe place. Chase is the only place I feel safe anymore.

★ ★ ★ ★

When I wake, I'm in bed. My face feels battered but nothing like I've experience before. The pain is tolerable. I look around and find Chase is sitting with his head hanging down, elbows on his knees in his standard worried pose. A woman I've met before enters the room. I think she's the doctor Chase hired to keep an eye on Phillip.

"Oh you're awake, I thought the medication would keep you out quite a bit longer," she says sweetly. Chase's head lifts up and his gaze meets mine. He looks as horrible as I feel. It's as if he's aged ten years in one night. "Gillian, how do you feel?"

Slowly I catalog my aches and pains. Instead of going through it, especially with Chase here, looking at me like

I'm a rare and precious gem, I respond, "I'll live."

Chase stands and starts pacing the room. His hands go right into his hair sporadically running through it and pulling at the ends.

"You've had a pretty serious traumatic experience today. It's okay for you to admit you're in pain."

I watch Chase as he paces. Every so often, he looks over at me longingly then anger slips across his face. I'm not exactly sure which Chase we're dealing with. I've categorized all that have made an appearance, but this one, it's beyond Angry Chase. It's possibly a few steps higher to downright Enraged Chase.

"Um, well, my head feels fuzzy and I don't remember what happened after I was punched the third or fourth time," Chase stops looking deadly furious. His hands are fisted at his sides. His lips are curved into a snarl and his eyes wild. "I'm okay, baby, I swear." I try to soothe his anger but it doesn't work. He shakes his head and continues his pacing.

A knock at the door startles me and I cringe as the pain in my head lances down my spine. A woman wearing a badge standing alongside Tommy is at the threshold of our bedroom door. "We need to speak with the victim, the woman announces." Tommy puts his hand on her shoulder. Chase inhales and clenches his teeth.

"She means Gillian. We need to find out what happened, Chase. Your guy, Austin, he's in cuffs downstairs," I open my mouth in shock, wanting to say something but nothing comes out. "He almost killed that man tonight. He beat him up so bad he had internal bleeding and they're trying to put his face back together," I gasp and tears form. Poor Austin. He risked himself for me.

"I wish he'd killed him," Chase says his face devoid of any emotion other than cold, hard, rage. Tommy pushes the door open and walks in. I turn away from him, not wanting him to see me right now. It's embarrassing enough that I wasn't able to get away, but to have Tommy see what Justin did to me, somehow it hurts more when its someone you know and care about.

The woman sits in the chair Chase vacated a few minutes before. "Hi, Gillian. I'm Athena, a detective with Special Victims. I'm going to need you to tell me what happened." I look over at Chase who's standing off to the side next to the doctor and Tommy. "Would it be more comfortable if we spoke privately?"

At the thought that Chase might leave the room, instant panic crushes down on my heart making it pound so loudly it's almost deafening. "Chase…" I whisper. He's to my opposite side in seconds.

"Baby, I'm not leaving. Never," his voice dips low and I clasp his hand.

"Can you have Tommy leave?" I whisper, and she nods.

"Thomas, we'll have the detective update you when we're finished here. A little privacy, please." Thomas nods and leaves.

"Okay, so tell us what happened?" she says softly. Her hair is short, a dirty blond color but her eyes are enchanting. A rainbow of colors. A mix between green, blue, and brown. They're honest eyes. Genuine. I know I can trust her.

"I went to the bathroom. Austin was waiting for me less than twenty feet away."

"Austin is the bodyguard?"

I nod. "Then as I opened the door to come back out,

the opposite door opened and there was Justin. He grabbed me, dragged me into the men's room and locked the door. I tried to scream but he covered my mouth. So I bit him."

"Good, baby!" Chase approves and I smile slightly. The detective looks at him in warning.

"Then he started saying these things like he wants me back, he'd heard that I was getting married and wanted to throw his hat in the ring," I swallow the bile that rises in my esophagus. Chase squeezes my hand for encouragement. Of course, he doesn't know how bad the story is going to get.

"When he dragged me over to the opposite side of the bathroom he slammed my head into the wall then gagged me with a bunch of paper towels. I couldn't breathe or scream through my mouth. That's when he started touching me. Saying how nice my body was and how much I'd changed over the years," The tears I had been holding back came rushing down my cheeks. I wipe them away angrily not wanting to give Justin even one more piece of me.

"Do you need a minute?" the detective asks.

I shake my head wanting to get this over with. "Then he pulled up my shirt and fondled my breasts," Chase's hand tightens on mine so hard I pull it away. "He punched me a few times, held me down, said he was going to fuck me quickly there in the bathroom, and then take me back to his house and do it slowly like old times. Said he liked that I was still fighting back. The last time he hit me things got really hazy. I remember hearing the door breaking down and pain on my chest," I lift my hand to my breast and pain splinters out like a starburst. I suck in a pained breath trying to breathe through the tenderness and throbbing ache.

"Did the attacker touch you anywhere else," she asks

writing something in her notepad.

A flash of Justin rubbing me between my legs comes to the surface. I glance at Chase under my lashes and then turn to the detective not wanting to see his face. "Yeah, he um held me against the wall while he played with my breasts, then cupped my sex roughly trying to encourage me to get excited and remember how it used to be."

The sound of something hitting the wall has all of us turning around. "Motherfucker," Chase roars. He pulls his hand out of a perfectly fist-shaped hole in the wall. The doctor rushes over to him. I slump in the bed exhausted and heartbroken. This is never going to get any better. We're never going to escape our pasts. This hell is forever going to be in our minds.

GILLIAN

CHAPTER SEVENTEEN

The doctor tends to Chase as I finish up with the detective. Just when I think I'm finished and can finally rest and deal with my man, the one that loves me beyond comprehension, who is literally doing a great job of beating himself up, she delivers the final blow.

"Gillian, I'm going to need to take pictures of your injuries." The doctor had asked me if I wanted her to do it while she did her exam but I declined. I shouldn't have.

Chase storms over to the detective. "I don't fucking think so." His anger is palpable as he stands in front of me breathing hard. He's a man on a mission, a mission to protect what he holds dear. Unfortunately, nothing can protect me. I'm a magnet for evil men.

"Look, Mr. Davis. I know your fiancée has undergone a lot tonight, but in order for Mr. Campbell's case to be adjudicated, we're going to need proof of the attack on Ms. Callahan's life and documentation of her injuries and the attempted rape."

Just the word rape sends Chase into a full meltdown. "I cannot fucking believe this shit. We have to protect the goddamned attacker's rights? That man"—he points to the bedroom door even though Austin was being questioned at the station—"saved her life tonight. He's a hero and should be treated as one!" I place a hand on his shoulder blade. The muscles bunch and tighten under his thin shirt. Heat radiates off him so strong it could power up an entire city with its electric energy.

The detective pulls out a camera from the bag she must have brought in. "I'm sorry Mr. Davis. Mr. Durham's injuries are life threatening. In order to prove that man is the hero you claim he is, we need proof. Otherwise it's he said, she said in court, and Gillian's not the one in surgery for a beating that could have taken her life. The attacker is." She finishes.

"Fine," he growls through his teeth. That jaw is working overtime and the muscle within is flickering like a lighter being turned on and off. "Let's get this out of the way so she can rest."

"Lights," she nods to Chase. He goes over to the wall and turns on the light to the highest setting. It's bright and blinding. It's as if I'm center stage and the big light is directly on me. Probably what Maria feels when she's dancing, only she flourishes in the light. Right now, I want to cower and hide, protect my body from pitiful gazes.

Athena looks at me, that soft, genuine glint I see in her eyes giving me the strength to do what she says. "Hold your hair away from your face," she instructs. Her camera flashes as she takes pictures of the bruises all over my face, and around my upper arms from where he gripped me and held me back. Then she snaps close ups of the bite mark and hickey on my neck. Chase actually growls when my hair is moved and that mark comes into view. Chase thinks of the space between my neck and shoulder as his special spot.

Now some other man has tainted that, for us both. I refuse to let the tears come back. It will be harder to pull through if I'm a sobbing mess.

"Okay, now your shirt," she says. I close my eyes knowing this is going to be devastating. I downplayed the treatment of my breasts in my recollection for Chase's benefit. When my shirt comes off, the finger print shaped bruises are everywhere. Chase tips his head back and grips his hair. I choke down the emotion raging a war inside me, wanting so badly to comfort him.

"Gigi, I'm sorry but you're going to have to remove your bra. I promise your face will not be in them but we have to be thorough." I knew it was coming but it doesn't change the gut wrenching fear of having to do this again. It's the first time in years that naked, battered pictures of me have been taken.

With a hand behind my back I flick the clasp of the comfy sleep bra I'd put on after the doctor checked me over. Taking a deep breath I finally I let my arms hang down in front of me. The detective's mouth opens in shock and her eyes close before she gets a grip and pulls the camera up to take the pictures. Chase looks at my chest and then falls to his knees, head hanging in defeat, fisted hands barely holding up his form. It's like a knife stabbing me in the heart watching him break down.

Bruises dot both of my breasts but that's not what's killing him. No, it's the full mouth bite mark around my right nipple. I recall the pain right at the end of the attack just before he must have been pulled off me. Looking down, I had no idea how bad it was. I'm greeted with angry, bloody indents, spaced evenly in a half moon shape from the top and bottom of Justin's teeth. The nipple is completely discolored a sickening purplish black where blood rose to the surface. Probably from the trauma of teeth clamping down prior to being yanked off.

The camera flashes just as I look up. Instantly I'm propelled to another time, another room where a detective stands in front of me.

Ms. Callahan, I'm going to need you to remove your shirt and underclothes so I can take pictures of the injuries. The detective is a large woman. I'd classify her as being very butch. Her hair is cropped short to her scalp and not a speck of makeup is applied to gentle her facade. It's clear this woman is tough as nails and just as pointy. She seems almost irritated that she has to take pictures of my beating.

"Um, can we just skip this? I don't plan on pressing charges," I whisper through a busted, bleeding lip. I can still taste the blood on my tongue.

The detective looks at me like I'm insane. "Are you kidding? You're just going to let some man beat on you like a punching bag and get away with it? This is for your own good," she lifts the camera and snaps a photo. "Take off your gown," she says and the tone of her voice reminds me so much of Justin I do what she says on autopilot, afraid she might lash out.

Tears slide down my face as she snaps picture after picture of my naked body. Then she crouches low in front of me and looks at my thighs getting really close to me. I step back as much in fear as embarrassment. "Don't move, I need to capture the bruising on your thighs where he forced open your legs and raped you."

Raped me. Did he rape me? No, Justin loves me. He just gets out of hand sometimes because he loves me so much. He tells me over and over how much I mean to him. How beautiful I am, how he loves to see his marks on me. He does it out of love. He doesn't realize how much force he uses.

I jump back and pull the hospital blanket over me. "I wasn't raped. Things…he uh, just got carried away. I wanted it. Him. He loves me and I love him. I'm not pressing charges. It was an accident," I nod repeatedly and wrap the blanket completely around my body and sit on the bed.

The detective comes close. I can smell cigarettes as she gets near. It reminds me of Justin. They probably smoke the same brand. She puts a hand on my shoulder and I flinch, she removes it quickly.

"What that man did to you wasn't love," she starts. I shake my head.

"I don't care what you say, I'm not pressing charges. I want you to leave."

The detective inhales then sighs loudly like she's being put out by being here. I wish she'd just go. Save someone else. Someone who's truly a victim, and leave me the hell alone. "Gillian, that man put his hands on you in anger. He punched you so many times your ribs are black and blue, two of them fractured," she starts.

"I fell down the stairs after we made love," I say in defense. That didn't happen but she doesn't need to know that.

"No you didn't. He. Beat. You. Up. Don't you get it? Can you be that dense?" The fear digs into my soul and I start to shake. "He's going to keep hitting you until you're fucking dead. Do you hear me? Dead. He doesn't love you, he loves hurting you."

If this is her way of trying to get me to see reason, it isn't working. Right now, I just want Justin. I don't think she should be talking to me like this. I'm only nineteen, scared, and I want my boyfriend.

"Where's Justin? I need Justin," I whisper.

"In jail until I get your statement. Without it, he'll be

released."

"You're not getting anything from me. My boyfriend and I had sex. He didn't rape me or beat me. Things got heated and after, I fell down the stairs. Now get out of here!" I scream.

The doctor rushes in. "I think she's had quite enough. Gillian, get back in bed. We need to wrap your ribs and tend to your wounds. Detective, have you gotten what you need..." the doctor asks but she doesn't answer.

Everything gets hazy, warps and fogs. A soft pinprick of light slowly opens at the center of my vision getting steadily bigger, bringing me back to a different room in the here and now. Arms are around me, a blanket covering my naked body. "Detective, have you gotten what you need?" Chase's voice clears the cobwebs of the past. "Baby, you're shaking. Was it another flashback?" he asks and I nod. "Okay, we're done here," he says to the detective.

"I've got everything I need. Gillian, I've got your statement recorded. We'll have it transcribed and you'll have to review it and sign it. It should be ready in a couple of days." I nod and turn into Chase's chest. For the first time I can breathe.

The detective leaves and Chase brings me to the bed. "I want to go home," I tell him. "Take me home," he nods and sits me on the bed. With great effort and extreme care, he puts one of his undershirts on me. I stand and he slips a pair of his boxers over my legs. Then he grabs a thick fuzzy robe from the closet and wraps me in it. He goes back into the closet comes out with pajama pants and a hoodie on, and my comfy slippers Maria bought me for Christmas. He bends down and brings each slipper to my foot as I step into it.

He links our fingers together, palm-to-palm and a sense of calm settles over me. Chase leads me out of the room. Jack sees us and grabs a set of keys. "Where to Sir?" he asks.

"Penthouse. My fiancée wants to go home." Jack curtly dips his chin. I'm certain he doesn't like this plan since the security at the mansion is much stronger but Chase is not a man you say no to when he's made up his mind. Jack snaps at two guys. I recognize them as Maria and Kat's bodyguards. "You two come with me tonight. I'll have reinforcements sent over within the hour." As we wait by the door, Jack goes over to Bree's bodyguard. "Don't let any of them leave until replacements have been sent. Got it?" he tells the tall beefy man. It dawns on me that I don't even remember his name. Too many whacks to the head this evening.

The big guy nods but responds, "Why are you so worried? We got the guy tonight, right? He's in jail?"

Then Jack says something that sends shivers down my spine and gooseflesh to appear on my skin. "We don't know that Justin Durham is the stalker. After seeing the guy, I don't think he is. Redding will know for sure by morning."

Chase rubs a hand down my arm. I wince but I don't tell him to stop. It's comforting more than it hurts. Having his hands on me is the only thing right now that can take away the filth of Justin's hands.

"Let's go," Chase orders as the two continue to argue about the stalker. I stop paying attention. There's nothing I want more than to be home with Chase.

The car ride seems longer than normal. When we enter the Penthouse tears prick at my eyes. This is home. Not some pink room with ugly pristine decorations. Chase leads me into the master bedroom. Even though the room is musty from being closed up it's still the best thing I've seen in a really long time.

"What would make you feel better, Gillian?" Chase asks softly as I scan our bed, the floor to ceiling windows, the decorations I haven't had a chance to change yet. Still it's more home than anywhere else. It's where I first slept the night with Chase and where I want to spend tonight wrapped in his arms.

I look longingly at the bed but my skin feels itchy and crawling with Justin's filth. "I'm dirty. Need to be clean," I mumble. He leads me into our bathroom. He dims the lights down so it's less glaringly obvious how ugly the marks are. Slowly he removes the robe then the shirt. I cover my battered breasts with one arm and tilt my head down. He carefully takes off the boxers and panties. Then he turns around and starts the shower, all without saying a word. I don't know what he's thinking or feeling and it's making me sick to my stomach.

When the water is the right temperature, he opens the door and leads me into it. I step under the warm spray protecting my chest and the raw flesh. Shivers wrack my frame until the most comforting arms in the universe encase me from behind. I lean into the naked chest of my man and close my eyes taking the comfort he gives just by holding me.

For long minutes, we stand there. He holds me until I wiggle and turn around chest to chest. It throbs when my breast hits his chest, but I don't care. Nothing could prevent me from being in his arms, hearing his heart pound in my ear, feeling his hands rubbing my back.

"I'm going to wash you now," he pulls back and grabs

my bodywash.

"No, yours," I say teeth chattering. Being surrounded by everything that is Chase is what I want right now. His scent makes me feel even closer to him. I want it flooding my senses. The shaking and chattering continues. It's as if I can't get warm enough. I turn around and set the temperature hotter. When I turn back, Chase is pouring the soap into a washcloth. "Hands," I say as his eyes meet mine. He nods stiffly. I put my hand out to have him squirt it into my hands. He looks at me, his eyes filled with hurt, anger, and sorrow.

He shakes his head. "I take care of what's mine," I shake my head hastily. He grips my hand with his, "Baby, I have to," his voice is horse and unsteady, full of raw need. I close my eyes and wait.

He lifts my arm and slides his hand up and over the limb, briefly washing over the bruises on my biceps and wrists. I've got the other arm over the wound on my chest. He rubs his hands over my clavicle making his way to the other arm. I switch arms so fast I'm certain he didn't have to see the worst of Justin's tirade. Chase lifts the arm and uses his hands to soothe up and down, effectively washing away the memory of that horrible mans' touch…at least for the time being.

Chase turns me around, pulls my wet hair into one long rope and sends it over my shoulder. He squirts more liquid into his hands and washes my back, down my bum and along the back of each leg and back up. I inhale at the familiar caress knowing it's Chase, the man who loves me and would never touch me in anger. When he makes his way all the way back he leads me to the water letting his hands follow the suds down my skin and to the floor. From behind, he leans forward and places his lips against the giant mark Justin left on my neck. He runs his tongue over the bruised flesh then kisses it no less than twenty times in soft baby pecks. "Still my spot," he murmurs and I choke back a sob, putting a hand out to the cold tile to hold me up as I nod my head so he knows I couldn't agree more.

With light fingers, he spins me to face him. Then he grabs the bottle of men's shower gel, adds another dollop, rubs his hands together and crouches low. He grabs a foot, smoothes his hand up one leg making sure to wash it completely, then repeats the same action on the other side. Every muscle is finally relaxing, turning to jelly under his comforting ministrations. Chase has always known exactly how to touch me. From the very first time until now, he just instinctively knows what's best for me.

He stands and squirts more gel on his hands and then looks at me sternly. "Remove your arm, baby."

"No, I don't want you to see what he did again." I allow all the emotion, shame, and disgust to fill my words.

"Every part of you is beautiful. Every inch of you perfect, and all mine. I'm taking back what he touched." His words brook no argument. "Non-negotiable," he uses the word that never ceases to make me smile. He's such a broody, but demonstrative man, and I love every inch of him.

"Only if I can touch you, too," I say.

"Always, I'm yours. Every atom, every muscle, every bit of skin and bone, it's yours for the taking."

Tears slip down my cheeks adding to the water already coating our bodies. On a deep breath, I move my arms from my chest and place my hands on his abdomen. The thick muscles bunch and tighten under my hands. I don't look down at his manhood because I don't want to know that he's disgusted with me, that my naked body right now isn't going to excite him, turn him on. I've never been naked in front of him without seeing his reaction to me *there*, virile and prevalent between his thighs.

Chase doesn't say anything. His eyes gobble up every inch of my wounded breasts. Slowly his hands cup the sides of the globes. He uses his thumbs to spread the soap over each nipple. I suck in a breath through my teeth as the soap covers the small open sores from Justin's teeth.

"Just breathe, baby," he coos coming closer. That's when I feel it, his hard flesh prodding my belly. I grip his shoulders and lean my forehead against his, emotions drowning me with relief.

"I was so afraid." My voice cracks.

"I know, but I'm here. He's never going to touch you again, I swear it." And I believe him but that's not what's bothering me.

I shake my head. "You don't understand…"

"What don't I understand?" He continues to wash my breasts, down my sides and belly.

"I didn't think you'd want me, now that you've seen me like this." I hug him close and he wraps his arms around me. The spray pelts against the sore muscles between my shoulder blades.

Chase kisses my temple. "Gillian, if you're naked, I want you. Bruised or not. You're still the most beautiful thing I've ever touched in my life. Will ever touch again," he promises.

"Then love me, right now," I plead.

He shakes his head. "Don't you see, me touching you…"

he swallows and I watch his Adams apple bob. "That is me loving you." And he's right. Every touch of his skin shaves away another layer of the attack from my consciousness.

I slide my hand down and fist his erection. "Then make love to me," I beg.

He pulls my hand away, brings up my fingers to his mouth and kisses each one individually. "I will Baby, when you're better," he uses that non-negotiable tone I'm usually so fond of. Right now I want to smash it into smithereens.

I hang my head and exhale. He's not going to touch me until I've healed. I hate Justin even more now. Chase turns off the water, wraps me in a thick towel then dries me slowly. He grabs another towel and ties it around his waist hiding away his desire from my greedy eyes. Again, he takes his time kissing each bruise one by one until I'm aching for him. He gets near the apex of my thighs and inhales. His eyes shoot to mine, "Christ, Gillian, I can smell you," he groans and I widen my legs offering myself. He mumbles something I can't hear, gets close, and nuzzles the skin inhaling. "That for me?" he licks his lips.

"Always," I whisper. He closes his eyes almost as if he's fighting with himself. I know the moment I've won because he moves my body to the vanity seat setting me down. Slowly he opens the towel and says the words that catapult me back to a similar, happier time.

"I'm going to give you some relief, but I'm not making love to you until you've healed," he says and I nod happily. I know my man so well. He can't ignore a wet pussy, especially when he considers it *his* pussy.

Chase lifts my hips, makes sure I'm leaning against the wall and comfortable before opening my legs. He bites down on his fat bottom lip and looks at the arousal waiting for him. The man is twisted in the sexiest ways. His hands slide under my bottom tilting my pelvis and opening me further. He's on his knees in front of me and it's the most sensual sight. Exactly what I need to see to erase the horror from earlier. Chase leans down and laps at the slick folds, delving his tongue deep. With one hand, I hold onto his hair and tug. He growls and sucks me harder swirling around my clit with the most talented tongue. Before long I'm panting, my head pounding in pain, though I won't stop grinding into his face. He takes me to the pinnacle of pleasure and then pushes me over it, into a blinding, satisfying orgasm. Chase licks and kisses me through my release.

When every tremor has left and I'm a lifeless bag of flesh and bones Chase kisses my lips. I can taste myself on him, and it tastes a whole lot better than the coppery acidic taste of my busted lip. He's careful as he kisses me, moving slowly down my neck. He makes it to my bruised chest and kisses each finger mark. Then his eyes settle on the dark nipple and bite marks. I cup his cheeks and he holds my gaze, then he gets close to the tortured flesh and with the tip of his tongue he licks around it, coating each wound with his gentle brand of ownership that's uniquely Chase. Using a softness I didn't think was possible, he brings the entire nipple into his mouth, swirls his tongue around the bruised aching flesh then pulls back, giving the tip a soft kiss. I can't control the tears as they wet my chest. He licks them away as well then kisses me again, making sure not to press too hard. He's the only man that's ever worshiped me.

Once he's made sure that every inch of my body is dry, cherished and replete, he dresses me in a clean shirt of his with no underwear. I can only hope that means good things for me tomorrow. He pulls on a pair of clean boxer briefs, his arousal still high and hard. I look down at it longingly. He shakes his head and pulls back the comforter on our bed. We both slip in, him behind me, spooned close so I can feel every bit of him plastered along the back of me. Moments later, his fingers tickle their way over my hip and under the shirt until his hand cups the breast that's not damaged. Well, not as damaged as its twin. With a heavy sigh he says, "I love you, Gillian."

I swallow down the lump in my throat, snuggle more deeply into his body and hold his hand against my body. "I love you, Chase. Thank you, for making it go away."

"I'll always bring you back to me." He reminds me of his constant promise. And he does. Each and every time.

X

"That's great news!" she exclaims into the phone. "Finally," she sighs. "Yes, okay, I'll make sure everything is cleared from his schedule for the next week. Thanks for letting me know, Jack," she says happily then hangs up the phone. She flops back to the bed, her small naked breasts jiggling. They're not as big as I usually like. Gillian's are at least a full size larger than hers but they'll do for now.

"What's going on?" I ask knowing something is up with the rich fucker.

Dana smiles bright in the dim light. She's really not bad looking. If she was a redhead with eyes the color of shamrocks she might do it for me. "They caught him!" she clasps her hands in front of her and bounces up to a seated position crossing her legs so I have a perfect open view of her cunt.

Sitting up, I extend a hand to hold myself up. "Caught who?"

"You know how I told you my boss and his fiancée had some crazy stalker following them around and hurting their friends?" Her eyes are happy and bright. This does not bode well for me.

Again, pretending to vaguely recall it, I crunch my brow together and lift a hand to my hair. "Yeah, you said something about it. Not much though."

"Well tonight, when I was at the pub with the fiancée and her three girlfriends he was there!" *Three* girlfriends. Should be two. I took care of Yoga Barbie.

"I thought one of her friends died? Didn't you say that?" I fist my hand into the blanket as her eyes narrow and she shakes her head.

"You see, that's what everyone thought, but it was actually this girl named Charity. So sad. She was only twenty but she looked so much like Bree everyone thought it was her at first. It wasn't. Bree's been laying low. Tonight was the first time she'd been out in the past couple months. And she's so cute with her tiny little baby belly," Dana smiles. The fucking bitch is alive? It takes everything I have not to punch this stupid cunt in front of me, but I need her. Deep breaths in and out.

After a moment I shake my head. "So, the one survived. But now you said the stalker was at the dinner with Gillian?" I ask.

Dana stops telling her story and looks at me. "How did you know her name?" Her eyes narrow.

I played it off with a smile. "Honey, I know who your boss is. Everyone knows who he's marrying. It's all over the smut mags," I grin.

She nods again and pushes her blonde hair behind her ears. "So the stalker was there and attacked her in the men's bathroom."

"What!" I yell then try to cover my outburst. If she doesn't start talking quick I'm going to have to cut her. "That's crazy!" I act surprised mostly because I am. Who the fuck attacked my woman and pretended to be me! Take credit for all my hard work? Fuck no!

"You see, it was her ex-boyfriend from years ago." That filthy dick. I warned him to stay away from her. "I think his name is Justin." Yeah, Justin Durham. I know exactly who he is. Last I heard he'd left town and disappeared when he found out Chase Davis and his goons were looking for him. "So anyway..." she smacks my thigh. I look down at the hand and cringe. She does that to me again and we're going to have a serious problem. As in she'll not have that hand any longer.

You need her to get to Gillian. Calm the fuck down.

"...and now he's undergoing surgery. Apparently, her bodyguard beat him up so bad he bled inside. Isn't that wild?" She finishes on a huff. "The horrible part is that he did a number on Gillian. He beat her up and tried to rape her." Her voice softens on that last bit.

Rape her? He tried to rape my woman! He's a dead man.

I look at Dana's naked body and think about how I'm

going to get out of here and not piss her off. I'll have to wait it out.

"What happens next? She's pressing charges right?" I ask knowing there were many times in her past where she didn't press charges that could have sent that fucker packing long ago.

"Yeah, Chase will make sure she has the best lawyers. He's definitely going to jail. Chase's lawyers are ruthless. Never lost a case," she says proudly. Again, I want to remove that from her face. Every time she talks about Chase like he's some saint I want to sew her lips shut and make a sick patchwork out of her lips, maybe like a scarecrow. She wouldn't be so chatty then.

I lean back and think about what I'm going to do to good ol' Justin. "So you say he's at the hospital now? Which one?"

"Why?" she turns her head and looks at me confused.

"Curious, is all," I pull her close and tweak her nipple. A moan slips from her lips. God, this cunt's easy. "San Francisco General" she says on a breath as I pull at the tightening tip. That's a good girl. I think I'll fuck her into submission then go check on Justin. Make sure he never makes it out of the hospital.

No one lays a harsh finger on my girl but me. And rape? Oh, he's going to pay for that. With his life.

GILLIAN

CHAPTER EIGHTEEN

"Keep your eyes closed," I cover Chase's eyes with my fingers and awkwardly lead him out of the car, down the dock to his yacht. If it hadn't been for Dana, I wouldn't have even known he had a boat. However, boat is the wrong word. It's definitely a water vessel, but the thing is ten times the size of my old apartment. It's white and aptly named "Angel" the words scrawled in gold cursive lettering just under the place where Dana is standing. All of our friends arrived at least an hour earlier. I wanted this to be special. He doesn't even know it's our combo bachelor/bachelorette party. Slowly, I assist him up the ramp.

Chase laughs and holds my hand tight as I trip over one of the rungs. "Careful," he smiles, eyes still closed. Even when he can't see me he's there, holding out a hand to catch me. I'll never get over finding my match, the man I'm going to grow old with and how in three days I'm going to be Mrs. Chase Davis. Like he always says, it boggles the mind.

We get to the top of the yacht and I lead him to the railing and set one of his hands on it. "Okay do you know where you are?" I ask, incapable of keeping the excitement out of my voice.

"Well," he grins and tips his head. "I hear water and can

smell the ocean air. I'd say we're at the bay on a boat." Smug bastard. Always guessing.

I come close to him and wrap my arms around his suit-clad body; I captured him directly from work not leaving him any time to change. "Yes, and no. Open your eyes."

He does and all of our friends and his cousins, sans Cooper, yell, "Surprise!" His eyes light up with merriment and something akin to joy. It's not a look I see cross his features very often, but right now, it's undeniably precious.

"What is this, Baby?" He slings an arm over my shoulder, bringing me close. "What did you do, gorgeous?" He kisses my temple.

I'm practically bouncing with glee. "It's our combined bachelor and bachelorette party! Dana and I planned it." I grin. She comes over and holds out her hand and I high-five her. "Thanks girl!"

"Anything for the big guy and his bride!" She clasps her hands over her heart. It's amazing how happy she is for Chase, especially when the whole time I was envious of their close relationship. Now I know they are far more like brother and sister, the same way Phil and I are with one another. Besides, she has a boyfriend. Speaking of…

"Hey, where's your boyfriend?" I ask.

Her entire face falls into a pout. "Had to work. He'll be arriving when we get to Cancun. Slave to the job, you know how it is," she glances at Chase and I giggle. Boy, do I ever. Usually Chase is knee deep in his work but lately, since the attack, he's been sticking close to home. We allowed everyone to go back to their homes but Chase still has people keeping an eye on everyone. Austin hasn't lost his job, and of course, Chase has Jack with him at all times, though I don't foresee us ever not needing security. As long as Chase is still bringing in crazy money and his companies stay successful, there's always going to be a risk. One he refuses to take, especially when it comes to my safety.

"Are you surprised?" I ask, wrapping both arms around Chase's neck. His hands go to my waist where he grips firmly.

He shakes his head. "You know, I've never been surprised or had anything planned for me. I'm flabbergasted." He blows out a breath smiling at all of our friends and family. "You constantly blow me away with your kindness." There is wonder in his tone and it fills me with warmth. Though it does sadden me that his mother, once she was back in good health never made a point to surprise him. At least she's meeting us in Cancun alongside her brother Charles. Wouldn't mind his Uncle here, but two full nights on a boat with Colleen Davis…this yacht is big but not large enough for that.

I smile and he kisses me softly. "I'll make note that you like surprises…like maybe the one I have for you under this skin tight dress." Wiggling back, I stealthily slide a hand down to caress alongside my breast, then ribs and over my hips. Chase sucks in a breath between his teeth, his eyes following the movement like a hawk watching its prey.

"There can't be much under there, baby." He grips my hip letting his fingers dig into the flesh there. He leans close and nuzzles my neck and ear. "Don't feel anything here," he slides a hand over my ass then squeezes the cheek.

"That's because I'm not wearing panties," I lick the side of his neck, letting my wild curly red hair hide the audacious move. He groans and hugs me close.

When I pull back and look into his eyes, they are dark and swirling with lust. "You temptress," he scolds. Now that one I like. I grin wickedly. "How am I supposed to enjoy my party knowing at any moment I can lift that dress and slide into home." He yanks me back to him, thrusting his very impressive erection against my belly. I laugh and kiss him several more times in succession.

"Um, hello, *amigos* here! *Conseguir una habitación!* Maria yells.

Chase chuckles. "What did she say?" I ask.

He grins and nips at my lips. "She said to get a room." I turn around and shoot daggers at her with my eyes. After all these years, I think it's time I get *Rosetta Stone* and learn Spanish. It's not smart allowing these two to have a secret way to speak to one another.

"Bring it!" she flexes her hands in a come-hither gesture.

"Only if you've got booze!" I holler as she walks over to the freestanding bar. Chase releases me as I take a few steps away to take in the view. Since we're the last to arrive the crew readies the boat to set sail. Once we're out, heading deeper into the horizon I finally allow myself to relax. It's been a horrendous few months but right now, a giant tranquil expanse of blue water and nothing but happy days are ahead for all of us. The time to let loose, be ourselves, enjoy one another's company and celebrate life.

A hand lands on my shoulder warmly. I turn and see Phil, brown hair blowing in the wind, a pair of Ray Ban knockoffs perched on his nose. He looks so good. Three months has done wonders for his healing. He's walking well, even with a little limp. Broken bones have mostly healed and he's doing well in physical therapy. One of his long arms curves me to his side and we both look out over the ocean.

"It's finally happening," his voice is a soft rumble over the sound of the yacht moving through the water. It will take a couple days by boat to get to Cancun but no one minds.

"What is?" I smile. I have a feeling I know what he's referring to.

"The elusive redhead is getting married. At least this man I wholeheartedly approve of," he grins.

I laugh and turn around locking eyes with Chase across the span of the boat. He's being entertained by Maria, Kat, and Carson. Those blue eyes sparkle as the sun hits the horizon. I blow him a kiss and he pretends to bite at the air. Phil laughs next to me. "You know, when I first told you we were dating you didn't think it was a great idea," I knit my brows together for effect.

He sighs loudly and then the corner of his mouth crooks up. "Well, in my defense, you were dating your boss, and my boss!" I continue to stare at him unimpressed. "Okay, okay, I was wrong, you were right, I owe you lunch or something. Will you drop it now that I've admitted the error in my ways?" He laughs.

I pretend to think about it bringing my finger up and twisting my lips. "Um hmmm…"

"Come on!"

"No, I forgive you for being an overprotective friend. It's okay. I've had a lot of practice between you and the girls. Chase though, his protective streak borders on insane. Sad thing is, I can't prove him wrong because of all the crap that's happened." I lean both forearms on the railing of the ship and look down at the water. "I just hope it's all behind us."

Phil pets my back. "Should we have reason to think otherwise? I mean they got Justin, he's going to trial for the assault and attempted rape. It's only a matter of time before they connect the dots between the gym explosion and killing that young girl."

My heart sinks. "I hope so. Right now, he's laying low but Tommy and Chase have people on him just in case. I don't really even know where he is. Last I heard from Maria was that he made bail and was living with his mother until the hearing."

"Good thing is in three days you'll be getting married and whisked away to your honeymoon. You don't have to think about any of it for a while. Unless you're staying in Cancun for the honeymoon."

I shake my head. "No, we're staying in Cancun for the ceremony and three days after to enjoy the resort and time away with all of you, but after that we're going to Ireland for two whole weeks. I can hardly wait!" The wind picks up and gooseflesh tickles my skin. Running my hands up and down my arms to warm them isn't helping. That is, until two much warmer hands cover the bare skin and run up and down.

"Cold, baby? I saw you from across the way and thought you might be chilly." Always aware of me. He's made it very clear that he plans to be a doting husband in all the ways that count. Apparently, my body temperature is included. "Here." Chase removes his suit jacket and places it over my shoulders. Sandalwood and citrus, the scent that has become a beacon of comfort, surrounds me as the heat from his body and jacket warm me straight through to my soul.

"Mmm, better. How about a drink?" I turn to Phil and he holds out a hand.

"Lead the way m'lady," he gestures toward the bar.

Chase nudges Phil in the shoulder. "I think you mean, *my lady*, Phillip," he says without an ounce of humor, but I know better.

"You were right, Gigi. Possessive much?" He shakes his head at Chase then hooks an arm around Bree as he passes. She whoops in delight when he swings her around. She's wearing a form-fitting turquoise blue dress that accentuates her perfectly round baby bump and swelling cleavage. The inflated breasts have been a much-appreciated side effect of pregnancy that Bree is riotously fond of. Even though she's only four months along, the bump is a nice size and the focus of attention. Maria constantly taunts Bree that it could be twins and one baby is hiding behind the other. I'm just excited to see her healthy, happy and glowing with Phil's baby.

Chase's eyes follow Phillip's move with Bree. "Takes one to know one, buddy," he grins.

"Oooh, he so got you, Phil!"

We all laugh and Chase leads me to the bar. I order champagne and down the first one in no time flat then hold my glass out for another. Chase leans over from behind me. "Not too fast. Wouldn't want you out of commission later on this evening." He uses that low throaty tone, the one that gets me hot faster than a hundred degree summer day in the California Valley.

I slam another glass and shimmy. "I'll burn it off on the dance floor." I grin sexily then make my way toward the most amazing women in the world. "Hey ladies…" I yell loudly with some serious voice inflection and wait for it.

Three instant rounds of, "Get funky!" come out of their mouths. Maria's hands go up in the air snapping her fingers. "Dana, get that DJ playing some tunes. It's time to *sacudir el culo!*" She shakes her ass. I watch the men around us. All eyes are on that tight dancer's behind as she rotates her hips like the expert she is.

All of a sudden, we're rewarded with a mix of techno pop and funky beats by none other than the Beastie Boys. Dana has some serious skill. I didn't even see a DJ but all of a sudden over in the corner is none other than a mixing board and a man spinning records. The moment we hear the cowbell it's on. If this was a "Dance for Your Life" competition, the four of us would win. The second the guitar gets going we are no holds barred dropping it like it's hot. Dana joins in, wearing her prim little business suit. Chloe, Chase's cousin bounces over shaking her breasts which currently look like two awesome ripe peaches jumping around in her tube top and blazer combo. How she hasn't been scooped up by a man I don't know but as soon as things settle down in my world, the girls and I are going to find a hot man to hook her up with.

For the next couple hours, the chicks get their dance on while the men either watch lustfully or join in. As I gyrate my hips I can hear a conversation between Chase and Carson. Instead of letting on that I can hear them, I just "Shake, shake, shake," as Taylor Swift's song continues on.

"Cuz, look at this. I feel like I've won the lotto. I'm… shit, you ever seen this many fine women who can dance like that!" he clucks his tongue.

Glancing over my shoulder, I can see Chase's eyes aren't on everyone else but solely on me. He watches my ass like it has a homing device. He runs a hand over his jaw and I imagine I can feel that stubble scratching delectably against my skin. "Lucky bastards, for sure," he swears.

After another couple songs it seems my guy has had enough of watching me shake it for everyone. Before I know it, I'm bumping and grinding into his body. Chase is a gifted dancer. I lift my hands up and sway, his hands running over my curves from behind. I clasp my hands behind his nape and rub into his erection. He groans into my ear and bites down on the side of my neck. Its slick with a hint of sweat but that only seems to turn him on even more. His tongue comes out and licks up the side to land at my ear where he nibbles. The beautiful torture of my ear, feeling his breath skate along my nape has me moaning and pressing harder against him.

"Careful, you don't want to unman me right here on the dance floor," he curls an arm around my waist holding me close. The DJ plays Christina Aguilera's *"Dirty"* which prompts a whole host of severely risky dancing all around. The men get the hint based on how the women are moving their hips sensually. Each guy cuddles up to his girl. Dana is nowhere to be seen. Probably missing her boyfriend. Chloe however is rubbing all over one of Chase's business associates.

"Who's that with Chloe?" I mumble getting into the music and the thrill of Chase's erection digging into the soft curve of my behind.

Chase slides his hands from my wrists around his neck, down my arms over the sides of my breast, ribs, then grips my hips possessively grinding harder into me. I moan while he continues to kiss the back of my neck. "Mmm," he exhales. Between seduction of my senses he finally answers. "One of my attorneys. He's a friend, but will also make sure the marriage license and documentation is taken care of after we're married." He bites the tendon in my neck and I swoon. Chase feels the moment I'm too far gone and twirls me around. His eyes are as black as the night sky over the open water. "I'm ready for my surprise under this dress. Say goodnight, Gillian."

"Goodnight Gillian," I say completely lost in him, this desire. If he doesn't touch me soon, I fear I may implode. He chuckles and lifts me into his arms. He really is my knight in shining Armani about to take the damsel in distress and make her sing.

Without a word, he walks through the crowd toward the door that leads to the rooms below. A bunch of raucous laughter and innuendos float over us as he makes his way down into the belly of the beast. At the very end of the long hallway is a set of double doors. He opens them with one hand, still supporting me with the other.

Once we're in the room he sets me down and pushes me against the door, lips greedily taking mine. Flashes of our first sexual encounter stream across my vision. His hands are everywhere at once, burning a fiery trail across the exposed inches of needy skin.

"Chase, I need…" comes out in a breathy whisper that loses steam when his hands yank up the slinky fabric of my dress to find thigh high stockings and nothing else.

"Christ on a cross, you'll ruin me," he says through the ever present clench in his jaw. Always trying to keep his control in tact but I want none of that when it comes to me. He's the only man I could ever trust to lose control and not abuse it.

The heat radiating off his body is enough to bring a small city to flames. His nostrils are flaring and his teeth are bared. He nuzzles the space between my breasts, pushing the top of my dress low in front before biting down on the expanse of smooth uncovered skin. He sucks at the soft swell of my right breast. With a swirl of his tongue, he soothes the quarter sized purple mark. Ever since Justin's attack, Chase has made an effort to leave his own passionate reminders of our coupling. He wants only his love bites to mar my skin. Now, fully healed from the attack, I'm ready to claim this man as my own.

Watching Chase lose his mind over me is exactly what I need right now. It's fueling the naughty side in me and I want to have some fun. I push Chase back, leading him backwards until his legs hit the bed and he falls into a seated position. I back up a few feet and slowly sway my hips from side to side, rubbing my hands all along my body seductively giving him a private dance. My guy's eyes are dark and hyper focused on each sway and dip as I twirl slowly around presenting him my backside. I move my hips bringing my dress back up over my bare ass. The moment he sees bare skin a slew of profanity fills the room. I curve my head over my shoulder holding the dress at my waist.

"See something you like, Sailor?" I grin.

"Fuck yes, and it's all mine. Come give it to me," he growls.

I would but I'm not done teasing him, so instead I shake my head no and wink at him. He tugs on his tie, pulls it over his head tossing it aside. Inch by inch, I remove the dress moving each hip from side to side in time to music only I can hear. Once the dress is off, I hold it in one hand still facing away from him and let it fall from my fingertips.

"Now Gillian, I won't ask again." He's losing his mind, and I love every second. Pride fills my heart and arousal slicks my thighs, readying me for what he's sure to make a memorable night.

"One minute, baby," I coo then go for the sucker punch and lean over still wearing only heels and stockings to remove my shoes.

"Fuck me!" he barks before his hands are on my ass cheeks holding them apart, his knees to the carpet and his tongue is devouring the dark little hole no man has touched but him. My hands are balanced on my shins as he licks up the arousal coating my thighs, delving his tongue where I want it most then back up to his newest obsession. "I'm going to take your ass tonight, baby. It's the only place my cock hasn't been and it's time."

Nervous fear coupled with equal parts excitement rush through me like a hot swallow of aged whiskey. My throat goes dry but that's the only part of me not soaking in pleasure.

"Chase…" I warn not sure about this step.

He spreads open the rounded globes of my ass even wider, sticking his tongue deep into the tiny rosette. The sensation is unique, different yet dark and exhilarating. Giving this last piece of me to Chase somehow makes our union seem deeper, darker in the most sensual ways.

"You going to give me what I want, baby? Let me take your little asshole, fill it full with my cock," he starts that dirty talk that never ceases to skyrocket me into a haze of unbridled lust. His words along with his seeking tongue are rocking me into a place of deep submission. I'm becoming a slave to his desire and I never want to be free.

"All of me. Everything I am is yours. Just touch me, Chase." I breathe out through the pleasure. At my words, he goes wild, standing, lifting me up and plowing his tongue into my mouth. I suck on his tongue and give him everything. Anything that I am and more. He brings me to the bed and lays me down, slowly peppering every speck with a kiss, a nibble, a swirl of his talented tongue until I'm so dizzy with the need to come I can hardly think straight.

Chase removes his clothes, and I watch as every inch of golden skin and hard earned muscle is revealed. He's the most stunning man I've ever known inside and out and in three more days he'll be mine forever. With a quick hand, he reaches into the side table next to the bed and pulls out a brand new bottle of lubrication. I'm not sure what it's for because I'm soaking wet.

With more boldness then I've ever had before, I open my legs letting him see how much I want him. "Don't think we need anything, baby," I lick my lips and trail a hand down between my thighs. With a quick finger I swirl two digits around the hard button of nerves moaning desperately before moving down to coat them with the proof of my need.

I hold out my hand, fingertips glistening. "See," I offer. He leans forward and pulls both fingers into his mouth swirling his tongue around the two digits. My sex clenches at the sight, so ridiculously turned on, physically aching to be filled.

Chase removes the rest of his clothes, his gaze focused between my thighs. He loves when I'm open like this, and with him, I'm not embarrassed. Much the opposite, I feel sexy, beautiful, and losing every ounce of control.

He leans down and kisses me long and hard. There's something different in this kiss, perhaps a bit more seductive. It works because I'm squirming under him. "It's not for your pussy, baby," he reminds me.

Chase kisses his way down my body and goes to work between my legs. Within minutes he has me screaming out his name, holding his face, thrusting wildly against his lashing tongue. After two back-to-back orgasms—he rarely allows for only one—he finally surrenders. When Chase Davis goes down on his woman, it's a feast, not an appetizer. I'm positive if I let him, he'd lick me relentlessly, bringing me to endless orgasms until I passed out.

I tug on his hair. "Had enough?" He smiles, my arousal coating his mouth and chin. It's fricking hot and makes me want to ride him. I pull a leg up and try to turn him around. He shakes his head then pulls a nipple into his mouth tugging and nipping at the erect tip.

"Mmm," I moan and hold him to me as he brings me to another sexual peak. The attention he lavishes on my breasts has me thrusting my hips up again, wanting him to fill me. Instead, he pulls away and rolls me over, and with a strong arm, he lifts me up onto my knees.

"Gotta have your ass, Baby. Need to make every inch of you mine," he whispers against the shell of my ear. Then he scrapes his teeth along my spine, pausing to kiss and caress as he goes. Once he reaches my bum he bites and nips on the space where the rounded part meets thigh. It tickles and I laugh. "Hmm, interesting," he says biting it again, eliciting another giggle. I fall down onto my forearms when he brings his fingers to my pussy, coating them with my essence before swirling them around my anus. He works one finger in pressing deep, the little muscle stretching against the intrusion. Then he licks my center as he fingers my hole. Soon I'm pressing back into his finger. He adds another finger and the muscle tightens and burns around the two questing digits.

With his tongue, he licks and flicks at my clit, the burning in my bum leaving completely as he stretches them out, I suspect making room for his cock. When he's got me moaning and begging for release he removes his fingers. The sound of the lubrication cap opening and closing breaks through the lust induced haze until a cold gelatinous sensation replaces his fingers at the small entrance. Chase leans over me and brings one hand around to flutter against that powerful bundle of nerves reminding my body I was just on the edge of orgasm when he pulled away.

Once he's got me moaning and delirious with pleasure he places the tip of his cock at the tiny puckered flesh. "This is going to burn a bit, but I promise it will go away and feel amazing. Do you trust me?" He asks. On that, I press back, pushing the head of his cock right into my ass. "Fuck!" he roars and grips my hips tightly. The invasion burns like a branding, fire hot pokers sizzling and centered at the spot where he's imbedded only a mere inch.

"Breathe, baby," he whispers as three fingers run over my clit then down to plunge shallowly into the wet heat between my thighs. He presses in further, centimeter by centimeter as sparks of pleasure skitter up my spine. I moan.

"That's it," another full inch and I exhale with the force of his girth. Those fingers of his slip up and down, swirling around my clit as he goes a little deeper.

Full, so full.

Every nerve ending seems to be prickling throughout my limbs. "Almost there, just a couple more inches and I'll be in you…" he groans and pinches my clit. Tingles ripple through me as if raindrops were suddenly pelting my naked body when he presses the rest of his thick cock in. He pinches my clit forcing the inner walls of my sex to clamp down hard. "Jesus, so tight. God, I love being in your little ass." He pulls out slowly and I feel every rigid inch of his massive cock sliding along swollen, pulsing tissue.

I close my eyes and inhale when he thrusts all the way back in. No pain, only fullness, pressure, and an enormous amount of pleasure moves through me. Chase shifts his giant erection in and out of me in soft, gentle movements. I can't take it. I need him to move! To take me *there*. Tremors and prickles of an oncoming monster orgasm rock through me. "Fuck me!" I yell completely beside myself with passion.

Chase's voice comes out strained, barely able to control himself. "Don't. Want. To. Hurt. You." He grates out through his teeth still moving his dick barely an inch or so in and out.

Those skilled fingers continue to run over my clit and into my pussy and back in a repetitive motion that's making my clit throb and ache. I clench down as hard as I can, using only my sphincter muscle. "Fuck me!" I beg. "Hard. I need it," I whimper my back arching pulling at his length. He feels like a metal pipe, strong and unbreakable as he fucks my ass in slow motion.

Finally, the words break through. His fingers move to my clit and twirl and pinch at the tight bundle. I scream out, "Yes!"

Then he's gone. He's a wild animal rooting into my body seeking his release. The constant pounding of his cock into the tight confines of my ass, feels like he's reaching high into my belly with his length. It shoots me into orbit. Gone. Every muscle I have tightens and cinches like a coat of armor, metal and unrelenting.

While I'm soaring, he lifts me up leaning my back against his slick chest. He curves one hand around my breast and the other around my hip for leverage before pulling back and slamming into me over and over. This angle has me hung up on his cock, reaching so deep inside me I see stars. Over and over he bounces me on his cock, allowing gravity to add to depth. When I think I can't take anymore, that I'm going to lose my mind, he tweaks my nipple tugging it hard, sending ribbons of excitement between my thighs. The pleasure is never ending, and then he proves he is in fact a God, by bring that hand between my legs, pinching my swollen knot and shoving that colossal cock deep into the tight dark hold wracking my frame with a brutal orgasm. Lights flicker behind my eyes and my body feels like jelly but I hold strong, *wanting,* no *needing* him to get there.

Finally, he loses it. "I love fucking you!" Chase roars, holding my hips to his, he leans me back over, my hands barely make it to the bed to hold myself up when I feel his balls slapping against my pussy. The grip of his hands on my hips is bruising, his body so tight and bowed back as he forces jet after hot jet of his release into my backside. With a shaking hand he lifts me to him, and we tumble to the side.

Both of us breathing so rapidly you'd think we just won a marathon.

"This proves it."

I can barely keep my eyes open, wonderland tipping me into darkness. "What does?" I mumble.

"We're definitely going to fuck each other to death."

A wide grin and two strong arms hold me in place. "It would be a good way to go," I whisper before blackness takes me.

GILLIAN

CHAPTER NINETEEN

Bang…Bang…Bang Screeches through the warm snuggly place, forcing me out of a really beautiful dream about marrying Chase. The noise continues to thud loudly against the door. I sit up and look at the offending piece of oak wishing a vortex would open up and swallow the entire thing whole giving me a full eight hours rest. Hell, I'd settle for a solid six hours. Chase hops up bare-assed naked and the banging starts again.

"Davis?" I hear Tommy's voice flit through the wooden door. Groaning I flop back down allowing the comforter to fall over my head and wait it out.

I can hear a ruffling of clothes. "Just a minute," Chase hollers, while likely putting on something. So much for a lazy Friday morning in bed with my guy.

The door opens with a rattle of the hinges. "What is it?" His tone is harsh and accusing.

"We've got a problem," he whispers and I pull the coverlet from my face and hold it against my bare chest. Clearing my throat both men look over at me. Chase is wearing a loose fitting pair of pajama bottoms I packed for him and nothing else. Drop dead gorgeous. I should be the one using that particular endearment he sprinkles in every so often. The long layers of his hair are a wild mop on top of his head making him look younger and less conservative. Tommy twists his head lifting his chin to the open hallway then the two walk through and close the door. Fine, leave me out of the loop.

Falling back to the bed, I wait and try to imagine every possible reason that Tommy could be knocking down our door at, I lean up and look at the clock, at seven in the morning. I'm certain we didn't get to sleep until well after two a.m. once we finished having the most intense and kinky sex of my entire life. Thinking back to it, the way Chase eased me into this new territory was so seamless. Made me wonder if that's how our marriage would be. Even though he's only five years my senior, it's as if he's so much more knowledgeable, wise in the ways of the world that I haven't scratched the surface of in my twenty-four years. Definitely in business, and between the sheets. With those two areas he's got a full leg up against what limited experience I bring to the table.

I fall back into a fitful light sleep until the bed shifts and Chase's woodsy smell enters my senses. Like a leech, I reach out, find his warmth and then pull him down to me. He oomph's and chuckles. Once I'm covered in a personal Chase blanket, I open my eyes. His, however, are not the sparkling ocean blue they usually are in the morning. No, they're calculating and a bit hard.

"Hey, what's wrong?" I worry my lip and slide my fingers through the hair just above his ears, letting my nails scratch along his scalp the way he likes. He closes his eyes then opens them.

He kisses me. "You know I'm going to protect you,

right?" he offers. Words like that are usually followed by bad news or information that's going to devastate.

I follow his gaze as his eyes seem to float over my features. "What is it?" I ask.

"Justin is dead. Hung himself." He says the words devoid of emotion.

Images of the four years I stayed with Justin flash across my mind like a strobe light, pictures of our life together in a twisted home video. Some of it was happy, beautiful even, but it doesn't outweigh the beatings, the degradation, or the loss of the child I carried. But for someone like Justin to hang himself? It doesn't add up. I shake my head. "Doesn't make sense, he was far too self-absorbed to end his own life. Are they sure it was self-inflicted?"

Chase shrugs. "We never know what goes on in a man's head when he's facing real jail time."

I knew Justin better than anyone. There is absolutely no way he'd commit suicide. "Did they find the connection to the stalker and Justin?"

Now I know something's not right. Chase tips his chin down and sighs. "That's what Jack is worried about. Thomas and the investigators have not been able to find a single link to any of the notes, phone calls, or the explosion and the murder of that innocent girl. He had to be the one. He attacked you, tried to rape you in that bathroom..." He ends on a snarl.

"Yeah, but as much as you hate hearing this, Justin would have done that to me anyway. He's always seen me as a plaything to do whatever he wanted. Smacking me around, fucking me in public, those were things that used to get his rocks off." I can tell Chase is having a hard time hearing this bit of information. He stands, fury a palpable wave rolling off his skin.

"All I know is the fucker is dead and I'm not sorry he is!" He tugs at his hair with both hands then forces the curtains aside to present the most startling view of the ocean. He opens the window and lets the salt air fill the room.

Not caring about my nudity, I stand and put my hands around his tense form from behind. The lines of anger and rage are physically showing through his skin as seen by the bulging veins and clenched muscles. Using his abs as an anchor, I nuzzle into his shoulder blades. "I'm sorry for his family and those who cared about him, but I'm not sorry he won't be hurting another woman ever again. He was a serial offender. If it wasn't me, it would be another unsuspecting woman. I'm sure the cops will find the connection they need."

His shoulders rise and fall as he takes a deep calming breath. I can feel the tension slowly slip from his arms and chest. Chase takes both of my hands, pulls them to his lips and kisses each finger like he's done a million times before.

"I have a present for you. I was going to wait until the day of our wedding but I want you to have it now. Wear it now. Then you'll understand how deeply gone I am for you," he says as if he's speaking to the open expanse of ocean not bothering to turn around.

I smile against his back and giggle. "I like presents," I say then nip the hard muscle of shoulder. He laughs lightly and spins around capturing me. His eyes take in my naked body from the tip of my red polished toes all the way up to the fiery strands of my hair.

"There is no woman in this world more beautiful than

you. I'm never going to forsake you or take advantage of the gift you bring to my life. You, Gillian, you make me a better man. Happier, stronger, and excited about life. I want to be that for you."

Leaning forward, I snuggle into his warm neck. "But you are, Chase. You're all that and more." I kiss the pulse point on his neck and appreciate the feeling of his heartbeat against my lips.

"Hold that thought," he lets me go then finds his suit coat that I wore last night. He pulls out a long, thin box. I take the cream satin robe that is lying over the end of our bed and pull it on. The fabric feels like butter smoothing across my naked skin. It's sensual and perfect for the moment. Chase brings me over to the large reading chairs facing the ocean view. The sea breeze blows his hair enticingly. "Open it," he murmurs as I settle into his lap feet up and tucked into the space between the chair cushion and arm.

Slipping the white bow off the teal Tiffany's box I look over at him. "Over spender," I chastise.

"Who me? Never," he mocks being offended.

I roll my eyes and open the box. Inside is a thin chain. At the very end is platinum infinity symbol pendant. The word "love" intertwined with the symbol in a cursive text. It's breathtaking and so magically Chase, there aren't words to describe how much this gift means to me.

"Do you like it?" he asks, tracing an infinity symbol over the fabric covering my knee. I think he does it subconsciously which makes this gift even more special.

"More than like it. I *adore* it and what it means…" I choke back the emotion. "Chase its perfect."

The smile he gives me is boyish, uncertain, depicting

a young man who wasn't sure he was going to please his girl. It's one of the first times I've ever seen him unsure of himself and completely unguarded.

He kisses me softly. "So you'll wear it on our wedding day?" he asks almost shyly. Shy Chase. An entirely new, yet lovely side I'm seeing for the very first time.

"I'll wear it every day if it means you're mine," I whisper against his lips. He grins so wide I can feel his teeth.

"We're going to be so happy," he says while he places the chain around my neck. The pendant lands perfectly just above my breasts. Chase turns me, opens the robe, and looks his fill of my bare breasts with his symbol twinkling in the sunlight. With ease, he leans forward and places a warm kiss directly over the symbol.

"Through infinity, my love," I say back to him before sealing it with my own kiss, only this time I've let the robe fall to my sides and properly thank my soon to be husband for his wedding gift.

★ ★ ★ ★

A private brunch has been set up on the sun deck where all the girls are waiting for me to arrive. When I get out of the shower there is a white bikini hanging on the door. It's a simple suit with a triangle top and strings that tie at each hip. The wow factor was the word "Bride" written across the booty in crystals or cubic zirconia. There was a little note sitting on the vanity in Maria's handwriting. The note simply said, "Wear this and meet us on the sun deck for brunch."

Not being one to ever rain on a parade I put the suit on

and it fits like a glove. So much so that the triangles seemed a bit revealing but this is a private party. I also secretly enjoy riling up Chase. When he sees this tiny bikini and how much of me is exposed, he's going to lose it. Hopefully, in the best possible way ending with the two of us in a tangle of limbs like earlier this morning. I snicker while putting my wild red hair into a messy bun on the top of my head. A little sunscreen moisturizer, a swipe of lip gloss and a layer of mascara and I'm off. As I head out, I grab the shimmery tunic cover up. It's mostly see-through but it covers the essentials making me feel a little less of an exhibitionist.

Once I make it to the deck, I hear some calming spa music playing. Maria and Kat are both lying almost completely naked out in the sun, getting a suntan massage, a towel over their bums. Dana jumps up and hugs me when I arrive. "Today's the private girl part of the bachelorette party!" The men are on the other deck drinking beer, smoking cigars and playing cards. I've got the chef making sure they have men type food and the big screen TV is on some live sports game. So it's just us girls," she practically squeals. This is an entirely different woman than the one I've known for the better part of a year. Regular sex must be doing wonders for her because this lady is sweet, fun, and excitable. The old Dana was kind, reserved, and staunchly professional. I decide I like this Dana much better.

"Is it normal for them to be lying in the sun while doing that?" I ask.

Dana shakes her head. "No, they wanted to get a tan while getting a massage."

Maria lifts her head and pushes her sunglasses up into her black hair. "Double whammy *chica*. You're looking nicely fucked *cara bonita*," she grins. "I'll have to pat Chase on the back for giving you that awesome glow," she chortles then stuffs her head back into the hole in the table.

"You're just jealous," I make a lame come back.

It's muffled but her reply can still be heard. "Now you know, I be getting mine, all day, every day, every way."

The rest of us laugh and Bree walks over in an awesomely crazy two piece suit. The triangles over her newly inflated pregnancy boobs are covered by twin Buddha heads. The bottom is also a string bikini with a circular sun right on her pelvis. The entire thing has paisley print and henna style swirls in rich yellow, orange and sienna. Her baby bump is out loud and proud. I lean down and kiss the bump and have a little chat with the baby. Bree just stands and allows it. She knows by now that if her sisters want to talk to the baby it's just easier to comply.

A server comes up and hands me a mimosa. The entire space looks like a comfortable mini spa. There are the two masseuses but there are also giant deck lounge chairs and quaint bistro tables. The entire ocean is in front of us, and behind, there's a huge spread of breakfast foods, a variety of juices and a server to fill drinks, clear away dishes, or get us whatever we need. There's also a person waiting in the corner with a bucket and tote full of stuff. I point over to her. "Dana, who's she?" I go sit down on one of the cushy lounge chairs in the shade. This white skin of mine turns lobster red under too much sun. I'm going to keep my skin as milky white as possible. New freckles are not my ideal accessory. However, this stunning chain and necklace is my new favorite.

"She's here to do manicures and pedicures. How about

we get her started on yours?" she offers and I nod.

"Sounds good to me." The woman is young, probably just out of cosmetology school but she has kind brown eyes and blonde hair.

Efficiently, she sets up her tools, the footbath and hand soak, and has me put my feet in the water. Bree sits next to me and Dana stands off to the side. "Dana, you're participating," I say firmly. "You can't just stand on the side. You've become one of our friends. And Chloe was invited too, right?" I ask.

Dana comes over and sits in another lounge chair. "She was, but I'm afraid we won't be seeing her. Apparently, she needs to sleep off last night," she clears her throat. "Maxwell, our attorney is also unable to attend the boys gathering preferring to recoup after last night's partying."

"Oh, I hope they feel better," I sip my champagne and Bree looks over at me like I'm an idiot.

"Seriously? They're both sleeping off last night? They were hanging all over one another. I'll bet you a hundred dollars cash they are in bed together right now."

I'm certain my cheeks are reddening as I realize how lame I was for not putting two and two together. "I'm not taking that bet. You're so right. They were all over each other, like white on rice!" I giggle and she nods vigorously.

"Speaking of all over each other, I want to talk about sex," I blurt out needing to discuss last night.

Maria's head pops up. Kat takes a bit longer but then leans her head up and pushes her glasses on top of her head. "Now you're talking," Maria sits up naked as a jaybird, breasts bouncing all over the place, and I mean *all* over the place, as our girl is very well endowed. Her body is like Jessica Rabbit only toned to the nth degree from her dancing career. Standing, she shoves her hands into her robe, ties it off and accepts the glass of champagne and orange juice handed to her. Kat is quickly on her heels only she's far more demure in her approach keeping her essentials covered.

Once the girls are all sitting in a circle Maria looks pointedly at me. "Spill *Hermana*. What's on your mind? I gulp down the rest of my mimosa and gesture for another. The steward brings over the champagne.

"Just the champagne this time, thanks," I smile and then turn to the four women waiting patiently. It's a little awkward talking about this with Dana present, Chase is her boss. "You can't spill this to Chase," I tell her honestly.

She shakes her head and crosses her heart. "I promise," she whispers and then looks around as if Chase was standing behind her.

"Okay, so last night, Chase and I had um…you know," I try to get the words out but they're stuck.

"Sex?" Maria offers.

I nod. "Well yeah, but we had the other type of sex," I gesture with my eyebrows. All four of them look at me confused. Sighing I suck in a deep breath. "We had anal sex for the first time!" The words tumble out of my lips as if they are rocks falling off the ledge of a cliff.

"And…?" Kat says completely unfazed.

Bree clasps her hands behind her neck and leans back into the chair closing her eyes. "Mmm, I love ass sex," she murmurs happily as if she's currently remembering a time when she had it.

Surprisingly, Maria doesn't say anything but I forge on.

"So you've all had it?" I ask dumfounded. My three soul sisters nod. Dana looks petrified and shakes her head.

"Okay, so Kat, do you do it all the time?" I ask shocked that we've never ever in all the years we've been best friends discussed this. Right now, it seems all the more important. Maybe because it was new to me, I feel like a virgin telling her besties about her very first time with a man.

Kat plucks a grape off the table between us that's filled with a bunch of finger foods and noshes and plops it into her mouth. "No, I wouldn't say regularly. For me it's kind of kinky and exciting. Plus, you have to be really relaxed in order for it to feel good. Carson and I have only done it a couple times."

"You've done it with Carson? How did I not know this?" Now I'm feeling like the loser in a group of cool girls.

Kat laughs. "What did you expect? I'm going to jump for joy and tell you every time I've had anal?" she snickers.

I shake my head rather annoyed. "Bree, what about you? What's your experience?"

"Well, I've not done it with Phillip yet. He seems to think it's going to hurt the baby. I'm betting he's never done it and afraid to try something new. But he was married." Her eyebrows pinch together prettily. Everything about Bree is pretty. "Don't all married people do everything?" She shrugs then pouts. "My last boyfriend was a serious ass man. He'd take my ass any time I gave it to him. Once the newness wore off it kind of got boring."

"No, I think that was your ex. He was dumb as a rock but hotter than Hades in the dead of summer," Maria chimes in.

"True dat!" I joke. Bree grins and nods excitedly.

Maria still hasn't contributed. "So Maria, what's your experience?"

She clears her throat and slams the entire glass of champagne in one swallow. Not a good sign. The steward immediately pops up out of nowhere and fills her glass to the brim.

"My experience isn't pretty." Maria says flatly. I know that tone. There be monsters hiding under the bed in that tone.

Just as I'm about to change the subject Bree asks, "Meaning you didn't like it?"

Maria shakes her head. Her face turns hard and her eyes lose their warmth. "No honey, it means I didn't choose it. Antonio took what he wanted, when he wanted, and didn't take his sweet time preparing for the big event." She stands, twirls on a toe her robe flapping in the breeze. "I have to tinkle," she says in passing.

"Fuck, fuck, fuck!" Bree slumps when Maria is out of earshot.

"Shit Bree, even I saw the signs!" Kat says and throws a grape at her.

"I didn't know. She never talks about Antonio. Gigi told us a lot about what Justin did to her but Maria has always been so tight lipped." Bree brings her hands up to her temples and rubs. Dana sits watching the verbal lashes back and forth.

"Honey, it's fine. Ria's a big girl and can handle it. Just don't say anything about it when she comes back or she'll get all grumpy and pissed. When she wants to talk about her experience, she will. I'm certain it won't be here while we're a couple days away from my wedding. Maria has this thing about tainting experiences."

The three girls nod and lay back switching the subject. Maria comes back in and sits in her seat looking refreshed and back to normal.

The elephant hangs heavily around the group when Dana blurts, "Gigi, that necklace is beautiful. Is it new?"

I narrow my eyes at her. If she had anything to do with picking it out I'm going to be extremely disappointed. "Why, have you seen it before?" There's a hint of malice coating my tone that I didn't mean to have.

Her head juts backward and a hand comes up to her chest. "No, I just thought it was pretty."

"So Chase didn't ask you to order this?" I need to know if this was as special to him as it is to me. She shakes her head. Immediately, the frustration poofs away and I smile wide and hold it out to the girls to get a good look. "It's my wedding present. Chase is always tracing infinity symbols on my skin when he's touching me, and he had this made as my wedding present. He's going to die when he gets his!" I laugh.

"Why? What did you get him?" Kat asks.

"I got him personalized infinity symbol cufflinks!" I laugh. The girls giggle.

"You guys are like living in a romance novel," Bree says wistfully.

I grin. "I know, right?" Closing my eyes I lean back and let the ocean breeze smooth over my skin and just enjoy the moment. "In two days, I'll be Mrs. Chase Davis."

Dana gets up to leave. "Need to go check on the guys, make sure everything is going smoothly." The four of us boo her announcement, but she hustles off ready to do her job. I give her credit. She's done an amazing job with the wedding plans, and making sure everything goes perfectly, this trip the icing on the cake.

"Toast!" Maria calls out when she's gone. All four of us bring our champagne glasses together. Bree's is filled with sparkling cider but she's enjoying it anyway.

"My turn for a toast!" Bree proclaims. She takes a deep breath and looks at each of us in the eyes. "To always knowing what's important." Her hand goes to her belly. "And remembering that with every breath we take, we are loved and connected by a bond that can never be broken. The four of us, it's who we are for the rest of our lives."

"Salud!"

"Cheers!"

"Amen, sister!"

X

The shadows and the dark clothing I'm wearing hide me from the other tourists, and I slip into the space where my girl is set to get married. Imagine my good fortune when I arrived two days earlier than planned and found absolutely no security around the location of the wedding. It was easy enough to get the details from the paperwork in Dana's office right down to the efficiently marked rooms on a map. Each room has a Spanish name, sticking with the Mexico theme. I never said Chase was stupid. He's smart enough to want the most perfect woman in the world. Just stupid enough to not know how to keep her. I scan the sheet of paper I copied from Dana's office.

Ceremony - Outside on the overhang with a perfect one hundred and eighty degree view of the ocean.

Reception - *Sala de Sol* meaning "Sun Room" in Spanish.

Grooms Quarters - *Sala de Luna* meaning "Moon Room"

Bride's Room - *Sala de Diosa* aptly named "Goddess Room"

The bride's room is open, filled with plush furnishings, nice for a woman preparing to marry her man. This is the perfect place. I scan the windows, the connecting doors and make a plan. There's one door that leads from this room out the back, down a pathway to where I can have the laundry cart waiting. I'll swipe a maintenance uniform when I'm done here.

The worst possible scenario is that Chase has a goon guarding the door. That won't be a problem. Nothing a little Etorphine won't cure. After a great amount of research, that animal sedative was the perfect plan and easy to get. All I had to do was break into an equine veterinary clinic. The sedative is designed to knock out horses. They had it locked up, but nothing a solid axe to the cabinet didn't fix. I even swiped the antidote, though I don't plan on using that on his goons. If they get medical treatment fast enough they might make it. Though I don't really care either way.

Laughter bubbles up and out into the dark, empty room. The noise echoes off the walls sharing in this moment of exquisite peace. It's going to be too easy.

Two more days my sweet and you're back to being mine.

313

GILLIAN

CHAPTER TWENTY

Contentment.

That's the prevailing feeling running through my veins, making my heart pound, wanting to jump out of my chest, as I look at the place where I'm going to marry Chase. The breeze is blowing softly, tickling my skin as if being caressed with a feather. In front of me are dark cappuccino-colored chairs with white fabric seats set up in rows of four across, split down the center where the aisle is. The aisle is no less unique. A spiral of white flowers lead up to the arbor in large sweeping swirls. The arbor was handcrafted for today's event and is flowing with sheer white fabric running down each wooden beam creating a softer effect. There's a variety of carnations, lilies, and more that I can't name in a long line of circular tufts running along the main beam that will be over our heads as we say our I dos.

"It's incredible," I whisper to Dana who's standing quietly next to me. "More than I ever dreamed I'd have in my lifetime…"

Dana smiles brightly. "I'm glad. You know, before you, Chase rarely smiled. Now he smiles all the time but mostly when he's near you. Honestly, I think you're the best thing that's come into his life."

I smack myself over the head as her kind words dig deep into my heart. How I could have ever been jealous of their relationship seems so utterly ridiculous now. "Thank you, Dana. I know Chase cares for you a great deal. So, your boyfriend, he'll be at the wedding, right?" The happiness she exuded completely dissipates when she shakes her head.

"He was supposed to come to the wedding. He showed up yesterday while everyone in the party was doing their own thing and you and Chase stayed in. We had a lovely evening of our own," she grins. "Then this morning he woke me up and told me he had to go back to the States. That there was *another* emergency with work. He's at the airport now, taking the next flight out. I mean, he's an accountant; what could possibly be so important that it couldn't wait a day or two?" she pouts.

I pull her into a hug. "Sorry girl. Maybe next time," I offer and she shrugs. Then I watch as she puts on her professional armor piece by piece. Her back goes straight, her eyes turn sharp and she looks over at me ready to take on the world.

"No worrying. Today is all about you and Chase and having the best day of your life! Let's go get you dressed."

I follow Dana to the *Sala de Diosa*, Goddess Room in English. We enter and my least favorite person in the world is waiting. "Hello Ms. Davis, how are you today?" Dana coos. "You look lovely as usual." She ladles on the compliments.

"Yes, well, some of us are early risers. You look perfectly put together, dear." Colleen Davis's thin lips tip up into what I think is the closest thing to a smile anyone has ever gotten. Dana goes over to her and kisses her cheek. Apparently, the distaste only extends as far as women who love her son.

"Wish I could say the same for Chase's soon-to-be wife," the remark biting and cold as she assess me with a calculating gaze.

Setting my essentials down on the bed, I look down at myself. I'm in a white velour tracksuit that once again has writing on the bum. Though this one says, "Bootylicious Bride." Chase thought it was the funniest thing he'd ever seen and promptly took a picture of my ass and saved it as his background on his iPhone.

"You realize that today is my wedding day, right? To your son?" I remind her with as much disdain as I feel she deserves for her comment. Super low class though I keep my mouth shut.

"Yes of course, dear. You needn't be so testy. I'm the one with the problem. My son is marrying a gold-digging whore with a John that wants her and anyone around her dead," her tone is as sharp as a serpent's tongue and just as evil.

Dana gasps, mouth opening in shock. At that moment, my salvation comes barreling through the room. Maria, Bree, and Kat plow through the door all laughs and joyful cheer. *"Goin' to the chapel and we're...gonna get married,"* they sing, pulling me into a little dance. When they've gone through a full rendition, I'm smothered in snuggles and love. Just what I need after Colleen's bitter words. Maria hold's me at arm's length, spins me around and smiles.

"Looks awesome and your *culo* is bootylicious for sure!" she says with enough Italian Spanish flare to outlive any Negative Nancy trying to ruin my mood.

"Mmm-hmm," Bree pinches her lips together and assess my rear. "That was the private yoga lessons for sure.

Damn, I'm good at what I do," she flips a lock of golden hair over her shoulder.

"Okay ladies, hair and makeup will take you in the room down the hall. Then once you're ready, we'll allow the photographer to get some shots of you." Dana announces.

Kat comes over to me, holds my hand looking over my shoulder at the sour-faced woman sitting in her wheelchair behind me. "You okay?" she whispers her brows pulling together. I haul her into a hug and nod.

The three women sing their way down the hall. This time it's a chopped up version of *My Girl*. Their mood is infectious and puts me back into my own happy place. I'm not going to let this ugly, sad woman destroy the best day of my life.

Someone knocks on the door. "Gigi, I'm going to have a private stylist come in here and work on your hair and makeup," Dana says as she opens the door. A man with a pink tackle box and satchel of gear enters the room like he owns the place.

"Where is my bride?" he says with cluck of his tongue and a snap of his fingers. It's obvious from the black skinny jeggings to the flouncy shirt pulled to the waist by a studded black leather belt that this is my stylist. His blonde hair is sleek and cropped into a perfect fauxhawk with a bouffant at the end. He's wearing the coolest shimmery lip gloss on a perfect model pout. I don't think I have to go out on a limb to say he's gay. "I'm Randi, it's my name and favorite emotion," he comes over to me and runs his fingers through my red hair. "Please…to the F, to the U-C-K yes, tell me you're my bride?" His eyes are a see-through blue and shining with mirth, reminding me of Maria's kind eyes.

I nod and he falls to his knees, clasps my hands and kisses the top of each one. "Randi with an "I" at your service, my queen," he grins and then pops back up. I love him already. Looking over at Colleen proves she definitely does not have those same feelings for Randi who likes to be randy.

"I'll be back after I check on things," Dana says. "Ms. Davis, would you like to come check things out? Make sure everything's as planned?" she offers.

"Thank you, darling. Don't mind if I do. Would you be so kind..." She gestures to the back of her chair. I'm one hundred percent positive the woman never pushes her own chair. It would be beneath her to get her gold dipped fingers dirty. Hell, she might even break a nail. The world would end as we know it if that happened.

Dana goes over and pushes Colleen to the door. I mouth a "Thank You" and she grins, leaving Randi-with-an-I to tend to my hair and makeup.

Randi is a master at his craft. Two hours later, my hair is styled to perfection and my makeup has never been more beautiful. I actually *feel* pretty. Randi air-kisses each of my cheeks then saunters over to his stuff.

"Don't mess up my art until after the ceremony," he warns.

I put a hand up to my forehead and salute him. "You got it, sir!"

"See you back in the States. I'm your new stylist in case you were wondering," he says grabbing his things.

"You are? I didn't know Chase or Dana hired anyone." I'm confused that I haven't been told about it.

He smiles, opens the door and turns back to me. "They didn't. You're going to. Someone has to keep that wild red hair in check and those cheeks a rosy hue for all the fancy-dancy pants dinners. Like I said, see you back in the States?" He holds his pointed look, clearly waiting for me to answer.

"Consider yourself hired, Randi," I say.

"Don't let anyone else touch you until we're back home," he says and turns right into a tall, dark, superhero. My fiancé.

Chase grabs Randi around the neck and waist and shoves him into the room and against the wall. Randi panics screaming like a little girl.

"Let him go!" I yell trying to be heard over Randi's desperate kicking and screaming.

Chase turns his head, "You know this guy?" he growls. Then he puts his face into Randi's frightened one. "That's my woman and I'll be the only one touching her. Who the fuck are you?" he roars.

"Mistake, mistake, mistake!" Randi's eyes are bulging, Chase's hand loosens up.

"He's my stylist, Chase! Let him go. He was talking about my hair!" comes out of my mouth so loud I felt my own teeth rattle. I suck in a breath once Chase lets the dangling man drop to the floor. I rush over to Randi, who's sputtering and chocking. I get him a glass of water and bring it over.

Randi takes a sip then looks at me, fear in his eyes. "Jesus H. Christ you're marrying the Hulk!" Chase barrels over and Randi jumps up and hides behind me, pushing me in front of him.

Instantly I lift two hands in front of Chase. His eyes are wild and his nostrils are flaring. "Baby, he's harmless. Breathe," I say while stroking his chest. Finally his eyes take in my appearance. My hair is done, my makeup perfect and I'm standing in the crème robe he plucked off me the other day. All of my special undergarments are on underneath. A sexy surprise for later.

"Why is he in here alone with you? Where's Austin!" he scolds. Austin pops his head in from behind the back door where he's keeping an eye on things.

"Sir, you need something?" Austin says.

"Who let this joker in? He could have hurt her," Chase growls. Austin cracks a grin but immediately rights it when Chase narrows his gaze at him.

Randi snickers. "What, with my makeup brush? Puh-leeze. Lighten up, big guy, you're going to give yourself a hernia," he jokes. Chase's jaw tightens in just that way and he grinds his teeth. Randi scampers back behind me.

"Chase, Dana hired him to do my hair and makeup. See," I point to the awesome work he did. Chase looks it over and his eyes soften, lips turning into a sweet grin.

With mesmerizing speed, he pulls me into his arms. "You look magnificent, baby." He takes a deep breath. "Sorry I overreacted." He nuzzles my nose and then kisses me slow, wet, and deep. Just the way I like.

Randi tosses his hands in the air. "Damn it! Now I have to redo that. Isn't there some bad luck mumbo jumbo about the man not seeing the bride before the wedding?" he huffs.

"Had to see my girl," He looks at me. "I'm going to marry you in less than an hour. You ready for it?"

I smile and loop my hands at his waist above his firm ass. "I can be ready in two minutes. Screw the hour," I say.

"Oh, no you don't!" I hear Dana enter the room. "You are getting married in an hour. Now, Chase you need to go take pictures once you have your tux on. *People Magazine* is waiting to shoot one with you, the groomsman and the bridesmaids." I cringe.

"I thought we agreed no media?" I slump in his arms.

"Couldn't avoid it. This way they have the exclusive and we don't have helicopters swarming the resort. So far everything's hush-hush but I don't' want to risk more paparazzi when we get home."

I nod and sigh into his warm neck letting the sandalwood and citrus take me to happy land.

Chase pulls back and holds my gaze with his. "Just another hour and you're mine forever."

"I'll willingly take that life sentence and raise you eternity, baby." I whisper against his lips.

His eyes turn the cerulean blue that makes my knees shake. He traces the symbol dangling from my neck. "Infinity will do," he promises and I nod.

One last kiss and my man is out the door as quickly as he came in. Randi brushes up my makeup and diddles with my hair making sure it's perfect.

Once everyone is gone, I slip on my wedding dress. Kathleen has outdone herself. I look at my reflection in the floor-length mirror. The dress is mostly satin with some tulle. Swarovski crystals and beads line the bottom as if they were sprinkled throughout the skirt. Every time I turn my hips side to side, they sparkle and wink a halo of rainbow light. The back of the dress dips low, leaving the entire back bare. Chase might actually drop to the floor once he sees it. He'll definitely spend the entire evening caressing my spine. He can't help himself. In the end, Kat made sure my wedding dress is sleek, elegant and everything I dreamed of since I was a little girl.

I, Gillian Callahan, am finally going to marry my prince.

While I'm ruminating on how amazing my life is going to be Colleen Davis is wheeled back in.

X

One hour left. The three bitches are flirting up the camera guy from *People* and Chase is hamming it up. Jack is watching the perimeter and the stupid fucks only left Austin Campbell at the back door. Sliding up the length of the wall I'm completely hidden by the large tropical greenery. Dumb asshole is standing a few feet in front of the door talking on his cellphone facing away from the door. Silent as a snake, I pull out the syringe and grip it tightly in my right hand. The element of surprise is once again in my favor.

Like a cheetah, I yank his chest back and strike his carotid on the right side piercing his neck. He whirls around and lands a cracking punch to my face. My jaw twists back and I fall against the wall, but not before seeing his hulking form sway. Those giant arms jolt out, looking like a mummy, trying to get a hold of me. Within mere seconds, his entire body falls to the ground in a giant heap. The bigger they are, the harder they fall. Grabbing his hands I drag him into the foliage alongside of the wall. At the very least, he won't be seen right away.

Getting myself back together, I lean my ear against the wood door. I can hear my girl talking to someone.

"You better be worth it and make my son happy," a

voice says.

"Ms. Davis, I swear I will. He's everything to me. I'm going to do everything I can to make him feel loved, happy and whole. It's the only thing I want in the world," Gillian says back.

God I hate that old crone. The way she's talking to my girl makes me sick. I lift up the sharp blade knowing what I need to do. It's now or never. I'm not going to let some old cripple ruin my chances of finally making Gillian mine.

Storming through the door I'm greeted by two equally shocked faces.

"Danny?" Gillian gasps. "What are you doing here?" Then her eyes scan my form, noticing the maintenance uniform and most specifically the blade in my right hand. "No," her eyes go wide, mouth opens and closes. "It's you!" Tears fill her leafy green eyes.

"Gillian," I whisper taking in her entire body, my eyes gobbling up the ethereal sight of her in her wedding gown. Then the white hot anger hits me like a thousand punches to the gut. The dress isn't for me. Her perfect beauty, the halo of light surrounding her, it's for *him*. The rich fucker!

"Young man, you need to leave before I call for help," the bag of bones screeches.

I shake my head walk over to the woman, hold her head and look directly at Gillian. "Let me go you vagrant! Do you know who my son is?" The scathing tone is too much.

"Do I know who your son is?" I grip her head yanking it back hard, tilting her chin.

"Daniel no, we can talk about this. Let's talk. Leave her out of it." Gillian starts to move closer. I pull out the knife and put it directly under the loose turkey-like skin of the old woman's neck.

"Don't fucking move. Go over there and sit on the bed. Now!" I contain my tone not wanting to bring any more attention. I have about fifteen minutes left before that blonde cunt I've been fucking comes calling for the bride.

Before I can make a decision, the old heap bites my wrist so hard she draws blood. In less than five seconds she has a new smile. Blood sprays out and pours down her purple dress. Her eyes go wide and then roll back into her head. I watch the life leave her body. It's the least I can do.

A scuffle behind me grabs my attention. Gillian has reached the door and is opening it. Lighting fast I catch a hand full of her satin and fabric yanking her back hard. I drop the knife and drag her back into the room a hand over her mouth. Like the old broad, she tries to sink her teeth into my hand.

"Fuck! Stop struggling or I'll kill you!" I breathe into her ear. She stops instantly. I kick the door shut, lock it then remove my hand from her mouth.

"You're going to kill me anyway!" she roars and then slams the spike of her high heel into my foot and pushes off my body. On a roar, I flail back, turn and punch her hard in the cheek. She falls to the floor blood spraying from a busted lip. My ring must have caught her lip when I cold cocked her. The hit gives me just enough time to get the other syringe out of my pocket and ready to strike.

Gillian is a quick one. She scurries back, her dress preventing her from moving too quickly. She screams at the top of her lungs and that's when I lunge. I'm on top of her. She's kicking and screaming her head off. I lock one hand down as the other scratches down the side of my face feeling like little knives skinning me alive. Blood oozes from the four wounds smearing all over her as we roll around. Finally, I'm able to get a knee up and hold her down. With all the strength I have I pin her down and plunge the syringe into her neck.

"No, please no!" her scream turns into a garbled moans as I hold her down a few seconds until she's out.

Quickly, I lift her body and toss her on the bed. Wrapping her entire body in the comforter I yank the sides together and drag her along the floor. Stripping the bloody uniform off I have an exact replica of it on underneath. Double layers is my friend. Besides, it was just as easy to steal two hotel issue coveralls as it was to steal one. Once I'm outside, I lift her into my arms and walk her quickly to the industrial sized laundry cart I had waiting at the edge of the path and toss her in. I cover her up with the linens and push the load towards my vehicle. A few patrons of the hotel walk by and I whistle as if I'm just a regular Joe doing my job. Nothing to see here.

Dead roses. The putrid scent swirls in the air like toxic gas waking me from a drug-induced haze. The scent is sickeningly familiar. Blackness engulfs the space I'm in. Only a sliver of light shows under what must be the door. The crystals scrape against the cold, hard foundation beneath me, sounding like a rat scuttling across concrete, its nails grasping for purchase. The lace and beads covering my dress swish and crunch as I try to sit up. Dry, thick rope abrades the skin at my ankles and wrists as I move, pinching the tender skin. Taking a breath is difficult, the air humid, stifling. Sweat slickens my skin trailing uncomfortably down between my breasts and hairline. My mouth is so dry I can't even swallow to rebuild the moisture.

This is not how I expected today to go. Right now, I should be kissing the man I love, promising him eternity. Thoughts of Chase rip through my mind tears swell and spill, carving a path through dirt and grit. I do my best to wipe them off on the lace capped sleeves of my gown, not wanting *him* to see me cry. The last thing I need is to prove how he has weakened me. If I'm ever to get out of this situation alive, get back to Chase, my friends, and my life, I'm going to have to play his twisted game and come out the victor. Otherwise, he will kill me.

My only hope is that someone saw him take me or he left clues. Daniel "Danny" McBride was never once on our radar. There was never a reason to suspect him. We broke up months before I started seeing Chase. It makes no sense. We dated for less than a year. Yes, I ended it, but he didn't seem fazed at all. Boy was I wrong. He killed Chase's mother. Oh, my God. Chase is going to find her like that with her throat slit and me gone.

More tears stream down my face. My arms ache in the joints where they're tied behind my back. The rope around my ankles is digging painfully into the skin shredding the surface. It's nothing compared to the hollow burn in my heart. I had everything I could ever want and within minutes, it was all taken away from me.

The door rattles and the sound of metal scraping across

metal reaches my ears. The light shines into the room landing directly in my eyes, blinding me with the yellow glow.

"You're awake. Finally, sleepyhead. I'll bet you're hungry, too?" he asks. Every one of his footsteps hitting the concrete sounds overly loud in the dim space. All of a sudden light floods the room.

Danny stands under a string that leads to an uncovered light bulb. I look into his black, dead eyes. The kind, sweet man I once knew is gone. This man, is a stranger, a very vile and dangerous one. His lips lift into a half snarl, half smile.

"It's been too long..." He crouches down and pets the side of my hair trailing a finger down the side of my face. I gag and push away, leaning my head against the cinderblock of my cell.

"Have you anything to say? This has been a long time coming," he says almost jovially.

"Let me go, Danny. Please," I beg, the words coming out of my mouth sounding as if they've been dipped in acid and rubbed raw with sandpaper.

Danny tips his head back and laughs heartily as if my request was the funniest thing he'd ever heard.

"Oh Gillian my love, I finally have you back. Look around, today is the first day of the rest of our lives together... forever."

THE END

The Trinity Trilogy is continued in…

Soul

TRINITY TRILOGY

BOOK THREE

ALSO BY AUDREY CARLAN

The Calendar Girl Series

January (Book 1)
February (Book 2)
March (Book 3)
April (Book 4)
May (Book 5)
June (Book 6)

July (Book 7)
August (Book 8)
September (Book 9)
October (Book 10)
November (Book 11)
December (Book 12)

The Falling Series

Angel Falling
London Falling
Justice Falling

The Trinity Trilogy

Body (Book 1)
Mind (Book 2)
Soul (Book 3)

ACKNOWLEDGEMENTS

For this one, I have to thank my soul sisters **Dyani Gingerich, Nikki Chiverrell, and Carolyn Beasley** first and foremost. Yes, I dedicated the book to you, but without the three of you letting me craft characters in your likeness, this trilogy would be nowhere near what it is today. It would be like baking cookies and not adding the sugar... the essential ingredient to make something sweet. You three are my sugar. Always. My love for you knows no bounds.

To my critique partner, **Sarah Saunders**, I always feel like I won the lottery every time I get one of your critiques. Each and every one is like a gift. I remember going through the process of trying to find a CP that fit well with me and thinking, "Maybe I just suck and no one wants to work with me?" Even though we were already friends, I think this process has strengthened our relationship and forged it in stone. I can't thank you enough for keeping me and my characters honest and consistent and making me laugh through every comment.

To my editor **Ekatarina Sayanova** with Red Quill Editing, LLC, I'm in awe of you. Not many editors would start in the middle of a trilogy, go back and read the first book and then continue on editing with a seamless transition. It just proves your professionalism and genuine concern for the author and their story. I look forward to working with you on Soul.

Any author knows they aren't worth their weight unless their story is backed by badass betas. I have the best!

Ginelle Blanch - You Dearheart prevent me from looking like an idiot. Your ability to find every single time I screwed up the spelling of words, used the wrong word, or just plain added words that shouldn't be there, blows me away. I'm pretty sure my readers would send you thank you notes if they knew all the errors you found right before each book goes live. And even though I made you cry, then made you mad at the cliffhanger I PROMISE to make you so happy you'll be bursting with joy at the end of Soul. Love you girlie!

Jeananna Goodall - How does one thank her favorite fan? In my case, I put you to work beta reading! <grin> You are not only my fan lovely, you're my cheerleader, my voice of reason, and my friend. You're in integral part of the creative process for me and I adore having you as part of my life.

Anita Shofner - You are my new QUEEN of tenses. How did I score an English major on my beta team? I don't know but I consider myself so damned lucky! Even though this was your first time beta reading it seemed liked you'd been doing it for years! Thank you lady for making my book better!

Lindsay Bzoza - I have never had a beta that was able to finish a novel and share her suggestions in two days. Blown away is an understatement. Thank you for dropping everything and making my book a priority. I love your pieces, girl!

Jennifer Cazares – Thank you for fitting me in at the last minute when you were bombed with other things. You are an angel and I appreciate you!

To my street team, **Audrey's Angels** I can hardly type these words I'm so filled with love and emotion for you. Each and every one of you gives me hope that one day my books will be read and enjoyed by the masses. You make me believe that one day my dream of being a New York Times bestselling author could come true. Thank YOU Angels for committing your time, energy, and effort into helping this indie succeed. BESOS Angels!

If you are interested in hanging out with the craziest, most loving, wild chicks in all the romance world, contact me via Facebook to get your wings and become and Angel.

And last but definitely not least to my husband Eric, your support and belief in me and my dream makes me love you like crazy. Hopefully my books will sell in the millions and you can retire early!

Special Thanks

Jess Dee – Even though I may not need the mentoring as often as I did earlier in the year, I still appreciate knowing that you're always there to lend some helpful advice. Thank you for replying to my feedback over a year ago. It was the start of a beautiful friendship, one I'm very grateful for. Love to you. www.jessdee.com

Carol Ray – Angel, you are tireless in your gift for spreading the word about my novels. I'm so lucky to have some like you in my corner. I could never thank you enough

AUDREY CARLAN

for all you do. BESOS

Drue Hoffman - DRC Promotions - For setting up an incredible blog tour and sharing your amazing advice about the industry. Thank you! Schedule your blog tour today! www.drcpromotions.com

Emily Hemmer - Author extroidanaire, thank you for always listening to me vent, going over ideas and sharing success and failures. It makes the world of being an author less lonely knowing there's another incredible author out there that just…gets it. Check out her books people! www.emilyhemmer.com

ABOUT AUDREY CARLAN

Audrey Carlan lives in the sunny California Valley two hours away from the city, the beach, the mountains and the precious…the vineyards. She has been married to the love of her life for over a decade and has two young children that live up to their title of "Monster Madness" on a daily basis. When she's not writing wickedly hot romances, doing yoga, or sipping wine with her "soul sisters," three incredibly different and unique voices in her life, she can be found with her nose stuck in book or her Kindle. A hot, smutty, romantic book to be exact!

Any and all feedback is greatly appreciated and feeds the soul. You can contact Audrey below:

E-mail: carlan.audrey@gmail.com
Facebook: facebook.com/AudreyCarlan
Website: www.audreycarlan.com